Murder in the Parsonage

The Maggie Monroe Series: Book One

Helene Mitchell

Praise for the *Maggie Monroe* series

"Helene Mitchell's *Maggie Monroe* mysteries are fresh, funny, and entertaining. The multiple layers of her eccentric characters kept me turning pages to find out what was coming next." — *Agnes Sowle*
Attorney-at-Law (Retired)

"Helene Mitchell's *Maggie Monroe* series offers readers fun and seemingly unsolvable mysteries by realistically blending criminal offenders' behaviors with the behaviors of those charged with managing them. Mitchell's mysteries kept me guessing, kept me entertained, and kept me wanting more." — *Christine N. Barrera*
Probation/Parole, Pre-Sentence Investigation Supervisor (Retired)

"Forty years of working in prison systems left me curious to read Helene Mitchell's *Maggie Monroe* books. I found them to be intriguing and captivating. From the first page I was enthralled with the eccentric, mysterious, and engaging characters. The books kept me guessing on 'who did it' while the small details brought me into the storyline. Highly recommend!" — *Pam Sonnen*
Idaho Department of Corrections Deputy Director (Retired), Prison Consultant

"Thirty years in law enforcement, I have seen all kinds of criminal behavior. Helene Mitchell's *Maggie Monroe* books spin those behaviors into quirky mysteries. Fun reads!" — *Shaun Gough*
Gooding County Sheriff

"Delightful! Having spent over 28 years in the Correction Industry, I found Helene Mitchell's *Maggie Monroe* mysteries to be spot on with the simple but effective interpretations of criminal behavior and manipulation. Very entertaining and educational—a must read that belongs in every corrections training library." — *Darwin Cameron*
Retired Correction Officer, Training Officer, and Parole Officer

This is a work of fiction. Names, characters, businesses, places, events, locales, and incidents are either the products of the author's imagination or used in a fictitious manner. Any resemblance to actual persons, living or dead, or actual events is purely coincidental.

Copyright © 2023 Gail Decker Cushman

All rights reserved. No part of this book may be reproduced or used in any manner without written permission of the copyright owner except for the use of quotations in a book review.

Edited by AnnaMarie McHargue and Anita Stephens

Designed by Eric Hendrickson and Leslie Hertling

ISBN (paperback): 978-1-7376288-7-3

ISBN (ebook): 978-1-7376288-8-0

www.gailcushman.com

Dedication:

To Tom,
Who started me on my journey.
Semper fi.

To Robert,
Who made my life whole again.

Acknowledgements

Murder in the Parsonage was written by accident. I had finished another story, yet unpublished, and was fiddling around one day and this story popped into my brain. I wrote it several years ago and it has sat on my bookshelf for about three years, while I contemplated its fate. But the thing is, I couldn't have done it alone. Many people, family and friends, helped me, sometimes baby-stepping me along this path and I am deeply indebted to all of you, especially Linda Alden, Joan Wenske, and Patricia Bennett. And of course, Anna, Anita, Leslie, and Eric…for making a manuscript into a book.

I hope you enjoy my efforts as much as I enjoy writing them.

Chapter 1

Barrier
Saturday

Brick O'Brien arrived in Barrier, Nevada, in early fall after a long day of driving. He was weary and parched after the trek from Los Angeles and dreamed of filling his throat with some cool amber liquid. He had driven the scenic Route 395 through Reno. It wasn't direct, but it was prettier, although some might argue more boring since, by actual count, the only things he saw were 27 vehicles, four dogs, a parked 1970 Peugeot with a *For Sale* sign on it, two Hereford cows, and one man in yellow shorts and a T-shirt talking on a cell phone while standing in the middle of the road. Alone. No vehicle in sight. Brick pulled onto the shoulder to see if he could assist, but the guy waved him on. Brick puzzled as to how the man had landed in that particular spot on Highway 50, the loneliest highway in America. Maybe a UFO?

He maneuvered his metallic blue Jeep Wrangler into a vacant space in front of the Eldorado Pizza Shoppe. The deserted street was mostly paved but bore no street markings and no parking meters. A couple stray yellow dogs lay on the wooden walkway, flicking their tails at Brick, clearly not thrilled about having their evening naps interrupted. In front of the shoppe sat two empty rocking chairs that seemed to rock without rhythm. The Saturday night rush hour must not have yet begun. He could park anywhere. No people welcomed him. In fact, Brick saw no people at all.

Brick stretched out his 6-foot, 2-inch frame and thought about doing a few reps of one-armed push-ups on the steamy hood of his Jeep to work out the long drive's kinks. But that thought instantly led to a blistered hand. He'd have to find other ways to limber up. He removed his dark glasses and ran his eyes up and down the street. Still, no one. He turned and entered the Pizza Shoppe, squinting as he strode through the swinging doors into the darkened café, as the overpowering scent of garlic wafted into his nose. He eased himself onto one of several red vinyl bar stools, all of which seemed to be spliced together with black electrical tape. The man behind the counter smiled and asked his preference. Did he want an Oly or an Oly? "I'll take a Bud," Brick answered.

"Ain't got Bud, just Oly, Olympia, nothin' else," the man behind the counter answered, "got Olympia. That's all." Brick knitted his eyebrows in question, but no answer came. Brick ordered an Oly. The man was wearing an apron that used to be white, and a backwards orange ball cap that used to be red atop his balding head. A few tufts of hair stuck out from under his cap while his well-fed belly hid his shoes from his sight. He jiggled as he moved around behind the counter. The ball cap, Brick could now see, read *Barrier Tigers*.

"One beer or another, makes no difference," justified the man behind the counter. "People who want a beer drink what you got. Everybody seems to like Oly, so that's what we got."

Now that he had made it to the little town, Brick felt it familiar, likely because it resembled every other small town in the West. Lining the street were a few churches, a grocery store, a single stop-and-rob drug store, a few more drinking establishments, a tiny breakfast café, and several second-hand stores. The owners often called them antique stores, but the merchandise was often younger than the people who browsed. You remembered a town like this because it was so forgettable that you couldn't help but think of it.

Brick peered out the bar's un-Windexed window and saw Wallace Johnstone's, the drug/grocery/liquor/dry goods store that he had visited on his last trip to Barrier. Below the store's name, a sign read, *We are never just out*. "Never just out of what?" Brick wondered. Of course, it could have meant anything. Brick had been surprised by the varied merchandise. Kitchen items sat next to food and cleaning items, and a variety of medicinal remedies, for humans or for animals, rested neatly next to those. It displayed some basic clothing items, including an extensive array of size large Pendleton brand shirts, underwear, socks, rubber aprons, and bibbed overalls. For shoes, he remembered choosing from rubber one-size-fits-all flip-flops, steel-toed boots, overshoes, and Converse tennis shoes. It was an eclectic collection by city standards but seemed to offer the basic needs of this dwindling mining community.

The one thing that brought a memory or two was his time spent with a priest who lived nearby. On his first visit, Brick was serving on transport duty. He was returning an escaped prisoner from a one-person jail in Horseshoe Bend, Idaho, to Los Angeles County Jail, which was filled to the brim with a waiting list. Brick smiled to himself as he thought of the prisoner. The offender located a blind spot in the Los Angeles County Jail exercise yard and wrapped his arms in three orange jumpsuits that he liberated from other prisoners. He then hoisted himself over two tiers of concertina wire. When he was free and clear, he made it all the way to Idaho to fish for Dolly Vardens. As November rolled around and cold weather set in, he robbed the local dump of $25. Later that night, he turned himself in to the local prosecutor handing him $18.52 and two unopened Keystone Lights. He and the prosecutor drank them down before he went to jail. The prisoner reasoned that it was already cold and bound to get colder. He possessed no bus fare and no warm clothes. He figured if he turned himself in, he would get transportation back to the warmth of California. Three hots and a cot. Sure, he would be incarcerated, but he could always escape again. No big deal.

Brick and his charge spent the night in Barrier. Brick registered his prisoner at the county jail and then checked into the local hotel, which was named the Panorama. The Panorama, the lone hotel in the town, was a beige colored cinder-block building, two stories high, with sleeping accommodations on the second floor. Its front door had lace curtains in the windows and was painted red.

Both the jail and the Panorama offered the necessities, but neither was elegant. The prisoner got a bunk and a hot meal that was provided by a local restaurant. Brick got a hot meal and a queen-sized bed, plus the bonus of a three-channel television. Both were paid for by Los Angeles County. Brick was certain that his dinner was tastier than the prisoner's.

On the off chance that something interesting might be happening that evening, Brick looked around the town but saw little. He ended up in the Panorama Bar and swallowed a few glasses of Irish whiskey with the local priest, Father Patrick Fitzwater. The two men turned one glass into several as they toasted Ireland, county by county, especially the half dozen—known as *strangers*—occupied by Northern Ireland. By 11 p.m. they considered themselves not only drinking buddies but also soul mates and compatriots. They ended their evening by singing *A Nation Once Again*. They didn't know all the words, but what the hell.

Chapter 2

Barrier
Saturday

The man behind the counter set the cold beer in front of Brick and wiped up the drips. "You want the Saturday Night Special? Order a beer and get a pizza for half price. Two bucks for the beer and six for the pizza. Full tummy for under a tenner. What do ya say? What do you want on your pizza?"

Saturday Night Special, Brick thought to himself. Quite a different meaning than in L.A. He regarded the offer without expression, then smiled. "You make it hard to resist. Pepperoni and onions. Large. And I'll have another cold one when this is gone. A salad would taste good, too."

"We have one size, large. Can do pepperoni and onions, but no salads. Pizza. That's all. Don't have salads. Too hard to keep the produce. We have pizza, Olympia, and Coca Cola. Don't need nothin' else." The man behind the counter ducked his head through the order window to pass on Brick's order. He opened the draft tap and poured Brick another Olympia before speaking. "What's your business in Barrier, if you don't mind me asking? Or are you passing through? We don't get many strangers here. People on Highway 50 most often keep on truckin' all the way to Eureka. Eureka calls itself the 'Friendliest Town in America.' Maybe they are cuz most people sure don't stop here. No more than a hundred cars a day pass through and only a handful stop for eats."

Brick smiled and answered, "I'm staying. I'm teaching school here this year. At the high school. Social studies. I've been living in L.A. but decided to make an adjustment to my lifestyle." Brick narrowed his eyes and wrinkled his forehead as he thought of the two near-misses he faced six months ago. "I've been a cop with LAPD for over 10 years, but decided it was time to move on. You know, big city, too many people, smog, too many cars. I needed something new. I was assigned a series of downer cases a few months ago, and it was time. When this job came open, Father Fitzwater invited me to take it, and I agreed. I never thought I'd use my college degree in education, but now, here I am with a teaching job. And coaching basketball." He smiled a quick smile followed by a frown.

The man behind the counter grinned and queried, "Are you Brick O'Brien? Hot damn. You're the new basketball coach. We've been waitin' for you. Basketball practice starts next month. We ain't had a winning season in a while, and we're hoping that you'll put it together. No pressure, of course. Fitz has been raving about you. And what he says, well, Sir, that's the gospel. The sun sure shined on this town the day he arrived. He is one fine priest. And he sure as hell keeps the kids in line at the high school. Father Fitzwater knows his stuff, all right. You must be terrific, or you wouldn't get such good words from Fitz. Let me be the first to welcome you." The man behind the counter reached across and shook Brick's hand. "And the pizza's on me."

Brick replied, "Thanks. Yeah. That's me. I only met Fitz twice, but we have a lot in common. He offered me this position a few weeks ago. I'm on my way to his house now, well, right after I eat some pizza, that is. I'll take what's left to him. I'm killing time, too. He's got Mass until about 6 o'clock. I'm not going to church tonight after that killer of a drive. I'll make confession tonight after a couple toddies, and he'll absolve me of all my sins. With luck, I'll receive enough absolution to go out and sin a little more." He winked at the man behind the counter and considered how he would make confession. After a couple glasses of Irish whiskey with the amicable priest, no sin existed save the English invading Ireland.

Chapter 3

Barrier
Saturday

The pay phone jangled, and the man behind the counter edged his expanded girth around the tabletop to answer it.

Brick took off his sunglasses but rethought the move as several nearby slot and video poker machines shot purple and orange beams of light across the room. Even the two pool tables seemed to be bathed in bright color. Across the room, though, was the antithesis. Darkness was lit only by a single beverage sign and a couple of clocks hung randomly around the walls. The Olympia sign's brightness had disappeared, and the flickering sign read *Oly pia*. The tables, decorated with red-checked plastic tablecloths, napkin holders, salt and pepper shakers, and ketchup, were lost to the darkness.

Brick hoped the place would come alive later that night. Surely patrons would emerge later in the evening. What did the town do for entertainment, he couldn't help but wonder as he finished his draft and waited for his Saturday Night Special.

Brick began thinking about his second visit to Barrier. He had used some vacation time to drive to Elko to watch a friend in a mine-safety competition. He stopped on his return trip to say hello to the amicable priest. They ate a late dinner at the Panorama followed by a couple toasts and a few songs.

But this trek from Los Angeles had left Brick famished. He had made so many changes recently, and the long drive forced him to rethink each one.

Had he really decided to leave his career and move to a town with only a single pizza joint, all because a priest he had met a few times offered him a way out? He reflected on that priest while he awaited the arrival of his order. Although their conversations were infrequent, Father Fitzwater shared his history, and Brick felt like he knew him well.

Brick thought he could avoid Mass if he extended his time at the bar, and he considered a game of pool or trying his hand at the slots. He slid off the stool and walked around the Pizza Shoppe, noting the posters on the walls that announced local events, some of which had long since passed. At one end of the restaurant was a display of mining supplies, sluice boxes, gold panning kits, rubber boots, and other mining gear. A sign read, *Gold Prospecting Equipment*. The paraphernalia was dusty. Maybe he would try his luck at panning some gold. Another new adventure. It couldn't hurt.

Chapter 4

Barrier
Saturday

"Oh, God. Oh, shit," the man behind the counter swore as he hung up the phone. "This can't be."

He collapsed onto one of the stools and with some effort continued his conversation with Brick. He stammered and shook his head. His voice squeaked higher than it had a few minutes before. His ruddy complexion was even redder, and his facial pock marks were even more pronounced. "You'll never believe it. You'll never believe it. That was my wife on the phone. The thing is, well, shit, I don't know how to tell you. The rumor is, but I don't think it's a rumor. The thing is, well, Father Fitzwater is dead. I mean deceased. Shit. That is, they found him dead at his house." He wiped his thumb at an unseen tear.

Brick gaped at the man behind the counter with disbelief. "What are you talking about? Dead? Father Fitzwater? Dead? You must be mistaken. I talked to him a couple hours ago on my cell phone. He was fine. Who found him?"

"Shit, I don't know who found him. It's Fitz all right. That's what my wife said. Murdered. I don't know nothin' else, just what my wife told me. You should speak with the sheriff, Sheriff Monroe. They're out at his house right now. Fitz lives across the street from me and my wife. That's how my wife knew about him. Murdered. Shit. Father Fitz. Damn. They got yellow tape around his house and shit, I mean, you know, that yellow tape you see on TV. It's up on the hill about a mile. Picket fence on the left. She said that an ambulance and some cop cars were out in front."

"Was she sure it was him? It can't be true. Was she sure? I know the house. I'll head over right now." Brick tossed a 10 spot down on the counter and rose to leave. The second beer would have to wait.

"Yeah, straight up the hill about a mile. You can't miss it. Hey, Mr. O'Brien, don't you want your Saturday Night Special?" the man behind the counter called after Brick as he passed through the door.

"No, keep it," Brick called over his shoulder. "I'll be back later. Damn, I hope this is rumor. Keep it warm. I'll be back." Brick situated his hat on his head and was out the door before the man behind the counter could answer.

Chapter 5

Las Vegas
26 Years Prior

Father Patrick Fitzwater, fresh out of the seminary, wanted to make plans. Priests crafted their own destinies. God's will be damned. A priest could go places, become a pastor of a large parish or maybe even a bishop. An archbishop. A cardinal. The Pope. The name Saint Patrick struck awe in every Irishman's heart, whether he lived in Ireland or had migrated to some other place. Father Patrick. Bishop Patrick. Pope Patrick. Saint Patrick. Another Saint Patrick wouldn't do any harm. The more he thought about it, the better it sounded.

Most of the priests in Patrick Fitzwater's seminary class were sent to serve God in the hinterlands of rural Oregon, Idaho, and Washington parishes. They would become mired down in parish work, and their bright futures would dissolve before their very eyes. They would recite Mass, anoint the sick, counsel the lazy, and feed the poor. Some would jazz up their lives with a discreet affair or two, while others would turn to alcohol, drugs, or in the extreme, fondling children to maintain some aura of power and self-worth. Recently, the Internet developed a whole new area of pedophilia, that is, viewing sexually explicit photos of children. Who could believe it? But then, who in a parish would ever know?

In Father Fitzwater's opinion, Garth Brooks' song, "Friends in Low Places," described their lives, a sorry house to live in, donated food, and when you retired, if you weren't dead, you could go to the priest's poor house. If you were lucky, you could find a patsy who would pay your green's fees and buy you a steady supply of whiskey to keep you warm at night. But that meant ponying up to some benefactor with extra Masses, prayer sessions, and obligatory appearances at various fundraisers. Patrick relished the priesthood, but not the accompanying financial bondage.

Father Patrick Fitzwater devised to be different. Even with his lousy paycheck, a solid investment would prove fruitful if he arranged it right. Obtaining money from a parish couldn't be very difficult. He would ask the parishioners. Most would do anything for a priest. With wealth came influence; with influence came power. An ambitious young priest could flourish, but he needed a way to begin. He needed money. Money would provide the influence that led to the power. An ambitious young priest could be influential if the parish finances were solid. Better yet if they were escalating.

Father Fitzwater deemed that he won the lottery of life when he learned of his assignment to the Diocese of Las Vegas. Money. Community wealth. Warm weather. Golf. Activities. Events. Fun and games. And, again, lots of money! If he were accurate in his strategy, the conceivable wealth of a thriving Las Vegas parish equated to power and influence, and he was ripe for both. Las Vegas. Hallelujah. God bless Las Vegas.

His first pastoral gig was as associate pastor at Our Lady of Perpetual Tears in a working-class neighborhood. The pastor was Father Kim Lin, a frail Vietnamese priest who came to the U.S. as a boat person. He awaited a lung transplant for two years since Mr. Lucky Strike outran him and eventually delegated all the Masses and parish work to the healthy and energetic Father Fitzwater. Father Fitzwater diligently checked in with the ailing priest every week for counsel and advice, none of which he took. The parish served merely a couple hundred families, and Father Fitzwater controlled the comings and goings well. He supervised meetings, committees, sacraments, personnel, and the day-to-day operations of the parish. The finances were stable. The collection plate generated enough revenue each week to handle the bills and to stow away some for a rainy day. Father Lin's medical bills were paid by the Diocesan insurance plan, but the finance council insisted on kicking in a little extra cash to keep him comfortable. They supplied enough cash for satellite TV and a cook. Father Lin fired the cook and used the money to buy a little marijuana from time to time to ease the pain.

The church council consisted of a group of working parishioners who scrutinized the parish finances monthly. The chairman, Alice Honeycomb—or "the hun" as she was called—analyzed every expense. She was very interested in increasing the parish coffers and kept an unwavering eye on the money that flowed through the parish. With Father Lin's increasing needs, she became discouraged. She was a cradle Catholic with dreams of adding both a new wing and eventually even a school to the church. Those dreams began to fizzle as more and more money went to support the ailing priest. When the youthful, ambitious Father Fitzwater arrived, she considered it a golden opportunity to increase the parish reserves and make some real progress in their financial state. The church was old and in need of renovation. The young, aspiring priest brought hope to the finance council, and they welcomed his new ideas with open arms.

Father Fitz enjoyed the freedom that Our Lady of Perpetual Tears offered. He loved people, and the parish adored him. Parishioners invited him to dinner and parties, and his single-digit golf handicap earned him invitations to play as a fourth. In his spare time, he expanded his photography skills and tried to publish his works. His salary was less than he hoped, but since everything was provided by the parish, he had more expendable income than he ever earned before. The parish provided Father Lin with a Buick to drive and Father Fitzwater with a Ford. A few months later, the council found a way to upgrade Father Lin to a Lexus, and Father Fitzwater inherited the Buick. He added a vanity license plate, FOTOBOY, to honor his new-found skills. It made him smile.

Chapter 6

Barrier
Saturday

On the way to the priest's house, Brick's mind drifted to an incident in late July when he was called to another crime scene. It was a Thursday night, a slower-than-average night for L.A., and Sergeant Brick O'Brien and his partner, Detective Mike Turner, responded to a call of a domestic fatality. As it turned out, it wasn't a fatality but rather a domestic dispute. The victim, Carl, was shot, but not dead. His wife/live in/one-night stand, her name was Dottie, shot his pecker off after he refused to take Viagra. Blood was everywhere. She was beyond horny and wanted to make a point, so she dialed 911. She was positive that the EMT's could sew or tape his dick back on, like they seemed to do on TV. They must have been able to do that, as the television character in question would appear in a later episode, healed and healthy. When Brick and his partner arrived, the victim had nearly regained consciousness. He somehow seized the pistol and discharged it, attempting to maim his female companion. Brick shoved the woman out of the way, and the bullet struck his vested chest knocking him flat. Dottie went to the hospital with a bruised boob from his push. Her love toy survived but would be peckerless for eternity. Dottie was suing the city for the bruised boob. She would probably win the suit.

The bulletproof vest took the brunt of the gunshot but forced Brick to spend a couple nights in the hospital with a cracked rib and massive bruising.

He knew he was fortunate that the vest took the hole rather than his chest. The department awarded him a Medal of Valor, which was nice, but he could have lost more than his pride in that incident. The Los Angeles city fathers made a fuss about his bravery and wanted him to be the model on the departmental recruiting poster. Brick's blue eyes, tanned skin, salt and peppered black hair, along with his physically fit frame, would lure the types of young men and women that they were attempting to recruit. Add the word *Hero* at the bottom of the poster, and the recruiting ad was perfect. The LAPD powers made the offer. "No way," was Brick's answer, and he began to search for a new career that would offer a safer challenge.

A second incident happened a short two weeks later. Brick was still recovering from consequences of the Dottie-Carl dispute when he and his partner responded to a call for a parole violation. It was a simple call. The 47-year-old female parolee was in possession of methamphetamines that the parole officer and drug dog found while making a routine visit. The P.O. called the police, and Brick and Mike responded. The problem was that she pulled a Ka-Bar knife out of the leg of her pants and wielded it at both officers. She tried to slice or dice whoever or whatever got in her way. She slashed Mike's arm, which landed him in the hospital. It took all three of them to hook her up, but not before she drew blood from the drug dog. It was after this incident that Brick decided to review his options more seriously.

That same week, Father Patrick Fitzwater phoned him bemoaning his lack of faculty, including a basketball coach for Barrier High School. Brick had retained his teaching certificate throughout his 10 years of police work, just in case he someday needed a backup job. He never dreamed he would make the change. He spent weekends coaching basketball for the Police Activities League (PAL) for inner-city kids and enjoyed watching the kids grow and stay out of trouble.

Father Fitzwater made a strong pitch to attract Brick to Barrier. Rural Nevada schools always had trouble recruiting teachers. This year, besides the social studies teacher, Barrier High School lost its math, music, and wood shop instructors. The basketball program had endured four winless seasons, leaving the school and town's morale low. Without a social studies teacher and basketball coach, the school was in disarray. Brick wasn't thrilled about living in rural Nevada, but, if nothing else, it would buy him a little time to figure out what to do with his life.

Brick considered the options. Police work paid more than teaching, but teaching was safer. Plus, summers and weekends off. That would be a bonus benefit. Between his vacation and sick leave, some savings and the job offer, he could afford to try his hand in the classroom. Nothing ventured, nothing gained. Being 35 years old and never married allowed him to make this decision quickly.

Brick gave his landlord notice, boxed up his goods, and placed them in a storage unit within a week. Perhaps he and the padre could take a quick trip to Ireland during one of the school breaks. They could have a hell of a time, visiting each county, sipping *The Creature*, as Fitz called Irish whiskey, while touring the country of their ancestors. The padre's uncles still lived in Galway. If they could stay with them, it would make for an inexpensive trip. Maybe they would even buy the whiskey. Brick knew that Ireland had six traditional brands of Irish whiskey, which meant at least six distilleries. Some Guinness breweries might be available, too. What a trip they could have chasing away their problems and enjoying The Creature.

Chapter 7

Saturday
Barrier

When Brick headed up the street toward the priest's cottage, he first noticed the yellow crime scene tape flapping in the breeze. Add to that red and blue flashing lights of the emergency vehicles and it felt like he was right back at the very thing he had come to Barrier to leave behind. Bystanders were clustered together, nodding and pointing, while the EMTs smoked and talked quietly as they leaned against the home's faded wooden fence. The one uniformed, rubber-gloved officer moved from house to yard and back again, holding a clipboard, camera, and tape measure. Brick got out of his Jeep and started up the sidewalk wondering who was in charge.

The two EMTs came to attention as one flipped his ashes onto the ground. "Whoa, Mister, where do you think you're going?"

Brick considered them and introduced himself, "I'm Brick O'Brien. I'm looking for Father Patrick Fitzwater. Isn't this his house?" The pair glanced at each other and returned their gaze to Brick.

"Yeah, this is Father Fitzwater's house. O'Brien? Hey, you the new basketball coach? I heard you were comin' this week. You need to see the sheriff. Sheriff Monroe. We don't know anything. We're waiting till somebody tells us what to do." The EMTs' name tags read Sid and Al. They were of similar height and weight, which is to say fat. Al was probably a few years older and took the role of spokesman for the two. He removed his baseball cap from his head and scratched his brow. "We got the call that someone was dead, but we don't know more than that. When we got here, Sheriff Monroe ordered us to stand by. We're standing by. That's Cagey over there with the clipboard. Cagey Garrison. He's the deputy sheriff. You can stand by with us if you want." Sid nodded in agreement and stamped out his cigarette in the dirt.

Brick regarded the house and glanced back at the EMTs pretending that he hadn't heard them. "Where's the sheriff? Is he in the house?" He scrutinized the rickety gate on the picket fence and then started up the walk.

Al grabbed Brick's shirt and replied, "Hold it, Mister. Didn't you hear me? You can't go in the yard. You have to stay out here, behind the yellow tape. Sheriff Monroe said no one can go in." Brick glanced down at Al's hand and glared at him.

"Let go of my shirt. Where's the sheriff? I want to see him," Brick growled. Al released his grip on the taller, younger, more athletic man's arm.

"Her. The sheriff is a her. Maggie Monroe. Sheriff Maggie Monroe. She said we should stand by. Behind the tape. That's her." He pointed toward the door that was opening.

Sheriff Maggie Monroe exited the house and took in the various groups that were huddled in front of the cottage. She then ducked under the crime scene tape that zigzagged across the sidewalk around the small house.

She was tall, almost as tall as Brick, with a boyish gait. Her long brown hair was tied up high on her head into a ponytail that dangled down the back of her forest green polo shirt. Brick watched it swinging freely as she walked down the sidewalk. She was young, perhaps in her late 20s, athletic, attractive, and carried herself with confidence. Her shirt sagged from her shoulders. Brick thought it was a size too large but would fit perfectly over a bulky Kevlar vest. She smiled as she approached the small group of citizens who were idling near the front door of the house. Brick ignored Al's advice and moved toward her. Al didn't say anything.

Brick watched her for a few minutes, learning what he could from afar. She was wearing a watch on her right wrist, a rather large pistol on her hip, keys clipped to her pant loops, and a badge fastened to her belt. Brick couldn't help but also notice that she wore no rings. She seemed to be at ease with the locals, and they moved back from the restricted area.

As she turned to re-enter the house, Brick called out, "Sheriff Monroe? Are you Sheriff Monroe? Can I speak with you for a minute? I'm Brick O'Brien. I'm, uh, supposed to meet Father Fitzwater tonight. I'm wondering about all this. What's happened?" He gestured with his hands at the ambulance and yellow tape.

She turned and responded, "Yeah, I'm the sheriff. Sheriff Monroe. Are you a friend or somethin'?" She cast her eyes over his muscular torso and then settled on his steel blue eyes. She ignored protocol and stepped over to get a closer look.

Brick regarded her saying, "Yeah, I'm a friend of his. Sort of. Father Fitzwater recruited me to teach school this year. I talked to him a couple hours ago. I am wondering what happened?"

The sheriff answered quickly, "What did you say your name is? O'Brien? The new basketball coach? I've heard about you. We don't know what happened. He didn't show up for Mass. It was after 4:30, and one of the deacons called him, but he didn't answer. Then the deacon came to the house. Found him dead."

Sheriff Monroe shook her head, her cheeks flushed, and her long hair bobbled a little. "Somebody shot him in the chest while he was sitting in his chair. Just sitting in his chair. Unbelievable. He was one fine man. And a fine priest, too. I can't imagine who would want to kill him. We got started but haven't been reading the scene very long. When did you say you talked to him?" Her green eyes seemed to get greener as she scrutinized him.

"Yes, I'm O'Brien, the new teacher and basketball coach. I called him on my cell phone a little while ago. I don't know exactly when. Maybe an hour. I was close to where that massive, odd-dressed tree is. You know, the one with all the shoes hanging from it?"

Sheriff Monroe responded, "You must be talking about the *shoe tree*, one of our local hot spots. It's about an hour from here."

The shoe tree located midway between Forsythe and Barrier wore a couple thousand shoes draped from its branches. It attracted interest from many of those traveling America's loneliest highway. It confirmed that the untraveled highway offered little for visitors to see or do except toss unwanted or unneeded shoes over its branches.

"You talked to him when? At 3:30? What did he say?"

Brick answered quickly, "Nothing really. He sounded good. I told him I would be here about 5 o'clock. He reminded me that Mass started at 4:30 and invited me to come. I told him maybe. But I didn't feel like it after that long drive. I knew if I dallied long enough, I would miss the opening prayers. I was thirsty and hungry and stopped at the pizza place downtown to wait until Mass was over. The man behind the counter told me that he was dead."

"That was Bob Givens. He lives across the street." She pointed toward a graying white stucco house with a faded red slate roof and green shutters. "His wife is home. I'm sure she called him."

Brick considered whether he wanted to tell Sheriff Monroe that he was a police officer or former police officer. Maybe she already knew. Still, it might be better to maintain his anonymity and let the locals do their thing without his intrusion. His instincts kicked in and told him that Sheriff Monroe was too young to have much experience. Nevertheless, he decided to take an observer approach. He requested, "Is he still in the house? Can I see him?"

"Oh, yeah, he's still sitting in his chair. He hasn't moved a bit. No. I'm sorry, you can't. Nobody is going in except law enforcement. I've got work to do." Sheriff Monroe turned on her heel and signaled the deputy to follow. She glanced over her shoulder at Brick before continuing into the house with her ponytail bobbing from side to side.

Chapter 8

Las Vegas
26 Years Prior

A simple game of blackjack launched Father Patrick Fitzwater's fondness of gambling. He needed some checks signed, and the secretary was on vacation. Alice, who worked as a casino pit boss, but who also had had an assistant role at church as a check signer, told him that she would be available during her break from 3 to 3:15 p.m. He arrived early with 15 minutes to wait. Everyone sang praises of Alice Honeycomb, the Pit Boss/Parish Finance Chairman. She was down-to-earth, no nonsense. As he watched her, he gained an appreciation of her vigilance and integrity. She kept a sharp eye on the players and the dealers. Nothing evaded her watchful eyes. She noticed him, checked her watch, and then flashed her hand three times to signal him that she would have a break in 15 minutes. He gave her a thumbs-up in return.

Father Fitz's previous visits to the casinos were to cash in the chips that parishioners placed in the collection plate. Casino chips deposited in the Sunday coffers were common, and sometimes were more common than cash itself. Father Fitz credited those offerings as thanksgivings for success at the various gaming tables. He could almost hear the prayers of desperation, "If I win, Lord, I will attend Mass every week and give You half of what I win." Certainly, those promises didn't last, but Father Fitz was glad to reap the rewards of good luck following a big win for those who did keep their promises.

Father Fitzwater was about 30 with wavy, strawberry blond hair that shagged over his ears and down his neck and accented his square face and flushed, ruddy complexion. His parishioners seemed charmed by the blue eyes and freckles he inherited from his mother's side of the family, but all that did nothing to hide the large nose he received from his father. Add to that, his slightly bucked teeth, pasty facial hair, and short stature of 5-foot, 8 inches, and there was little to find attractive. And, while he savored good food, he was far too busy for exercise. This was proven by the saggy gut that hung over his belt. Each day, he smoked and enjoyed a good glass of Irish whiskey, although never partaking in either to excess.

Today he was clad in his priestly uniform of black pants, a black short-sleeved shirt, and white collar. He perched on a stool at a blackjack table while he waited for Alice. He seldom gambled except for a few all-nighters during his seminary years when the seminarians used unconsecrated wafers instead of poker chips. He thought he was a pretty good player as he always accumulated more than his share of wafers. Eventually, the other seminarians refused to play with him.

It would be a few more minutes until Alice was available. On a whim he extracted a couple of twenties from his wallet to play a few five-dollar hands while he waited. He never fancied the casinos, but smoking was allowed, which was a plus. He lit up and watched the dealer for a few minutes before passing over his $40.00. The red-vested dealer gave his white collar the once over, nodded, and returned eight $5.00 chips. The dealer's name was Gerry. Gerry with a G.

Father Fitzwater placed one chip on the green-felted, half-circle table in front of him and waited for Gerry to deal. A king face down followed by a queen up. He pursed his lips then immediately hoped the stone-faced dealer didn't notice. He rolled the king over, put out another chip and asked, "Can I double?" The dealer nodded without expression.

Gerry dealt him another face down card to go with the king. He peeked at it, saw an ace, and rolled it over. Twenty-one. The dealer dealt him another face down card. He peeked at it again. Another ace. Twenty-one. Again. The dealer said simply, "Congratulations, Sir. Uh, Father." He didn't change his stoic expression. Father Fitz placed another chip on the felt and repeated his luck. Again. And again.

Father Fitzwater started, "I never, I mean, I never thought I'd...," when he felt a firm hand bite into his shoulder. It was Alice. He turned and responded, "Alice, it's a miracle. I mean, how'd I do that?"

"Come on, Father," she whispered. "Trust me. It's no miracle. I need to get you out of here before you send my boss to the poor house. This is no place for you. Let's go sign those checks." Alice grasped his arm and began pulling him toward her. "Come on, Father."

He resisted and shook her off. "But I won. And then I won again. I'm sure I could...didn't you see, Alice? I turned $40 into $80. I'm sure I could..." She grasped his shirt sleeve, hung on, and pulled him from the table. He looked at her and then turned his head to view the table. He heard it calling his name.

"The casinos don't pay my salary with their losses," Alice whispered to him. "Quit while you're ahead. Come on."

Gerry double blinked at the priest and passed him the chips of his bonanza. "You did well, Father. Come back and see us again," he invited the priest in his dealer's monotone. He nodded to Alice as if to say, "Good call, Alice."

Father Fitzwater and Alice left the gaming area to sign his checks.

Chapter 9

Barrier
Saturday

Brick answered back, "Look Sheriff, it looks like you've got your hands full. I don't want to intrude but...."

"Then don't," Sheriff Monroe snapped, turning back toward him. This time her eyes landed on his ball cap. "LAPD. I didn't notice that before. Are you a cop? I thought you were a teacher." He had forgotten about his cap. It was well worn with a frayed bill. He took it off and stroked his hair with his hand.

She gazed straight at him and stated, "We aren't quite finished here yet. Hang around if you want, but outside the tape. By Al and Sid." She pointed toward the ambulance and the EMTs. She reached down and retied her shoe before taking an extra-long stride to reach the sidewalk.

Since his cap had given away his anonymity, Brick decided to take another tactic. He stepped back over the crime scene tape and called after her, "Yeah, I was a cop with LAPD. A sergeant for homicide investigations. Sheriff, I don't want to intrude, but I have some experience in homicides." He whacked the cap against his pants leg and dust bounced off it, evidence of the long hot ride. "Father Fitzwater invited me here to teach school this year. I just now arrived in town, but if I can be of any help, I would be happy to..."

Maggie narrowed her green eyes and cast a sideways glance at him. She interrupted him before he finished. "Perhaps later. I want to spend a little time working on it with my deputy. Maybe later but not now. I'll talk to you tomorrow after things have settled down a bit. You can come by the office, and I'll see you then."

He appreciated the young sheriff's position. She desired to take control of a situation that might make or break her. He considered his answer for a second and saluted, "Yes, Ma'am. You're the boss. You only have one deputy? I'll hang out with the EMTs for a while."

Brick stood near the gate of the tiny adobe house with its peeling white adobe plaster brown shutters and door, and red-tiled roof. It easily could have been something on loan from central casting for a turn-of-the-century western. Constructed in the early 1900s, the well-maintained, but tired looking cottage would be considered minuscule by today's housing standards.

But for a bachelor priest, it was entirely suitable. Three sides were adobe with the fourth side reinforced with empty liquor bottles and canning jars. They were inserted horizontally and lay prone, both supporting and supported by the adobe. In rural Nevada during the early part of the 20th century, builders searched for techniques to construct without wood, which was scarce and pricey. Adobe became that standard.

Brick remembered the priest explaining this kind of craftsmanship. Packed with mud and rock, as the structures rose and the weight of the stones increased, the stress caused the walls to give way and sometimes crumble. They switched from stones to empty whiskey bottles and glass jars and laid them on their sides, necks toward the interior. They pounded mud between them. Windows were an expensive luxury that were difficult to move by wagon. The bottled walls served two purposes: They filtered minuscule rays of sunlight into the structure, while also serving as insulation and filler for the walls.

From the outside, one would see a myriad of bottle colors winking in the light. From the inside, a prism effect shifted light through the day, colors twinkling on the adobe walls. A constant supply of empty liquor bottles created a marvelous recycling opportunity as they were emptied during the long cold winters and the long hot summers in rural Nevada. Barrier might well have been the first green city.

Brick shifted his weight and surveyed the cottage, noting that a roof hung over the front door's entry way, shielding it from the never-ending wind and infrequent rainstorms. The front yard was dirt-packed, surrounded by a faded and peeling picket fence with a few patches of parched grass and shriveling weeds that were struggling to survive. Lack of rain and a coat of dust on everything emphasized the dreariness, even on the rusty mailbox that hung on the fence. A planter displayed a couple of dead and dying tomato vines and served as a resting place for a weather-worn statue of the Virgin Mary. Brick saw that the hot wind waved the ribbon that had been tied to its base.

A small dog broke his concentration as she waddled toward him. It was a pink-eyed, mostly white, piebald mutt with a hot pink collar. She wagged her tail once and then scowled, giving a croaky yap as if to say, "Who are you, and why are you interrupting my day?" He leaned down to pet her and looked at her tag. *Bridget. Owner: Patrick Fitzwater.* He rubbed the back of her head, and she perked her prominent ears. "Hi, Bridget," he said. "You live here? I've got some bad news, Girl."

Chapter 10

Las Vegas
26 Years Prior

Father Fitzwater felt euphoric over his 10-minute winning streak while he waited for Alice at the blackjack table. He felt power. He felt triumph. He felt alive. In those brief moments, he became completely aware of his destiny. He knew he was born to lead with money and influence as only Las Vegas could bequeath. And now he knew how to get it.

The next morning, he arose early, recited Mass, and made a few phone calls. He reviewed his calendar and saw nothing that couldn't wait. His excitement from his casino victory did not subside as he switched out of his clerical clothes into normal street clothes. He donned a black baseball cap and drove across town to an area where he wouldn't be known and that housed the Irish Casino, *Hanover's*. It was in an obscure location, but what's not to love? Irish name. Irish pub. Irish casino.

He pulled into a parking spot and ducked through one of the back entrances toward the bright neon lights and chimes of the machines. The small, dimly lit game room held only a couple of blackjack tables. Stale smoke entered his nostrils, and he was aware of the constant din of coins being dropped into the machines. The occasional delight of a few returned coins enticed the players to keep playing. It was mid-morning, and girls in lime green bikinis and black fish-net stockings offered drinks to the players while expressionless security officers hovered near the entrances watching and waiting for wayward activities.

Patrick Fitzwater took it all in: the impropriety, the immorality, and the bawdy behavior. It simultaneously offended him and enticed him. He shook his head at the represented sins and recited a silent prayer for redemption and for financial triumph. He lit a cigarette and made his way to one of the blackjack tables.

That day he won $1,700 on an initial $100 investment.

Father Patrick Fitzwater continued to visit the casinos and gradually increased the time he spent playing. One day a week, two days a week, and within six months, he was fitting Mass into his playing time. He alternated casinos to avoid being cast as a regular. By frequenting one casino, he risked being identified by a parishioner or other holier-than-thou Catholic who worked or played there. He was a risk-taker but didn't want to damage his stellar reputation. He preferred the smaller casinos, but the larger ones provided more anonymity, although he seldom wore his white collar while gambling fearing it would draw attention to himself. If he wore the collar, he inevitably won a few games, but it was crucial that he remain anonymous. He wanted to be one of the many gamblers who sometimes got lucky. He always carried a small bag of casino chips from the parish offering plate. If he saw someone he knew, he could claim he was trading in chips and got caught up in the moment. He would avoid that casino from then on. The downside of this alternating pattern was that he never was able to observe the routines of the dealers. He wasn't sure if his winnings ever reached their full potential, regardless of whether he played blackjack, poker, or craps. He dabbled with various machines and enjoyed blackjack, but knew his odds were best at craps.

***

Father Kim Lin died of lung cancer during Fitzwater's first year in Vegas. At the young age of 31, Fitzwater, after filling in for the ailing priest that year, was appointed Pastor of Our Lady of Perpetual Tears. This placed him in charge of everything and gave him influence within the Diocese and community. The Diocese, which was headed by the bishop, oversaw the various parishes. A Diocese allows the churches to be independent but can also restrict or change programs as it pleases. An overly ambitious bishop can create havoc for an individual church.

Since he had already managed the parish, Fitzwater had distinguished himself from the rest of the Diocese as a go-getter, a take-charge priest, one who could deliver the goods. He reported that he added some programs that seemed to be working. He reported that attendance of the weekly faithful had increased. He reported collection dollars were up. He reported that membership was up. Although the reports were somewhat exaggerated, the bishop took him at his word and was ecstatic that this previously waning parish had gained strength, which meant more money.

Father Fitzwater's Vegas success plans were becoming a reality. He had gained the influence he desired. Now he was keen for power.

Chapter 11

Barrier
Saturday

About 40 minutes later, Sheriff Monroe and her deputy came out of the house and signaled to the still-smoking EMTs. "Al, Sid, we're ready for you." They stubbed out their cigarettes and started toward the ambulance to get the gurney. Brick sat in his Jeep rubbing Bridget's neck. It was warm enough that he left the top down. Bridget was enjoying her new perch.

Brick stepped out of his Jeep and called, "How about it, Sheriff, I'd like to see the padre before the EMTs take him away. Any objections to my coming in now?"

Maggie considered him for a minute and liked what she saw. He was handsome and muscled. He obviously frequented the gym. His T-shirt clung to his torso with no bulges. His belted jeans rode low on his hips accenting his slim waist. He tipped his LAPD cap back on his head and revealed his salt and peppered hair. She moved toward the Jeep and answered, "Tell me again, Mr. O'Brien, how did you know Father Fitzwater? Could I see an ID?"

Brick adjusted his hat and pulled out his California driver's license and a duplicate LAPD badge that he retained when he left the department. "Yes, Ma'am. I have these, Miss, uh, I mean, Sheriff. Will they work?" he inquired. "I didn't know Father Fitzwater well, but we met on a couple occasions, and then he invited me to Barrier to teach school."

Maggie read the badge and driver's license before saying anything.

"I read about you in the Forsythe newspaper, but I don't recall that you are or were law enforcement, too. I'm not sure about this. But I guess it's okay. Just don't touch anything. I assume you have seen a dead person before." She handed his identification back to him and assessed the sky considering how much daylight was left, then nodded at the EMTs. "Al, Sid, you guys wait a few more minutes. We'll get him out of here before it gets much darker though. I want you to drive him to Forsythe tonight. Can you do that? Cagey, would you check with the neighbors to see if they saw anything. Be sure to ask Anita Givens. She usually keeps an eye on the neighborhood's comings and goings."

Al and Sid nodded and leaned against the ambulance again.

Brick answered, "Yes, Ma'am. I've seen a few bodies. I know the rules about touching things in a crime scene. I appreciate your letting me come into the house. Do you have some extra gloves? I want to glove up."

Maggie watched Brick and challenged, "How does it happen that you arrived today? School started a month ago. It seems odd that on the day the new teacher comes rolling into town, the principal of the school is killed. I don't much believe in coincidences."

Brick paused before he spoke, "I don't believe in coincidences either. But to answer your question, Sheriff, I drove from Los Angeles today. I was at the Eldorado Pizza Shoppe when I learned he died. I'm not your killer. Father Fitz and I weren't close, but we have been in contact now and again for the past few years. We met four years ago when I was passing through Barrier with a prisoner, transporting him from Idaho to Los Angeles. A couple years later I stopped to see him when I went to Elko to see a friend. We drank a few toddies both times. We hit it off and stayed in contact. It's an Irish thing. He called me once when he was attending a convention in Los Angeles. Then last month, out of the blue, he called me and invited me to teach at Barrier High School. He needed a social studies teacher and a coach. He knew I wanted to get out of L.A. It was perfect timing, and here

I am. I know school's already started, but I understood that I simply needed to arrive before basketball season began."

They started up the walk. "You quit being a cop, just like that?" she wondered aloud. "What happened?"

"Yeah, just like that. I experienced a couple incidents that made me rethink my priorities. The time seemed right to try my hand at something else. I'll tell you about them sometime."

Sheriff Monroe nodded in response as she handed him a pair of disposable gloves. They entered the house slowly. Slumped over in his green vinyl recliner, the priest was indeed dead. His black shirt and white collar were drenched with blood, and a gaping hole pierced the middle of his chest. His mouth lay slightly agape as if he were about to say something. A few gray strands of his thinning faded hair were clumped and tangled and spread across his forehead. Dried blood flecked his face and clung to his hair and eyebrows. Brick also made a mental note of the pile of books, one of which held a red ribbon marking his place, that sat on the lamp table beside the body. The daily mail, a half-empty glass of milk, a couple antacid packages, and a remote control filled the tabletop.

An eerie dust shown through two faint amber beams that passed through the house's whiskey-bottle walls and converged into a fuzzy point atop his shiny head. A sallow ghost-pall replaced his ruddy Irish complexion and seemed even fuzzier in the glow of the ancient television. Judge Judy's face appeared on the silent screen.

Sheriff Monroe leaned against the wall and crossed her feet. She raised her chin to express confidence and control, when in reality she had no experience in working a murder scene and was apprehensive about the task before her. Her youth alone announced her greenness to Brick, but she didn't consider that. She tried to appear casual but conveyed restlessness within her attempts to stay collected and calm. She tied, untied, and retied her ponytail, then she repeated the motions.

"I called the coroner, but he couldn't come. He owns a mortuary in Forsythe, and he returned from a burial a few minutes before we spoke. He said

I should send the body to the Forsythe hospital as quickly as I could. I can't image who did this. Everybody loved him."

"Well, somebody held a grudge. That's a big hole and a lot of blood. I'm sure the coroner will agree that he's dead, all right," Brick announced flatly. He noted that the priest looked frailer than the last time he had seen him. He didn't know Father Fitzwater very well, but still he had moved to Barrier for him.

"I don't see any sign of violence or other disarray," Brick muttered to himself, although a whole lot of blood and tissue remnants created a gruesome scene. As a homicide detective he had witnessed many death scenes, some natural, most unnatural. "I'd say off-hand that he knew his executioner. What do you think? No struggle, no muss, no fuss. He and someone were talking and that someone shot him cold."

Maggie had observed Brick keenly as he spoke and agreed with him. "I think you're right. But, unfortunately, he knew everybody, although I'm not sure he had lot of friends, real friends. I always thought he was modest. For example, he came to our house for dinner before my dad got sick, but I don't think my parents considered him a close friend. Although, out of respect, I am guessing the town will shut down the day of the funeral Mass."

Brick countered, "I don't know if he was modest, but he loved to have fun and was full of mischief."

"We'll autopsy the body to rule out other possibilities. I'll get the EMTs ready to transport him."

Brick glanced out the front door. "If you don't mind, I'd like to look around the house for a few minutes before the EMTs come in. They're still smoking. I don't think they'll mind the wait." He rose and started toward the kitchen.

"Sure, have at it. Don't touch anything. We've taken a lot of photos already, and we'll take some more after Father Fitzwater's body is removed." She arose to follow him. "He's a pretty good housekeeper. Things are nice and clean. That'll make our work a lot easier." Brick raised his eyebrows but made no comment.

They entered the kitchen and looked around. Sheriff Monroe was right on target. The house was tidy, considerably tidier than the last time Brick visited. The fresh smell of the house revealed that the interior was recently painted. The white rooms were accented in turquoise at the ceiling and mid-wall. A small crucifix and photographs of Mother Teresa and the Pope hung on one wall, and a Ducks Unlimited calendar, open to the month of August, graced the other. The empty sink glistened. Two hand towels lay folded on the counter with a full cup of coffee and an opened can of soda resting on top of them. A large wooden cross studded with gems on a wooden base was positioned on the counter but seemed out of place considering its size and beauty. Brick opened the refrigerator. Two or three plastic dishes of leftovers, the usual condiments, and a half gallon of milk were the only edibles inside. A carton of pistachio ice cream waited in the freezer. Neat, tidy. Everything in its place.

Chapter 12

Las Vegas
26 Years Prior

Father Lin was a mere 40 years old when he passed away. The rumors about Lin included a variety of priestly wrongdoings including pedophilia, homosexuality, AIDS, and drugs of several kinds. As far as the Diocese was concerned, the rumors were unsubstantiated and were just rumors. Nothing to worry about. Father Fitz heard some of the rumors but ignored them. After all, Lin was the senior priest, and it was not his job to question him.

Throughout his brief career, Lin shuffled from parish to parish, serving only a few months in each. Lin had served in parishes in California, Idaho, Oregon, and Alaska. At one point the Diocesan office assigned him to investigate allegations against other priests but was removed and reassigned amidst allegations of his own pedophilia by an angry parishioner. His longest stint was his four years at Our Lady of Perpetual Tears, but Father Fitz had performed most of the ministerial work during the last year.

Within four hours of Lin's death, an assistant from the Diocesan office arrived and boxed up all his personal belongings, with the exception of a few things that Fitz kept for himself, and had them immediately loaded into a moving van and whisked away. She arranged for his body to be moved to a mortuary in Phoenix where he would be buried.

On the one hand, the congregation appreciated the quick response of the Diocese. On the other hand, Father Fitzwater became more anxious about the allegations and rumors and worried about what people—and the Diocese—knew. He knew of Lin's indiscretions, having kept silent through all the past year, but he didn't know why the Diocese sent his belongings to Phoenix instead of keeping them in Vegas. Why did they move him so quickly? Who else knew of the transgressions?

Father Fitzwater's seminary roommate managed the canon law office at the Diocese. He called him, but his friend would tell him nothing. He declared that no information was available. The files were confidential and were either concealed or destroyed. At any rate, no one was talking. Likewise, Father Fitzwater didn't answer the questions of his parishioners. The secrets of Father Lin's reign would remain just that—secrets. As far as the Diocesan records were concerned, Father Lin never existed.

Chapter 13

Barrier
Saturday

The last time Brick visited Barrier was about two years ago. He heard that his buddy would be involved in a mine-safety competition consisting of two events that demonstrated how miners rescued people who became trapped in small enclosures like walls, wells, or large pipes. Brick needed a break from policework so headed to the competition. He could have flown to Elko more quickly, but he wanted the down time. Driving through rural Nevada allowed for plenty of that.

The first of two events simulated extracting an injured miner from a horizontal, 42-inch-diameter pipe that was 50 feet long. The two rescuers who competed were both over six feet tall with wide shoulders as was the purported injured miner. All three were positioned within the pipe. The problem they encountered was that rebar crossed within the pipe every 10 feet. The rebar was positioned six inches off the floor of the pipe. The rescuers were required to maneuver the 175-pound miner over the rebar within the compact space. All three were battered and bruised before the simulated rescue ended. They were successful at pulling the trapped miner out of the pipe and Brick's friend won the timed competition. They were also dehydrated and exhausted from the heavy lifting and tight fit.

The second event simulated the rescue of a trapped person who fell down a well or into a deep hole. This part of the competition was held in an auditorium with an escape hatch in the ceiling over the stage. In the simulation the rescuer suspended himself head-first from the roof onto a dangling rope. His task was to haul the trapped miner up the rope to the roof. While the two were still suspended 10 feet from the ceiling, the judge ordered the rescuer to administer CPR to the victim while both were hanging on the unanchored rope. The rescuer performed the seemingly impossible task, but Brick doubted that an actual trapped person would have survived in a real situation. As it happened, the rescuer who was upside down was quite drunk at the time, making it doubly interesting. At the end of the competition, everyone guzzled a lot of beer.

***

On his first visit to Barrier, the condition of the priest's house made Brick wonder if the priest was a hoarder. It was cluttered from stem to stern with piles and stacks throughout. Every room was piled high with papers and magazines except for a narrow path through the house.

Maggie and Brick continued through the house. Nothing seemed out of place. The dresser tops lay bare and dusted. Clothes hung on hangers or in drawers. Bathroom sparkled. Trash cans emptied. The extra bedroom uncluttered. The bed contained a pale blue patchwork quilt and fluffed pillows.

Maybe his old buddy the priest hired a housekeeper, as today the house was spick-and-span. "We haven't searched everything in the house," Sheriff Monroe offered. "It doesn't look like anything else has been touched."

Brick looked at her and recommended, "I don't want to meddle, but I think you should search the entire house. You can wait until tomorrow though."

Bridget trotted through the open door and with some effort, scrambled up onto the quilted bed. "What are you doing here, Girl? You don't belong here." Sheriff Monroe told her, leaning down to stroke her head. "You're not supposed to be in here. You need to go outside." Bridget wagged her tail at the attention but gave a low growl when Maggie escorted her from the house.

Brick answered, "This is Bridget, Fitz's dog, at least that's what the collar says. He didn't have a dog when I was here two years ago. I can take care of her for the time being if you like. Do they let dogs stay at the Panorama?"

"You want to do that? I think the Panorama owner likes dogs," Maggie responded. "At least they have a sign in the entry that dogs are welcome. It says something like, *Dogs welcome. They don't fight, chew, spit, get drunk, or steal the towels, unlike their masters.* My guess is that they will let her stay. I'd keep her, but we already have an old black lab at home who thinks that he is the king pin in Barrier. If it doesn't work out, give me a call, and I'll have someone pick her up and take her to the shelter in Forsythe until we figure out what's what."

They finished walking through the house and didn't see anything out of order. Sheriff Monroe beckoned for Sid and Al to take the priest to Forsythe to await the coroner.

Brick returned to the kitchen to gather up some dog food and her dish. A box of dog chews sat on the counter, and he added those to his pile. He looked for a leash but didn't find one and returned to his Jeep. Bridget hopped into the front seat like it was hers. He gave her a dog chew, and she yapped a thank you. She held it in her mouth like a cigar.

Chapter 14

New York
46 Years Prior

Father Patrick Fitzwater was a professional Irishman. He considered an Irish heritage as one's only path to heaven, fame, and fortune but not necessarily in that order.

His mother, a headstrong lace-curtain Irish woman, emigrated from Ireland when she was merely 18. She saw no future for herself in Ireland, so she got on a ship and sailed to America with no money, no education, no family, no friends, no job, and limited English. She had worked as a house servant for more than two years to save enough money for the voyage, and when she finally had enough, she told her parents she was going for a walk on the beach. She failed to mention that the walk would take her to a pier that moored a ship that would take her across the ocean. She became seasick the day she boarded the ship and stayed nauseated until the ship finally made port on Ellis Island. She never contacted her parents; they didn't know where she went.

By the time she had disembarked in New York a few weeks later, her one dress sagged with the loss of 25 pounds. Besides the clothes on her back, she owned nothing except the determination to become a new American.

She thought she had found some good fortune on the boat when a family she met there offered her some employment, but they left before she got through the Ellis Island interviews. For two days she sat on a bench waiting for them to return for her, and likely would have stayed there far beyond that had an immigration worker not taken pity on her. The worker fed her and helped her gain employment as a nanny for a local family. Over the months, she strengthened her English with help from the children and assimilated to the American way of life. The family supported her until she married Patrick's father, Seamus Fitzwater. Seamus and Dora married and birthed 12 children in the Irish Catholic tradition. All were boys. Seamus and Dora wanted one of their sons to become a priest, in thanksgiving for their way of life, meager as it was, and they sent five sons to the seminary. Patrick was the youngest and the only one to take the vows.

In the streets of New York, Patrick learned what he believed to be an essential life lesson: Money was the most important thing for survival. Dora, as the center of the family, tried to keep the boys on the straight and narrow, but being hungry also taught them a few things. The boys learned how to distract a shop owner long enough for one of them to filch a few vegetables or fruit for the family. She never questioned where they got the extra food. Maybe it was a gift from God? No matter. Dora and the boys attended Mass regardless of whether food filled their bellies.

Seamus worked on the production line of a photography manufacturing company and became fascinated with cameras and photography. He began moonlighting as a photographer for weddings and other community celebrations, and his new love became well known and sought after. But none of the boys really wanted to learn about photography except Patrick. The camera captivated him, and he eagerly pursued his father's passion. Using his father's camera, he photographed everything from people to landscapes and learned to display his work. His father photographed for money; Patrick did it for art.

Everybody on their street was the same: hardworking, hungry, and doing whatever they could to survive. But the church was different. It was filled with riches and money, but still the priests were able to eke out more and more from their impoverished patrons. It tormented Patrick that those in the church possessed so much and still asked for more. The priests, Patrick couldn't help but notice, looked healthy and well fed. Patrick knew, from an early age, that this was the life for him.

Chapter 15

Barrier
Saturday

Brick drove to the Panorama Hotel to obtain a room for the night. The two-story hotel had seven rooms to rent, all on the upper floor. Four were already taken by the servers and hostesses, but he could pick any of the other three. He chose one on the back of the building with a view of the empty parking lot. He and Bridget loped up the stairs, and he tossed his duffle bag on the bed. He would unpack later. Bridget enjoyed a long taste of toilet water and left a trail of drops on the faded orange carpet as she flapped her jowls. Brick reviewed the hotel literature and stretched out with Bridget, trying to decide what to do. Soon they were both snoring.

The Panorama Hotel served as a halfway house for female immigrants who had come to Barrier through a government program that allowed them to work. They could stay in Barrier until they found a steady position in Las Vegas or Reno or some other Nevada town. They received their transportation to the United States plus board and room, but no compensation for their work. After a stay in Barrier, the women generally would find work in casinos in larger cities and were groomed for those jobs. By then, they would have attended classes to learn English, American culture, and etiquette. If they were overweight, they slimmed down. If they were underweight, they gained a few pounds—in just the right places.

Harvey Cooper, the owner and operator of the Panorama, was connected to a variety of enterprises throughout Nevada. He received a healthy stipend when the women joined one of the many establishments with which he affiliated—particularly if they were young, pretty, and enjoyed men. He recruited young women through travel agencies in Europe, Africa, or Asia and made a steady profit. With their charming accents, the immigrants were always in demand. He treated them well, and they stayed for their year before moving on to a more lucrative life.

Brick rallied before 10 p.m., and he and Bridget double-timed it downstairs. The bar was empty, as was the dining room. The dinner menu featured only two dishes each night, each of which was European and upscale. Meals like Beef Wellington, Duck L'Orange, Pheasant Under Glass, or Sauerbraten were unusual for a village like Barrier, but Brick looked forward to dining there as he had during both of his previous visits. He enjoyed the white tablecloths, linen napkins, and candelabra, as well as the charming young women who served him.

He stopped to glance at the menu that was posted by the door. Tonight, they offered Veal Scallopini or Steak and Kidney Pudding. He remembered the pizza, sure to be cold by now, and decided to return to the Eldorado Pizza Shoppe. He could order a pizza for Bridget since he was sure the menu offered no hamburger. He hoped she liked pepperoni.

Brick and Bridget devoured their pizzas and listened to the Eldorado chatter for about an hour. The man behind the counter was gone, and a young woman had taken his place. Her apron was also almost white.

The previously empty pizza joint was buzzing with noise from families and singles of all ages. Brick heard bits of conversation: Fitz was such a great man. Did he have friends or enemies? Loved taking photos. Who in the world? I loved Fitz. He was always kind. Brick watched and listened. The town obviously adored him, but at least one person didn't. Sooner or later, that person would show his head, but how long would it take?

Chapter 16

Barrier
Sunday

Rural Nevada could test a person's patience, and Barrier was no different. Originally a mining camp, the town's character vacillated between tourism, gold mining, and ghost town. The beautiful valley attracted loners and hermits who banded together in their common bond: reclusiveness. The residents hunted and fished, and some even lived off the land if they were creative and lucky. Natives often lived in Barrier their whole life—from birth to death. The newbies came in for very short periods of time, drifting in and out, disappointed that the answers they searched for did not emerge. The mix of native Barrier-ites and transients created its own unique definition of cultural diversity.

The ghost town side of Barrier was nestled into the west side of a mountain. The mountain protected its inhabitants from the harsh elements of both winter and summer. U.S. Highway 50 skirted the town. Before the system of highways was developed, town centers were constructed near railroad stations. When the railways ceded to the automobile, the growth left city centers behind.

Barrier was one of those cities that progress forgot. Like a step back in time, boarded walkways, rocking chairs, and checkerboards filled old porches. Old men played checkers, while girls hopscotched and boys shot marbles. Even still, Barrier had made strides with cell phones and electronic games simplifying, yet complicating, their unassuming lives. Several stores post signs reminding patrons to *Turn off your cell phone*, recognizing, but not accommodating, the current technology. Dogs, however, were always welcome.

A vacant four-story stone castle with its man-made moat and drawbridge watched over the town. The moat was empty except for a few dead birds and snakes. Weeds encroached the moat while patches of asters and verbena enjoyed the breeze. The top of the castle held a battlement, and a 20-foot spire capped the roof. Windows in the spire were positioned 360 degrees around and overlooked the entire valley. The lead-glass windows were cracked, and errant graffiti demonstrated disrespect of the vacated building. Erected by a wealthy Swiss gentleman to be used as a winter home in the early 20th century, the house fell into disrepair after the untimely death of its owner. Rumored to be haunted, the castle offered teenagers a place to hang out on Saturday nights. Used condoms and cigarette butts tainted the once elegant stone-tiled floors.

Marking the existence and demise of Barrier's former residents, a trisected cemetery rested below the castle. The Catholic section of the cemetery was protected by a padlocked gate, rendered useless because of the collapsed wooden fence. It was guarded by a statue of the Sacred Heart. Most graves had not only headstones, but also wrought-iron fences surrounding them.

The Jewish section contained 31 graves and was fenced off with large white chains. A Star of David was engraved into each headstone.

The largest section, the Protestant section, likewise contained three parts. An older section with high ornate headstones and walk-in vaults offered tribute to Barrier's previously thriving community. A newer part held smaller, plainer headstones. The third area consisted of crude hand-made wooden headstones etched with first names only. A small, hand-made, wood-burned sign hung on the fence and read, *Lady Lane*. This marked the passing of the *ladies of the evening* whose occupation was legal in parts of Nevada.

Lack of zoning and the transient nature of mining brought a mile-long series of mobile homes, trailers, metal storage containers, and sheds erratically placed on the outskirts of Barrier. People entered the town with no intention of leaving. The non-existent zoning laws allowed any type of building to be brought in, lived in, added to, and abandoned without consequence. Dogs wandered around at their leisure, and cats skulked from behind buildings and discarded vehicles. The sparse brown foliage did little to conceal the prairie dogs and jackrabbits that scampered through dormant lawns and unkempt vegetable gardens. They searched for mice and snakes and in turn, were part of the food chain of hawks and larger animal predators.

More than a decade earlier the Barrier Mining Company discovered gold under the town and determined that it was a major strike. They bought the entire town, house by house, razed the structures, and mined the town, lot by lot. Seven years and over 200 million ounces of gold later, the former housing development lay dormant. It now attracted roadside artists, who wrote their names in pebbles in the sand, announcing their existence in this section along the lonely highway.

Chapter 17

Barrier
Sunday

Brick arose early. He and Bridget descended the stairs to the Panorama dining room. The Sunday morning buffet consisted of Eggs Benedict, English muffins, and marmalade. The fresh fruit tray held pineapples, kiwis, and various citrus. Beverages included an expansive variety of juices and tea.

Brick noticed the deputy dining alone and invited himself to join him. The deputy didn't answer the question, but asked, "You're Coach O'Brien, right? The new basketball coach?"

Brick took the interaction with the deputy to mean that he was welcome to join him. He moved to the deputy's table and ordered bacon and scrambled eggs but was disappointed to learn they were not on the menu. He scrunched his face and instead ordered the breakfast of the day: bruschetta with roasted mushrooms with a poached egg. And tea.

"I would like coffee," he told the server when she took his order. "Black and strong."

"No can do, Honey. We got tea. That'll have to do." She smiled and gave no explanation.

The deputy rolled his eyes and started the conversation. "You'll get used to it."

Brick queried, "What's with no coffee and the European menu? No bacon and eggs?"

"The owner has his own agenda. The original owner tried to expand the culture of Barrier. People got used to it and like it now. Buy a coffee pot. That's what I did. You can get an all-American breakfast across the street.

"You were out at the priest's house last night, but I don't think we formally met. I'm Cagey Garrison, the Washington County Deputy. Such a shock about Fitzwater, don't you think? We haven't seen any real crime since I moved here. Of course, I haven't been here very long." He paused and took a bite of his English muffin. "We're glad you're here. This community is eagerly anticipating a decent basketball program. Not much to do in Barrier in the winter. Everyone in town goes to the games whether they are home or away. You will find the support for the school is terrific."

Brick stated, "That's good to know. I hope I can put the program together quickly. You can build some skills, but it helps if you have some natural talent and height to establish a good program. How'd you end up in Barrier, Cagey? It isn't exactly the center of the universe, even for Nevada."

"That's true. I was a freshman at UNLV and needed to work to pay for it. I joined the Nye County Sheriff's Department where I worked at the jail watching prisoners. I wanted to be a deputy, but I didn't have enough schooling or experience to work in Vegas. I also wasn't doing that great in school but knew I first needed to learn a thing or two. I joined the police force in Conifer Mountain, but then saw an opening here in Barrier. I knew a couple people here, and the pay is decent. It pays better than Conifer Mountain anyway. I went to work for the former sheriff when I arrived. When Sheriff Monroe was elected, she promoted me to chief deputy. The other deputy quit, and now I'm the lone deputy. I guess I'm still chief deputy."

Cagey had dark brown eyes with a weathered face and arms, and his nearly black hair was almost non-existent. He sported a mustache and straggly beard. His conditioned arms strained his sleeves. At 6 foot, 3 inches with a barreled chest and muscled arms, he appeared to be able to handle himself. He bore a small scar on his left cheek that became more noticeable when he smiled. His teeth were yellowed from cigarettes, and he wore a baseball cap with WCSO on it. A few tattoos decorated one side of his neck and both of his arms.

The two men conversed a bit more and finished their breakfasts. The room filled with people on their way to or from church.

Cagey stood and tossed cash on the table. "I've gotta go back to work," he said.

"Thanks for the company, Cagey, if you don't mind, I'll tag along," Brick said before calling to Bridget. "Come on, Bridget, we've got work to do. Let's go visit the sheriff. Maybe we can help her with something." Brick was remembering her amazing green eyes.

Chapter 18

Barrier
Sunday

Brick held the door open for Cagey and Bridget, and they walked to the sheriff's office. They greeted the sheriff, and Cagey took his spot at the front desk, which was piled high with papers and files and books. Sheriff Monroe was in her office on the phone. She stood rocking her tall body from heels to tiptoes as she conversed on her phone. She motioned for Brick to enter.

"Damn," she said as she hung up the phone. "This is a new one. One of our overnight guests ate a light bulb last night. Now he is moaning and groaning about police brutality and insists that he needs to go to the hospital where, of course, he'll try to escape. He's done it before. I was just on the phone with the ER doc in Forsythe."

"They told you to feed him a loaf of bread, right?" Brick offered.

"How did you know that?" she answered. "That's exactly what they recommended. A loaf of white bread. It would absorb the glass and minimize the damage." She shook her head at the thought and went to the front office to tell Cagey of the incident and the remedy.

"Cagey, go buy the cheapest loaf of bread you can find and make him eat it. Give him as much water as he'll swallow and tell him he is not going to the hospital. If he refuses, try it again in 15 minutes. When he hurts badly enough, he will hopefully cooperate." She shrugged her shoulders as if to say, *What next?*

Brick told her, "It used to happen on a regular basis in L.A. until they started putting cages around the bulbs. It still happens but less often. I saw a guy drink a half can of Drano one day though. Whew, that was ugly."

She returned to her office and closed the door. "What was he thinking? My predecessor had a favorite saying, 'If stupidity was a misdemeanor and gross stupidity was a felony, we would have the same people in jail.' I think he was right. Sgt. O'Brien, I am glad to see you."

"I've been involved with enough investigations to know that an extra set of ears can help sort things out, and you are welcome to use mine," Brick answered.

"Can I call you Brick? Is that your real name? I was thinking about you before the light bulb emergency because I planned to drop by the Panorama to see you. We were so busy last night that I didn't really get the opportunity to properly welcome you to Barrier. The whole town has been waiting. Basketball is king here."

Brick smiled at her. "People are always curious about my name. My parents named me Rockford after the James Garner character, but they always called me Rocky. When I started playing basketball during elementary school, my basketball skills were the pits. I threw basketballs like they were bricks not balls. My brothers started calling me Brickford. I grew tall in the 8th grade and was taller than the rest of my class before high school. My skills improved, but I didn't lose my nickname. Even though I attended college on a basketball scholarship, I never could ditch the name."

She chuckled. "Interesting. I like to hear how people got their nicknames. Barrier's population has a lot of nicknames. For starters, Cagey and Thumper."

"Thumper? Now that's one I haven't heard before. I never tried to change my name back to Rocky. It reminds me that I need to work hard at things to succeed and never give up. Now it is normal. I just go with it. I like the last sheriff's philosophy though. He was right. People do dumb stuff." He smiled and shook his head. "Anyway, anything new on Fitz's death?"

"I wish I could tell you we had something," Maggie started, "but we don't. The EMTs took Fitz's body to Forsythe last night. I tried to call the coroner, but besides being the local mortician and coroner, he is an evangelical preacher. That's typical for a small town. We all have a bunch of jobs. He held his own church service in Forsythe this morning, and nothing has been done yet. I will try to get ahold of the Father's family this morning. One of the deacons came by and told me that he called the bishop in Reno. I also called the bishop and left him a message, but he hasn't returned my call yet. No one answered, likely because it is Sunday. I'm hoping we can find some phone numbers in Fitz's house. I don't know if he owned a cell phone, but I should be able to find family addresses and phone numbers somewhere, maybe the church, or the school. I don't even know for sure that he has a family."

Brick nodded, "I know a little about his family. I took the liberty of calling his brother, Arthur, in L.A. this morning. I met him once when his car was stolen last year. I never met the rest of his family, but Fitz told me that he was the youngest of 12 children, all boys. His parents and at least four of the other 11 are also dead. All of the others live back east. Arthur offered to call the other brothers, but he doubts they'll come out. Father Fitzwater didn't have a good relationship with any of them. He never returned home after he went to the seminary." Brick paused. "How about we go have some coffee and a bite to eat? I've already eaten, but it wasn't enough. I'm still hungry and need coffee."

"I'll bet you ate breakfast at the Panorama this morning. It offers wonderful European style food but no coffee, right? Sure, it'll give us a chance to talk," she answered. "Unless you want pizza and Oly for breakfast, we'll have to go to the Barrier Café. You can have a normal breakfast, including coffee. We'll get Bridget something tasty, too."

Chapter 19

Barrier
Sunday

The three of them crossed Main Street to the Barrier Café and ordered the early bird breakfast special of ham, eggs, toast, hash browns—and all the coffee they could drink. They ordered Bridget scrambled eggs and a bowl of milk, which she gobbled down before Maggie and Brick even received their meals. They took their time eating while Brick told the sheriff more of his law enforcement history and his intermittent relationship with Father Fitzwater. Maggie confessed that she called the Los Angeles Police Department and spoke with the lieutenant in his division. She wanted to verify who he was. While his identity was confirmed, she still had questions that needed answers.

"How often did you see Father Fitzwater?" she inquired.

Brick answered, "I met him three times, but we called back and forth a couple times. I was in Barrier twice, and when he went to see his brother in L.A. last year, we met for a drink. That's when his brother's car was stolen. He called me late last summer to ask if I was interested in the teaching/coaching position that had come free. I liked him well enough, but when you get right down to it, I didn't know him. He was a good drinking buddy and could spin a yarn, but I don't know what he liked or didn't like. He enjoyed Barrier and the high school. He bragged the kids kept him young."

Maggie smiled, "He was great with teenagers. Our high school used to be an all-Catholic school but merged with the public system when the mines closed, and people moved away. He was the principal back when I was in school, too. He was very involved, attending extracurricular activities, visiting classrooms, and he never missed the games. He knew all the students and kept them honest. If we got out of line, he'd haul us into his office and chew us out. If we were Catholic, he'd require that we go to confession. Nobody got away with anything. He reamed me out a couple times. I'm not Catholic and didn't get the confession thing though." She blushed as she thought of his scolding. Brick wondered what she did to gain the principal's attention.

She asked Brick a few more pointed questions about his relationship with Father Fitzwater. When she was satisfied with the answers, he again offered his assistance with her case. This time she accepted.

Chapter 20

Barrier
Sunday

Sheriff Monroe invited Brick to help search the house while Cagey was busy with the light-bulb-eating prisoner. Besides locating more phone numbers, they were hoping to find something, anything, that might lead them to the killer. The yellow tape still encircled the house, restricting entrance from beyond the picket fence. Several had ignored the barrier and placed flowers at the base of the statue of the Virgin Mary, creating a small shrine. Surrounding the statue were high school keepsakes, including a football helmet, a basketball, and a pair of volleyball knee pads. A Teddy bear with a pink bandana looped around its neck had blown over and was matted with a powdered layer of dust brought by a gust of Barrier wind. Bridget hopped out of the Jeep and dashed up to the house, wagging her tail as she nudged her nose against the locked door.

"How's Bridget doing?" Sheriff Monroe inquired. "Do you think she misses the padre?"

Brick stepped out of the Jeep, "She's a peculiar dog. She always has a gloomy look on her face like she's mad at somebody. At the same time, she seems to be at home wherever she is. When I mention Fitz, she puts her tail between her legs, lowers her head, and skulks off as if I were scolding her. If she weren't a dog, I'd think the padre instilled some Catholic guilt in her. In one moment, she ignores me, but the next thing I know, she is my best friend, and I'm tripping over her. When I get into the Jeep, she hops in like we've been friends forever. I wonder if she saw the person who shot him."

Maggie ducked under the tape and led the way up the walk to the front door. She pondered aloud, "Let's see if we can find something that will help us. We went through everything obvious. I guess we are searching for the not-so-obvious now."

Brick countered, "Yup, it's the not-so-obvious that I like. My experience says that the scene often holds the answers." Maggie handed him a pair of rubber gloves before she removed the seal and unlocked the door. She led the way in and stepped over Bridget as she entered.

"Let's start with the living room," Brick suggested quietly. "Let's see what we see."

Brick sent the dog back to the Jeep before entering the house. Maggie turned the television on. A Sunday morning news program showed a fuzzy picture, and the sound was scratchy. She pushed the mute button.

Brick observed, "From his chair he could see the door, see who is coming through the door, see the hall to the bathroom, and the kitchen door. He would know pretty much what's happening in the whole house. He knew the killer all right. I'd bet a bundle on it."

"I am sure you're right, but how do we find out who he is? I mean, where do we start? What are we looking for?" This was Maggie's first murder investigation. It was her first death scene since becoming sheriff. She welcomed some expertise and was eager to learn.

"We start right here. I think this house contains all the information that is available about who killed Father Fitzwater. Right here. This is where we start." Brick pulled a notebook from his pocket and began to take some notes. "What do you see, Sheriff? You talk. I'll write."

Maggie answered, "I don't see much. Nothing seems out of place. Everything is immaculate. *Time Magazine, Catholic Digest,* and *People*. The magazines are current. The mail has been opened and stacked. Junk mail and a couple bills, Visa and Nevada Power and Light." She pulled the bills from their envelopes and whistled out a long breath. "Whew, look at this. The new Visa bill is over $4,000. It was $2,500 last month and paid off. I wonder what he bought from Amazon.com that cost $4,000. It says 'electronics.'"

"I dunno but we can check that out," Brick answered while writing in his notebook. "Four-thousand-dollar Amazon purchase. It could be anything. Maybe a TV with the works or some appliances. It seems like Amazon sells everything and anything. I imagine they are essential in a place like Barrier where people don't have a lot of choices in merchandise. This might be for a flat-screen TV or a super-duper computer. Of course, my whole electronic inventory plus the rest of my furniture didn't cost $4,000. I don't see a computer anywhere, and this clunker of a TV must have been here since *I Love Lucy* was a hit, if you know what I mean."

Add to that, Maggie returned, "He was of the age where his computer literacy might not be the best. I doubt that he could turn on or use a computer. We should ask the school about his computer literacy. His secretary will know. Maybe he ordered a new TV, but it hasn't arrived yet? That's something to investigate, too. What about those books on the table? What was Fitz reading these days?"

Brick leafed through the pile of books. "Two Louise Erdrich books have bookmarks in them. I've seen her name but haven't read anything by her. The newest Greg Iles novel. Maeve Binchy. She's an Irish author, more of a girl novelist if you ask me. No offense meant. But she's good."

"None taken."

Brick continued, "Last year's high school yearbook and that's about it." Brick leafed through the yearbook and noted the graduation class of 26 beaming faces. "Not many kids." Glancing through the rest of the book, he observed about 10-20 students in each of the grades with the usual photos of ball teams, cheerleaders, dances, kids being kids. Some of the photos were signed with remembrance notes recorded in the margins.

"Yeah," Maggie answered, "not many, but it was the biggest class in several years. A dozen a year is the norm ever since the mine stopped producing, and the company pulled out. Not many kids finish school here, and those who do leave and don't come back. After they get a taste of the real world, they put Barrier in the rear-view mirror. The drop-out rate is high, higher than folks believe. My class was over 35 students, but that was the last large class."

Brick grinned at her, "You are a Barrier High Tiger-ette? You didn't ever leave?"

"You bet I left. For a while anyway. I left and swore never to return except to visit my parents. I graduated from UNLV with a major in criminal justice and a minor in hotel-restaurant management. I had lots of job offers. After I graduated, my mom needed me to help her with my father. He has early onset of Alzheimer's disease and gives my mother holy hell. She needs a lot of support. I decided to come back for a while and went to work for the sheriff. It was either go to work for the sheriff, Barrier Café, or Eldorado Pizza. I went to work for the sheriff. No way would I work for the Panorama. The sheriff retired a year ago, and I decided to give it a whirl. I ran for sheriff and won. Not many people voted. I ran unopposed and won with 586 votes. Eleven votes were recorded for Mickey Mouse or Donald Duck. Twenty-eight votes were for Clint Eastwood. Since Washington County has about 5,000 people, I guess that's a mandate. So here I am, doing what I said I would never do. I live in Barrier and, worst of all, I live with my parents," Maggie answered as she clinched her jaws. "I hope it isn't forever, but who knows? I remember my parents saying they wouldn't be here forever either, and they're still here. Maybe when Dad dies. But I guess I'll cross that bridge when I need to. I'm worried that he'll outlive my mom, and I'll have to deal with the Alzheimer's alone."

"That's hard. You've got a tough job ahead. I don't envy you." Something caught Brick's eye. "Hey, here's the padre's checkbook. It was shoved down into the side of the chair." He scanned the ledger. "He wasn't too precise. He seems to have written the amount of the checks down, but skipped the dates, payee names, and check numbers. We need to see if we can find a bank statement around here somewhere. Why don't you see what's in the desk?"

She moved over to the roll-top desk and opened the center drawer. "Here's August's bank statement right on top. I guess he didn't get around to filing it."

"See if there are any canceled checks, too," Brick stated casually. "Or photocopies of the checks."

"Nope, neither. The statement and a couple ads for checks with flowers and names on them."

"What's the balance?"

Maggie reviewed the various subtotals on the bank statements and exclaimed, "Whew, more than I've got. He has $4,200 in checking and about $314,000 in savings. Wow! He has moved money around some as the daily balance for his checking account has been both very high and low. The savings account has been up and down as well. $314,000 appears to be the high, but the low was under $5,000."

"I wonder what that's about," Brick mused. "My experience is that most people don't keep hundreds of thousands of dollars in their saving accounts. Give me those numbers again, would you?" Maggie reread the exact amounts and dates as he wrote them in his notebook. She pulled out a plastic evidence bag and placed the bank statement in it.

"Did he gamble?" Brick asked. "What did he do for fun?"

Maggie looked at him incredulously, "Fun? A priest? How would I know? Do priests gamble? I can't imagine that. We don't even have any real casinos here. Maybe a few slot machines, but they wouldn't reap this kind of money. I thought they did priest things for fun, like pray or go to confession. I know he attended all the sporting events at the school. Basketball, football, volleyball. He was often invited to people's homes for dinner. My mom invited him over about once a month before Dad got sick. He liked watching the ballgames, I know that much. We could ask Thumper, his administrative assistant. She works half-time at the school and half-time at the church. She probably knows something."

Brick retorted doubtfully, "Thumper? I've wondered about her ever since you mentioned her earlier. Where'd that name come from?"

"It's a nickname. It's a combination of her first and last names. Thelma Ampere. She was given that nickname during her elementary school years, and it stuck. When you meet her, you'll see that it fits."

Maggie paused before continuing, "Maybe for fun he hunted or fished? Lots of people here enjoy the streams. Others love to hunt grouse or antelope and deer. I have to say though that he didn't look like a hunter, and I didn't notice rifles or other weapons yesterday. Maybe they are stowed someplace. If he does have anything, we will need to lock 'em up until we decide how to handle his personal effects. Rifles will attract riffraff, and I don't need any of that."

Brick recommended, "We should search for weapons in all of the rooms. I didn't notice a gun cabinet when we were here before, but we'll check again. We'll need to look under the bed and in the back of the closets. Let's also search for a door to an attic or basement."

Brick recorded in his notebook. *Gambler?* Hmm. Interesting thought. Father Fitz never mentioned gambling. *Hunter?* Brick knew that he liked to drink Irish whiskey and smoked, but those were about the only activities that he had mentioned.

Maggie searched through the rest of the desk drawers but didn't find anything that seemed important. Some postcards from travelers and a few mementos of trips and some photographs. One drawer held about 50 or 60 worthless Vegas casino chips, mostly from places that were out of business or renamed. A two-drawer filing cabinet held several randomly filed folders, and the top drawer contained several years' worth of statements, invoices, and advertisements from various hospitals and assorted Catholic social service agencies. The lower drawer held a couple of unframed photos and some memorabilia of his youth. "There's nothing here," she announced. "Nothing that might lead to his being murdered."

"We need a weapon," Brick responded. "Get the weapon, and you'll find the killer. That's my rule. Without the weapon, we'll have a tough time finding the guy who did this."

"We need to check the rest of the house," Maggie said. "We've been thorough, but another look won't hurt." They turned to the kitchen where they spied a pile of money on the kitchen counter. The wooden cross they had noticed yesterday held it in place. It was over an inch high. "Holy cow. What's this?" Maggie exclaimed. "This wasn't here yesterday. There must be a hundred of them. Maybe more. Fifties. A few tens and some singles. There's no way we would have overlooked these yesterday." She reached to pick them up but immediately thought better of it. "I think we might want to send them to the lab. What do you think?"

"You're right. These were not here yesterday. Remember? Cigarettes, a coke can, a cup of coffee, and the big cross. But the cross was moved. It was sitting on some towels. No money. Where's your camera?" Brick walked over to the back door and checked the lock. "The door is still locked. And the front door was padlocked. Does someone else have a key? And why would someone leave a pile of money on the kitchen table? You've got your gloves on. Why don't you count them?"

"Who would have a key? Before I count, let me take a photo." she remarked, returning to the living room for her camera. She snapped a few photos of the kitchen counter with its stash.

"What do you think? How much do you think is here?" Answering her own question, she replied, "I don't think it's a thousand. Maybe $500 or $600?" She reached for the cash and began counting, placing them in piles by denomination. She tallied 31 50-dollar bills, four 10-dollar bills, and 28 one-dollar bills. Over $1,500. More than she thought.

"This is weird," Maggie remarked as she bagged the money in another plastic evidence bag and placed it in her hip pocket for safe keeping.

"You got that right. Let's keep on searching. Something else might turn up," Brick replied. They continued through the house, room by room, looking at both the obvious and the obscure. Brick's experience and Maggie's diligence made a good team. They patted down the house, as if they were patting down a cell for contraband. Nothing slipped from their eyes or hands. When they finished, they had located the kitchen money plus another $1,000 from various other stashes. Under a pile of books. In his sock drawer. Behind a statue of the Virgin Mary. In one of the priest's clothing drawers, they found a small pile of papers and letters that seemed worthy of reviewing. But no weapons. Maggie snapped a photo to record the locations of the money and papers. She then stored the cash in an evidence bag.

They walked through the house again double checking everything. With the exception of the money, nothing seemed out of place.

It was after 2 p.m. when Brick said, "Let's get out of here and go have a cup of coffee and a sandwich or pizza, if that's our only choice. We can drop the cash by your office. Do you have a vault or safe? We can examine these papers and letters after we enjoy our pepperoni and onion." Sheriff Monroe and Brick headed outside and paused at what they saw.

The few flowers that had been placed at the statue of Mary had expanded into a small garden with several bouquets. Someone had left more school memorabilia in the array. The shrine had mushroomed.

Chapter 21

Las Vegas
21 Years Prior

Father Fitzwater carefully counted and double-counted the offering after each Mass making sure it was correct. He visited the bank to deposit the money and gave a receipt to his administrative assistant, Mary Grace O'Toole. From time to time, he advanced himself an additional smidgen of his salary. Not much, he reasoned. The advance was barely enough to cover his losses, but it kept him from going in the hole. Sometimes he lent himself a little more to keep him solvent. He planned to repay the money when he reached his goal, which he was sure would be any day now.

After most Masses, the collection plate held a variety of casino chips which he carried to the various gaming houses. It was an act of kindness that saved Mary Grace time and gas money. He could use those chips to his own advantage without anyone knowing how many were deposited in the offering plate at each Mass. Some chips were worth a few dollars. Others were in the $500 range. Once someone dropped a $5,000 chip into the collection plate. Mary Grace never saw them. He deposited what he wanted and fed her a number. Sometimes accurate. Other times almost accurate.

He believed that the church's money was under his control, and if it evened out in the end, what difference did it make? His system was easy. Whether he gained or lost money at the gaming tables, it was shared between him and the church. 50-50. Or 60-40. Whatever was fair. And he was sure that his losses were temporary. God was on his side, and Fitzwater vowed to make a big donation when his ship came in. It was sure to happen soon. He hadn't been hurt very much at the casinos. He had some losses, of course, but nothing to cause him difficulty.

Shortly after Father Lin died, Father Fitzwater ran into a streak of good fortune. He was at the Cantina Regala playing craps—and winning. It was his first return visit to a casino since his predecessor's passing. The casino manager, Lucinda, stood behind him for a few passes after he pulled in over $50,000 with an investment of $2,200. The floor managers always summoned Lucinda when the wins were high. As he cashed in his chips, Lucinda waved to the bar maid for a drink on the house for Father Fitzwater.

"Father Fitzwater! I didn't realize that you enjoyed the games. It is a pleasure to see you here. You did well, my padre. What are you drinking?" Lucinda queried. This afternoon the priest was not wearing his white collar. He wore black jeans and a polo shirt with a baseball cap riding on his brow. He didn't recognize Lucinda although she looked vaguely familiar. It was her nametag that told him who she was. A crowd gathered and cheered him, which made him nervous. He glanced around concerned that someone else might recognize him. *She must be a parishioner*, he thought a little fearfully. He didn't like being recognized by employees or patrons of the casinos. It could get back to the bishop.

"L…Lu…Lucinda." he stammered as the bar maid handed him a drink. "How nice to see you."

"I'm happy for you. You won big. How about letting me buy you dinner tonight to celebrate? I'm still working but will be off shortly. It would be my pleasure to treat you to a steak and a glass of wine. Why don't you have a drink, and I'll join you in about half an hour?" Lucinda offered, as she winked at him.

With an Irish whiskey in his hand, the priest sauntered over to the cashier's booth to cash in his chips. He requested a check and was issued one for $35,783 after taxes. He pocketed it and glanced around for

Lucinda. He thought he might as well have dinner before heading back home, especially if she was buying.

Lucinda, having donned fresh clothes, reappeared behind him and tapped him on the shoulder. "Hi again, Handsome." She was wearing a black and white dress that fit like a glove. Her long black hair, now unpinned, draped over her shoulders. She took his arm and led him into a private dining area.

He was stunned. What a beautiful woman. And she was buying him dinner. "I'm starving!" she announced. "What are you hungry for?"

Chapter 22

Barrier
Sunday

Bridget, Maggie, and Brick left the priest's house and returned to the sheriff's office. Maggie grabbed a couple of bottles of water from her mini-fridge and handed Brick one. She took off her jacket, and Brick noticed that she replaced her T-shirt with a white turtleneck that clung nicely to her slim, athletic body. She still wore black Levi's that rode low on her hips. They looked new—and she looked amazing.

Maggie opened the vault and placed the money inside. "This will have to do until tomorrow when the bank's open. How do I handle having money as evidence anyway? Do I deposit it in a trust account? Or leave it in the vault. I know that I can't deposit it in a checking account, but don't want to risk it being stolen from here either. They didn't teach me this in sheriff's school." She wrinkled her brow while considering this puzzle.

Brick knew the answer. "It's fine here if you keep the vault locked. Who else has the combo?"

Maggie didn't answer but looked at the flashing light on the phone on her desk, indicating that she had voicemail messages. Four messages. She listened. Two were from anxious parents worrying if their children would be safe at school. One was from her mother wondering if she was all right, and how could this have happened while she was sheriff? The last was a call from an anonymous caller. She listened to that message three or four times.

The caller ID listed the caller as *Restricted*. "What good does it do to have caller ID if it is restricted?" Maggie mumbled to no one in particular. She hit replay and the speaker button so that Brick could listen to the message. Loud music played in the background. It sounded like a bar or noisy restaurant. A falsetto voice rang out in a sing-song manner, "Ding-dong, the warlock's dead." The music boomed with a mix of voices. The message was clear, but the speaker spoke indirectly into the phone, perhaps talking to another person.

Maggie asked Brick, "We have to assume that the caller is referring to the priest's death, but what does it mean? I can't imagine anyone in Barrier would consider him evil. He was more like a saint. What is he—if it even is a he—talking about?" Brick liked that she said *we*.

"It sounds like a crank call to me or maybe a butt dial. Murder scenes bring out all kinds of crackpots, and this case will be no different. Don't erase it. Save and record it on another device. You might need it and don't want it erased accidentally. It could mean something. Why would someone think him evil? Maybe the papers we found will hint at something or someone."

Maggie and Brick sat down and laid out the paperwork that they brought back to the office with them. They made three piles. One contained correspondence, one pile was for bills, and the third was for financial statements. The mail pile contained five pieces. Three picture post cards, all from Ann and Jeff, whoever they were. Mailed from Hawaii. The substance of each was, *We are having a great time. Cheers.* A letter from the priest's brother, Arthur, in Los Angeles was dated three years ago and shared that their brother who lived in Illinois had fallen ill and wasn't expected to live. The last piece was a handwritten note card from somebody but was unsigned. It looked old. The ink was faded, and the paper was crumpled as if it had been read a few times. It read, *Moving to Barrier. See you Thursday.* The postmark read Las Vegas but the date was smeared. Brick added, "I wonder who was moving to Barrier. It could be from anyone. Let's bag it and see about fingerprints, although that's probably a waste of time."

"Not much to go on," Maggie mused aloud. "Ann and Jeff are the Winstons who live here. He is a retired miner, and she works at the library. I am sure they are Catholic. Maybe they traveled with Father Fitzwater in the past. I know he often took cruises or tours in the summer when school was out."

Next came the pile for bills. There were only four. The Visa and power bills were unpaid. The phone and water bills were marked paid. The Visa bill was the most curious with drastic fluctuations and high balances in recent months.

The bank statement pile included statements from two different banks. The one that they previously viewed was mailed from a bank in Lake Tahoe. The statement from the Forsythe bank showed a balance of over $20,000. "How much does a priest earn anyway? I always thought priests were poor as they took a vow of poverty," Maggie pondered aloud. "These amounts jump around a lot. They go from $600 to $25,000 in one month. What is going on?"

Brick said, "Look at this. This LVN Investment statement shows his assets of nearly half a million. I'm not used to seeing these kinds of balances in normal bank accounts. They look more like the ones that are either laundering money or have drug money coming in. I think we need to think of this from a different vantage point. My first thought is drugs. At least that's how I would investigate it in L.A."

Maggie responded, "This isn't L.A., and Father Fitzwater wasn't selling or buying drugs. No drugs. No way. He was a real straight arrow and too well respected for any type of drug issue. You can ask anyone in town. They would all say the same thing."

Brick nodded, but his experience told him that no one was perfect. They should not take anything or anyone for granted.

Maggie then set to making a few phone calls. She started with the coroner but got an answering machine. She left a message. Then she called the Diocesan office in Reno but got a recording saying the message box was full.

"It's hard to do law enforcement stuff on Sunday in Barrier. Everything is closed. Let's go grab a bite to eat," she suggested.

They returned to the Pizza Shoppe where Bob Givens, the man behind the counter, met them at the door. He looked at Maggie and asked, "Have you found out anything yet? Who done it?" Then he turned his attention to Brick. "Hey, Coach O'Brien, I saved your pizza from last night. Do you want me to warm it up for you?"

Brick answered for both of them. "We're still working the case. Last night I came back and got a fresh pizza. In fact, I got two, one for me and one for Bridget. You had already left, and I didn't know that you'd saved it."

"I see you got Bridget. I was curious where she went. She seems like such a sad dog, and I thought maybe she got stolen or somethin'. You keepin' her?"

Brick ignored Bob's comments while Maggie ordered. "We'd like a pizza and cokes. Could you make a fresh pizza for us and then warm up that leftover pizza for Bridget? Not too warm though. We wouldn't want her to burn her mouth. And, could I also have a pineapple and Canadian bacon pizza and a Pellegrino?" Maggie inquired innocently.

Chapter 23

Barrier
Sunday Afternoon

"I am going back to the house. Do you want to come?" Maggie offered after they finished the pizza.

Bridget, Maggie, and Brick piled into the sheriff's car and drove back to the priest's house where the memorabilia pile clearly was growing. This time, though, three teenaged girls sat on the front steps to the house. Two of the three held cell phones. They wore black shorts and T-shirts emblazoned with orange letters spelling *Barrier Tigers* on the front. They sat atop square bandanas to avoid getting gray dust on their black shorts.

"The memorabilia pile has doubled in size since lunch time," Brick noticed as they walked up the sidewalk. "Maybe we should have a look at those items. What do you think, Sheriff?"

Sheriff Monroe ignored him and sat down on the steps beside the girls. "Pretty awful, isn't it?" she inquired. Brick waited on the doorstep while the sheriff was conversing with the three.

"Yeah, it is. We loved him as a principal and a priest. Did you find his murderer yet?" the blonde girl asked. "Do you know when the funeral will be?"

"Who are you?" Maggie queried. "What are your names?"

They answered in turn.

"I'm Reese," the blonde girl replied. Her long blond hair was tied back in a ponytail. A breeze pulled strands of hair out of the pink hairband, and they floated around her pretty face.

"I'm Marianne." Marianne was also blonde, but her hair was chopped in layers and streaked with lime green. It stuck up all over her head like a green porcupine. She had a nose-ring and a star tattoo on her wrist.

The third girl responded, "Cassie Santos." Her massive wavy, jet-black hair fell loosely down her back past her waist. She was striking, far prettier than the other two but seemed shy.

"It's nice to meet you all. Reese Brownley, right? I should have recognized you," the sheriff answered. "I babysat you a few times when you were little. I think you were four or five, and we ate pizza together. And weren't you selected as homecoming queen last week? Congratulations."

Reese grimaced and snapped. "No. First runner up. I lost to her. That one." She pointed at Cassie who blushed.

Maggie stretched over and fist-bumped Cassie. "Congrats. I know how exciting that is. It's a real honor."

Reese continued, "Father Fitzwater himself crowned us. He was proud of me. He was my godfather as well as my priest and principal." She paused, then added, "We were very close."

"Homecoming is always a lot of fun. I was the homecoming queen for my class when I went to BHS. Cassie, you're new to town, aren't you? Didn't your dad move here last year to work in the mine's skeleton crew? I met him a few weeks ago. He's a nice man." Cassie nodded in answer.

"Marianne, what's your last name?"

"Franklin."

"Oh, I know now. Isn't your mother a teacher? Science, right? Aren't you related to Thumper?"

Marianne nodded, "Yeah, she's my aunt."

"You girls shouldn't be hanging around like this. We don't know who killed your principal, and he still could be in Barrier. I know you are sad about

Father Fitzwater, but it isn't safe for you to be here. Not yet. Do you know if any kids were mad at him or anything?"

Marianne answered, "No, everyone loved him. Do you think one of us killed him? I mean like one of the students at Barrier High? No way. No way any of us could hurt him." She turned and faced the sheriff with wide eyes.

Reese and Cassie nodded in agreement while Reese quickly repeated, "No way. What's going to happen to Bridget? He hasn't owned her very long, but he was crazy about her." Bridget shuffled over to them and sniffed their sandaled feet. When she heard her name, she wagged her tail and licked Reese's knees.

"Where did he get her?" the sheriff inquired. "She isn't a puppy. Did someone else own her before Father Fitzwater?"

The three of them shrugged their answers. Reese said, "Don't know. She started coming to school one day, and next thing we knew, Father Fitz told us that she was our unofficial mascot. We think somebody dumped her. People do that sometimes. She hardly looks like a tiger though." That brought a smile to Maggie's face.

"If you hear anything that might help us, will you call me? For now, my deputy will keep her," she declared looking at Brick. "She seems cranky but isn't much bother."

Brick raised his head, startled at his sudden promotion.

Maggie started to rise and apologized, "Oh, I'm sorry. I should have introduced you. This is Mr. O'Brien, my newest deputy sheriff. More importantly, he will be your teacher this year. Social studies. Like U.S. History and American Government. And basketball coach." She handed each of them a card with her phone number on it. The girls turned and gave out a weak wave but didn't say anything.

Finished with the conversation, Maggie rose and signaled for Brick to follow. They entered the house stepping over Bridget who growled at her being left out.

Chapter 24

Barrier
Sunday Evening

Brick spent the evening driving around Barrier searching for a place to call home for the remainder of the school year. He drove by the houses that were advertised on the community bulletin board and was not pleased with what he saw. His apartment in Los Angeles was modest, but these houses made his old apartment seem like a palace. The first needed a new roof, and number two's windows were boarded up. God only knew what the inside looked like.

A third one was more promising, at least on the outside. It looked livable. Maybe. A *For Rent* sign drooped from the wire fence, which was in good shape except in a couple places where it hung from the pole. The weather-beaten sign must have been hanging there for a while as it dangled from its wire. He took that as a bad omen but peeked in the windows anyway. The house was vacant. He tried the door, which was unlocked, and went in. He hoped he wouldn't be arrested for trespassing.

The house was very clean and had a few serviceable pieces of furniture. That was a plus. If he repaired the fence, Bridget could guard the house from the exterior. It might work. But as he looked further, he noticed that the house was inclined. The living room was positioned toward the front of the house, and it seemed to be a good foot higher than the kitchen to the rear. The floor lay on a slant and sloped several inches front to back. To test his depth perception, he laid an empty coke can that was discarded by previous occupants on its side and gave it a little push. It rolled all the way to the kitchen picking up speed as it went. Entertaining maybe, but limited in its appeal. It banged into the kitchen cabinets with a slight clunk.

Bridget toured the house looking for food remnants of which none were to be found. A couple deceased cockroaches lay in the kitchen, but they didn't interest her. Brick checked out the other rooms, all of which had similarly angled floors. He went outside to inspect the foundation. It had collapsed. Its cement base was compacted in the rear of the house. This upset him more than he expected, as this home seemed to be his best alternative. He would ask Maggie and Cagey to see if they could suggest others. Of course, if he rented this one, he could be entertained by watching Bridget roll from the living room to the kitchen as she slept. He wrote down the phone number in his notebook but also wrote *sloping*.

Other housing pickings were sketchy at best. He saw trailers and a shabby duplex, which were scary even for Brick. Four stacked container houses completed the tour. Windows and doors had been inserted, but they were still shipping containers. No way. He drove around the main part of town while he considered his options. The Panorama, the scary houses, a trailer, a container house, or the sloping house. None of them was good. For the time being the Panorama was his best option, if he could buy a coffee pot. Housing was important, but morning coffee was, too.

Chapter 25

Barrier

Monday Morning

Monday morning Brick donned his Dockers and a blazer, and he and Bridget drove to the high school. He was not sure of the formality of the Barrier High School faculty but thought it would be better to dress up for his first visit. BHS was located across the tracks and was one of the few structures that had not been relocated when the mining company purchased the town. The football field lay to the north of the building and was bedecked with left-over ribbons and posters from the previous week's homecoming activities. The building itself was brick, and the outside needed paint and polish, to say the least. The cornerstone read, *1910*, making it well over 100 years old. The grounds were primarily grass, but weeds encroached the sidewalks and flower beds. The original structure was doubled in size by an addition that extended away from the road. A painted banner above the front entry read, *Barrier Tigers*.

He parked the Jeep in the parking lot in front of the building that was marked, *Teachers Only*. It was still warm enough to have the top down. He reminded the dog to wait in the Jeep until he returned. She blinked her eyes in acknowledgment and lay down on the seat. As he began to walk up to the school, a host of emotions overwhelmed him. Law enforcement had been his life for 10 years, and now he was leaving it behind. In recent months, though, he reminded himself that he had enjoyed his job less. Perhaps after a couple years in the classroom, he would return to law enforcement, maybe run for sheriff in some small town. After all, he had arrived in Barrier only a day or two ago and already had been promoted to deputy sheriff. The thought made him chuckle.

His life's dream could be accomplished in more than one way. Perhaps this path was better. He could steer high school students through academics and athletics and help them capitalize on their strengths. He also found himself thinking of Maggie. She was bright, pretty, tenacious, and athletic, all good qualities for a sheriff. He didn't think she had a boyfriend. Maybe their relationship could go farther. He could always dream.

Holding on to his dream would help him make the life change he sought coming to Nevada. He just hoped he didn't end up like so many others who moved to rural areas only to discover they couldn't find happiness. Too isolated or lonely. *One day at a time.*

Six well-worn steps led up to the front double doors. Their deep grooves hinted at all the tennis shoes and boots that paraded up and down for a hundred years. A handwritten sign on notebook paper read, *Classes Cancled til after Funral Mass.* It was taped to the front window. Brick noticed the misspellings but shrugged it off. He tried the doors, and they opened. He met another six steps that led up to an office and six more that led somewhere below. The school's interior smelled of cleaning solutions, and the floors glistened beneath his feet.

"Can I he'p you? The school's closed. The principal got himself kilt, so we ain't having school today." A short, stocky man in jeans, a plaid flannel shirt, and baseball cap double-timed it up the steps from the lower level. The cap sat back on his head revealing thick black hair. He held a push-broom in one hand and a dust cloth and dust pan in the other. A squirt bottle dangled from his back pocket with blue liquid dripping out. He smiled a broad smile but was missing part of a front tooth. "The fun'ral will be Wednesday at the church. You should come back Thursday, and somebody'll be here to he'p you."

Brick extended his hand and introduced himself, "I'm Brick O'Brien. I'm supposed to start teaching here this week. I was hired by Father Fitzwater to teach history. Is someone here who I can speak with?"

The custodian grinned even more widely and reached out to shake Brick's hand. He balanced the cleaning equipment under his other arm. "Oh, you're the basketball coach who is here from California, aren't you? I should have recognized you. Your pit-cher was in the paper. I wondered if you was comin' or not since the principal got kilt. He said you was tall and athletic and all. My name's Harry. Harry Bird. My folks had a sense of humor that I got to live with my whole life. I'm the janitor." Harry rapid-fired his words. "Your folks must have had a sense of humor, too, giving you Brick for a name."

"I thought I might meet whoever is in charge. Do you have an assistant principal or somebody else here? I wanted to come by to see what I need to do to get ready for the students. Even though Father Fitzwater is dead, I would like to stay and fulfill the contract that I have. I need to speak with somebody."

Harry shook his head and answered, "Nope, nobody but me. I guess I'm in charge, at least for today. The only teacher who's here is Mr. McCrone. He heard him come in the building a few minutes ago. I haven't seen him yet, but his car's in the parking lot. He's in the bathroom. I think he has prostate trouble. He teaches Latin. Mr. McCrone and I've been here longer than anybody. Anyhow, I'll show you the social studies room. You need to talk to the superintendent to see what's what. He don't live here though, but he'll be here for the fun'ral. That's day after tomorrow, I guess. They don't tell me nothin.'"

Harry Bird led Brick down the hall to his classroom. Harry was a tad over five feet tall but walked faster than anyone Brick had ever met. Despite the difference in their height, Brick found himself almost running to keep up. Harry talked as he walked announcing which room was which. He quietly cussed the students as he stooped to pick up a wayward scrap of paper or remove invisible finger prints from a locker door. He was a cleaning machine. He didn't allow any smudge, visible or invisible, to escape his eyes and cloth.

Harry deposited Brick at the social studies room telling him, "Dang kids. Things are a mess around here. Homecoming was last Friday. The kids taped stuff all over the place. I'll get it back to normal real soon. I thought I'd get it done over the weekend, but then the principal got kilt, and I got off track. Let me know if it isn't clean enough. I can't stand a dirty room. I'll get you a key tomorrow." Harry scurried out the door, and Brick could hear him talking to himself as he re-swept the hall.

Brick glanced around his classroom and thought about his student teaching experience. This was certain to be different. No metal detectors. No school resource officers with wands. No cameras. And no locked, bulletproof windows. The schools in urban areas were more secure but only because of the extrinsic fortifications. In L.A., he considered the schools' defense mechanisms as circling the wagons while waiting for the attack of unknown intruders. In addition, it was reported that classes now surged to 40 or more students. Barrier High School would be a welcomed change.

The pale green room contained an old-fashioned blackboard with chalk and a lone computer. Three spools of maps and a TV were mounted on the wall. A teacher's desk, about 25 student desks, a room-length, waist-high bookcase, and a table were the only furniture. An overhead projector sat on a table. It was not an electronic one, but the type that used plastic overlays. Teaching social studies in Barrier certainly was going to be different. In a rural school, a teacher taught everything. He would have five different subjects—U.S. history, world history, American government, psychology, and economics—to prepare for each day. This was the tradeoff. He was in a safer school but had lots of daily preparations. Nevertheless, it should be an easy schedule. He stood near the middle of the room considering this when his thoughts were interrupted.

"Greetings and salutations. Are you here to praise Caesar or bury him? I am Philip McCrone, the lone intelligent person in this academic institution of lower learning. I present Greek and Latin to the prodigy who attend this school. Note that I don't say they learn it. I merely present it." A meticulously dressed, white-haired man leaned against the door jamb, shifting his weight uncomfortably. Brick thought he might topple under the weight of the large black umbrella over his left arm, or the tall stack of books tied with a belt under his right arm. He held a brief case in one hand and a Glengarry hat in the other. He looked soft and even a little pudgy, as if someone applied small pinkish pillows to his arms and face. His skin flushed red against his blanched complexion. He wore a pastel pink and blue plaid oxford button-down shirt with a baby blue bow tie and navy-blue trousers belted high on his waist. His bushy white hair was uncombed but not unkempt.

Brick walked over to shake his hand. The other teacher dropped the books as he reached out to take Brick's hand. Brick stooped to pick them up. "A pleasure, Mr. McCrone, I'm Brick O'Brien, and I'm trying to find my way around the school. Finding out that your boss is dead isn't the best way to start a new job."

"Ah, yes, you're Father Fitzwater's friend. Brick is an interesting sobriquet. I'd like to hear how you acquired it." Instead of waiting for a response, he continued, "Fitz's demise is a tragedy, a real tragedy. Almost Macbethian. He spoke very highly of you. He divulged that you and he were affected by many commonalities," Mr. McCrone said. He shuffled his armful of items and set some of them down. Brick was curious about the umbrella. It was unnecessary in Nevada in September. Mr. McCrone's cheeks puffed in and out as he spoke. His face colored, "Most people call me 'Doc.' It's a dignified moniker that I find endearing. It represents a type of symbolic affection that I have come to accept. The deceased and I spoke at length about your proposed tenure here. He regarded your presence as a definite rectification of the prevalent situation, which is a paucity of competent faculty."

Brick was having difficulty following the conversation of this well-spoken teacher. He needed to concentrate on each word that Mr. McCrone, that is, Doc, pronounced. Nevertheless, this was his first contact with his new job, and he wanted to make a good impression. "Thanks. I'm going to be coaching, too. Basketball. Do you coach anything?" Brick asked, instantly regretting having mentioned it. Brick couldn't believe that this man coached anything.

"Indeed, I do. I am an assistant football coach. All faculty members must, out of necessity, demonstrate competency in at least one non-academic area. Academic accountability plays second fiddle to the playing field at Barrier High School. If I am to improve the minds of these adolescents, I must improve their bodies first. Rah, rah, rah." Doc pushed his hand past his ears as he repeated the chant, grinning widely. He then set the rest of his items down and threw a pretend pass at Brick. "We are not having school until after the funeral. But naturally, we are having practice today if you would care to join us. It is always a jovial outing to witness these lads throwing around the 'ol' pigskin,' as they say." He arched his eyebrows and chuckled as he commented.

They chatted a while longer. As far as Doc knew, the information coming from Harry Bird, about a temporary principal or changes in the schedule, were warranted or anticipated. School would resume on Thursday after Wednesday's funeral. Harry Bird seemed to be the gateway to all information even though he claimed, "They don't tell me nothin'."

Doc unlocked the school office door to allow Brick to find the superintendent's phone number. He wanted to verify that he still had a job. He would call later. Brick scanned the office. He noted a second office that allowed the principal to view everyone who came in through the door. The doorplate read, *Father Patrick Fitzwater, Principal.* It was locked. His desk was piled high with mail, folders, and miscellaneous reading material. It resembled the disarray of the padre's house during Brick's first visit, 180 degrees from the current housekeeping.

Doc nodded toward the office. "The padre liked to preach that cleanliness is next to godliness, but I never noticed him taking it to heart."

Brick wasn't sure what to make of it. Thinking aloud about how the priest's house was, he said, "Maybe a housekeeper helped him keep his house clean. It's as slick as a whistle."

"A housekeeper at the parsonage? No, I don't think he would have one unless it was provided by the church. Fitz was a miser, a splendid reincarnation of Ebenezer Scrooge. He would not pay for anything as frivolous as a housekeeper. Remember that he was clergy and took a vow of poverty as a young man."

Brick thought to himself, *Vow of poverty? Hardly.*

Doc returned to his own classroom while Brick reentered the social studies room and sat down to ponder the situation. The death of his friend. The priest. The principal. His arrival shortly after the death. The uncertainty of his new position. And Sheriff Monroe. Doc might be an interesting addition as well. He thumbed through the books on his desk: the attendance book and lesson plan book. He mindlessly opened and closed the drawers and cupboards considering what he needed to do before school started again. The single computer sat in the back of the classroom. It was ancient. Brick wondered if he would have Internet.

He used his cell phone to call the superintendent who reassured him that he still had a job. The two decided to meet in person after the funeral on Wednesday.

Brick grabbed the teacher's textbook editions for each of the five subjects that he would be responsible for and strode quickly out his door. He noticed Doc standing at the blackboard of his room with chalk dust sprinkled over his blue pants. He stopped and said, "Thanks for your help today, Doc. I'll see you mañana."

Doc's eyes lit up, and he replied, "Mañana? Do you speak Spanish? I could use some cultural expansion. I'm finished with my little Latin brain exercise. Hic, haec, hoc. Amo, amas, amat. And a few more declensions to entertain myself." Brick looked around the room and noted that the entire blackboard on three walls was filled with Latin words and phrases, none of which Brick recognized. "I'll start on the Greek verbs as soon as I finish these. These exercises keep my mind sharp. I bid thee farewell." he said with an exaggerated bow.

"Later, Doc," Brick uttered, shaking his head. How did this teacher fit into Barrier High School?

Brick exited the building taking the steps two at a time. He tossed the books into his Jeep and signaled to Bridget to jump down and follow. She danced at his heels with her hips wagging from one side to the other as the two made their way over to the gym. The door was unlocked, and Harry Bird was running the length of the gym floor with a push broom preceding his path. The gymnasium, attached to the much older building, was no kid either. The cornerstone for the gym read *1955*. The spectator seats sat on two levels. Brick thought it would seat about 1,000 people and considered if it would fill for a game. The floor gleamed, awaiting fast and hard competition. Forty years of orange and black banners hung on either side of the polished wooden bleachers. District Championships were on one side and State Championships on the other. A stage that was used for storage was located at the far end. A few of the more recent banners were for girls' athletics, volleyball and basketball, but the majority read "BBB." Boys' basketball reigned king of winter sports in rural schools for more than half a century. The most recent banner was from 10 years ago, the same year the gold vein diminished, and the town began its downward spiral. He saluted Harry but didn't stop him from his cleaning and polishing duties.

Chapter 26

Lucinda
26 Years Prior

At age 24, Lucinda had already had a life filled with both fortune and misfortune. She had escaped from insurgents who ravaged her Indonesian village and killed her parents, a few of her neighbors, and her best friend. They had beaten and raped her before the Red Cross could evacuate her to Australia where she spent several weeks in the hospital and in counseling. Eventually, the organization connected her with a wealthy and generous American sponsor who paid her passage to the United States and promised her a job in Nevada.

The benefactor and entrepreneur was named Harvey Cooper. Harvey met her at the airport in Los Angeles and flew with her to Reno, Nevada. The short flight and long drive to Barrier brought her to a new and exciting life where she began training and working at the Panorama Hotel. Harvey's standing offer for young women from other countries was one- or two-year's room and board, transportation, and clothing. He trained them in elocution and manners, and also refined their English skills. He taught them to dress American style and kept them safe.

Harvey introduced these young women to casino managers in larger cities. In return, he received a healthy finder's fee for his efforts. They could serve as part of the waitstaff or be assigned to encourage the big spenders to gamble even more. The young women's accents charmed these whales, as they were dubbed, to spend even more money than they planned. Good for business. And it was a wonderful opportunity for the young women. It was a win-win situation for the casinos and for Harvey. Helping the five to 10 women each year was his contribution to peace in the world.

Lucinda quickly became one of Harvey's favorites. She was his star pupil who spoke English as well as several Indonesian languages. The casinos wanted to expand their South Pacific and Asian clientele, and she could be crucial in that expansion. She finished college while she was in Australia, majoring in business and English. She was five feet, eight inches tall and weighed a bit under 120 pounds. She smiled easily and often, revealing straight white teeth that contrasted with her pure ebony complexion. She wore her long hair pinned up, stylishly displaying her long slender neck. She was eager to learn all that she could to make her own way in America.

Within a year, Lucinda left the Panorama and moved to Las Vegas where she took a job as a hostess in one of the large casinos, the Cantina Regala. Her job was to cajole the whales, keeping them happy while they spent their money. She called them her "paus," Indonesian slang for whale. When she drawled it out, it sounded amorous, and they swooned. She told them that it meant lover, and they believed her. Her language acuity and her beauty made her a popular hostess with a stream of return clients.

It wasn't long before she was promoted to floor manager, which was followed quickly by casino assistant manager. She loved her work, and her bosses loved her. More importantly, though, she was thankful to be out of Indonesia, in Las Vegas, and safe.

She fell in love with Jack Garrison, who was a few years older than she and was finishing his MBA at UNLV. He doted on her and spoiled her in every way imaginable. A year later, their marriage produced a baby boy. She named him Vijay honoring her deceased father in Indonesia. Two years later she gave birth to son number two, Kenneth, whom she named after Jack's father. By this time, she was in a position to become casino manager and her salary and benefits were high. Even still, she aspired to become a general manager over other casinos in the corporation, which would position her to gain even more opportunity.

Jack graduated and used his MBA degree to launch a successful real estate career in Las Vegas. The market was flush, and although he was successful, he learned quickly that he was less than fond of Vegas, the heat, the people, the traffic. Before long, he began to push Lucinda to consider a move, maybe to Reno or to Tahoe so they both could take advantage of the hot real estate market and cool temperatures. His request, she knew, would cost her plenty. Not only would she have to start over, but her handsome boys would, too. They were both straight-A students and popular with their teachers and friends. How could they replicate that good fortune?

Not to mention Our Lady of Perpetual Tears was within walking distance of both their home and school. The boys became involved with church activities as well as basketball and cross country. It gave them something to do and taught them responsibility. In addition, the priests were positive role models for them.

Chapter 27

Barrier

Monday, Late Morning

Brick returned to the sheriff's office. He wanted to see if the sheriff had received an autopsy report yet, and, truth be told, he wanted to see the sheriff. She was entering the building as he arrived and invited him into her office. "Want a Coke?" she offered. "Or a bottle of water? It's gonna be a warm one if the weather forecasters are correct."

"Water would be fine. Thanks, Sheriff," he replied. "Or coffee even better."

"My name is Margaret, but you can call me Maggie. I'm named after my grandmother. It's an old-fashioned name, but I like it, and it fits me and this town. A little backward, a little old-fashioned like me."

Brick smiled and said, "I like it, too. And I don't think you are either backward or old-fashioned. Did you get the autopsy report or hear back from the coroner?"

Maggie shared what she knew, "Yeah, he called this morning. No surprises. Someone shot Fitz once and killed him. It was a .38 with nothing special about the bullet or how it arrived in his chest. The toxicology scan was negative for drugs or poison. He was murdered by a bullet. The mortician is fixing him up, and the funeral Mass will be Thursday. Cagey has been fielding some phone calls, and the whole town is buzzing about who did it, but we haven't heard anything that makes any sense."

"Thursday? Harry Bird said Wednesday and posted it on the front door of the school. I'll run over to the school to tell him the correct date.

I am sure he doesn't have a cell phone and isn't getting updates. So, what have you heard so far? I've got fresh ears. Maybe I'll catch something that seems out of the ordinary to me." Brick enjoyed looking at and listening to the sheriff.

"Harry has a cell phone, all right. He keeps track of everything that goes on in Barrier. Trust me on that. I'll ask Cagey to tell Harry to change the sign," Maggie retorted. She took a drink of water before resuming. "Three rumors have raised their ugly heads. The first is that it was a teacher. That seems a bit far-fetched but here goes. This summer four teachers left. A math teacher, the social studies teacher slash basketball coach." She motioned to Brick, "Obviously, that's who you replaced," and then continued, "the music and the woodshop teachers. The issue of the math and music teachers created quite a stir. In the middle of the year, the music teacher's wife up and left, and the math teacher moved in with the music teacher. It didn't look good. Did I mention that they both were men? Fitz didn't think it was right, and they ended up leaving the school at the end of the year. I don't know if he didn't renew their contracts or they left on their own. The bottom line is they left. He controlled the school with a steady hand. Not everyone on the faculty felt the love, if you know what I mean. Most people liked him, but naturally a few didn't. You know how it is in a small town."

Brick did a slow blink and answered, "I have never lived in a town this small, but I'm learning. Are those teachers still here, or did they move out of town? Do you know where they are now?"

Maggie continued, "The music and math teachers moved to Vegas where they got positions for the fall. No one bats an eye about who lives with whom in Vegas. But that's not true in Barrier. What happens in Barrier haunts us forever. They were replaced by one person, a former college teacher who can teach both subjects. She retired from her professorship at University of Nevada Reno and moved in with her kids. I think she grew up here. Maybe. She divorced her husband and wanted to be near her kids, according to the local chatter. We have two classes of music a day. Band and choir. It was an easy way for Fitz to save money.

"The woodshop teacher wasn't very well liked and got tired of the hassle and left. He'll earn a higher salary elsewhere anyway. I think he ended up in Washington or Oregon somewhere. The school board hired a man out of Winnemucca to replace the woodshop teacher, but I haven't met him yet.

"The basketball coach hadn't had a winning team for at least 10 years, and the parents were about to tar and feather him. He knew his subject matter but couldn't win even a scrimmage to save his soul. I haven't heard where he went, but someone will hire him. Some school that has a basketball team that's worse than the Barrier Tigers, if that's possible. The teacher angle doesn't ride with me. They're all gone and haven't returned, at least as far as I can tell. The two guys in Vegas were glad to be gone. The woodshop teacher didn't have much to do with anyone, but I don't think he wanted to pick a bone with Fitz. The basketball coach, your predecessor? No, I don't think so."

Brick nodded. "We ought to approach them anyway. I will do that for you. I'll get their names and addresses from the superintendent."

"The second rumor that has even less credibility is that he was killed by one of the *ladies of the evening*. The Chicken Dinner Ranch, which is our local brothel, is out on Highway 50, less than a mile from town."

"Barrier has a brothel?" Brick exclaimed incredulously. "That's something I didn't know. I don't recall seeing it."

"You drove by it when you came in. You didn't notice it though because it's an obscure two-story adobe building painted beige. It is a very plain looking building and doesn't have a sign or anything. There's not even a yard. Just a few Mesquite trees and a very large parking area. These days, only a few women work at the Ranch, and I've heard that they aren't very busy. They don't stay at the Ranch very long from what I hear." She blushed as she hurriedly continued. "I mean I don't think they are busy. I haven't ever been in it. As sheriff I could visit it, but the opportunity has never presented itself. I haven't seen the need to go into the building." Brick thought it charming that she was suddenly so nervous as she discussed the inner workings of the whorehouse. He smiled to himself as she continued her update. "Except on Sundays when they go to church, we don't often see the ladies in town. They have things delivered or sometimes Jay, the owner, comes into town. I think it is closed on Sunday mornings. I can't imagine that any one of them could have come into Fitz's company. I would bet my bottom dollar that he never darkened their door. It is totally out of character."

Brick smiled at her and said, "Maybe the sheriff and her new volunteer deputy should make a courtesy call, and you can satisfy your curiosity. What do you think?"

Maggie flashed her eyes at him. "The ladies don't bother anyone. Why should I bother them? They are licensed and, so far, they haven't caused any trouble. I don't see any reason to interfere with what they are doing. This is something that most Nevada sheriffs don't have to deal with. I have chosen to ignore it as well. Growing up here, it was something we giggled about but didn't discuss. Sort of like the proverbial elephant in the living room. We knew it existed but largely ignored it. Glossed it over." Half a dozen counties in Nevada have legalized prostitution. Maggie didn't approve of it or even like to admit that prostitution was alive and well in Barrier.

Brick frowned and raised his eyebrows, "We can put it on the back burner, but if I might give you some advice as your new deputy, I think you, Sheriff Maggie, need to be a presence at the Chicken Dinner Ranch. It might be legal, but it isn't a normal establishment. And you should assert your authority before you need to." He paused before continuing, "So, what's rumor number three?"

Maggie cocked her head at Brick, "You're probably right, although it's out of my comfort zone. The previous sheriff advised me that the best thing to do about the CDR was leave them alone. You know, live and let live. I don't know Jay well, even though he has been running the Ranch for about five years. Anyway, the third rumor makes the most sense to me and Cagey. It is that a drifter came through the town. Maybe someone who met Fitz before. Somebody had to know about the cash we found. Besides you, me, and Cagey, the killer might be the only one who would have known about it.

Twenty-five hundred dollars is a lot of money in this town. Cagey is talking with the neighbors and local businesses to find out if they know anything."

Brick agreed, "The whole money thing makes this even more curious. I think that the first thing we should do is figure out where that money came from. Follow the money."

Chapter 28

Las Vegas
21 Years Prior

Lucinda arrived home after a particularly trying day at the casino. *It was just one of those days*, she thought to herself. A pit boss came to work drunk, and she needed to find a replacement, which necessitated overtime and its approval. A woman fell off her stool while playing the slots and broke her shoulder. She would be released from the hospital soon and was likely to sue the casino. The incident took a chunk of time out of Lucinda's day. She verified what happened and wrote an accident report. She then located the woman at the hospital to have her sign the report. The main bar ran out of their most popular brand of gin, and several customers were not happy. They were offered free drinks of a better brand of gin but preferred the other. Of course. The head chef threw a fit about a suggested change in the menu and threatened to quit. And the day was topped off by her suspending one of her dealers who had made derisive remarks to a gay couple. The usual annoyances of drunks and people angry about losing their money rounded out her day, and she was exhausted.

Jack was already home when she arrived, but he had appointments to show houses that evening. It was a school day, and the boys attended their youth group at the church after school. They were both unusually quiet during dinner. Lucinda thought they might like to go to a movie and offered to take them, thinking it would give her some time to relax. The boys said *no* and went to their room.

"That's odd," she observed aloud to Jack. "I suggested the new Harry Potter movie at the LV Show House, but they weren't interested, which is weird because I know they haven't seen it, and it was on their want-to-see list. It sounded like a very cool film to me, but I guess I will offer up something else. It doesn't matter to me."

"I'll talk to the boys and see what's up. I could drop them on my way to show the houses, and you could pick them up in a couple hours." He rose and headed to the bedroom. When he went in, he found Kenneth in bed under the covers. He had been crying.

"What's going on, buddy? Why the tears? You don't have to go to the movie. You can stay home with Mom if you want."

Jay answered for Kenneth. "We already saw that movie. Don't ask. He doesn't want to talk about it. We'll stay home."

"When did you see the movie? Mom said you hadn't seen it, and she thought it would be a good one. Was it terrible? Who took you?"

"Leave me alone," Kenneth moaned from under the covers. "I don't want to see anybody. Leave me alone."

Chapter 29

Barrier
Monday Afternoon

Brick loaded Bridget into his Jeep and revisited the school, so he could see the boys' locker room and learn about the equipment status. If he needed anything, he would have to order it, but he didn't know if he would have a budget for equipment. He thought Harry Bird might be able to answer that question and hoped that he would be working. The door to the school was open, and the sign announcing the correct day of the funeral had been rewritten. The sign also noted that school would not be in session until the following Monday, which gave Brick a bit more time to find a place to live and perhaps even take the sheriff on a date. The extra days allowed him more time to read his text books. He greeted Doc and asked where he might find Harry Bird.

"Harry will be re-polishing something that is already glistening," Doc told him. "I think that this school has stood all these years because of Harry and his relentless war against dirt. If a cleaning college existed in Barrier, Harry would be valedictorian. I speculate that Harry will be busy in the gymnasium."

Harry Bird was still cleaning the gymnasium when Brick walked through its doors. He had finished re-polishing the hardwood floor and had set to dusting the bleachers. He grimaced with his disapproval of Bridget's presence, and his eyes warned her to stay off the newly waxed floor. Bridget parked herself in the doorway and glared back at him intending to stare him down.

"I thought I would take advantage of no kids at the school. The gym is always in use for PE or volleyball. It needed a real cleaning. I'm getting the bleachers ready for basketball. You can expect a crowd when the season starts. Everybody will want to see how you do," explained Harry. "Between you and me, a couple parents will cause you stress. Larry Sparks thinks his five boys are headed to the NBA. His oldest kid can put the ball in the basket but can't keep the other team from scoring, if you want my opinion. The younger kids are not out of junior high school yet. You'll see."

Brick, Harry, and Bridget surveyed the equipment room. They found that the previous coach maintained it well. Three dozen new basketballs, a dozen nets, and scoring equipment sat ready to go. The locker room was freshly painted, and the floor and benches gleamed, thanks to Harry's diligence.

Harry asked, "Have you met Jay Guzman yet? He's the basketball program's biggest donor. He loves basketball and makes sure you have what you need. It wouldn't surprise me if he was responsible for all this new equipment. I know he went in to see Father Fitzwater during the summer. He paid for the locker rooms to be painted and ordered these new uniforms for the players this year." He pointed to the boxes against the wall.

Brick was taken aback. Wasn't Jay the name of the guy who owned the local happy house? How many Jays could live here? Brick bluffed his answer. "The name sounds familiar, but I don't think I have been introduced to him. I am sure I would have remembered. Where can I find him?" He could kill two birds with one stone.

"If I were you, I would ask him to come to see you rather than go to his office. He, uh. Most people don't want to go visit him at his office," Harry stammered. "You see, uh. My wife would kill me if she thought I knew this, let alone went to see him. Dang. He, uh. He runs the Chicken Dinner Ranch. Have you heard of the Chicken Dinner Ranch?"

"Really?" Brick answered as though he hadn't heard of it before. "The Chicken Dinner Ranch? Yeah, I've heard about the Chicken Dinner Ranch. Isn't it a brothel? You know, Harry, I don't have a wife to keep me in line. I have always been curious about those places. Maybe I should pay him a visit."

"I'd be careful, Mr. O'Brien. Goin' to the Ranch might cause you big trouble. You're in the public eye now. Your Jeep at the Ranch will get everyone yakking."

Chapter 30

Las Vegas
21 Years Prior

Kenneth's teacher called later that evening. "What's going on with Kenneth? He sulked all day and didn't want to go out to recess. Instead, he sat alone in the corner and rocked. He took a spelling test and got all the words wrong when he usually aces them. He turned his math assignment in without any answers. He told me that he wasn't sick, but I don't know. He mumbled when he spoke to me. This is not the usual happy-go-lucky Kenneth I know."

This concerned Lucinda. Kenneth was the more serious of the two, and he enjoyed school. He liked his teachers and worked hard. He was a quiet boy but always happy.

"Did something happen at school?" she asked his teacher.

"Not that I know of," the teacher responded. "The usual, boys being boys, chasing each other and racing to the top of any playground equipment that is being used by girls. I didn't see anything unusual, and the playground aide didn't alert me to anything."

"Thank you for calling. I don't really know. He was quiet at dinner tonight as well. Maybe he will talk to me." She went to the boys' room and found it locked. "Hey," she yelled, "let me in. No locked doors, boys." It was a couple minutes before Vijay opened the door, but only after she pounded on it.

Vijay poked his head out and scowled, "What do you want?"

Lucinda stuck her foot in the door and opened it wide. Kenneth was in the bed, lying still on his stomach with his head under the covers. She went to him, sat down on the bed, and cooed, "Hey, my man, what's up with you? What's wrong?"

She pulled the blanket from his head, and he burrowed down farther and yanked the blanket back over his head. She pulled it down again and began to rub his back. "Don't touch me. I hate you," Kenneth barked as he twisted away from her. "I don't want to be touched. Go away."

She removed her hand and moved away. Without his telling her, she knew what happened. Her mind flashed back to Indonesia and the rape she endured. She felt the same way. Hate. Withdrawal. Hiding. Shame. But who? How? Where? And why?

She called Jack and demanded that he come home right away. He had finished with his clients and stopped for gas before returning. He heard the desperation in her voice but didn't ask.

She took Vijay by the arm and led him out of the bedroom. "Tell me what happened, and tell me right now. Tell me what you know."

Vijay started crying, and he sobbed, "I don't wanna tell you. Kenny doesn't want you to know. It wasn't his fault. It wasn't my fault either. It was after school at the movie."

"Movie? You went to a movie after school? Who did you go with, and where did you get the money?"

Vijay was nearly hysterical. "Father Lin wanted to go to the movies and asked us what was a good one. We told him we wanted to see the new Harry Potter movie. He said he hadn't heard of Harry Potter, but if that's what we wanted, we could go. He paid. Then bought us popcorn. Two. One for each of us. The big ones with butter. I wanted to sit down front, but the Father wanted to sit in the back. He said sitting too close to the screen made his eyes hurt, and it would be too loud. Kenny wanted to sit with me, but Father Lin said he wanted to share the popcorn, and Kenny had to sit with him."

"What did Kenneth tell you?" Lucinda asked gently.

"He told me…he told me…but he doesn't want me to tell you. He doesn't want you to know. He made me promise."

"You have to tell me, Vijay, I won't be mad."

"He told me that Father Lin held his hand and put his arm around him and kissed him on the cheek and neck. And then he put his hand on Kenny's leg and started rubbing all over, even right here. He held Kenneth's hand and made him rub him in the same place," he said, as he pointed to his penis area. "That's not right, is it, Mom? Kenny tried pushing him away, but he wouldn't stop. And this wasn't the first time. It was just worse this time."

Jack burst in and saw Lucinda and Vijay talking and Vijay wiping tears away. "What happened? Where's Kenny? Is he okay?"

Lucinda told him about her conversation with the teacher and then what Vijay told him. "No, he's not okay. We need to take him to the ER to have him checked out. You get the car, and I'll get Kenny. Vijay, go get your library book. You can go with us, but it might be a while."

Chapter 31

Barrier
Tuesday Morning

Bridget woke up early. When Brick rallied, she was sitting on the bed scowling at him. One ear was perked up. The other drooped across her eye.

"Come on, Girl, let's go for a run before we have breakfast. We both could use some exercise." He tossed her a dog biscuit to munch on while he threw on his running gear.

Fifty steps into the run, he determined that Bridget was not an athlete. She ran atilt with her eyes looking to the side rather than ahead. She led with her ear instead of her nose. She sidled along with brief bursts of speed to catch up with Brick before faltering back. After a few minutes, she sat down and refused to go farther. She apparently did not approve of her new master's exercise regimen. Brick finished his run, a quick three miles, and it felt good to stretch his legs again. He trotted back to where Bridget sat pouting and whistled for her. She dawdled behind him for the last few blocks, stopping often, and then reluctantly trying to catch up.

"Bridget, my friend, you've got to get better. Let's go to the Barrier Café for breakfast. I need coffee."

After coffee, ham, and eggs over-easy for Brick and two scrambles, milk, and toast for Bridget, they headed back to the Panorama to change clothes. Brick wanted to talk with Maggie before launching into his other errands, one of which included a visit to see Jay at the Chicken Dinner Ranch.

"Good morning, Sheriff Maggie," he teased. "How are we doing on crime solving?"

"Oh, hi, Deputy O'Brien. I was headed back out to the house. It occurred to me this morning that we haven't checked out Fitz's car. It must be in the garage. Want to come?"

"Sure," Brick responded. "I didn't see a garage attached to the house on our previous visits. And I didn't see a car anywhere. Where is it?"

"It isn't attached to the house. It is obscured toward the back of the lot behind some trees. Most of the garages in Barrier are detached. That's because they were built before people owned many cars. His garage lies behind a copse of pine trees. I don't think he drove much. I used to see him walking, first alone and later with Bridget. He walked to school and church, or he'd bum a ride."

"What kind of car did he have?"

"I don't know. Never paid attention. Might have been tan."

The trio got into the sheriff's rig and returned to the parsonage. The garage was larger than they expected. Two cars could fit in it with room to spare. The graying paint on the garage was peeling, and the lone window was cracked and coated with grime. Curled, gray wooden shakes topped it with several missing. Wind had propelled some of them off, and they lay in the dirt that doubled as a driveway. The dirt driveway was adorned with a variety of dying weeds that led to the door. It was secured with two extra-heavy keyed padlocks on bolted hasps. They were not scarred, rusted, or even dirty.

They tried to peek in the garage by rubbing dirt off the window to no avail. The grime was thick, and they could not see anything. "We need keys. Let's look in the house. If we can't find them, we can use some bolt cutters."

They walked around the garage through the yard toward the house and noticed that the shrine had swollen once again. Hundreds of objects were deposited for the dead priest. Flowers, ribbons, cards, and school memorabilia paid him tribute.

Maggie and Brick re-gloved before entering. The backdoor of the bungalow was unlocked and ajar. Another pile of money lay on the kitchen table. It was nice and neat and as high as the one recovered on Sunday morning.

Brick and Maggie turned toward each other. "What in the world is going on? Who is leaving this money?"

Brick shrugged, "I don't know, but we need to find out. For starters let's get somebody to take fingerprints from the door jamb, the table, and the money. Can Cagey do that, or do you have someone else?"

Maggie answered quickly. "A retired deputy lives here in town. He should be able to come right away. He's not well, but he likes to help when he can." She scrolled down the list of numbers on her cell phone and spoke with someone. She then picked up the money and began to count. After a few minutes of counting, she put the money down and announced, "Eighteen hundred dollars. I wonder what the hell is going on."

Maggie's phone rang. It was Cagey. Trouble up at the castle again, and it required her presence. The garage would have to wait. She picked up the stash of money. They locked up and left the house.

Chapter 32

Las Vegas
21 Years Prior

The Cantina Regala eventually became Fitzwater's casino of choice. It was several miles away from the church but near his home. A small, rarely used parking lot was situated behind the casino and off the Strip. It was perfect because it was hidden from people walking or driving by. He hoped no one would see him coming or going. The casino was large enough to create anonymity but small enough that he got to know the staff and their schedules.

Father Patrick Fitzwater grew to love the Cantina Regala and improved his game. Playing craps became a daily habit. With each appearance, the international staff of hostesses greeted him, bought him drinks, and encouraged his play. Early mornings were the best times to play because fewer people lingered about. After he recited Mass, he performed his few duties and drove to the casino. Alice worked nights, and he didn't think she was aware of his gaming. If anyone recognized him, nobody mentioned it. The waitresses showed him many kindnesses, and he found it hard not to play at the Cantina Regala. They were enchanting young women who seemed to care for him, and they went out of their way to make sure he was happy. An Irish whiskey was always waiting, even early in the morning.

Father Fitzwater felt the Cantina Regala brought him good luck. At first, he won almost every time he played. Later, when his luck soured a little, he ordered some books from Amazon and studied how to win the games. His skill and good fortune improved. In fact, his luck seldom ran bad for very long. He soon built his $50,000 to over $100,000. It was time to use some of the winnings for himself. After all, he was the one who was winning. The Cantina Regala grossed plenty of money. The hostesses repeatedly insinuated that they were glad to see the money passed to such a handsome and worthy fellow. He traveled to Reno, opened a personal finance account, and began squirreling money away.

The money grew rapidly. He bought a Cadillac. It was used but not too used. He didn't want it to look too ostentatious. He seldom washed it and whacked a front fender gently with a hammer. He thought the ding made it seem older, more weather beaten. He bought himself a new gold watch to replace his old Timex. He donated $12,000 to the church, which brought them into the black. He told Mary Grace that he inherited a little cash from an old aunt in Ireland. She would never know the difference. He confessed to himself his sin of fibbing and atoned his sin with a few Hail Marys.

By this time, Father Patrick Fitzwater had served as a parish priest in Las Vegas for several years. He continued gambling and sometimes switched casinos, but he always returned to the Cantina Regala to take advantage of the amenities and favors of the hostesses. He enjoyed the ups of the casino life, the food, the shows, and the lights. He especially took pleasure in the cocktail servers in their provocative frocks. The downs were the days that he used a line of credit but never over $10,000. Now and then he would see a parishioner, but most of the locals gambled in the downtown casinos on Fremont Street. The uptimes outnumbered the downtimes.

When Father Lin oversaw Our Lady of Perpetual Tears, the offering hovered around $2,000/week. Since Father Fitzwater arrived, the collections tripled and hovered around $6,000/week. Father Fitzwater attributed the increase to his excellent sermons and charismatic personality. He didn't consider that the newly constructed homes in this area of town made any difference. His ego reported that the success was because of him. Nothing else.

He reasoned that the extra money that came in belonged to him. At least part of it. He could make a personal deduction of $2,500 a week, and as long as he counted the money and made the deposits, no one would be the wiser. Mary Grace simply wrote the checks. That was all. He signed them and took care of everything else, including mailing them. Even with his weekly deduction of $2,500 from the church's money, he was able to report that the income for each week was now over three grand. It was much more than when Father Lin was pastor.

The bishop was happy. Very happy. His Las Vegas gig was everything he hoped for. Elvis was right—Viva Las Vegas.

Chapter 33

Las Vegas
21 Years Prior

Lucinda proved to be the perfect hostess. Father Fitz was amazed that he did not recall her from the Masses he served. She was beautiful, smart, and a good listener. He admitted only to himself that she was quite sexy. He watched for her during Mass on Sundays but never saw her. Puzzling.

She led him into a small private dining area that was reserved for the high rollers. She ordered for them: French onion soup, Caesar salad, Idaho trout with rice pilaf, and Tiramisu for dessert. Candles and flowers adorned the table. White-vested waiters whisked napkins on their laps and bowed low as they served the pair. They knew Lucinda and predicted that she would tip them generously. They brought her wine before she ordered, already knowing what her choice would be. The second bottle arrived before the first one was depleted.

Father Fitzwater was somewhat taken aback with the elegance of the meal. He was a celibate bachelor after all and ate what parishioners brought to him. Left-over casseroles and halves of dinners that were cooked the day before were his usual fare. The donated meals that he received, while sometimes tasty, did not have much ambiance and arrived in plastic bowls. He was regularly invited to dinner at the homes of the flock, but seldom went out to a restaurant for a meal.

The priest considered himself handsome. His fair hair and Paul Newman blue eyes had attracted the attention of young lassies all through high school and college. Attending the seminary put a damper on his love life, but he could always watch and mostly they watched back. Father Lin's illness interrupted his exercise routine, and he had let himself go recently. His tummy was protruding over his belt a bit. As he ogled Lucinda, he wondered if he knew anyone who would donate a gym membership for him.

Lucinda knew how to make men talk. She spent 10 years in Las Vegas working in the casinos, encouraging her clients to gamble. She understood how to charm men and cajole them into talking about themselves. She was as successful with Father Fitzwater as with the whales. She had watched him for a long time could clearly see his narcissism and confidence.

She learned about his family, his Irish heritage, and his dream of becoming a bishop. She learned about the difficulties of being a priest whether living in Las Vegas or a small parish in the middle of nowhere. He invited her to call him "Fitzy," the nickname of his youth. He told her of the frustrations of working with Father Lin during his last days and the drudgery that accompanied his chosen profession and calling.

As they finished their meal, Lucinda said, "I have an unopened bottle of Bushmills waiting for an excuse to be opened. I think tonight would be a good night."

Father Patrick gaped at her not knowing if this was a seduction or an invitation to have a drink. He would soon find out.

Chapter 34

Barrier
Tuesday

Maggie dropped Brick and Bridget at the Panorama while she hightailed it out to the castle with lights and siren blaring.

Two things lingered on Brick's mind. Well, three actually. He wanted to have his own place, preferably one that came with a coffee pot and microwave. He needed something furnished and clean. He might want to entertain a guest if that opportunity presented itself. Although Bridget was welcomed for the few days he resided at the Panorama, he wasn't sure they would agree to a permanent four-legged guest.

The second thing on his mind was that he wanted to meet Jay. His interest in the school seemed a bit odd considering his profession, but who knows?

The third thing on his mind was Maggie. She was becoming more fascinating. He found his attraction to her growing and wanted to spend some time alone with her without the sheriff badge on.

Perhaps nothing on, he thought to himself coyly.

Bridget set herself up in watchdog mode as she and Brick went into the Panorama. She glanced around the restaurant, saw no people, and sat down. "Come on, Bridget, let's go see what mischief we can get into while the sheriff's out at the castle. I wonder what the Panorama will serve tonight for dinner." He looked around, and then looked at Bridget, "I don't think this will do for long-term digs. I hoped that Fitz would help us, that is me, find some place to live, but that's not going to happen, is it, Girl?"

Brick perused the Forsythe paper. He noted a couple more possibilities and decided he would scout them out. The restaurant was idle. Three of the European waitresses were playing some card game, and Brick sat down at the table with them.

"How did you three happen to end up in Barrier?" Brick queried. "Do you have relatives or friends who live here? I would have imagined you in Las Vegas or Los Angeles or Chicago, somewhere big and full of adventure, instead of being on the loneliest road in America."

Greta, a buxom blonde, answered. "You see, I'm from Sweden." She pronounced it Sveden. "Carla here is from Spain, and Anne is from London. We all came the same way. We answered an ad for employment in America, and here we are. I've been here six months and have six more to go. We each got airfare, room and board for a year, and money for clothes. We don't receive a salary but can keep all the tips we earn. The only requirement is that we have to stay here a year."

"Stay in Barrier a year? With everything paid for? Who paid for all this? The owner of the Panorama?" Brick puzzled.

"We don't know," Greta answered. "We have no idea. It's a secret. The manager says he has a silent partner with plenty of money who decides what happens. All we know is that we get an airplane ticket and room and board. After a year, we can take off. Poof, we're gone. It's the same for all of us. It's an easy job, and we have lots of time to spare. We waitress five days a week although we don't always have a lot of customers. We are required to go to Mass on Sunday. We also are expected to improve our social skills and language skills, kind of like charm school stuff. If we don't have a high school education, he'll even arrange for us to get a GED. But that's about all."

"Hmm, that's interesting. Did you know Father Fitzwater by any chance? If you attend Mass, you must have known him."

Greta and the other two young women paused their game while Greta answered Brick's question. "Everyone knows Fitz. We call him Fitzy. All of us go to Mass because it's part of the agreement. I'm not Catholic, but I live up to my part of the contract. Fitzy was a wonderful man. He came in for dinner a couple times a week. He favored corned beef and cabbage. We made it every Monday for him. We called it Fitzy-time. If he didn't come in on Monday, he wouldn't mind eating leftovers later in the week."

"You can go anywhere after a year? Anywhere you want? Where do you want to go?" Brick was curious.

"Most of us go to Las Vegas or Reno to get a job in the casinos because that's where the big money is. We can work and go to school if we want. People think we end up lying on our backs when we leave here, but most of the GG's, that's what we call ourselves, Global Girls, want to find a husband, raise some kids, and go to school. Like American girls. We know some have ended up as working girls, but not many," Greta explained.

Chapter 35

Las Vegas
21 Years Prior

Father Fitzwater liked Lucinda and enjoyed being with her. He never knew a woman he could be as comfortable with as Lucinda. She was fun and a good conversationalist, educated, and smart. Her flirtations were something he enjoyed. She was beautiful. He learned about her childhood in Indonesia. Her ebony skin glistened, and she glowed as if she were blushing. And most importantly, he was sure that she could keep a secret. Their secret. Their trysts.

They saw each other every now and then, although not often enough in his opinion. They met in one of the vacant casino-owned apartments on the top floor of the casino. Their meetings were always spur-of-the-moment, not real dates. It wasn't like an affair. That would not be right as he had taken a vow of celibacy. She seemed to enjoy seeing him, and he cherished their time together. They made love a few times, and he always apologized afterwards. And the next day he would send her a rose and make confession.

She told him about her early life, her brother's fatal injury, her time in Australia, and the move to Barrier a few years ago.

"Where is Barrier?" he asked. "I've never heard of it, but then again, rural Nevada has never appealed to me. I don't think I would want to live in the boonies. I like the big city. No small town drudgery for me."

"Barrier's not much, but it's better than Indonesia," she challenged.

He learned, much to his surprise, that she had two sons, both in junior high school. They were born in Vegas but now lived with their father. They moved out of Vegas a few years earlier.

"Don't you miss them?" Fitz queried. "It must be hard to have them grow up without you. What does their father do?"

She paused for a moment considering how much to tell him. Should she tell him anything about her husband? About her boys? "My husband's in real estate and successful at it. He is a great parent. His job lets him spend lots of time with them. I see them when I can in the summer and holidays sometimes. My days off are Monday and Tuesday. I can make that work, too. It's harder for them to come here because of school. It has been complicated, but it was best for them to go to Reno. Neither he nor the boys liked Las Vegas much. Life here was too hectic, and it caused the younger one to have problems. He even talked of suicide."

"Suicide? That's tragic. I hate thinking about kids who might be suicidal. I suppose it evolves from too many violent video games. You know nearly every church has some religious programs and priests who specialize in helping kids who are suicidal. I can get the name of one of the priests in Reno if you would like. They can be good influences on kids. Especially boys."

She didn't answer, leaving a void in the conversation. "When we split, Jack took the boys with him. His mother lives in Reno and needs help, so they all moved in with her." Lucinda didn't want to tell him why they moved. He would learn soon enough if her plans worked out.

Chapter 36

Barrier
Tuesday

The sheriff had busied herself with the latest crisis. Another castle event. Someone bludgeoned one of the transient guests with a toilet seat. An anonymous caller reported that a castle guard had been hurt and needed medical attention. She called the EMTs.

Maggie and Cagey proceeded to the castle to see what was happening. It was mostly vacant these days, but drifters moved in and out as the weather changed. It sheltered the transients from the harsh elements that could occur in both summer and winter. It had no electricity but did have running water. The original owner tapped an artesian well and piped the water to its roof. Gravity did the rest and made running water available to the freeloaders who poached on the property. Castle maintenance and cleaning had been suspended when the original owner abandoned the property. Some weekends, high school students arrived with six-packs of beer and pizza or other food-stuffs. They would share the food with whomever was present. Sometimes willingly. Sometimes not.

It appeared that this poacher had resided at the castle for quite some time. His personal belongings included a bedroll, two half-full bottles of Mogen David wine, a plastic grocery bag of prescription medicine with a variety of names on them, a jacket, and a bike. A partially eaten pizza rounded out his supplies.

He told them he was asleep on his bedroll and someone attacked him, although he didn't know who assaulted him and could not describe the person or much about the incident. Between the head injury and his sporadic recollection, information gathering about the incident shrank to almost nothing, especially since the victim had no identification. After a quick physical exam, the sheriff dispatched him to the hospital in Forsythe with Al and Sid. Cagey took some photos and gathered up his belongings.

Maggie gloved her hands before picking the purported weapon, the toilet seat, hoping for fingerprints and bagged it as evidence. It was black with grime, and she doubted that any could be found, but they would try.

Chapter 37

Barrier
Tuesday Afternoon

Brick continued to fret about housing and returned to the school Tuesday afternoon to seek advice from Doc or Harry. Bridget glared at him as he entered the school but remained in the back of the Jeep. She seemed to be learning the routine. The perfect 70-degree temperature swayed Bridget to take a snooze.

Brick spent a little time in his classroom reviewing the previous lesson plans. He examined the roster of students and tried to familiarize himself with their names. Having a new teacher is difficult, and he wanted to put his best foot forward. The lesson plans seemed routine. The substitute teacher used the textbook lesson plans and hadn't expanded on her own personal knowledge and experience to fortify the lessons. He, as well as anyone, knew that sterile lesson plans led to student boredom. He wanted to add some colorful stories to help the students apply what they were learning to their lives and world events.

Doc came by for a visit. "*Tempus fugit,* doesn't it? Especially in the classroom. How are you proceeding with your new vocation?"

Brick paused and answered, "Indeed, time does fly. It certainly does." Brick was thankful for his long-ago Latin teacher who forced him to memorize a few phrases.

"I'm wondering, Doc. Sheriff Monroe requested my assistance with her investigation. You seem pretty in tune with the school and community.

Do you think any of the students or parents might have been involved with Fitz's death? Did any of them hold a grudge against the padre?"

"Not that I ever heard. If someone resented him, I was never privy to that information. Conversely, the students adored him, even doted on him. Some seemed to worship him. They utilized him as a counselor, mentor, and parent, as well as a priest. I have never known a person who could cast such a spell," Doc answered. "It was extraordinary to observe him. He would enter a room and the countenance of the class would glow. He charmed them all, especially the young virgins of the school, if any still exist."

"Charmed them? What do you mean, *charmed them*?"

"Yes, he charmed them. Enticed them. Cajoled. Wheedled. Seduced. Sweet-talked. To use the revolting vernacular of the day, he sucked them in. And they loved it. They loved his dance and how he worked them. He could have been a carnival barker or a salesman or a drug dealer if he wasn't our principal and priest. We should be thankful that he didn't deal drugs. He was the most charismatic, hypnotic person I ever knew. As for your interrogatory regarding conflicts with his priesthoodness, I doubt it. He wouldn't allow conflict."

"He wouldn't allow conflict? I must say, Doc, that's an odd statement. I've known people who hated conflict, but never knew anyone who wouldn't allow it. He must have been controlling?" Brick was feeling more like a cop in this conversation than a schoolteacher.

Doc pondered his answer, "Controlling? Maybe? Magnetizing might be a better word. With his charm, I don't think the students and most of the parents realized the power that he possessed. He cast a spell over them, so to speak. I am the most intelligent person on the faculty without question. Even I didn't realize how he had mesmerized them until he was killed. Whoever murdered him abhorred something about him. I believe it was his prodigious power."

"Would you explain or give me an example to help me understand better?" Brick asked. "What kind of power did he wield?"

A high-pitched voice interrupted them. "Hiya, Doc, aren't you coming home? Honey, we've got plans tonight, don'tcha 'member?" They both turned to see a diminutive, thin woman in strapped high heels standing in the doorway puffing a cigarette. She wore a short, white denim skirt with eyelet lace and a baby blue sweater. Her auburn hair perched atop her head in an old-fashioned bun. Her red lipstick and nails complimented each other. Her makeup was flawless.

"Janey, Honey. Hello, I won't be long," Doc beamed from ear to ear. "Come in, I want you to meet our new teacher, Mr. O'Brien. Brick, this is my bride, my bride of many years, Janey."

Janey was filled with questions for Brick, "I saw Bridget outside the school in a Jeep. Is that yours? It's a pretty one. Is she staying with you? Aren't you the new basketball coach? I've heard about you. Father Fitz thinks you're the cat's meow. Oops, thought you're the cat's meow. I forgot that he's dead. It's terrible, isn't it?" Janey balanced her cigarette in her mouth as she caressed Brick's hands in both of hers. "Are you a priest, too, Honey?"

Brick clasped at her spindly hands and grinned, "I'm pleased to meet you, Janey. No, I'm not a priest. I'm a school teacher, like your husband. I spent some time in law enforcement as well."

"Janey, my darling, you can't smoke in here," Doc reminded her. "It's against the law."

She took another long drag on her cigarette and flicked its ashes to the floor and winked at Brick, "Oh, Doc, screw the law. With Fitz dead, who's going to turn me in? Besides, Sheriff Monroe's got her hands full with his murder. She won't care if I smoke a cigarette or two in the high school. Half the students smoke between classes anyway. You told me that. Do you have football practice this afternoon, my love?"

"That's true, Janey," Doc agreed. "She probably won't care, but Harry will. He's liable to have a heart attack when he sees ashes on the floor. The sheriff is engaged in finding the perpetrator of that horrendous crime and won't arrest you, but watch out for Harry. To answer your question, no, I don't have football practice tonight so we can head home. Brick, we're having a little get together tonight. Would you join us for a couple toddies? Say around five.

And then again around six if you can't make five. Or both would be fun, too. What do you say?"

Brick considered the suggestion. "Thanks for the offer, Doc, but I was going to spend the evening trying to find a place to live. Bridget and I are at the Panorama, but I don't want to stay there much longer. I have a couple rental advertisements. Could you tell me if you think they would be okay before I take the time to see them in person? Maybe after I have a look, I can stop by."

"A house is a house is a house in this town. I think the one consideration will be your little friend downstairs. Some rentals won't take dogs. I find that incongruous as dogs are allowed in all business establishments. In restaurants but not in a trailer park. Other than that quirk, I conjecture that the houses in the real estate market are all about the same. See you at 5 p.m. or so?"

Brick spent a little more time in the classroom before returning to his Jeep to see what Bridget was up to. The heat of summer stretched into the chilliness of fall, and Bridget enjoyed her afternoon nap in the sun. Nevertheless, she greeted him eagerly. She wagged her tail and hopped from the back to the front seat and back again. While Brick was gone, someone had tied a pink kerchief around her neck. It matched her hot pink collar.

"Where'd you get the scarf, Girl? You have an admirer? It seems to fit you, kind of girlish. But where'd you get it?" Brick fingered it as he surveyed the school. Some students dallied near the school on foot and in vehicles, but no one lingered in the vicinity. "It's harmless enough, but I don't like people touching my stuff, that's all. You are part of my stuff now, Bridget. I don't want anyone touching you either."

Chapter 38

Las Vegas
18 Years Prior

During Fitz's eighth year in Las Vegas, a new bishop was selected for the Diocese. Bishop George Schmidt. A German. Mr. Conservative. Mr. No-Nonsense. Bishop Schmidt determined that an audit of all the parishes was in order. He stormed the Diocese like a tsunami inserting himself where he had no business. At least that's what the priests thought. They all agreed that the new bishop was a little bit too eager. Too intrusive. He announced that he would review everything: The membership roles. The directory. The baptismal registry. The marriage records. And most of all the finances. Intake. Outgo. Usage and long-range plans.

When the audit team of four priests, led by Father Murphy, arrived at Our Lady of Perpetual Tears, they were sure they would find everything in order. In the eyes of the bishop, Father Fitzwater created stability and growth in the previously stagnate parish. He reported that collections and attendance had increased by 50 percent. The parish calendar that he submitted to the bishop was crammed with events, and the bishop received few if any complaints about the priest. He knew that the church leaders were interested in developing a school, and he also knew Alice Honeycomb was still chairing the parish council and ran a tight ship.

The audit team arrived on a Thursday afternoon at about 3 o'clock, a full month ahead of their scheduled visit. Bishop Schmidt juggled the times and dates of the audit team's visits as a surprise tactic. He thought he might obtain a better picture of what was happening.

The schedule on the parish event calendar for Our Lady indicated that the Diocesan auditors could anticipate a marriage encounter session with 12 couples. It was scheduled for Thursday, Friday, and Saturday and would finish before the Saturday evening mass. Father Fitzwater was scheduled to facilitate the marriage encounter with some assistance from a deacon.

The door to the parish hall was locked and no cars were in the parking lot. It was apparent that no meeting was being held. Had the event been rescheduled? Was it being held somewhere else?

"This is odd," Father Murphy offered. "I wonder if they canceled the encounter. Let's ask the administrative assistant what's going on."

The four priests walked around the building to the office located at the rear of the church. That door was also locked. The *Be Back Soon* sign on the door did not indicate when *soon* would be. They speculated that perhaps she was ill or running errands.

They waited for a half an hour, and when she still hadn't returned, they decided to call it a day and hit the golf course before the 5 o'clock rush hour.

They returned the following morning, anticipating seeing a women's group meeting regarding liturgical music in addition to the marriage encounter. But again no one was at the church. They tried to call Father Fitzwater but could not reach him. Voicemail. They went to his house with no success. They tried the number of the administrative assistant. Again, no answer. Voice mail. That afternoon they returned to the parish and found the office door unlocked. Mary Grace O'Toole, the administrative assistant, was busy at her desk. She was a joyful soul and greeted them cheerfully.

Father Murphy, the leader of the audit team, winked at Mary Grace. "We're here to do the audit. Where is Father Fitzwater? Is he facilitating the marriage encounter?" He flirted with all women, and his eyes twinkled as he spoke with the diminutive Mary Grace.

Her eyes grew large. "Marriage encounter? Audit? You must be mistaken. We aren't having a marriage encounter this year. And the audit. It isn't until next month. Father Fitzwater? You know. It's Friday. Naturally he's not here. Friday is his day off. He might come by tomorrow in the early afternoon though," Mary Grace answered. "He usually drops by for a while on Saturday. You know, to prepare for Saturday night Mass. Can you come back then?"

Father Murphy seated himself on the edge of her desk and cooed, "You're right, darlin'. Of course, you're right. The audit is scheduled for next month, but we changed the date and are here today. Do you think you can find him? I'm sure that Father Fitzwater mentioned that Bishop Schmidt is auditing every parish. Maybe we got the date wrong for the marriage encounter."

"I know that we're having an audit, but I'm sure you made a mistake. Our audit is scheduled for next month. I am positive. Father Fitzwater is meeting with Alice next week to prepare for it," Mary Grace sighed. "I don't think that Alice is ready for the audit either." She grimaced at the thought of having to deal with this team of four priests alone. Where was Father Fitzwater?

Chapter 39

Barrier
Tuesday Afternoon

Brick decided to stop at the sheriff's office hoping that Sheriff Maggie would be working. He wondered how the second castle emergency panned out. He wondered if she was going to return to the parsonage. He also wondered if she had a boyfriend.

It was not quite 5 o'clock. The door was locked, but a sharp rap brought Maggie to the door.

"Hi, Sheriff, are you still open for business? What was the castle's trouble about? Anything new on the murder? Can I assist you with anything? Did you go back to the parsonage yet?" Brick's questions came fast.

"Hi, Question Man, I'm glad to see you. Which question shall I answer first? I've been dealing with the castle. It draws more flies than it's worth. Transients move in. Then they get hurt or sick, and we get to deal with it. Personally, I would like to see it demolished. It would make my job a whole lot easier. Have you ever known a toilet seat to be a weapon?" She shook her head at the absurdity of it.

She continued, "I've been collating all the photos and my notes on Fitz. I know you took some notes, and I'd like to see them as well. Do you have them with you?"

"I thought you might like to see them, so I brought them with me, and I'll even help you decipher them. Did you find out anything about the money that was in Fitz's house? Who in Barrier would have that kind of money?"

"I haven't learned anything new about that. I'm driving out to Fitz's house in the morning. The garage beckons. You wanna tag along?"

"Sure, I'd like to do that. How about I pick you up here first thing in the morning? We can take my Jeep."

Chapter 40

Las Vegas
18 Years Prior

"Mary Grace, darlin'" the redheaded Father Murphy cooed, "Why don't we review a couple things today? We want to take a look at the current membership roster, all the sacramental records, and the financial records. I'd like to start with the check register and the bank statements for the last year. Father Couch and I will review those while Fathers Schwartz and Bernini peek at the membership roster and sacramental records."

Mary Grace stared at the four priests in disbelief. No one was allowed access to the records except Father Fitzwater. No one ever requested to see the records. She wasn't even sure where they were. She supposed that Alice knew, but Alice was at work. She looked over the calendar and found nothing for that day. Mary Grace didn't know where her boss might be. She knew that the financial records were in the filing cabinet, but she didn't have a key. Disobeying a priest was a sin, and sin meant confession. She didn't want to have to go to confession this week. She and her fiancé had recently started living together. If she was forced to go to confession, it wouldn't be pretty. She tried his cell phone but reached his voice mail. Again.

Mary Grace had worked at the parish for eight years. She was pretty with a quick sense of humor. Her laugh echoed through the building most days but not today. She had already been working for Our Lady when Father Fitz arrived during his first year of priesthood. She knew that he did things differently than the former priest, especially since Father Lin was sick and contributed nothing. She never questioned Father Fitzwater about the parish finances. She knew that he personally counted the collection each week, traded in the chips that were left in the collection plates, and made all the deposits. He brought her the deposit slips every week or two.

She made the deposit entries and wrote out the checks. He signed and mailed them. He had not given her check-signing authority.

Mary Grace offered to help him once, and he flared up at her. She never offered again. She was sure things were on the up and up. After all, he was a priest, which meant he practically was without sin. She loved working at Our Lady as the work environment generally was pleasant. She was overqualified for her job but had no aspirations other than to work as a parish administrative assistant. Even with an MBA from UNLV where she had graduated magna cum laude, she still was paid only minimum wage. But that was fine with her. All she really wanted was to get married and have kids. Her last job had been stressful, and she preferred a low key, no stress job. This was perfect.

Mary Grace never questioned anything that Fitz did or said. He was the boss, no matter what. They fell into a routine, and he made Monday her night. He called it Mary Grace Monday. They spent a little extra time together for dinner or a show or something else, whatever he wanted. He was handsome and charming and always showed her a good time. He loved her laugh, and she loved everything about him. Too bad he was a priest, she mused. He'd make a good father, too.

The Diocesan benefit package was meager. It was no sacrifice when the priest suggested that she opt out of the program. After all, Father Fitzwater reminded her that her fiancé made a good salary, and he could support her. She wouldn't need that much money. She didn't like that sort of comment, but priests were holy men. It was not her place to question him. It would help the budget if they didn't have to pay for her benefit package. Father Fitzwater reminded her if she turned her needs over to God, He would take care of her.

"Mary Grace, darlin,'" Father Murphy purred again. "Can you open the filing cabinet for us?"

Father Fitzwater's desk could have been the aftermath of a Kansas tornado, but Mary Grace scrounged in the drawers and came up with a few keys that might open the filing cabinet. She handed them to Father Murphy. "I'm not sure which one it is. You see, Father takes care of everything." Her smile faded, and her cheerfulness evaporated.

The four priests set about their work. Fathers Couch and Murphy opened the filing cabinet and rifled through two drawers. They selected a ledger and several months' bank statements. They closed the drawer and began reviewing the records.

"Thank you, darlin,'" crooned Father Murphy, as he winked at her. She smiled weakly, turned her back, pulled a rosary from her pocket, and began to pray.

Chapter 41

Barrier
Wednesday

Brick, Maggie, and Bridget linked up early to inspect the priest's garage. It was another ideal, smogless Barrier day.

His concern over housing began to dominate his thoughts. He knew he needed to find somewhere to live, and soon. "While you were rousting out the homeless and toilet seat weapons at the castle, I spent the rest of yesterday trying to come up with a place to live," Brick announced. "Bridget and I can't stay at the Panorama indefinitely. I talked with Doc, and he has no recommendations. How about you? Do you have any good ideas?"

"Not really. Decent housing is scarce here. You can always find a few trailers for rent or mouse-infested container houses. The mobile home park is always trying to find tenants, but I wouldn't want to stay in one of those. Our office gets called to it a lot, and Bridget wouldn't be welcome."

"Are there any apartment buildings here? The only one I've seen was boarded up."

"Nope. There used to be some before the town was leveled. Your best bet is a house. Did Fitzwater ever mention anything to you about living arrangements?"

"No. He suggested that I live with him, but I was reluctant as I thought his house was too small and cluttered for an additional resident."

"I wonder who owns his house," Maggie mused aloud. "It's vacant. Obviously. It's still got yellow tape wrapped around it, but it might be available later. What about it?"

Brick nodded his head at the thought. "That's a thought. It's looking more and more like I will be at the Panorama for a while, which is fine. I'll just need to buy a coffee maker for myself. Bridget already knows the lay of the land, so we'll be good until I can find something else."

When they arrived at the house, Bridget hopped out of the Jeep and rolled in the dirt. Some brambles stuck to her new pink kerchief and Maggie brushed them off. "Did you buy the scarf for her?" Maggie asked.

"No, somebody left it on her while I was at the school. I don't know who."

They entered the house to search for the key. "I should have brought the bolt cutters," Maggie complained. "If we can't find a key to the garage, I'll call Cagey to bring them by. I don't want to destroy the lock unless I need to." Bridget curled up in one of the chairs and began to snore.

They set to work, rummaging through the various drawers and obvious spots that one might leave a key. No more money piles. They searched for an hour and came up dry. Maggie called Cagey and a few minutes later he appeared with a giant bolt cutter.

They cut the locks off the garage and entered. The priest's car was a champagne-colored Cadillac. It was coated with a layer of dust shielding its shine but seemed to be in good condition. The expired license plate read "FOTOBOY." It, too, was locked.

Maggie and Brick looked at each other and shrugged. Cagey stared at it and said nothing.

From the exterior, the garage appeared large enough to house two cars but when you entered, there was only one bay. The crowded aisle around the vehicle was littered with overflow. As they examined further, they noted two generations of construction. One matched the age of house, and it contained the garage bay and Cadillac. The other side was newer and was not part of the original garage. This section was walled off with sheet rock, which had not been installed by a professional. It was misaligned and leaned into the garage-half of the structure. It hadn't been taped or painted.

Several shelves and their contents lined the walls. Typical garage stuff occupied the shelves. Tools. Christmas decorations. Lawn care equipment. A box of weed killers and grass-growing chemicals. Paint. Miscellaneous sealed but unlabeled boxes that held who knows what. Partially hidden behind a tall box of tools stood a metal door with double locks that prohibited their entry into that half of the garage.

"Cagey, snip these off, too," Maggie ordered.

When Cagey cut the bolts off the door and opened the second half of the garage, the room revealed a side of the priest they did not know.

Chapter 42

Las Vegas
18 Years Prior

Father Fitzwater's luck ran hot and cold. For the past two months it was cold. Very cold. He still played regularly at the Cantina Regala, but things weren't working as well as in the past. He lost $13,000 last month, followed by $8,000 this month. Another $5,000 last week as well as his $2,500 weekly allocation this week. It was only Tuesday.

He was growing apprehensive. His normally ruddy complexion paled and became flushed and blotchy. He knew the audit was looming in the next few weeks and wanted to impress the bishop with a very healthy balance in the parish checking account. God placed him in Las Vegas. He was sure that his continued losing was not a part of God's plan.

Lucinda was paying attention and brought him a complimentary Irish whiskey. "Need a line of credit, Padre?" she queried in her husky voice. "I can make you good for $25,000. You have taken $10,000 in the past, but why don't you try for the big time. I'll be gone for a few days. This'll give you enough to make a major comeback by the time I return. You've had amazing luck over the past few years. You can chat with God, and by the time I get back, you'll be flush for sure. This streak of bad luck will pass once you regain your rhythm."

"Where are you going? I'll miss you. I love seeing you watching over me like a guardian angel," he flirted.

"I've got some family issues to tend to. I'll be back before you know it."

Father Fitzwater gaped at Lucinda without blinking. He thought of his current losses and the forthcoming audit. He was used to winning not the reverse. This was a temporary setback to his master plan. "Yes, I'll take it. Just this once. By the law of averages, I know I have a win coming to me. It's my time. I'll turn it around." He signed the line of credit for $25,000.

Chapter 43

Barrier
Wednesday

The room was dark, but Maggie found the light switch and flicked it on. The windowless room remained dim. They gaped at the room, appalled at what they saw. "Oh, my God," Maggie exclaimed. "What is this? Oh, my God."

The trio stopped in their tracks as they fixed their eyes on the sight before them. Pictures and clippings covered the walls on three sides. On one wall, photos of high school students were displayed with plenty of black and orange. It was memorabilia from school events. But attached to the other two walls were photos that were more unnerving. They displayed pictures of young girls and boys between the ages of five and 12 years old. The children were in varying states of dress or undress. A few babies, too. Some hid their faces and tried to cover their bodies with their hands. Others bowed their heads as if hiding or praying. A few stared angrily into the camera like they were defying the photographer. "Get your camera, Sheriff," Brick said. "Get your camera. And bring in three sets of gloves."

Maggie turned toward Cagey and commanded, "Do you have a camera in your rig?" Cagey paled white as he bolted out the door. He vomited twice before he reached his rig.

The photos and clippings were taped, stapled, or pinned to the wall. Some photos were black and white. Others were color. Some clippings were curled and faded. Others were sharp. Some contained hand-written dates. A few photos of boys were set apart from the others and framed with golden borders. It was unlike anything Maggie had ever seen. Maggie, too, headed outside to release her breakfast.

The fourth wall contained a cupboard system with an extended counter and what appeared to be a walk-in closet door. It had no knob. Just a lock where the knob should have been. The cupboards were pine but stained dark, which made the dimly lit room seem even darker. The counters were deeper than kitchen counters and stretched nearly the width of the room. The cupboard drawers and doors had cam locks flush with the surface. The countertops were empty except for a computer, server, and printer.

Cagey and Maggie returned with the camera and gloves and observed Brick. "Where do we start?" Maggie's eyes were wet and red. Her skin was ashen. "I need water and air. This is unbelievable. How could Fitz have been involved with these atrocities."

Brick had seen crime scenes like this but had never been involved in investigating one. But he knew what to do. "We start here. I didn't know the man well, but he clearly kept some deep, dark secrets." He walked over to the computer and hit the space bar. It lit up with even more pictures. He scrolled through a couple pages before motioning a somber Maggie and Cagey over to view the computer screen.

While Cagey took pictures with his camera, Maggie began to scrutinize the photos on the wall. She was horrified at the number of pictures but was shocked to see photos of a couple kids who seemed familiar. She couldn't remember their names. Had she babysat them or gone to school with them? She counted them quickly. One hundred forty-six photos were on the walls, 16 of which were babies. She reported aloud, "One hundred and forty-six friggin' pictures. This is appalling."

Brick seated himself before the computer and busily began recording in his notebook. He glanced up at her and nodded. "Yes, it's sickening. It's horrible. Truly horrible."

Not much else was in the room. They saw no keys but needed to open the locks. With no keys they would have to find a locksmith or remove the hinges or break the locks. Maggie resisted the idea of calling a locksmith, fearful that it might breach confidentiality. No locksmiths lived in town anyway. They reasoned they would have to re-search the house.

Maggie, Cagey, and Brick spent the better part of two hours in the garage room. Cagey photographed each picture individually and in groups. Naming the kids in the photos was impossible. Kids change as they grow up plus the age and condition of the photos reduced any chance of identification. One girl was familiar to Maggie, but she no longer lived in Barrier. They discussed the protocol of taking them down versus leaving them in the building. Taking them down won.

They still needed to deal with the cabinets. God only knows what they would find.

Chapter 44

Las Vegas
Friday, 18 Years Prior

Father Fitzwater took a sophisticated view of sin in Sin City. When he addressed sin in his sermons, he intimated that atonement could be theirs if they placed extra money in the offerings each week. There was a two-fold advantage to his plan; more money in the collection plate, and fewer parishioners making confession, which meant that he didn't have to listen to the hackneyed list of wrongdoings that were laid at the feet of most priests. Infidelity and late-night trysts. Drinking, smoking, and gambling. Living with boyfriends or girlfriends. Not honoring their aging parents. Frustration with their kids and spouses. Blah. Blah. Blah.

He reasoned that financial sacrifice would impact them more than a visit to the confessional. It was a win-win situation. The faithful didn't have to go through the Rite of Holy Contrition, and he didn't have to listen to confessions, leaving him additional time for his avocation. Besides, many of those attending the Sunday masses were Vegas guests who passed through and tried their hand at gaming. Sometimes they were successful, and when they won, the parish did as well.

Bishop Schmidt visited Our Lady once in the past year, and the church was full. As he greeted the flock after Mass, the parishioners raved about Fitz. They complimented the bishop on his foresight in placing this priest at Our Lady of

Perpetual Tears. They loved him and his more cosmopolitan view of sin and the world.

Father Murphy, the chief auditor, was the quintessential Irishman. Nothing pleased him more than a good joke. He was second generation American, and his parents taught him of the hardships of the Motherland. He became a priest because his mother expected him to. When she gave birth to her first baby, she decided that the first born would go into business and the second born would become a priest. The third son would take care of his parents. His older brother became an accountant, and he became a priest. The baby was the baby and took good care of his parents. That was the way his mother willed it.

As it turned out, his mother got it wrong. His older brother was the one who should have been the priest, and Father Murphy should have gone into business. His older brother had compassion for the underlings, which caused him to fail at every business he tried. Father Murphy, on the other hand, had a head for figures and enjoyed the business end of running a parish. He enjoyed flirting with the ladies and developed intimate friendships with many of the women who happened his way. It didn't matter if they were seeking forgiveness for their indelicacies or if they were serving God. They seemed to enjoy his attention. He would offer them a glass of wine, and they offered him something in return as well. Sometimes at least. Luckily, no one reported him, and as far as he knew, no little carrot-topped Murphys were running about.

Father Murphy had shifted parishes through the years, but no matter where he landed, the rumors and accusations seemed to follow. There were rumors of his affairs with women, as well as young boys; rumors and accusations of sexual harassment; claims that he drank too much and got out of control. Wherever he landed, turmoil followed.

Bishop Schmidt placed him on the audit team to take him out of the day-to-day challenges of parish life. It seemed to work. Father Murphy could audit. The rumors stopped. He didn't have to be moved around, and the bishop's difficulties lessened. It couldn't have been planned better.

Chapter 45

Barrier
Wednesday

Cagey returned to the sheriff's office for some boxes, envelopes, and file folders. Brick and Maggie searched for the car and cabinet keys. Doubtless the cabinet keys would be small, but another search might discover them. They could take the doors off or pick the locks, but finding the keys would be a less invasive way to open them. Maggie called the local prosecutor to relay their findings and told her about the locks and lack of keys. The prosecutor directed that they should try to find the keys first. She was at an out-of-town conference. It would be impossible for her to come to the scene this week, but she would stay in touch.

Maggie started with the shelves in the car bay. Shelf by shelf she searched for hidden keys but located none. Brick fingered the wheel wells under the Cadillac but came up empty.

Cagey walked in with several boxes. He and Maggie began taking the photos down and putting them in order. Cagey suggested arranging them in three boxes. Babies. Boys. Girls. That way, he guessed, they might be able to identify the victims.

Maggie agreed. "That sounds as good a method as any. When we get back to the office, we can try to put names on them. I'll bet we will recognize one or two of these kids, even though some of the photos are old and faded. Those kids are adults now. I know he was in Vegas before coming to Barrier, so I am betting some of these kids are from his church there. Let's take the computer back to the office. I'll contact the National Center for Missing and Exploited Children and the Vegas police. I am pretty sure they can help us."

They began to remove the photos from the walls, handling each of them gently as if it were a precious jewel. They found themselves conversing in low voices, almost a whisper, like they were trying to shelter these children. Maggie moved from youngest to oldest. Cagey started with the older boys. He glanced over at Maggie and secretly pocketed five of the photos.

Chapter 46

Las Vegas
Friday, 18 Years Prior

This wasn't the first time Fitz took advantage of the line of credit. He had used it several times. It was an accepted practice among those who gambled regularly. It was sort of like going to a pawn shop except you didn't pawn stuff. You pawned yourself. Interest rates were high, but it was easy to access the money. You could do it without leaving the casino.

This week's line of credit was the largest he had ever taken. And he was good for it. He regularly invested money with his LVN personal finance advisor and could cover the credit line. He deposited funds under a different name, Paddy Waters, in his Reno account, but he didn't have access to it today.

Lucinda was good to him. He had grown fond of her in the past year and thought of her often. Even though they had made love those few times, she was always a little standoffish. It was possibly her upbringing. He wasn't sure of her relationship with her husband. Most likely they were divorced, although he never questioned her about it. She didn't wear a wedding ring, and that was usually a sign. At least in Vegas.

Lucinda was a dream casino manager as far as Fitz was concerned. He didn't think that she was all that bright. She obviously adored him and would help him in any way she could. She always came through. He considered her a good friend and his good luck charm.

If things went awry, he could tap into the line of credit without raising questions. And who would know? After all, priests got special privileges all the time. Everyone knew it and took care of the clergy. Speeding tickets fixed. Special interest rates for loans. Discounts on cruises. Show them the white collar and all was good.

Chapter 47

Barrier
Wednesday

Brick returned to the cottage alone, marveling at how the makeshift memorial swelled in the past day. He thought about the photos, speculating if any current high school students were victims. It seemed puzzling that Father Fitzwater was beloved yet maintained a sordid secret and lifestyle that nobody identified and reported to law enforcement. On the other hand, he was a priest. They received special privileges in many situations and communities. He had seen it many times in L.A.

He ducked under the windblown tape and entered the house, gazing around looking for what they might have missed. He called to Bridget. She didn't move a muscle except for squinting an eye when he entered the house. They already had combed through the various drawers and found no keys.

He started in the living room not believing that he would find anything. He removed everything from the desk top and the corner hutch and re-searched the various drawers. Nothing. He went into the bedroom. He checked under the bed and in the pockets of clothes in the closet. He wasn't sure if the deputy searched them but found nothing.

The kitchen was next. Bridget rallied at the thought of food and led the way. She partially skipped and partially bounced while twisting her rear around to see if Brick was following. She wanted to do her own search for food. She'd been asleep for a while and was hungry and thirsty.

She snorted and growled at Brick to remind him that she was unhappy.

Brick ignored her and systematically began searching the kitchen. He removed all the items from the cupboards and felt toward the backs and bottoms of the drawers. No keys and nothing that might lead him to the keys. Most drawers were sparsely filled. The cupboards each held a few items, including dinnerware, a couple pots, and a frying pan. Two drawers were what he considered junk drawers with a little bit of everything in them. He focused on them, thinking they would be likely spots to toss keys. They held a few key rings but no keys. It took a bit longer, but he went through each drawer item by item. Nothing.

Bridget started poking his ankles. She wanted food or attention or both. He found a bowl and gave her some milk and a biscuit. While she slurped her milk, he opened the refrigerator. Nothing. He sat down at the table wondering where else to search. She drooled the last of her milk onto the floor and soon she made a rather large slimy puddle. Brick scolded her and grabbed a towel off the counter tipping over the coffee mug and soda. They crashed onto the floor spilling their contents.

"Dammit," he growled to himself as Bridget retreated to the corner cowering and still drooling.

The mess was a two-towel job, and he grabbed a second. As he did, he knocked the wooden cross and its wooden base from the counter, and they crashed onto the floor. The base flew open and about 30 keys clattered down. He pulled out his cell phone and took a couple photos before calling Maggie.

Chapter 48

Las Vegas
Friday, 18 Years Prior

Father Fitzwater had no plans to return to the church on Friday. It had been a stressful day. He won, then lost and then lost some more. He tried to be complacent but agonized at his continuing misfortune. He worried about the ups and downs. He tapped into the line of credit, but his winnings didn't cover it. He played all day and lost $2,500. Thankfully, he hadn't seen anyone he knew, which was good.

His eyes were glazed over, and he wanted nothing more than a glass of Irish whiskey and a steak. A bottle of Jameson waited in his office to be opened. He decided to drop by and pick it up before returning home. He had clicked his cell phone off that morning and thought some messages might be waiting. He hoped for a call from Lucinda but would wait to check until he got home. He would call her later. Perhaps she would treat him to a meal followed by some playtime in one of the casino apartments. He would enjoy the company.

He arrived back at the parish at 6:30. Mary Grace usually left at 5 o'clock each day, and he wanted to avoid her ever-constant question, "Can I do something for you?" It was an annoyance. He didn't want to be bothered with her mindless fussing over him.

Only a few cars sat in the parking lot when he arrived, including Mary Grace's battered Toyota. Five black Lexus sedans that he had never seen before were grouped toward the front of the lot. He did not know to whom they belonged.

"I wonder what she's doing here at 6:30. It's Friday. She should be out with her boyfriend," he complained aloud to himself. "I guess I'll have to endure her cheerful nagging after all. Damn." He decided to go in through the back door, hoping to avoid her.

He circled to the rear of the church and was startled to see some black shirts and white collars exiting the building.

Who....might...that...be? He began walking again and recognized three of the four priests. Fathers Couch, Murphy, Schwartz, and some other young priest he didn't know. Behind them leaving the church building was, oh my God, Bishop Schmidt. He knew that Murphy, Couch, and Schwartz were on the audit team, which meant the other guy probably was also. Mary Grace was standing in the doorway. It was obvious that she wasn't happy.

Warily, he steered himself toward the office door and smiled at them. "Hi! I wasn't expecting you. What's going on? Has something happened?"

Chapter 49

Barrier
Wednesday

Maggie and Cagey were part way through their task of taking the photos off the walls and placing them in boxes when Maggie's phone rang. She answered and said, "I'll be right there, Brick." She turned to Cagey and said, "Stay here and keep working on this. You might have to finish my half as well. I'll be back as quickly as I can." Cagey didn't say anything. He was glad to see her go.

She went into the house and guardedly stepped into the kitchen and gasped at the array of silver keys that had dropped to the floor. "Whoa, keys. Where were they? How did we miss them? We have keys. Lots of them."

Brick nodded, "Yeah, we have keys. Lots and lots of keys. I took a few photos, but I thought you would want to see them and their hiding place. You can thank Bridget for this. She drooled milk on the floor. When I went to wipe it up, everything fell off the counter. I knocked the cross and this box to the floor. Magically these keys spilled all over the place. Some are still wet from the coffee and soda that spattered. The cross was sitting on top of that little box which hid the keys."

Maggie took a set of photos with her cell phone. The keys. The box. The floor with milk on it. She snapped one of Bridget, too, for the hell of it.

"We need to get the prints off the keys and the box before we try to open the cabinets. I don't see any locked cabinets here in the kitchen. I'm sure that these keys belong to the locks in the garage room. Unfortunately, none of them are marked with lock location. No tags or writing. I saw a cabinet with a lock in the bedroom, but it was open, remember? We'll need to test that one also when we get the prints off these keys. How are you coming on the pictures in the garage room?" Brick asked.

"Cagey's on that. We were about half done when you called me. It's going quickly. He should be done in a few minutes. It's all surreal, but I gotta tell you, seeing those babies on the wall made me vomit. They were the worst. Let's go back out to the garage to help. Cagey has a finger-print kit with him."

With gloved hands, they picked up the keys and put them back in the box that the cross stood on. The 30-some keys were all about the same size. They each exhibited a different cut indicating that they would have to find the right key for the right lock through trial and error. Thirty keys. Not that many locks. With no tags, it would be a crapshoot as to what they might open.

They relocked the house and adjusted the yellow tape, securing it from the ever-blowing wind. Maggie returned to the garage and the work that needed to be done there, while Brick and Bridget left for his appointment with the superintendent. It would be a good idea to be on time.

Chapter 50

Las Vegas
Friday, 18 Years Prior

Bishop Schmidt came forward and stretched out his hand to Father Fitzwater. "Hi, Pat, we have been here for a while. Mary Grace has been taking good care of us. We came to do the audit."

Fitzwater shook hands all around still baffled as to why they were at his parish on Friday afternoon, not to mention, a month earlier than planned. He would have thought they would be golfing or doing something else.

"But. But. Your letter indicated it was next month, and we could have time to get ready. I'm not ready yet. When did you change your mind? Why did you decide to do it today? I could've been here if you'd let me know. It's, uh, it's not exactly ready yet." Father Fitzwater was stammering for words. Images of Dante's *Inferno* flickered through his mind.

"We decided to perform the audit a few weeks early. We have many things to review, and they take a lot of time. You know, reviewing all the records. We audit your accounts and analyze each parish's potential so that we can make recommendations for growth and improvement," the bishop explained. "I find Fridays to be the best day to review as the week is over, and things are always a bit more relaxed. We still have a couple more days' worth of work to do though. Can you be here on Monday? We would like to visit with you. We'll try to see Alice sometime this weekend when she is off from work. Then on Tuesday afternoon, one of us will review our findings with you. You'll be here next week, won't you? Will that work?"

"Uh, sure. Mary Grace, Alice, and I will meet this weekend and make sure everything is ship-shape." He glared at Mary Grace, and she saw her weekend scurrying away.

The four priests and the bishop got into their cars and drove off. Father Fitzwater turned angrily toward Mary Grace, his fists clamped shut. "You stupid cow. Did you know about this? Shit. Did you? Why didn't you fucking tell me? Shit. You should have called me and sent them packing. Why didn't you fucking call me? You know that we're not ready for the stupid fucking audit. You know it, and you let them in anyway. You've got to be the stupidest fucking person in the world. Fuck the bishop. Fuck 'em all. Fuck you, Mary Fucking Grace. We're done. Mary Grace Mondays are over."

"Listen to your voicemail!" she shouted back, as she grabbed her purse. Her face turned beet red, and tears streamed down her cheeks. She was overwhelmed with the stress of having four priests, not to mention the bishop, interrupting her afternoon. And her weekend. And the audit. Her job depended on it. And now Father Fitzwater turned on her. Swore at her. Screamed at her. She turned and ran toward her car not saying another word.

Chapter 51

Barrier
Wednesday

When Brick arrived at the school, it was nearly lunchtime, but the cool morning allowed dew to linger on the school yard. He had not refastened the Jeep's top, but he knew its days were numbered. Nightfall was coming earlier, and the mornings were brisk. As he strode over the dewy grass to the school, he left foot impressions marking his way.

Several vehicles sat in the parking lot. Brick hadn't met any school personnel except Harry and Doc, and he was anxious to meet the rest of the faculty members, as well as the superintendent. He knew he was labeled as the basketball coach but didn't want to be categorized only as a coach and not a teacher. Coaches became the focus of wins and losses, right or wrong, and he recognized that he would need some faculty support through the year.

One vehicle in the lot belonged to Doc, who appeared to be always at the school. It was obvious that he adored Janey but loved his work as well. It was puzzling to Brick as to how Doc arrived and survived in this small Nevada village. Wouldn't a New England prep school suit his personality better? *I'll ask him*, he thought. *But not today. I have enough on my mind.*

Brick was still disturbed by the gruesome discovery in the parsonage that day. It was like the amicable priest owned two personalities. Fitz the angel and Fitz the demon. Fitz the school leader and Fitz the manipulator. Fitz the beloved and Fitz the betrayer. These acts were sordid, but especially when done to children. He knew it would all come out, and the community would be in an uproar or worse. The sheriff's office would be central to the chaos. People would point fingers and make accusations, and where would it end? The next few weeks were going to be prickly.

When he entered the school, he saw Doc first, and they visited for a bit. Brick apologized for missing their gathering the previous evening and conveyed he didn't have housing yet. He remained silent on his morning's activities; the school would soon be filled with rumors. Being the new guy in town, he didn't want to light the fire. He would leave that to the sheriff.

Another vehicle he saw in the parking lot belonged to the school administrative assistant. She was a tall woman, about 40. She had wild flaming red hair that was bound with a bright yellow sweat band around her forehead. She grinned at Brick as she eyed him from head to foot. She wore neon green and yellow running pants and a white T-shirt, aware that few parents or students would drop by today. She was neither skinny nor heavy but would have looked comfortable in an athletic club if Barrier had one.

"You must be Mr. O'Brien. I heard you were in town. I'm Thelma Ampere," she said. "Most people call me, 'Thumper.' Except the students, of course. I am glad to meet you. Bummer about Fitz, though."

"Yeah, bummer. I'm glad to meet you too," Brick answered. He reflected on what she would think when the whole story came out.

Thumper continued, "He was the best. You know, I did double duty with him. Half time here, half time at the church. I'm going to miss that old fart. He loved the kids and the school and the town. Not just anyone can live and work in a town like Barrier. The sun was shining brightly the day he became principal at Barrier High School. How lucky we were."

Her phrase sounded familiar, he thought. Isn't that what the pizza restaurant guy told him? Probably just a localism.

"Yes, he was the best. I enjoyed my visits with him, and I'm sorry he isn't here for my introduction to the classroom." Brick didn't want to say too much. "I see that you are busy, so I'll leave you to your work. It was nice meeting you, and I'll see you tomorrow. By the way, I'm waiting for Superintendent Felton to come. Could you call me or direct him down to my classroom when he arrives?" He told her his cell number.

"I can call you on our intercom system. Just push the button by the blackboard, and answer when the sound chimes. See you tomorrow at the funeral. If you need anything, just holler," Thumper told him. "Fitz said I should fix you up with whatever you need."

Chapter 52

Barrier
Wednesday

Twenty minutes later, Superintendent Alan Felton arrived, full of energy and excitement. He had hired a basketball coach at long last. The teacher credentials didn't matter. It was the unhappy basketball parents who caused him trouble. If this coach could solve that problem, he would do as much as he could to retain him forever.

Alan Felton resembled a basketball player himself. He was long-limbed with huge hands and held a few small scars on his arms and face. He might have endured a broken nose along the way too, as it was off center. He pulled his baseball cap off his head. "Hi, Coach," extending his lanky arm. "I'm glad to meet you. You know we have great hopes for you this year, and you'll make my day if you can get the basketball parents off my back!" He drawled *make my day* as if Clint Eastwood were saying it. "It's been a long, dry season for Barrier basketball. I hope you're ready. At any rate, if you have any trouble, give me a call. Fitz was wild about you. Oh, yeah, by the way, terrible thing about Fitz. Awful, just awful. Any news on that account?"

Brick expected an interview about social studies and instructional philosophy and teaching methods. He had thought about questions that might arise and the appropriate answers. Superintendent Felton appeared to be disinterested in educational methods, but he was very interested in school hoops.

Brick answered, "You'll have to see Sheriff Monroe about Fitz and how the investigation's going. I arrived in town on the weekend, and I'm not privy to much," he fibbed. "I met the sheriff the night I arrived. I was going to have dinner with Fitz, but he was already dead. Other than that, I'm still trying to find a place to live. Pickings are scarce."

"I can't imagine who would shoot Fitzwater. He was one in a million. One of the good guys. I have dealt with a lot of principals, but none could hold a candle to him. I never experienced any issues with him or the school while he ran it. Except for the basketball program. And that's where you come in. By the way, do you need anything? For the program? For basketball, I mean? Anything at all, give me a call." Felton shook hands with Brick and was out the door.

Quick interview. I guess that means I'm still hired, Brick thought.

Chapter 53

Barrier
Wednesday

Brick waved goodbye to Thumper and left for his initial visit to the Chicken Dinner Ranch. He wanted to meet Jay and thank him for the generous donation to the BHS basketball program. He had never visited a brothel before and was unsure what to expect. He drove the Jeep around to the back of the house and parked near a few other cars.

The Chicken Dinner Ranch's front door faced the back of the lot. The house was bordered on all four sides by barbed wire, supported by solid 4-inch x 4-inch wooden posts. The fence drooped in a few places, weathered by high snow and constant wind. The metal gate creaked as the hinges swung open, while a gust of wind banged it shut as he passed through, then repeated. The wind whooshed it open again and closed a couple more times before he got to the house.

The adobe building was beige, tarnished by wind, and it needed a repaint. The black metal door held a sign reading, *Enter at Your Own Risk*. Brick looked at the door considering if he should knock or just go in. It was one of those businesses that lent itself to either. He decided to knock. It was answered by a young woman dressed in denim, wearing a brown and pink flannel shirt and cowboy boots. She had a pink bandana tied around her neck. Her hair was in pigtails, and she looked like she was ready to go for a horseback ride. She eyed him up and down and uttered in a husky voice, "You ready to ride, Cowboy?" A double entendre for sure.

Brick grinned at her and wondered if he was blushing. She was rather cute and charming in that outfit. He nodded and considered her question for a second then asked to see Jay.

She invited him in, and while she went to get Jay, he surveyed the room. It was decorated in blues and grays, and although tasteful, it seemed a little dingy. The furniture consisted of a few deep, well-used, overstuffed chairs, a wooden desk, and decorative lamps. A lava lamp sat alone on a small end table. He hadn't seen one of those in years. Several framed photographs of Nevada hung on the wall. Some were black and white and others color, photographed from a plane. They appeared to be old, or maybe just the frames were old. It was hard to say. Most were titled or bore descriptions, and with some scrutiny one would be able to identify their locations. A large, handmade sign scrawled with felt-tip markers read, *Tips are appreciated!* with a picture of a cowboy tipping his hat. Another sign over the door was bright yellow and read, *Chicken Dinner Ranch where everyone's finger is lickin' good.*

Jay entered the room and immediately took it over. He filled the room with his smile and outward demeanor and offered a hearty handshake. "Jay Guzman. I'm glad to meet you. I was planning on coming to school next week to meet you. You know, basketball stuff. After things settle down."

Jay wore a full-face black and gray beard on his round head. His eyes were blue with a soft glow to them. He wore blue jeans and a flannel shirt, like the one that Pigtails wore. He stood well over 6 feet, 6 inches and was a bigger-than-life kind of guy with a bigger-than-life belly. He grinned a toothy grin over bright red lips. "I've been wanting to meet you. I can't wait for basketball to start. We've had a run of bad luck on the court. Too bad about Fitz. We were stunned. I'm sure glad to meet you though." Evidently, he felt no discomfort meeting the basketball coach in a brothel.

"Brick O'Brien, my pleasure."

"Want some coffee?" Jay asked. But before Brick could answer, he yelled out to one of the employees, "We need coffee and donuts. Bring 'em here, would ya? You take cream and sugar? If you are staying at the Panorama as

I have heard, you won't find any coffee there. I own it, so you can blame me if you want." He laughed a hearty laugh. The donuts appeared as did two steaming mugs of coffee. Jay handed Brick one.

"Sounds good. The coffee is welcome. Thank you. You own the Panorama? I didn't know that. It's a good place to stay with a nice staff. I do miss the coffee, however. I definitely welcome this cup," he hoisted the cup as a thank you toast. "Why no coffee? I can't be the only one who would like it."

Jay nodded. "We ain't Seattle, that's for damn sure." He slapped his hand on his leg and gave a loud belly laugh. "Coffee was always an issue, good coffee, bad coffee, too strong, too weak. This brand, that brand. Then you have all the foo-foo coffees. I got tired of it. I made the decision a few years back to eliminate coffee from the menu. The international menu is popular, and tea fits better. At that time, I had never traveled to Europe. I didn't realize how popular tea was there, as well as throughout the Americas. But people got used to it, and I let it be."

"That's interesting, but I still like my coffee in the morning." Brick smiled as he made his point.

"Then drive out here and join us for a cup," Jay responded. "We can give you coffee and a whole lot more. Just ask for it." His grin widened even more. He pointed over his shoulder to the yellow finger lickin' good sign.

"Actually, I stopped by to thank you for all the basketball gear you donated to the team. It was very generous of you. It should help with the practices. I was stunned at how much you contributed."

"No problem. And give the girls some of it, too, if you want. I'm sure they need new balls. Smaller. But then they don't have any balls at all." He guffawed at his pun and continued, "Tell the girls' coach to order what he needs, and I'll pay for it. If you need something, don't hesitate to call me. Barrier offers very few programs to help kids in this town. Basketball gives them exercise, identity, and pride. It's a small price to pay. It keeps them out of trouble and alcohol and drug use is lower than you might expect. You know I played for a few years in high school and then college. I was headed to the pros when I was in a car accident and injured both knees. Goodbye scholarship and goodbye pro career. They are healed now for the most part, but I couldn't play after that. The knees didn't work right. Still don't."

"Where did you play?"

"Reno High School, then UNLV. UNLV's program was a lot better than UNR's back when I played for them."

Their coffee and donuts were gone, but Jay continued, "By the way, my brother thinks you'll be great. When does practice begin?"

"I haven't set a date yet. I plan to have a players' meeting sometime next week. I'll get a feel for the potential team. Your brother? Have I met him?"

"K. G. Garrison. You know him. He works for the sheriff." He pronounced the name K. G. rather than Cagey.

"Cagey's your brother? You have different last names.

"Our mom and dad used different names. We were born in Las Vegas and used Guzman, which was our mom's name. That was her maiden name. She was Indonesian. I think it's customary in Indonesia for kids to take their mother's name. Then we moved to Reno and used our dad's name, Garrison. The school insisted on it. I thought it was stupid. My last year of high school, we rebelled. Each of us took one of their names. I took back Guzman to honor Mom, and he kept Garrison. I changed my name legally. We felt it would honor them both. I know it's a bit confusing, but it's what we wanted. We are both tall and big like our dad and dark like our mom. K. G. got our dad's calm temperament, and I got our mom's outgoing personality. We used to look alike before I got this," he laughed as he patted his extended gut. "K. G. got the bald gene, and I got the love-to-eat gene."

Chapter 54

Las Vegas
18 Years Prior

Father Fitzwater went to his office. His head was reeling. Damn Mary Grace. He had always liked her, but today she betrayed him. Damn her. Damn the bishop. Damn the audit team. Fuck 'em all. He needed a couple more days. That's all. Things were on the upswing, and he knew that he would be back in the chips soon. He was due.

He worried about what they found or didn't find. He paced through Mary Grace's office into the storage area and conference room. He didn't see anything out of place. In fact, her desk was spotless, cleaner than ever. No wayward coffee cups, pens, pencils, note pads, or file folders.

Slick as a whistle. Was that good or bad?

He sat down at his desk and started moving things around to regain some semblance of order. He inspected the drawers to see if anything was amiss. It was hard to tell as his desk held piles of stuff. Mostly stacks of nothing except junk mail and advertisements. It seemed undisturbed. Everything was there. That's good, he thought to himself. He dug out the memo from the bishop of three months prior. It outlined the proposed audit, what it would entail, and what records would be reviewed. It listed baptisms, marriages, parish roles, deaths, and parish attendance. Documentation, it stressed. Documentation. No problem, Father Fitz thought. No problem.

But the biggie was parish finances. It wasn't a problem three months ago, but dammit, it was today. Shit. Mary Grace did a good job with recording income and writing checks. He could count on her to do that correctly. He always counted the offerings, took the cash to the bank, and gave her the receipt. She didn't have access to the accounts or have check-signing authority. He did. No one else. That might have been a mistake. It would be difficult to blame financial inconsistencies on her since she was not privy to the bank accounts. He pulled out the parish checkbook and the most recent bank statement, which was still unopened. He ripped the envelope open and gaped at it. It didn't seem to be correct. It was definitely off, in fact, way off. It showed that they were in arrears. The bank must have made a mistake. Damn the bank.

He sat at his desk and considered his options. Lose the bank statement. Maybe. Put some money from his own account into the church's account. Yes, that would work. Except that he invested it with a brokerage house in Reno, and they were closed and wouldn't open until Monday. He didn't have his broker's cell phone number. He could claim an emergency and leave town so he wouldn't be around on Monday morning. Hmm. That's a thought. Maybe he could borrow the money.

Who would loan it to him?

While he was considering his options, his cell phone chirped. He debated whether he should answer it or not. The screen read, *Lucinda*.

"No, not now. I can't deal with this now," he muttered to himself. On the other hand, perhaps she could help. He answered it. "Lucinda? I am very glad to hear from you. I was thinking about you. Can we have dinner? I'm starving." He wasn't really starving. In fact, he had no appetite, but maybe she was the one who could help him.

Chapter 55

Barrier
Wednesday

Brick had a lot of things on his mind but most importantly right then was his stomach. He was hungry. The donut tasted good, but it didn't fill him up. The coffee was amazing, but he hadn't been offered a second cup so his hopes of getting to know Jay Guzman better would have to wait.

Brick decided to invite the sheriff to lunch. He liked being with her and was anxious to hear about any progress she might have made. He also wanted to report on his trip to the Chicken Dinner Ranch and ask her a few questions about Cagey and his brother Jay.

With school starting back up in a few days, he hoped he'd be settled into his own digs. He would search again this afternoon. He gave some thought to Maggie's suggestion for him to live in the parsonage, but he would have to dust off a lot of skeletons. Literally.

The funeral was tomorrow. He speculated who would attend. Perpetrators often showed up at funerals, and he was eager to see who was there. The bishop from Reno was officiating, and undoubtedly a few other clergy would be present as well.

He drove by the sheriff's office. It was dark, and it didn't appear that anyone was in the building. He turned around and drove the few blocks to the priest's house. Maybe she was there.

When he arrived, the parsonage appeared different. Six black or gray shiny sedans and SUVs, along with the sheriff's squad car, were parked beside the fence. The yellow tape had vanished, and the makeshift memorials had been removed. It resembled a regular, non-crime-scene house. He had been gone for barely two hours. A lot had happened in that short time.

He decided to go inside even though he was unsure of where the sheriff and her deputy were. He had a feeling that they were in the back shed gathering more evidence and were completely unaware of what or who was inside the priest's home.

He hesitantly walked up to the door. He owned no weapon with which to ensure his safety. He had surrendered his weapon to the LAPD when he retired, and, generally speaking, teachers don't carry weapons as they are prohibited on school grounds. He didn't know who or what would be on the other side of the door. He opened it cautiously and went in. The house was filled with more than a dozen priests, all decked out in their black and white clothing. Some were sitting; others were standing. He didn't see the sheriff.

"Uh, what's going on?" he demanded, uncertain of what to say. Seeing a dozen priests in their black shirts and white collars in one room was a little intimidating, even for a non-Catholic. "I'm trying to locate the sheriff. Is she here?"

"Who are you?" a white-haired priest demanded in return. "Do you belong here?"

"I'm Brick O'Brien, a friend of Father Fitzwater. I'm working on his murder case. Who are you?"

"Do you have a badge or ID?" the same priest prodded while his eyes searched for a badge. "We haven't seen the sheriff."

"Let me call Sheriff Monroe. She's close by, I believe," he responded and punched her number into his cell phone.

He turned his back to the group and whispered, "Sheriff, you better come back in the house. Some folks are here who want to meet you."

Chapter 56

Las Vegas
18 Years Prior

Lucinda was waiting at the restaurant when he arrived. She was as beautiful as ever. Her pale-yellow dress accented her dark complexion, and it clung to her curvaceous body. He greeted her with a kiss on the cheek.

"I'm famished," she declared. "I didn't have lunch today and was on my feet since morning. If anyone ever said managing a casino is fun, he was nuts. Dealing with the smoke and the drunks and people who grab you all day long is frustrating. Oh, who am I kidding, even though I am complaining, I really do love it. It's exciting and stimulating and makes me want to get out of bed every single day. How was your day? I saw you come in earlier, but never saw you leave. Did you win anything today?"

"Oh, my day, where can I begin? Let's order a drink and dinner, and I'll fill you in."

They ordered. He ordered a double Irish, and she ordered Pinot Grigio. New York steaks for both.

He began. "No, today was not a good day for my wallet. I won for a while, but then my luck went south. I ended up in the hole. It is frustrating beyond words."

"That's why they call it gambling." Lucinda winked at him with a sympathizing half-smile. "If you could win all the time, they would call it winning, and I wouldn't have a job."

Fitzwater thought for a moment, deciding how much to say. "Yeah, whatever. When I returned to the parish, the Diocesan audit team was standing outside. They were supposed to come next month, but they showed up today, a month early. It's that damn German bishop. He always thinks that not only do the trains run on time, but they must be early. I was here at the casino when they showed up. My idiot secretary didn't call me. I bumped into the damn audit team as they were walking out to their cars. I had no idea they were here. The team was only supposed to be four people, but the bishop showed up as well. All of them are coming back on Monday morning, and I've got to be ready."

"So, what's the problem?" Lucinda inquired. "Aren't you ready? What are they auditing?"

"The usual. Births. Deaths. Marriages. Attendance. Membership," he listed before adding the last piece. "And the financial records of all the accounts. They are going to audit the books."

"I still don't understand the problem," she repeated. "I'm sure that your assistant keeps the records up to date. If you are off by a couple babies or dead people, they'll forgive you. You can always blame your secretary. What's her name? Mary something?"

"Mary Grace. Mary Grace O'Toole," he repeated her name slowly to emphasize his annoyance. "She's not the problem. Or maybe she is. The problem is that she's an airhead. I have to take care of the money and the books. She is a birdbrain, and I can't trust her to keep accurate records."

"I thought you told me she earned an MBA? I thought she was a pretty sharp cookie?"

He snapped at Lucinda, "She does have an MBA. But she's also got a boyfriend who can be very distracting for her. Her work has been suffering because of it." He switched gears and said, "Lucinda, I need some money. I looked at the church's bank statement, and we are in the hole. I can't imagine how that happened. I know my luck has been up and down here recently, but I always keep track. Do you know someone who can help me?"

She looked at him in disbelief, "You used parish funds for your gambling? Oh, my God, Fitzy. You are in big trouble. How much do you need?"

"Not that much," he growled. "About $68,000. By Monday."

Chapter 57

Barrier
Wednesday

Sheriff Maggie Monroe didn't waste any time getting to the tiny house. She sensed the urgency in Brick's voice and entered within a few minutes. Brick stood near the door and the roomful of priests fell silent. No one knew what to expect from the sheriff.

Sheriff Monroe paused for a short moment when she saw all the priests. They were a daunting group, but she didn't miss a beat.

"Who are you? How did you get in? The door was locked, and yellow tape surrounded the house. You're trespassing. Did you break in?"

The priests who were standing shifted and looked at each other, wondering how to answer. A couple of them stood when she entered. After a long silence, the white-headed black shirt began to talk. "You're the sheriff? A female sheriff in rural Nevada?"

The bishop introduced himself, "I am Bishop Harold Cassidy from the Diocese of Reno. We came for the funeral. We didn't know where else to go and came here. You realize how long the drive is from Reno to Barrier? We couldn't possibly drive both ways in one day, so we decided to come today. I am presiding at the funeral Mass tomorrow. These other gentlemen will be assisting me. I have a key to this house. Father Fitzwater gave it to me some time ago. The yellow tape was flapping in the wind, and we took it down. It didn't seem to be very well tied down. Somebody left a lot of junk in the front yard, and we dumped that, too. It's in the trash can on the side of the house. We do not need to draw more attention to this tragic event. If we can't stay here, Sheriff, you need to find us someplace else to stay.

"By the way. A rather large pile of money is sitting on the table in the kitchen. It seems to me that you and your posse have not been very thorough in your investigation." He nodded at Brick. "We left it on the table, so you might want to pick it up. We didn't count it, but it's probably a few hundred dollars."

The sheriff was furious and didn't hold back. "You have to leave. All of you. Right now. This is a crime scene. Do you not understand? Father Fitzwater was murdered. We are trying to find the person who did it. I could charge you with the crime of interfering with a police investigation. I don't care where you go but leave. Go to the church, or find a hotel. Or camp out at the castle. I don't care. Are you really not capable of making your own housing arrangements? You cannot be here."

"Oh," the bishop answered. "I didn't think of that. Crime scene. Sounds like CSI. We don't mean any disrespect, Sheriff. We are trying to get over this awful tragedy. Does Barrier have any hotels? What's the castle?"

"Whatever," she ordered. "Leave now. Call my office, and let me know where you are staying in case I need to get ahold of you. Out. Out." She went to the door and held it open while they reluctantly filed out. She handed the bishop a card as they left.

"What nerve," she said. "What arrogance."

Brick nodded in agreement and then laughed at the random thought he had of them bunking at the Chicken Dinner Ranch. Wouldn't that be interesting?

Chapter 58

Barrier
Wednesday

After the priests departed, Brick and Maggie quickly searched the house. The mentioned money still sat on the table waiting for someone to retrieve it. Everything else seemed untouched.

Brick turned to her and invited, "Let's go have lunch, shall we? We can take the cash to your office and then go wherever you want. I really want to tell you about my morning. I interviewed with the superintendent and then visited the Chicken Dinner Ranch. Both were interesting, and I've got a lot to tell you."

"That sounds great. We have been tied up here all day, and I could use a break. I'm hungry. Let me tell Cagey where we're going. We have things together in the garage. We'll lock it and come back later if we need to. We obviously need to change the lock on the front door, too."

They opted for lunch at the Eldorado Pizza Shoppe. The menu was predictable. Pepperoni pizza. Coke. Beer.

Brick started with his interview with Superintendent Felton. "He was pleasant and happy to have me here. He didn't seem to care about if, how, or what I'd teach but was very interested in the basketball and how I would run the team. He didn't ask me one question about social studies or teaching or anything having to do with actual student learning. He's kind of a jock himself. I got the feeling that he's under a lot of pressure from the community about the quality of the basketball program. Mostly from the parents of the players. I hope I can live up to his expectations. Otherwise, I'm certain I'll be looking for a new job."

Maggie answered, "I've met him a few times. He's a nice guy but doesn't like to come out to Barrier much. I'm sure it's too rural for him, and it's a long drive. I'm pretty sure that Fitz didn't bother him very often except with the basketball stuff. The girls' program doesn't get as much attention as the boys' program, but they win a lot of games and do well most years. A lot of GBB banners hang in the gym. You'll meet that coach soon. He's a local guy who doesn't teach at the school. He used to farm but is retired now."

"My second stop," Brick stated, "was more interesting. I visited the Chicken Dinner Ranch."

Maggie jerked her head up at him and widened her emerald eyes. "Oh, really."

"I met Jay Guzman. He is a bigger-than-life kind of guy who takes over the room. He didn't appear to have any qualms about his business, although I learned that he owns both the Chicken Dinner Ranch and the Panorama. It seems like the Ranch is clean and organized. The one young lady I met was friendly and nice. And attractive. I didn't ask for a tour because it didn't seem like a good idea. We talked basketball, too. It seems everybody wants a winning team."

Maggie finished her pizza slice and agreed, "Yes, Jay is a gregarious soul. He likes to talk and always has a joke. I met him when I first moved back to Barrier but don't know him well. I've been here about three years and, as far as I know, he took over the CDR a few years before I returned. I didn't know he owns the Panorama. We can ask around to learn if he owns other businesses. Cagey might know. He puts a lot of money into the school for sports. I know that for sure. Primarily basketball, although I heard that he spent some money on the gym last year. He paid to repair the bleachers, redo the court floor, and paint the gym. That type of thing."

"That sounds like he's spending a lot of money on the school. Speaking of Cagey, Jay told me that he and Cagey are brothers."

"What? They're brothers? They don't have the same last name. Are you sure? They're as different as night and day. Jay is outgoing, always has a story. He truly likes people. Cagey is a loner. Some days he hardly says a word. It seems like he doesn't like people at all. Cagey never told me they were brothers."

"That's what he said," Brick replied.

Chapter 59

Las Vegas
18 Years Prior

Lucinda examined him with her big eyes and took a sip of her wine. Her brain was on overload, and she remained silent as she processed her thoughts. *I've been waiting a long time. Has the opportunity finally arrived? Be careful now,* she warned herself. *Go slowly. Don't blow it.*

Fitz took a long swig of Irish, chugging half the glass waiting for her response.

After a few moments she spoke, "Let me get this right. You borrowed $68,000 from the church and gambled with it? How did you do that? Does anyone else know? That's a lot of money, Fitzy. I might be able to help. Maybe. I don't know. It will be tricky."

Father Fitzwater was in awe, "You could help? I don't care if it is tricky. I need to get out of this jam. My own money is with my personal finance person, and I can't access it immediately. Through the years, I have won quite a lot of money and invested it and done well for myself. My other investments prospered, but I can't get to those funds, at least not today. I need a fix for this. Now. Do you really think you can help me? Do you know someone?"

Lucinda's brain was doing a happy dance. "Yeah, maybe. Possibly. Do you have any collateral, anything to borrow against until you can free up your personal money? Like property? Land? A boat? Jewelry? Credit cards? A Lamborghini?"

He took another swig of Irish. "No, I don't have any of those. I live in a house that belongs to the church. And they own the car that I drive.

No jewelry. My credit card is not maxed, but it has a $5,000 limit on it." He didn't tell her the truth about the Cadillac.

Lucinda paused for a moment before proceeding, "How about the church building itself? Do you have access to that deed? Who owns it? Our Lady or the Diocese?"

"Our Lady. No, that's not right. The Diocese. But I think that we have the deed," Fitzwater admitted slowly.

"Who is we, Fitzy? YOU?"

"I dunno, Lucinda. I'm sure Mary Grace knows, but I can't ask her. I am positive that Alice knows, but I absolutely cannot ask her. She would have a stroke. I think it's in the church's vault. At least it was."

"My dear Fitzy, perhaps we should go take a peek. I can arrange to provide you with the cash quickly, even tonight. I can help you fix your books. They'll look good. But I must have some collateral. That's non-negotiable. Something concrete or my bosses will come down on me. I manage the casino, but I answer to a general manager. He answers to a board of directors. The GM's at a conference in New Jersey, and the board met last week. They won't meet again until the end of the year. It shouldn't be a problem. We can do a switcheroo between the church and the casino fast, even tonight. We'll switch it back before the GM returns. Piece of cake."

Lucinda could hardly contain herself. She had been waiting a long time for this. Years. She had stayed in Vegas and lived apart from Jack and the boys for all this time. She felt like a cat about to pounce on its prey. She almost meowed but instead said. "No problem."

"You can do that?" Fitz marveled aloud. "You can really do that? I thought you might know someone who could help me, but I never considered that you could do it." He was starting to repeat himself and was giddy with glee. This could be the answer to his problem.

He would lend her the deed until after the audit was over. No one would be the wiser. After the audit, he would tap into his personal accounts and make the trade. Brilliant. Yes, he was!

Chapter 60

Barrier
Thursday

It was the day of the funeral when Father Patrick Fitzwater would be laid to rest. The day awoke sunny and crisp and calm. Barrier enjoyed four seasons, and this was a typical fall day. Sun, no wind and no humidity. A little chilly but not cold. The whole town would turn out, and Maggie wanted to eye the crowd. She didn't know what she was looking for, but maybe she would see it anyway. She and Brick would go together, and Cagey would join them later.

The Mass would be held in the Catholic Church with Bishop Cassidy from Reno presiding. It was set for 10 a.m. to allow the bishop and his entourage to return to Reno the same night.

The priests obviously spent the night at the Panorama, as it was the sole hotel in town. The manager moved his serving staff around and found ample room for the priests, although they needed to double up in their rooms. Brick was the one true guest and management left him alone.

It seemed the whole town was at the funeral. Students, parents, teachers, and business owners. Jay was present along with several young women, including Pigtails. Brick assumed they worked with or for him. The Panorama restaurant was closed as was the Eldorado Pizza Shoppe. The town was quiet.

Brick and Maggie sat toward the rear of the church. It was packed. Brick thought that Maggie looked very official in her uniform. And stunning.

He had only seen her in T-shirts and jeans. She had pulled her long hair back into a bun. She did the uniform proud. And he loved a woman in uniform. Cagey entered a few minutes later. He was also clad in his uniform and sat with them.

She whispered, "I am sure the perpetrator is here, but since everybody in town is here, that would make everybody a suspect."

"That would be my guess," Brick whispered back.

All three of them silently reflected on the mood of the town and how it would change once everyone learned of Father Fitzwater's transgressions.

Chapter 61

Barrier
Thursday

The funeral was predictable and smooth. The community had decorated the church hall and filled it with memorabilia of the priest. They were mostly school remembrances. Black tablecloths with orange ribbons waited for the potluck lunch to begin. Someone opened an impromptu bar that offered a variety of wines, beers, and sodas.

The room hummed with a combination of crying, head-shaking, and hushed conversations about how this fine man could have been murdered. Who would do such a thing? Why? He was a holy man and all. Salt of the Earth. The visiting priests consoled people and lauded Father Fitzwater for all his good works.

Maggie and Cagey kept their eyes peeled but didn't see any tell-tale signs of impropriety among the mourners. The funeral goers bombarded them with questions about the murder and what progress they had made. Some offered to assist with the investigation while others voiced resentment and fear that the killer was still on the loose.

The priest fraternity left for their hometowns a few minutes after the food was gone. Father Fitz accompanied them in a hearse that had been arranged by the Diocese. The people in the hall gathered outside to wave goodbye as Father Fitzwater and the rest of the priests departed. As soon as they were out of sight, several townspeople headed to their cars after they gathered up a few more bottles of alcohol. It was time for more lamenting.

Brick found Doc, Janey, and Harry Bird and linked up with them. They introduced him to some of the other faculty and staff at the high school. Superintendent Felton soon joined them and confirmed that they would not start school until Monday. This would give staff and students some extra days to mourn and regain their peace of mind. He planned to send a temporary administrator to manage the school until they found a new principal. Another option would be to appoint a teacher as administrator. He eyed Doc as he spoke. The faculty and staff found a place to gather and soon Brick was surrounded by students and parents, all hoping to introduce themselves. Brick shook hands until his palm was sticky and hurting.

A deluge of questions directed at Brick floated in the air: When does practice start? What kind of drills are you going to run? What was the best way to reach him? The questions from parents kept coming.

Brick retorted, "It takes time. I understand your concerns, but it takes time." It was the same answer he gave to victims while working homicides in Los Angeles. These parents didn't like his answer any more than the crime victims in L.A. did.

Chapter 62

Las Vegas
18 Years Prior

Father Fitzwater and Lucinda finished their dinners. She paid as usual, and they drove to the church. It was empty. No cars in the parking lot. That was good.

They entered the church and went right to the vault. He pulled out his wallet, found the combination, and dialed it in. It took more than three tries, but he finally got it open.

He identified the objects as he removed them from the vault and laid them on the table. "Not much is stored in here. Insurance policies on the church and me. Here's an envelope with some cash from a recent bake sale. The envelope says $104.38. John Andrews gave me a set of diamond earrings that his wife owned before she died." He held out the earrings to show them to Lucinda. "It is an earring and a half, but I think it is worth some money. The diamonds are big. Maybe a quarter karat each with five diamonds total. They might be worth some money." He probed, "Would they be worth enough collateral for the $68,000?"

Lucinda shook her head. "No, Fitzy." He sighed and continued.

"Here are a few casino chips that I forgot about. And some rosaries that Mary Grace found in Father Lin's desk after he died. She says they were blessed by the Pope. And here's the deed to the church. Finally. Here it is."

Lucinda took the deed and reviewed it. It was exactly what she needed. It was perfect, unless something had not been revealed. She questioned Fitz about encumbrances, and he assured her that none would be found. She hoped she could believe him. "This'll be fine. I can use this. I can give you the whole $68,000 cash, and you can deposit it tonight. Early tomorrow morning I will meet you here and repair your books. Everything will be kosher. Wednesday afternoon after the audit, we'll swap the deed for cash from your brokerage firm. Just like that. Everything's square. Fitzy, I want to remind you, though. You should not be borrowing from the church. It's a bad way to go."

"I am pretty sure the church and land are worth far more than $68,000. A half a million for sure. Possibly more. Can I get a receipt?" Father Fitz gritted his teeth regretting his predicament. "Can we do the swap on Monday? I think that would be better."

"No, no, no. Not Monday or Tuesday. That's when your audit is happening. You need to get through that first. Then we'll do the swap."

"I'm not sure, Lucinda. I think it would be better on Monday."

"Don't you trust me, Fitzy? It's a loan. Nothing more. You'll get it back on Wednesday after you call your personal finance guy. Don't worry." She leaned up and gave him a peck on the cheek. "Here's where you sign. Trust me."

Chapter 63

Barrier
Thursday

The funeral broke up, and Brick accompanied Maggie back to her office. "Oh, God," she thought aloud, "How are we going to do this? The town will go crazy. Did you see how many people were at the funeral?"

Brick nodded. "The good thing, which isn't good, is that Fitz is dead. That means we won't have to confront him, arrest him, try him, or put him in jail. The citizens of Barrier do not have to be told today about the awful things we found. I have some ideas, but this is your case, Sheriff. How do you want to handle this?"

"Who could have thought that this would happen in Barrier? We are a small town and things like this don't happen in small towns. I've been thinking this through and called the sheriff in Reno to get his thoughts. He has been sheriff for a long time and is always willing to give me advice. I didn't give him any specifics, but his immediate response was to call the National Center for Missing and Exploited Children and get their input. The Feds will be interested. We can call them as well or maybe the Center will call them."

"That's exactly what I was thinking," Brick agreed. "Good job on calling that sheriff."

Cagey walked through the front door with a cup of coffee in his hand. "I finished fingerprinting those keys, so maybe we can try to open some of the cabinets. Any chance you are able to do that so I can send in those prints and catalog the photos of the kids? Since they are all sorted by gender and approximate age, I'll number each of them so hopefully that will help us to identify some of them."

Maggie agreed, but added, "Put them all in clear plastic sheets, and insert them into a notebook. Individually wrapped. You can get some plastic sheets at Johnstone's or from the school. Call the school and see if they have any. Thumper will be able to find some for you."

Chapter 64

Las Vegas
Friday, 18 Years Prior

Lucinda and Father Fitzwater returned to the Cantina Regala to swap the deed for the money. They went to the cashier's cage. Lucinda sent the cashier on a break and told her she needed to make a deposit adjustment in something from the previous day. The cashier eyed her oddly but did as she was told. Father Fitzwater waited outside the cage. He watched as she counted out $68,000 in cash.

"If you deposit it in the ATM tonight, you'll have time to make the adjustments in your checkbook," Lucinda murmured into his ear. "It'll work. You'll see. I'll come by early tomorrow, and we can work on the books. It won't take long. They'll be perfect, and everyone will be happy."

"Okay, thanks, Lucinda. I'm headed to the ATM right now." He started to leave to go to the bank but turned and whined softly, "Can I come over tonight?"

"No, Fitzy," she whispered. "I think we should stay apart tonight. You don't want anyone to be suspicious. I'll call you tomorrow, but you should stay away from here." She kissed him on the cheek and nudged him toward the door. "Don't worry. It'll work. Don't worry. Trust me."

Fitz left with the money in hand, eyeing the various gambling tables. He considered taking a detour but rethought that idea and beelined it to the parking area.

Lucinda picked up her cell phone and dialed her son in Reno. It was his birthday, and she hadn't talked with him all week. "Hey, happy birthday! What did you do today? The next time you come to Vegas, we'll have a party. I have the best thing for you for your birthday." They talked for a while and hung up.

Lucinda sang "Happy Birthday, Dear Kenneth" to herself while thinking, *Fuck you, Fitzy.*

Chapter 65

Las Vegas
Monday, 18 Years Prior

The bishop and his team were scheduled to return bright and early on Monday morning. Father Fitzwater came in even earlier than usual, purchasing donuts on the way. He put on the coffee and laid out the sweets. He hoped that they might help him charm the bishop into delaying the audit for a few more days.

He spent Saturday and Sunday afternoons reconstructing his checkbook, straightening his desk, trying to organize what he could. He called Mary Grace several times, but it went to voicemail. He considered whether he was too hard on her. He sorted the various bank statements and put them in the filing cabinet. Some were missing. He didn't know what to do with the most recent bank statement, which showed them in arrears. He needed to hide it from the team and Mary Grace.

He thought for a second then grabbed some duct tape and taped it to the bottom of the center drawer of Mary Grace's desk. He could reclaim it after the audit. "That should keep it from being found. If they do find it, she'll get the blame," he convinced himself. He had deposited the money into the ATM Friday night and would blame his lack of a bank statement on the post office. He hoped they wouldn't call the bank.

It was still too early to phone his broker, but that was on his agenda as soon as the brokerage opened.

He continued to call Lucinda all day Saturday and after his sermons on Sunday, but finally gave up. She wasn't at her apartment or the casino and didn't answer her phone. It was as if she completely disappeared.

Alice burst through the door as he was getting out from under Mary Grace's desk. He held a pencil high as if he recovered it from under her desk. "Dropped my pencil," he chirped.

"Good morning, Father," Alice Honeycomb greeted him. "The bishop invited me to come in this morning for an interview regarding the audit. I thought it was next month, but today will work, too."

Father Fitzwater smiled faintly as he greeted her. *She is not who I need right now*, he thought to himself. *The Hun. I don't think she will understand.*

"I am glad you are here, Alice," he lied. "I don't know how I can get through this without you. You understand this much better than I."

Mary Grace arrived, and the two women kissed each other on the cheek. She gave Father Fitzwater a dirty look but didn't say a word. "They're a month early," she whispered to Alice. "I didn't know they were coming on Friday, and things were sort of a mess. My boyfriend and I attended a wedding in Pahrump and were gone all weekend, so I didn't have a chance to come into work and organize some of the things they are bound to need. I'll do my best, but I'm sure we'll have some gaps."

"Don't worry, Mary Grace," Alice whispered back, "it'll be fine. I reviewed everything a few months ago, and nothing was out of place. I'm sure that nothing has changed. I know we have the documents they need, even if we have to hunt for them." The three of them sat waiting in Mary Grace's office. The women chatted about their lives and families. Father Fitzwater munched on a donut while he prayed.

Chapter 66

Barrier
Thursday

With the keys in hand, Maggie, Bridget, and Brick drove to the parsonage rectory. They first went into the house to see if any more cash emerged. It seemed to appear regularly. They didn't want to leave it on the table where someone might see it and take it.

Sure enough, another stash. About $800 this time. Where was this money coming from?

They counted, bundled, and bagged it before going out to the garage. One of the keys opened the car door, and they turned over the engine. It hummed on the first try. No issues. They opened the trunk, and it was empty except for the spare tire and the tools to go with it. They had not replaced the padlocks on the door to the room. It opened easily and revealed the room as they had left it, without the pictures of the children. The non-pornographic pictures of high school students were still posted on the wall.

Of most interest was the full-sized door with no door knob. Was it a door to a closet or another room? Without a knob it would be difficult to know. A keyhole was located where the knob should have been. Brick tried several keys, but none of them worked. It needed a larger key, something like a house key. "Back to the drawing board," he resolved. "Maybe we'll have to get a locksmith after all."

They each took a few keys and started checking the cabinets by trial and error. Six cabinet drawers and two doors needed to be unlocked. It didn't take long before all the doors and drawers were open.

"Oh, my God. Here are more," Sheriff Monroe said. "These three drawers are filled with pictures. I can't tell if they're the same ones or not. And here is a camera. It's old. Not digital."

Brick was searching through different drawers, "This one has BHS memorabilia, kind of like the stuff that was on the front lawn before the priests tossed it. Orange and black. Some tools, too. Screwdriver. Flashlight. Pens and pencils. Extra batteries."

He opened another drawer. "Ah. This one has sex toys. Here is a dildo and some vibrator stuff. I don't know what these are." He thought of Dottie, the woman who shot her boyfriend in L.A. She could probably identify them all.

The last two drawers were empty. Good. The doors hid some camera equipment, including a video recorder and an ancient Polaroid. Two HP laptops had been shoved in the back corner of the cabinet. They appeared to be new, but neither of them knew for sure. Three sealed boxes held a new, high-end computer, a color printer, and a Pentax camera.

Brick and Maggie looked at each other and shook their heads. She pointed out, "Here sits $4,000 worth of Visa charges."

Maggie dialed Cagey to bring more boxes.

Chapter 67

Barrier
Thursday Afternoon

Brick drove back to the Panorama after all the new evidence in the garage was packed up. He didn't think it was a good idea to hire a locksmith because there'd be too many questions and information might get leaked. He would hate for the sheriff's office to lose control of the investigation. It would be better to try to open the locked cabinets by themselves. He hadn't confided his lockpicking skills to Maggie but being a detective in L.A. required some skills that were not necessarily licit. The ability to pick locks, not as a formal skill, but as a supplementary ability, came in handy on more than one occasion. Only his partner, Mike Turner, knew about it.

Even though he wasn't an expert, he could get the job done. All he needed were tools and time. A former girlfriend in Los Angeles gave him a bump key set with a note that said she was offering him the key to her heart. He learned that bump keys were keys with their pin positions cut down. Using a small hammer and a little jiggling, the experienced user could persuade most locks to open. He thought it a strange gift at the time but later realized its usefulness. Hindsight proved that she was a very strange woman, but perhaps she had predilections that could help him. He had been unsure if she meant that the nefarious activity of lock picking was something she wanted to learn or if she meant a more romantic flavor. Perhaps she was intimating that her heart could be opened by using a key. Either way, he never used this kit. Perhaps that was why she dumped him a few weeks later.

Now, though, the gift might actually come in handy. He watched a YouTube video and gained the general idea of how it worked. Picking locks wasn't something he ever felt good about, and he guessed that Maggie wouldn't like it either. It was better if she didn't know. It is easier to ask forgiveness than permission sometimes.

He and Bridget went upstairs to their room and stretched out on the bed. Bridget slept immediately, but Brick tossed and turned with jumbled thoughts. Maggie, the still-closed lock, and whether or not his move to Barrier was a great decision all occupied his thoughts.

After an hour of trying to fall asleep for a nap, he decided to go for a run. He considered the sleeping Bridget who was staring at him while she was snoring. Her wide-open eyes focused on nothing during her slumber.

Not sure he had brought his lock-picking kit, he was relieved to find it at the bottom of his duffle—a clear sign he should put it to use. He tossed on a pair of running shorts and tennis shoes and pocketed his phone and the kit.

Bridget didn't act like she was ready to involve herself in exercise, but he was. He told her to stay, and she immediately and defiantly hopped down from the bed and followed him out the door. He could leave her in the Jeep. Maybe. They hurried down the stairs where he saw Greta, who made a fuss over Bridget, and he inquired if she would keep an eye on her for a while. She agreed and offered to feed her. That made Bridget tail-wagging happy.

Brick sprinted up the road considering the town. It had livened up since the funeral. Restaurants were open again, and people were visible in the streets. There were even a couple of cars were parked in front of the Pizza Shoppe. Brick passed the sheriff's office and spied her rig in front. "That's good," he thought. He didn't see Cagey's car, but that was no surprise. Cagey seemed to go off by himself a lot.

Ten minutes later Brick was in front of the garage eyeing the padlock. *Okay*, he said to himself, *Let's give it a try*. He pulled out the bump key kit and inserted the key. First try, no go. Second try, same. He wiggled the key in the lock and tapped it with the hammer. Attempt number three: success. The lock clicked open, and the shank fell free.

It was nearly dark, but he didn't want to turn on the lights. He passed through the door into the disturbing room. He remembered that he saw a flashlight in one of the junk drawers and felt around until he found it. It emitted a weak lamp but was bright enough to see the keyhole. He held the flashlight under his armpit and started jiggling the bump key around. First try. Click. He was getting good at this. If teaching didn't work out, he could try being a locksmith or even a criminal. Brick smiled at the thought.

Chapter 68

Barrier

Thursday

Brick opened the door...a door with no knob. Weird. He supposed a knob was on the other side.

He entered with the flashlight still squished under his arm. It flickered, and its dim lamp dimmed more. Why hadn't he thought to bring his own? The space was about the size of a typical walk-in closet. A closet bar held a few garments. Robes, stoles, priest stuff. The room was carpeted, which was odd, as the room with the cabinets was tiled. The flashlight continued to flicker with more off time than on. He banged the flashlight against his leg hoping it would revive itself. It didn't. He knew his cell phone could double as a flashlight but didn't know how to access it. What to do? Why would someone install a knob on the interior of the closet with no apparent access? It made no sense.

This can't wait, he thought. *She needs to see this*. He called Maggie and told her where he was and what he discovered. He told her to bring flashlights. With her in the room though, they could flip on the light switch.

Fifteen minutes later, Maggie burst through the door, turning on lights as she entered. "What are you doing? How did you get in here?" She sounded angry but grinned at him as she strolled into the room. "Why do I always feel like you are one step ahead of me?" Her glumness quickly turned into joviality when she saw him.

Brick sheepishly returned the grin. "I thought if I could figure out this lock thing, you could save some money and frustration by not having to call a locksmith. I got the door open as you can see, but it's still puzzling. I picked the lock. My bad. I admit it. When I was in L.A., I learned a few seedy skills, one of which is lockpicking. I am not very good at it, but this lock was pretty easy to pick."

"You picked the lock?" she retorted. She was unsure whether to be angry or happy.

They went into the walk-in closet. The few garments that hung in the closet undoubtedly belonged to the priest.

"I am curious as to why the doorknob opens from one side but not the other." Maggie, too, was baffled. They studied the room. "It has no ceiling entry, no exterior door or window. How would someone get in here? But. What. About. The. Floor?" she punctuated her last sentence out. "The floor. Barrier has tunnels all over it from the gold mining a few years ago. What about the floor? Do you smell that? It smells like new carpet." She dropped to the floor and started picking at the carpet. It lay snug to the wall but wasn't tacked or glued down. It pulled loose after a few quick tugs.

She continued talking as she freed the carpet. "I never thought about this before. The tunnels."

"Wait. Explain the tunnels again." Brick said with renewed interest.

"One of the mining companies discovered gold under the town a few years ago and determined it would be worthwhile to mine it. They bought all the houses, razed them, and then rebuilt them where no gold existed. They dug pits and tunnels and mined the hell out of the area until there was nothing left to mine."

"They razed the houses and rebuilt them? That would be expensive, wouldn't it? How many houses are you talking about? Didn't the people in town balk at the mining company's practice and sue them?"

"Remember, almost everyone worked for the mining companies. More gold meant more and higher paying jobs. A few tried to hold out. When the mining company offered double the current value of their home, they couldn't say no. The company paid top dollar to buy the land and everything on it, including mineral rights. They estimated over 3 million ounces of gold. Much of it was microscopic, but occasionally they hit a vein. At that time, it was selling for $300 an ounce. The potential was a billion dollars over the course of four or five years. They could afford to buy the houses and move them. The houses were wooden or adobe shacks or mobile homes, so the cost of razing the houses was minuscule to the return on the gold. They ended up taking out about 700,000 ounces a year for two or three years. Add it up and that's over $200 million a year. Not their target, but nevertheless, it's a lot of cash.

"But, up here on the hill, the estimates were much lower. They dug tunnels to assay and estimate the potential gold production throughout the area. The tunnels were never filled in and still lie under this area of Barrier. Some tunnels were used for actual mining, but others were used to move tools or people into gold-producing areas and move the gold out. They tunneled all over, and 30 or 40 tunnels still exist in and around the town. Some are short and shallow. Others are long and deep. I've seen parts of some of the shallow ones. I'm talking hundreds of feet or maybe thousands. Some were wired with electricity, but the mine disconnected it when they closed. The lines are ripped out now. It was quite a feat, but they pulled out a lot of gold."

When the carpet fell free, a trap door became visible. They opened it to see what lay beyond. "It's a good thing I brought the flashlights. It is pretty dark down in that hole." Maggie jumped up and retrieved the flashlights from the main room. She handed Brick one, and they flickered the lamps down. Brick shoved a folding ladder with his foot, and it collapsed into the space below. The tunnel. Brick took the lead with his flashlight in hand.

She descended after him, and they started following the tunnel, not knowing what they would find.

Chapter 69

Las Vegas
18 Years Prior

Lucinda was elated. She had conned the priest, and he didn't have a clue. She had been scheming for a long time and had never been able to come up with exactly the right plan. Then this one fell into her lap.

She felt it was imperative to leave Las Vegas the moment she had completed her mission. She wasn't sure what would happen to Fitz but didn't really care. She knew that he would be in hot water with the church. It was fraud at the very least, so she expected that he would go to prison. At the same time, she could be in trouble, too. She could feign ignorance, and that would probably work. Hopefully.

Lucinda wasn't a revengeful person, but the abuse of Kenneth defied her ability to cope. She hadn't told Jack of her revenge strategy because he probably wouldn't have approved. She told him she was staying in Vegas for better career advancement and a higher salary than she could earn in Reno. He accepted that. Her real reason was to avenge the wrongs that Fitzwater and Lin had done to Kenneth.

Jack and Lucinda were happily married. Their careers didn't complement each other and living apart became normal. The boys had been desperate to leave Las Vegas and settled easily into school and activities in Reno. No church stuff, however. That incident scarred them from ever darkening the door of a church again. At one point in their young lives, both boys mentioned becoming priests, but those thoughts were long gone.

Lucinda walked down to Human Resources and filled out a vacation request. She marked the boxes reading "two weeks" and "emergency." Two weeks ought to be enough time for the casino to sell the church or at least scare the living daylights out of the bastard. Either one would be good. Jail would be better. It was enough time for her to decide if she would return to Vegas or stay in Reno.

It would be a hard decision. Her career was on the rise, and she loved what she did. The corporation even hinted that they were interested in her being General Manager over two Vegas casinos. But Jack's business also was booming in the Reno real estate market. California's high taxes and density pushed people to move to smaller states, and he was reaping the rewards.

Jack's mother also was a consideration. She suffered multiple health issues, including diabetes and COPD. And recently, she had been forgetting things. They thought she might have Alzheimer's disease, but didn't want to have it diagnosed. That would end some of her freedom. Lucinda would be an extra person to lend a hand.

Lucinda would phone her boss in the morning and explain things. It was sort of an emergency, or at least she could sell it as one. If she left tonight, she would be in Reno before dawn.

Chapter 70

Barrier
Thursday

As they searched the tunnels, they quickly learned that they were ill-prepared for the temperature change down below. It was at least 20 degrees cooler; they would need to do their search quickly. Their flashlights beamed a few feet ahead, but they saw nothing except the hard-packed path and earthen bulkheads and ceilings. They walked about 50 yards and came to a fork in the tunnel. They could either go straight or left. They went left. This path appeared to be an offshoot of the main tunnel. The path narrowed quickly, and they were forced to walk in single file. The ceiling in this part of the tunnel was so low they needed to crouch as they moved through the passageway. It was but a few yards long, and the ceiling suddenly rose to about 12 feet. Their flashlights lit an overhead hatch with four metal clasps and one padlock. The wooden door, which lay above them, was oblong with rusted hinges. Spider webs covered the door. A folding ladder suspended from the ceiling door above, and a rope dangled down. Brick jumped for it but could not reach it.

Maggie offered, "Let me try."

Brick wrinkled his brow and said, "Sheriff Maggie, if I can't reach it, you won't reach it. You are a few inches shorter than I am."

"That's for sure, but how about you boost me up? I can stretch for it."

Brick stooped down allowing her to perch on his knees. She stepped up, teetering for a few seconds before balancing each other. She stretched up a few inches and grabbed a loop in the rope that was hanging down. Using two hands, she hoisted herself up off Brick's knees and did a Tarzan move to pull down the ladder. It slowly arced down, and they grounded it.

Brick stepped onto the ladder and climbed up until he could reach the lock. He unhooked the four clasps but couldn't open it without unlocking the padlock. "Damn, it's locked." He reached in his pocket for the bump key kit and realized he left it in the closet. "That idea is gone," he grumbled.

"Let's go the other direction then," Maggie said. "We can try to unlock it later. What do you think is on the other side?"

"It must lead to Fitz's house," Brick predicted.

"But there are a couple more houses in that little cul-de-sac. It could go into one of them. We never saw a trap door in Fitz's house. It could be somewhere else."

They turned around and retraced their steps to the main path and kept walking. After about 15 minutes they had seen nothing except the footpath and earthen bulkhead. Parts of it were crouch-worthy, which strained their necks and shoulders. They saw no sign that any person or animal passed through the tunnel for a long time and noted no more forks in the tunnel or alternative paths or trap doors.

As the tunnel expanded, they could walk side by side again. They discussed turning back to get the bump key kit, but Maggie thought it would be a waste of time, "The tunnels are just tunnels, vacant, nothing to be seen. We've seen nothing here, and we are likely to end up in a pit somewhere," she fretted. "Perhaps we should turn back."

"No, not yet," Brick answered. "If we end up in a pit, I'll save you," he joked, "or you can save me. Do you have a boyfriend?" This was a question that he had wanted to ask for a while. He hadn't seen a sign of one, but then he hadn't known her long. Less than a week.

"It all depends on the pit," she laughed. "If it's full of water, I'll get you out. I am an excellent swimmer. However, if it is full of spiders or snakes, you are on your own. No, I don't have a boyfriend. I'm not engaged, I've never been married, and don't have kids, if those are your next questions. I don't like snakes or spiders either and scorpions even less."

"Yep, those were my next questions. I'm glad. We should go on a date. What do you say? After we get a little farther along on this case? It is consuming both of us right now, and I'd rather go on a date when things are not as intense, so we can focus on something other than high crime. But I would like to go on a date. Yes? No? Maybe?"

Brick was glad she couldn't see his face because he was sure he looked like an idiot. To himself he thought, *Did that really come out of my mouth? Not smooth, Brickford, not smooth at all.*

But she said, "A real date? Wait. My turn to ask a few questions. Are you married? Have kids? Or a girlfriend?"

"Yes, a real date. The other answers are no, no, and no."

"In that case, yes. It could be fun. I haven't been on a real date since I became sheriff. But no dates in Barrier. I'm sure we can come up with something more creative. Let's talk about it in a week or so. School will have started again, and maybe we'll know more about the case by then. I hoped that finding this tunnel would fill in some of our information gaps, but so far, nothin'. Too bad we don't have a golf cart down here. How far do you think we've walked? A mile?"

"No, not a mile. Maybe three quarters. It seems longer because it's dark. Let's keep going a few more minutes. If we don't find anything by then, we might be out of luck."

A few minutes later they saw a light. *The proverbial light at the end of a tunnel*, Brick thought.

Chapter 71

Las Vegas/Reno
18 Years Prior

Lucinda's phone rang at least 18 times on the drive to Reno. She didn't answer. She saw no reason to speak with anyone, especially Fitz. Highway 95 was an easy drive, especially at night as it was a direct route from Las Vegas to Reno passing through Tonopah, Forsythe, and Hawthorne. All nice little towns. They weren't much bigger than wide spots in the road, but they were bigger than Barrier. And bigger than her village in Indonesia.

So many thoughts raced through her brain as she viewed the barren landscape. Highway 50 was designated as "the loneliest highway," but this might be the spookiest highway since there was really nothing at all to see. She sped up. *Get off this road as fast as you can*, she thought. *Get home to Jack and the boys.*

Lucinda arrived in Reno as the sun was peeking over the mountains. She turned off her phone, removed the battery and crammed it deep into her bag. *I'm not going to answer phone calls until I return to Vegas. If I return. I'll let him sweat.*

She stopped at the local McDonald's and bought Egg McMuffins for all. She doubled up for her husband and tripled up for her high schoolers. She was anxious to see them and let herself into the house easily. Everything was quiet when she looked in on the boys. They were still asleep. The soft snores and even breathing made her smile. They were in the first stages of puberty, but to her they're still little boys.

She went over and tousled their hair. "Hi, guys, I'm home. Are you ready for breakfast? I brought Egg McMuffins and OJ. Get up! Get up! Time to get moving."

They each rolled over and yelled almost simultaneously, "Mom, you're here? Egg McMuffins? Let's go!" They jumped out of bed, gave her one-handed hugs, and raced past her to the kitchen where they thought the food would be. They had their priorities.

"Save some for Dad," she called after them.

The raucous noise rallied Jack, and he jumped out of bed. "Oh, Luc, I am so glad you are here. I missed you so much," he crooned as he grabbed her and hugged her with both arms and a generous kiss. He nuzzled her ear and whispered, "I'd rather devour you than Egg McMuffins, but I'm hungry, too." They joined the boys in the kitchen.

Chapter 72

Barrier
Thursday

Brick and Maggie glanced at each other as they approached the light. The walls narrowed again preventing easy movement. The electric light sputtered, and they felt around hoping to find a hatch or secret door but there was none to be found. Maggie and her flashlight crept down the tunnel a little farther seeking an egress like the ones in the garage and house. Nothing. She noticed a crumpled Hershey's candy wrapper on the floor, the first sign of the presence of people. Brick gave up on his secret door idea and joined Maggie. They continued to squeeze their way down the tunnel.

The ceiling receded to less than four feet and they found themselves on their hands and knees.

"It's odd to have a light but no door. Somebody has been here recently." She pointed at the wrapper. "How far do you think we've come?" she queried, as she glanced at her watch. "We've been in here about half an hour but weren't in a hurry. I'm guessing a mile by now? The tunnel was reasonably straight so I am thinking we are about a mile west?"

"What lies a mile west of the priest's house?" Brick queried, looking back at her. "Maybe a little more?"

"Not much. A couple of deserted shacks, which were vacated after the mine closed. The castle and the Chicken Dinner Ranch are out that way, too," she guessed uncertainly. "So, more than I thought," she added quickly.

They crawled a few more feet and were happy to have a people-sized ceiling again. Brick was wearing his running shorts and his knees felt gritty and were starting to get a little sore. Another light shined in the dark, but it was dimmer than the first was. It emitted so little light that they still needed their flashlights. They saw where an old trapdoor that had been constructed in the low part of the tunnel. It was gone now, and a single hinge dangled from the jamb. In front of them, a locked wooden door barred their entrance. Brick rattled the knob, hoping it would break away and open but had no luck. It was a full-sized door, not an overhead hatch. If they could open it, entering would be easier.

"Okay, Maggie, we've got to open these two doors. I need the bump key kit. Do you want to stay, and I'll go get it? Or do you want to go get it, and I'll wait for you? It's in the room on one of the counters."

Maggie was skittish about either option. "We should stay together. Who knows what we will encounter when we return to the house? For that matter, who knows what might greet us inside this door? This whole thing is creepy. Why don't we both return to the garage to get the kit? We should open the lock in the other tunnel, then come back here. We can see where short tunnel leads first. That entry might be more available if any snoopers are lurking about. Then we can return here to open this door."

They crawled and then double-timed it back to the house. Returning felt quicker than going.

Chapter 73

Las Vegas
Sunday, 18 Years Prior

Father Fitzwater was as nervous as a cat. He was having second thoughts about his deal with Lucinda. "Oh, what have I done? What have I done?" He dialed her cell phone. No answer. He didn't leave a message. He was sure she would call him back. She always had. Later, he called again. No answer. What's going on? Did she say something about going out of town? Maybe. He forgot. He drank some more Irish. It was more than his usual limit, but he needed to calm down.

He went to bed late and tossed and turned all night waiting for her to call. He arose at 4 o'clock and was wide awake. "If I could hear from her," he reasoned, "it would set my mind at ease. I didn't have any choice. The bishop would go berserk if he thought someone was messing with church money." He went to the church and pulled out his rosary beads and prayed the rosary. He prayed for forgiveness. He prayed for ideas. He prayed that this would work. He prayed that Lucinda was okay. Maybe she was involved in a car accident. He prayed. For everything and anything.

She promised she would be here first thing in the morning. But it was now 8 o'clock, and she wasn't here.

He recited his 9 o'clock Mass but skipped the homily. The parishioners wouldn't care. Luckily, it was a small turnout. Another Mass at 11 o'clock. It was larger, but he scooted out after he was done.

He departed for home and called her again and again. He left a message each time. She would surely call when she got the messages. No return calls. He called the various hospitals. She wasn't at any of them.

He decided to go to the Cantina Regala and meet her in person. He couldn't find her car in the parking lot, so he decided to look for her. He walked through the entire casino and went to the cashier's window. They didn't know where she was. They hadn't seen her. He talked to a couple of pit bosses. Lucinda had vanished without a trace.

Chapter 74

Barrier
Thursday

Maggie and Brick quickly retrieved the bump key kit. They retreated down the ladder again and double-timed it to the first leg of the tunnel and then to the hatch they found earlier. The ladder had eased itself upward, and they were required to repeat the acrobatics of pulling it down. Brick led with his flashlight in his mouth and used his bump key. In a few seconds, the hatch scratched open to a closet in the laundry room. It smelled like detergent, soapy but not unpleasant. The closet was dark, and Brick left his flashlight on. Maggie crept up after him. Brick forced his wide shoulders through the sliding wooden door that restricted outside light. It was slightly ajar but jammed and stubbornly refused to open wider. It took Brick several hard shoves to free it.

Maggie passed through more easily, but she also was forced to maneuver her small body through.

"Both of us were in this closet but neither of us saw the trapdoor in the corner. Between the closet darkness and the jammed door, we missed it," Maggie lamented. "I smelled the detergent and figured that was the only thing in the closet."

The laundry room was adjacent to the kitchen, and they walked in expecting to see cash on the table, but it was empty.

They passed into each room expecting mischief, but the cottage remained unharmed. They jiggled the locks and assured they were intact. They reversed their direction and squeezed themselves into the closet and down the ladder, then relocked the hatch and resumed their trek through the tunnel.

In 15 minutes, they were recrawling through the low-ceilinged part of the passageway and reached the other door. Brick picked the lock, and the shaft fell free easily. "You are getting pretty good at that," Maggie teased. "Are you sure you don't have a previous criminal career?"

When they opened the door, massive strands of spider webs and a short flight of steps greeted them. They brushed away the webs and discovered another door. It was unlocked.

They entered and were surprised by, "Well, hello, Sheriff, what are you doing here?"

Chapter 75

Las Vegas
Monday, 18 Years Prior

The bishop came out of the conference room and greeted Mary Grace, Alice, and Father Fitz. "Thanks for the donuts and coffee," he said as he patted his ample belly. "None of us needs those extra calories, but they tasted good. We have a few routine questions. We want to conduct a real assessment of the parish. Alice has an appointment this afternoon and needs to be interviewed first, so we'll start with her. Then Mary Grace and then you, Pat. We'll try to wrap this up today."

The bishop turned to Mary Grace and requested, "Mary Grace, could you locate the information we need while we're talking to Alice? The titles to the church and other property are customarily maintained at my office, but as you know Father Lin brought the deed here several years ago. He was a sneaky one. That happened before I was bishop. He told my assistant that he needed to keep it safe. I guess he didn't trust the Diocese, but we never got it back. The lawyers say you need to return it. If you can gather these items, we'll be able to get out of your hair today." He read it aloud and handed her a handwritten list of several more bulleted items.

- List of marriages, baptisms, and confirmations for the past year.
- Average amount of money collected in the offerings.
- Attendance numbers, weekly, total, average.
- Most recent bank statements.
- Deed to church.
- Title to the car, other property, if any.
- Salaries and benefits paid to each of the employees.
- Estimated volunteer hours performed each week.
- Insurance policies on the church, cars, employees, other property.

Mary Grace scanned the list and answered, "Sure, no problem. Everything should be right here."

Father Fitzwater hastened into his office and slammed the door thinking, *Yeah, right. Shit. Everything should be right here. Oh, shit. The deed, the fuckin' deed.*

Chapter 76

Barrier
Thursday

Today was a busy day for Jay at the Chicken Dinner Ranch. Nevada law controlled all brothels and required him to keep detailed records of who, what, when, and where, in case something happened. His administrative assistant was out for the day, putting the record keeping squarely in his lap. He relied on her part-time work as she performed her duties promptly and thoroughly. After her deadbeat husband depleted all their savings, Jay offered her the bookkeeping job at the CDR. First, because he felt sorry for her, but then he realized that she offered excellent office and people skills. Without his assistant, Jay would have to complete the in-depth reports and handle the bookkeeping himself that day. He detested paperwork. His business was a cash business, and although they owned a credit card reader, most people paid in cash, not wanting the paper trail. A double row of slot machines chimed throughout the day. Records were required for those, too.

Little haggling occurred when his assistant dealt with the visitors. He couldn't figure out why. Perhaps they knew she either didn't have the authority to negotiate or that it wouldn't do any good. Or maybe it was her personality and constant smile that charmed people into paying without negotiating. Either way, she did a damn good job.

The brothel generated more business than people imagined. True, it was located off the beaten path, but a lot of lonely people traveled that road.

Jay's reputation was solid among those who visited, and the word spread. With home-cooked meals and some gambling options available, he was busier than ever. A lot of truckers considered themselves regulars. Jay hired attractive young women and made sure they were clean and healthy. It was good for business. His enormous parking lot accommodated 18-wheelers, and the CDR entertained a healthy supply of overnight visitors.

It was a two-crisis day. One of the working girls was beaten up, and one quit. The woman who was beaten up was doing okay after applying some ice to her bruises and taking some Tylenol for the aches. She would lay off work for a couple days and be fine. The girl who quit claimed she needed more excitement and clients, so she hit the road with her purse, a backpack, and her last client of the day. She left for what she thought would be a better house in Elko.

On top of that, the CDR was hopping with one guest after another. Some days were like that. Prosperous, but also taxing. And now the sheriff showed up through the tunnel. What next?

Maggie smiled skeptically as she greeted Jay. "Hi, Jay. I guess it is obvious what we discovered," motioning to the tunnels. "Those last few yards are killers on the knees." She dusted off her jeans and explored them for holes. You've met my deputy, Brick O'Brien, right?"

Jay was sitting at his desk counting money from the day's business. A big pile of cash, Maggie observed.

Jay stood and rounded the desk to shake hands with both. He beamed a big grin on his bearded face. "Yes, we've met. He dropped by this morning. Not through the tunnel, however." He paused and let out a brief chuckle. "We have a common love. Basketball. Great game. I didn't know about the deputy thing though. I thought K. G. was your deputy. You know he's my brother, right?"

Maggie responded, "Brick told me that you and Cagey were brothers. Cagey never said anything though. We found the tunnel by accident and weren't sure where it led, but here we are. I didn't even know that this tunnel existed. It's up on the hill, and most of the Barrier tunnels lie down in the flats. It passes from Fitz's house to the CDR. Do you know if it goes any farther?"

"No, this is its first and only stop."

Maggie asked, "We noticed another tunnel before we arrived here. It branches south. Where does that one go?"

"I don't know. I haven't been through it in a long time, not since Fitz built the garage. It's a tight fit," he patted his sizable belly. "I don't think anyone uses it now. That short, knee-crawling area plays havoc with my knees, and the spiders and their webs creep me out, especially if I don't have a flashlight." He shuddered.

Maggie did not assume that was true. She didn't trust Jay. The tie-in between Fitz's extracurricular activities and the Chicken Dinner Ranch could make for an interesting conversation with Jay. For that matter, Cagey, too.

"It came as a real surprise to me that you and Cagey are brothers. Did you move here together? He and Brick are both my deputies, although Brick is unpaid. I deputized him today." In truth, she thought about deputizing him but hadn't yet. "He's helping me unravel the murder but will conclude his work on the case on Monday, once school resumes. Kids and basketball will be on his mind then." Brick didn't say anything. He was wondering about his promotion.

Jay listened to her explanation and responded, "I'm glad K. G. is still your deputy. You know how standoffish he is. He's always been a loner. His moodiness started when we moved to Reno as kids. Keeping a job has never been one of his strengths, but he sure loves being a deputy. I don't think he and I would work together very well. You know how brothers are," he chuckled.

"We've talked about reopening the tunnel, making it part of the attraction to the CDR, but we'd have to dig out the low-ceilinged section. The knee crawling isn't good. My partn...," his voice trailed off, and he paused before resuming, "I guess now it will never get done.

"Originally the tunnel terminated in the little group of trees behind Fitz's house, but then he added that storage room to his garage. That was a few years ago. He thought the tunnel should be somehow connected to his garage. He never told me why. I wasn't sure why he did that or why he built a trapdoor into his new room. I never saw this new addition, but I am guessing he needed it for extra storage."

Maggie caught the "partn…" but didn't address it and noticed that Jay used *we* throughout his conversation. She wanted to ask but didn't. She would investigate. After all, the ownership of the CDR was public record.

She reasoned that Cagey and Jay discussed the garage room and its contents. She hoped not, but that was no sure thing. "This is the first time I've ever been in the CDR. I'd like a tour if you have time. It would be good to know the general layout of your business in case I ever get called out here. I know you keep a good house, so this is just precautionary."

"Sure, no problem. And I'll give you a history lesson besides."

Maggie thought she knew the history, but Brick didn't. She nodded and agreed, "Thanks. I'd like that."

"The house was built in the 1800s, originally as a stage stop. Barrier was a terminal for the railroad then, but that's defunct now. The stage stop was about halfway between Reno and Salt Lake. The stage would lay over for a day or two while the passengers rested, ate, and cleaned up. It was named Chicken Dinner Ranch because they were famous for the fried chicken dinners along with mashed potatoes, green beans, and apple pie. And corn on the cob in the summer. Passengers looked forward to it at the end of a long stage ride from Reno or Salt Lake. I'm glad they didn't specialize in chicken livers. The Chicken Liver Ranch wouldn't do much for drawing in customers." He chuckled at his little joke.

"It started out as a one-story building with a parlor, bar, and two sleeping rooms plus a lean-to kitchen. As the wagon trains started to roll in, the passengers wanted to rest before continuing their dusty journey. They reconfigured the kitchen and added the second story with quite a few bedrooms. The bar expanded and became a watering hole for northern Nevada miners, travelers, and ranchers. Then, after World War II, the owners modernized it again. Lots of people moved west during that time. Vegas became a gambling mecca, and the gaming business throughout Nevada boomed. This time they added another set of bedrooms and bathrooms. They planned to build a resort, but the resort thing didn't work out. The brothel was born after that.

"Today lots of tourists still stop for meals and drinks on their way to or from California. Nevada gaming was stabilized during the 50s. A few years ago, the CDR became licensed for slot machines and a card room. Then I added a spa, which is complete with Jacuzzis and massages. Our special bubble baths are quite popular." He raised his eyebrows finishing with a wink. "Especially among the truckers. We have a small museum that shows the history of the world's oldest profession, and we now employ about 18 women, although the number varies with the season. About 20 brothels operate throughout Nevada right now. I like to say that we are the best and most prosperous. We employ over 25 people.

"Even though Barrier is a small town, people still have a lot of interest. You'd be surprised how many people stop in. They want to be able to say that they've been to a brothel. Like a bucket list thing. Some want to partake, while others are snoopers. They search for comfort on the loneliest highway in America. And yes, we still have fried chicken dinners. They are served every day." Jay laughed out loud. "You should join us sometime for dinner, Sheriff. You would enjoy it. You, too, Brick."

Jay led them into a large, well-stocked kitchen. A man with a white apron and cook's hat stood molding crusts into metal pie plates. Three wooden tables sat center floor. Placemats signaled where guests should sit. Faded plastic flower arrangements and salt and pepper shakers topped the tables. And ketchup. Nothing fancy, but functional. An oversized refrigerator and a six-burner stove had been installed along the wall. Wafts of fried chicken, green beans, and coffee filled the kitchen.

Jay escorted them up the winding staircase where a long, wide foyer disclosed several closed doors. Maggie counted 12 bedrooms and half a dozen baths. Jay did not invite them to enter the rooms. They stayed in the hall.

It was painted white with translucent curtains, which allowed lots of window light, and paintings. Maggie and Brick would not have been surprised at country scenes or western art, but the walls were lined with full-sized, floor-to-ceiling murals of contemporary action figures. Brick stared in awe as they resembled the graffiti that was sprinkled on buildings throughout L.A. Graffiti collectors would pay a pretty price for some of it. Maybe L.A. and Barrier had similarities after all.

Chapter 77

Las Vegas
Monday, 18 Years Prior

The conversation between the audit team and Alice Honeycomb revolved around money. She felt confident about the finances of the church. She informed them of the planning committees, building and education, both of which she oversaw. The committee wanted to open a school for elementary children. It would contain four grades to start, but they planned to add more classes as demand and finances allowed. "This section of Vegas is growing by leaps and bounds," she said. "Young families are moving in every day. Vegas is losing its casino gambling image and becoming a nice city for families and children.

"Father Fitzwater is the perfect priest for this parish. He is young, smart, and personable. He likes people, and they like him. Maybe even love him. I can't imagine what the church would be without him. Father Lin was amiable, too, but he didn't have the charisma that Fitz has. Plus, Fitz manages the finances well. He always asks me before making a major purchase and attends the finance committee whenever we meet. I haven't reviewed the checking account statements in a couple months, but the last time I did, our bank accounts were flush. Attendance is up, which means offerings have increased. He always follows through with his commitments."

When the conversation turned to Mary Grace, Alice had nothing but praise.

"Mary Grace has been a godsend for us. She is smart and earned her MBA from UNLV, graduating magna cum laude. She is a people person and loves her job. She is always happy and her laugh! Oh, my, everyone loves her laugh. She is dedicated to her job and her faith. Father Fitz told me that she requested her salary and benefits to be reduced to save the parish money. I think that's a first for anyone. Anyway, she is a good administrator and manages both the priest and the congregation. She's getting married next year. I hope we can keep her. We have no real problems that I know of."

Once finished with Alice, the committee turned their attention to Mary Grace. The conversation with Mary Grace centered on the daily routine of the church and Father Fitzwater. After his rampage, she was less than enthusiastic, but still made positive statements. "Things are good," she said hesitantly. "He takes care of almost everything. He tries to help me and when he does, I can complete my work quickly, leaving time for me to help Alice with her projects. He deals with all the money issues, like tallying the collection, taking it to the bank, and cashing in the casino chips. I don't have to worry about anything. I answer the phone, write out the checks, record the information he gives me, and do whatever computer work needs to be done. I don't even have to sign or mail the checks. He does it. I always get good support from your office, too. I love both my job and the priest. Things are much better than when Father Lin was here."

The audit team wanted to review the various items on the list they gave her. She handed them to the team one by one. She was organized and ready.

"One problem," she admitted, "or maybe two. Verifying the bank accounts is sometimes slow because Fitz doesn't provide information right away. He picks up the mail from the post office but doesn't always give it to me. Because I don't get the bills, unfortunately a couple bills were paid late. It was because I didn't get them on time. I don't think it affected our credit or reputation. He's very busy with all his duties. I think he takes the mail home and forgets to bring it to me. The demands on his time get bigger and bigger. For example, I haven't seen the bank statement for two months. It should have come last week, but I don't have it yet. I don't think I got the one before that one either. Father Lin did nothing with the money or anything else. I hated taking the poker chips to the casinos to cash them in. The smoke and noise. Ugh. Father Fitz doesn't mind it at all. He says it gets him out into the community more often, and he enjoys it. I think he smokes, and the casinos allow smoking. Sometimes we get chips from a half dozen casinos."

The audit team nodded and wrote down some things while she was talking.

"The other problem is that I can't seem to find the deed to the church." The audit team stopped writing and looked up at her. "It should be in the vault, but it's gone. I am certain that I saw it last month when I stored some diamond earrings that someone donated. I need to take them to a jeweler to have them appraised. But the document has disappeared. I looked twice. It's simply gone. I can't imagine where it is. We don't have any titles for cars. Father Lin's car, the Lexus, was given to someone else. I don't know who. The Buick that Father Fitz drove was sold after he bought himself the Cadillac."

The audit team started reviewing the materials. After a few minutes, they handed everything back to her. "All your records seem to be in order, Mary Grace. You do a great job. But we still need the deed. Could you try other places? Do you have a safe deposit box at the bank or another safe somewhere?"

"I don't know. I don't think we do, but I'll do some scouting. Maybe Fitz knows. I'll ask him. And Alice."

"It's lunch time, and we're going out to eat. We'll see you in a while. Could you ask Fitz if wants to join us?"

Unfortunately, Fitz was nowhere to be seen.

Chapter 78

Barrier

Thursday Evening

Jay offered Brick and Maggie a ride back to the parsonage rather than returning via the tunnel. He picked up a metal cash box saying that he needed to make a deposit at the ATM. Maggie wondered how much money was in the box.

Jay expounded, "I've been in the tunnel a few times, but it's a tight fit for me. I'm so tall that I have to stoop down the entire distance, not to mention the crawling. My knees acted up the last time I crawled through it. I'm not the slim person I once was. Too much food and too many cocktails. Now, when I was playing basketball, I was the tallest and skinniest on the squad. I used a belt to keep my shorts on. But not now." He drummed his tummy.

"Thanks for offering us the lift," Maggie said eagerly, not waiting for Brick to answer. "We'll take you up on that. I am not sure the knees of my pants can withstand another trip through the tunnel either." Brick was happy, too, as his knees were raw and his back ached from stooping. His previous injuries screamed for attention.

Jay dropped them off and left.

They were both tired from the tunnel trip and thought they should debrief. Maggie admitted, "I don't know about you, but I need a break. I need to see about my mom and dad and change clothes. I am hungry and need to eat and would enjoy a glass of wine."

Brick answered. "How about we meet in an hour at the Panorama and have some dinner and that glass of wine that you mentioned? We do have a lot to talk about. Doesn't the Panorama have a little private dining area off the bar? That would work, and we wouldn't need to worry about anyone overhearing us. Who knows what they are offering for dinner tonight?"

"It's a date," Maggie replied. "Not a date-date because we are going out of town for that date. This can be a preliminary date or business date, whatever you want to call it, just not a date-date." She knew she needed to stop talking.

Maggie got in her car after offering Brick a ride back to the Panorama. He declined, deciding to finish his run, and they went their separate ways.

Chapter 79

Las Vegas
Monday, 18 Years Prior

By the time the audit team returned from lunch, it was 2:30. No one was around. Father Fitz was still missing-in-action. Mary Grace called everyone she knew but couldn't locate him. She even called Alice to see if he had dropped by the casino but no luck. She drove over to his house to verify that he was not there. His car was not parked outside, and he didn't answer the door.

Mary Grace returned to the church and resumed her search for the deed. She pawed through every drawer and cubby hole that she could find. It was nowhere.

The audit team came into her office several times asking if she was able to locate the priest or the deed. "We are anxious to finish," the bishop complained. "We have a golf match at 4 o'clock and some meetings later tonight. Why don't we return tomorrow? I am sure that you will have everything sorted out by then. And tell Fitz that we need to talk with him. Let's plan, uh, 10 o'clock? Will that work?"

She nodded to the team as they left. Immediately, the office phone rang. She expected Fitz to be calling. "Where are you?" she yelled into the phone, believing the caller to be Father Fitzwater. "The audit team is waiting for you. Did your car break down? Do you want me to pick you up?"

The voice on the other end of the line replied, "Uh, no, Ma'am. This is Tim Smythe at The Bank of Las Vegas. I have a couple questions about something that deals with your church."

"Sure," she answered curtly. "Mass times are posted on the web. You can check our website."

"No, Ma'am. It's not that." Mr. Smythe replied. "The CFO from the Casino Regala came in this morning with the deed to your church. He inquired about foreclosing on Our Lady of Perpetual Tears to build a new casino. Apparently, someone signed it over as security for a gambling debt. Do you know anything about that?"

Chapter 80

Barrier
Thursday Evening

Brick was waiting for Maggie when she came in. She looked fantastic. She wore a pink denim skirt and a lacy shell, rather than her uniform. Her hair fell down her back in generous waves. She was attractive in a pony tail, but spectacular with her hair loose and flowing. He requested the use of the private room, and the servers opened it for him. They eyed him skeptically when he first asked, but the little room was vacant, and they ushered him in. When Maggie arrived, they quickly got to work.

One table was set up for six diners. The servers removed the four extra place settings and reconfigured the table, creating a table for two. "Are you having a little romance tonight? I'll get the candles," Greta teased, winking as if she knew a secret.

"No, it's business," Brick answered while thinking of pleasure as well. "We are trying to put some stuff together and need a place where we can talk privately."

"Are you two talking about the murder? We all feel bad about him, his being such a nice man and all. I hope you can find his killer soon." Greta left the room.

Brick and Maggie ordered dinner. The menu was limited to two items: Beef Wellington or Wiener Schnitzel. Beef Wellington for both.

Maggie queried, "Brick, what do you make of the tunnels and the garage room and all the ugly stuff we found in the garage? What's our next step?"

Brick responded, "Have you already called the FBI? If not, I think you need to call them as soon as you can to ask them for help. School starts on Monday, and I won't be available as much as I'd like. Cagey is a good deputy, but he is overwhelmed with keeping the office and jail going. He seems to have handled the sorting and labeling of the photographs well. That will make the Feds' work easier."

Maggie said thoughtfully, "He bought the plastic sheets at the store and inserted the pictures into a 3-ring binder. That'll make it easier to work on. We have 141 pages. He hasn't even started on the photos that were in the drawers. The 141 pictures are only those that were displayed."

Brick looked up and responded, "141? That's not right. We found 146 pictures. You said 146 when you counted them on the first day."

"No, 141. And yes, I am sure. Each of the packets held 10 sheets, and he bought 15 packets. He used one plastic sheet out of the last packet."

Brick insisted, "I'm sure you told me 146. I wrote 146 in my notebook. I was headed back to the house to find the keys, but I wrote it down. Is it possible Cagey lost some or that you miscounted? You and Cagey stayed to pack up the pictures. Are you sure you got them all?"

Maggie was getting a little miffed. "What I'm sure of is that he labeled 141 photos, not 146. He placed numbers on the plastic sheets, and they end at 141. We can ask him. Maybe he lost them or something. Or maybe you heard me wrong. Either way, 141."

They both fell silent waiting for dinner. Maggie was stubborn and didn't like being challenged. When the meal arrived, they agreed to stay away from the subject of the priest's death during their dinner. They both needed a break.

The meal was superb, and the wine was welcome. Maggie broke the silence, "Let's talk about something else. Have you found a place to live yet?"

"No, not yet. I'll keep looking. Maybe one of the other teachers knows of a place I can rent."

"I doubt it," she denied. "Everyone who moves here has the same difficulty. Eventually a house will come open. Have you ever thought of living in a shipping container? You'll find a couple of those on the outskirts of town," she grinned mischievously. "It isn't a joke. People fix them up and live in them, sometimes for a long period of time. But don't throw in the towel yet. Someone will give up on Barrier and move back to the big city. Then you can either rent or buy that house. Father Fitzwater's house might still be an option. I checked with the bishop when he was here. He informed me that the house belonged to Fitzwater not the Diocese. The sooner we find his murderer, the sooner you could have that house. We can review the tax rolls to see who owns it. How do you feel about living in a house with a murder in its history?"

Brick responded incredulously, "My choices are a shipping container and a murder house? You have got to be kidding me. I'm not sure how I feel about residing in Fitzwater's house. It might be kind of weird. On the other hand, if the money keeps rolling in, that would be a plus!" He raised his arms in a shrug and continued, "In L.A. apartments were everywhere. I could move as often as I wanted and could still find a new place to crash. Back to the case, did you notice that Jay started to say *partner* when he was talking? He immediately corrected himself but used *we* throughout the tour and history lesson. Does he have a partner? If so, who would it be?"

"Yeah, I noticed that but don't know anything about the CDR. We can look at that, too. The laws governing brothels are strict and ownership is public. Let's put that on our list for tomorrow."

"I have a question," he said. "Do you have brothers and sisters? Do they live here, or are they off to the city?"

"No, I'm an only child. After I was born, my parents decided that life in a mining town was too difficult for kids. They gave up trying to have more. Besides, when you get a perfect child with try number one, why keep at it?" She raised both hands in a semi-shrug and grinned widely. "I was the perfect child, you know."

"But you said that Fitz punished you for something. I doubt that you were perfect," Brick teased.

"Oh, that. It was nothing. I ditched school once. It was President's Day, and the other schools were allowed the day off, but we weren't. So, I skipped. It was more of a protest. Just once. He got cranky about it and called my parents. They grounded me or something. No big deal." She took a last bite and resumed, "Another case issue. How can we find out who's leaving the cash so we can figure out where it's coming from?"

"Maybe it's just a gift from God," Brick offered.

Chapter 81

Las Vegas
Tuesday, 18 Years Prior

Mary Grace started to stammer. "Mr. Sm-Smythe, you must be wrong. A casino has the deed to Our Lady? No, that's not true. You are wrong. The Diocese owns the church straight out, and no one else could possibly have access to it. You must have read it wrong." Her head was ringing as she thought of the missing deed. How on Earth?

"No, Ma'am. It is the deed to the church property all right. The CFO from the Cantina Regala uses our bank whenever they are going to build something. I am sure you have noticed all the aggressive growth issues in the newspaper lately. The gaming industry is building more casinos to try to keep up with the population growth. Your property lies in a prime location. The corporate officers are already talking about tearing down the church to build a new casino right there on that property. It is a very desirable location with all the growth around it. The lot size is perfect, and it is already zoned for a casino. I can't read the signature on the deed that transfers it over to the Cantina Regala. It is scribbled but I think it starts with an E or maybe F. I need to speak to your boss, the priest. What's his name?"

Mary Grace cringed at his comments. She was horrified. "Father Fitzwater is the priest here. He's gone, I mean, he's not here today. I'm not sure of anything right now. I'll call you back. I've got something else to tend to."

"That might be what it says, Fitzwater, yeah Fitzwater. That's what it says. Sure, Ma'am. What's your name? I can call you tomorrow morning if that's more convenient."

Mary Grace turned her head at the sound of the door opening and slammed the phone back in the cradle.

"Mary Grace." The bishop had returned.

Chapter 82

Barrier
Friday Morning

Friday morning dawned early. Brick rallied and pushed Bridget off the bed so they could go for their morning jog. At least Brick jogged. Bridget lagged after him, grumbling all the way. Every now and then, she parked herself on the walkway and barked. She waited for him to come back and gave out a feeble yap every few minutes. When she realized that he was not returning, she yapped louder and scrambled to catch up. Once he noticed that she was lagging and trotted back to encourage her. It did no good, and she lay down and pouted. She was stubborn and not an athlete. Brick jogged his three miles; Bridget maxed out at less than half a mile.

They ate a quick breakfast and returned to the school. He wanted to see Monday's schedule for classes and also see Doc if he was at school. He wanted to ask him some questions that had been bouncing around his mind during the past week regarding the schedule.

Brick had been in Barrier for one week and a lot had occurred. The death of Fitzwater. Meeting Maggie. Finding pornography on the dead priest's property. Visiting the Chicken Dinner Ranch with its tunneled access. Bridget. And still no place to live. He had what felt like an unending list of unanswered questions. The primary ones were: Why was Fitzwater killed, and who did it? Did someone find out about the pornography? Who? How did Fitzwater become involved with child pornography? How did Doc and Fitz arrive in Barrier? The town didn't seem to fit either of them, yet they were both here. Were Doc and Fitzwater connected? Who was involved with the CDR besides Jay?

Harry Bird met him at the front door of the school. "I know'd you'd be here today. I know'd it. Let's go see your room, Mr. O'Brien. Bridget can come, too. I don't like dogs in the school, but Fitz decided she'd be the mascot. I fixed your room up last night, and I wanna know how you like it." Harry took off at a near trot and left Brick in proverbial dust. Except no dust would dare enter the building with Harry around. Bridget skipped behind him barely keeping up.

Harry had rearranged the furniture and placed the teacher's desk toward the front of the room. The student desks sat in five neat rows, polished, and waiting for students. He'd buffed the hardwood floors to a shine. And best of all, he had replaced the dusty blackboard with a brand new, sparkling white board. Someone scrawled, *Welcome Mr. O'Brien* in black and orange markers with sketches of brown basketballs drawn around the edges of the board.

"Wow! Thank you, Harry. Did you do this? I appreciate it. A white board. What a surprise! I have to say that I wasn't looking forward to all that chalk dust constantly soiling my blue jeans. Thank you, Harry."

"Don't thank me, thank Mr. Felton. He was the one who ordered it. He musta lit a fire under somebody because it arrived yesterday afternoon. You met him Wednesday, and he was at the fun'ral yesterday. You're the one person who got the white board. The rest of the teachers still have blackboards and chalk. It was easy to install though. I came back to school and did it last night. Fitz never gave teachers nothin' new. He thought that what they had was good enough."

Brick took a deep breath and held it as Harry talked. He had a sudden worry that this favoritism might rankle the other teachers. He knew instantly that he was right. Doc stuck his head in the door. "Well, well, well, Mr. O'Brien. Don't you rate? This must be an accolade from Superintendent Alan Felton, former UNLV basketball star."

"I didn't ask for it, Doc. It arrived without my knowledge. I'm worried this might upset the other teachers, too."

"Don't worry about it," Doc answered. "The teachers recognize King Basketball and know that the town will be more supportive of the school if hoops are played well here. They'll be fine. You need to make sure you win some games. Soon. You know, to the victor goes the spoils."

Chapter 83

Las Vegas
Monday, 18 Years Prior

The bishop reentered the room. "Mary Grace, was that phone call from Father Fitz?" He sent the audit team to the golf course without him and said he'd catch up with them before their tee time. He focused his attention on Mary Grace, and again asked her about the deed. He hoped she'd feel more comfortable talking to him alone. "Mary Grace, you can talk to me. Is it possible you misplaced it?"

Mary Grace snapped at him. "No, that wasn't Father Fitzwater, and no, I did NOT misplace the deed. I don't lose things!" She realized she was shrieking and regretted it immediately. "Oh, I am sorry, Bishop. I didn't mean to yell at you. I am exasperated right now. I can't find the deed. I can't find Fitz. I don't know what to do. Please forgive me."

"Well, hopefully both will resurface tomorrow. We really need to talk with him, and we can't leave here without the deed." Bishop Schmidt waited around a few more minutes. Neither Fitz nor the deed magically appeared in that brief time, and the bishop headed out the door to the golf course.

Mary Grace was relieved when the door closed behind him and he drove away. Not sure what to do, she raced to her car and drove straight to the Casino Regala. Alice would straighten this out. She had to.

It was a Monday afternoon, and only a few people were at the gaming tables. Flashing lights and loud cha-chings interrupted the constant din of chiming video and slot machines. They signaled that someone won big. At least she thought that's what it meant. Mary Grace was not a gambler. She took classes in gaming when she got her MBA but never considered it a very good retirement plan. She would take her chances with the IRAs she managed to invest on her meager salary. Still, seeing all the lights and hoopla was exciting.

She eased her way past the gaming machines to the tables that were overseen by Alice. She glanced around for Alice's boss, Lucinda, hoping to say hello. Mary Grace knew Lucinda because her sons served as altar boys with Father Lin, but that was a few years ago. She hadn't seen Lucinda or the boys for a while and wanted to greet her. She never found her but did see Alice as she was leaving on a break. Mary Grace flagged her down.

"What are you doing here?" Alice demanded in her no-nonsense way. Alice seldom wasted time with niceties. "Aren't you still doing the audit? Are you finished?"

"No, Alice, that's what I need to talk to you about. The team left for the day because they couldn't go any further. Father Fitzwater is missing, as is the deed to the church. I don't know what to do." Mary Grace was almost in tears. "I've searched for him everywhere, and nobody knows where he is. He doesn't answer his cell phone or his door. He isn't at the church. I don't know where he is."

"What about the deed to the church? What do you mean when you say it's gone?" Alice was concerned that they couldn't locate the priest but panicked at the thought of the missing deed. "It's always been in the vault. Father Lin brought it over from the Diocese when he first arrived. We never returned it. We should have given it back, but nobody seemed to care, and we didn't think much of it. Did you check thoroughly? I mean take everything out? Is anything else gone? Were we robbed?"

"I don't know. I don't know," Mary Grace wailed in a whispered voice. "I am very upset, and I am so scared."

"Calm down, Mary Grace, the deed is somewhere. I'm certain you overlooked it. Let me ask my boss if I can leave for a while. It's quiet in here today.

Lucinda is gone. Some sort of emergency. I'll check with her replacement and be right back."

Mary Grace didn't tell Alice about the phone call from Mr. Smythe at The Bank of Las Vegas. She decided to wait on that detail as Alice could only handle one crisis at a time.

Chapter 84

Barrier
Friday Morning

Harry left the classroom to continue cleaning things, most of which didn't need cleaning. In fact, he mentioned something about power-washing the goal posts. He thought it might help the football team score.

Doc offered Brick a cup of coffee, which he accepted with thanks. He had not purchased a coffee pot yet and skimped on breakfast in favor of his run. The coffee was hot and tasted good.

"How's the house hunting coming?" Doc ventured. "Houses are at a premium here. Inexpensive enough, but hard to find. Have you had any luck at all?"

Brick shook his head and laughed. "The sheriff suggested a shipping container. I don't know if she was kidding or not, but that's not going to happen. I'm still trying to locate something inhabitable. Do you have any ideas?"

"I do have a thought. Maybe it won't work, but it's worthy of considering. Why don't you try to rent Fitz's house? It's one of the better abodes in Barrier. The sheriff should complete her investigation within a few days. You could hire a housekeeper to clean it thoroughly, and it would be ready forthwith. My suggestion is Mrs. Brownley, who does exceptional work. She's Reese's mom. Have you met Reese? A very polite and cordial young woman, who is a hard-working and delightful student. Her fellow students nominated her as one of the Homecoming Queen candidates, which apparently is an important honor for a young lady in high school. The faculty thought she would win. I don't know what happened, but she was awarded second place, the Princess level of achievement," Doc explained before continuing. "Anyway, Fitz's house actually belongs to the school. It is owned by the school district for the principal to live in. We don't have a principal, and it will be vacant anyway. I am sure Mr. Felton would be delighted to have the basketball coach in it. Basketball coach trumps principal in the Barrier High School hierarchy."

Brick looked puzzled. "The bishop said Fitz owned the house. Are you sure? I've never heard of a school district providing a house for the principal."

"Yes, I'm sure. Before the town was demolished, the school district provided housing for teachers, too. Those houses were razed, and the practice was terminated. Now they provide a house for the administrator. Nobody else. I believe that was one of the reasons that Fitz took the job as principal. Housing was very scarce when he came, exactly like it is today. I'm sure that he didn't want to live in the church or in the Panorama. Or the ever-vacant container housing. He lived in Las Vegas before he arrived here. He was accustomed to a more enhanced housing situation than Barrier could provide."

"I'll consider that. It is sounding more and more like a good idea. Would I call the superintendent? I have to call him anyway to thank him for my white boards," Brick said while deciding to take the plunge. The timing seemed good. "Why did Fitz come to Barrier anyway? He didn't fit the town very well. Did he ever say anything about why he left Vegas?"

Doc answered, "Fitz told me that he was desperate to leave Las Vegas due to the high crime rate and cost of living. The gambling, too. It brought a destructive element to his community and church. He was afraid he might get caught up in it himself. He always stressed that gambling was a sin. He knew that rural Nevadans needed his religious expertise, and he requested a transfer. The bishop moved him without question. Rural Nevada has a very hard time attracting priests and ministers and teachers. All professions really. You've no doubt noticed the dearth of doctors and lawyers. His move was fortunate for Barrier, but a misfortune for Las Vegas."

"Did he return to Vegas often? To see friends or have a meal out? That type of thing," Brick prodded.

"No, I don't think so. As far as I know he never returned to Vegas. He was content to remain in Barrier. His brother lives in Los Angeles, and I know he visited him occasionally, but I think that's about it."

"Yes, I met his brother, Arthur, some time ago myself. Somebody stole his car, and I investigated. How about you, Doc? You and Janey don't seem to be an exact fit for Barrier either. You strike me as one who might use your abundant talents in a private New England academy. More an academic setting than rural Nevada can offer."

"That's a good story. Janey and I hail from New England. That's where we were born and reared. Janey's heritage evolved from a privileged family. Her father was a beloved family physician in a Lilliputian town in Connecticut. Saybrook. My parents owned an expensive department store in Boston. You might have heard of MCC's. It's a small New England chain store that specializes in high-end men's and women's clothing. A bit upscale from Walmart, if you know what I mean. It had, correction has, a loyal, and I might add, prosperous clientele. It remains one of the classic New England department stores. Its name is a shortened version of my family's name, McCrone, the first three letters, you see?

"In college I preferred literature over economics and business courses. I obtained my undergraduate degree in English literature with minors in Greek and Latin and graduated top in my class. My father, however, didn't think it was a very worthwhile course of study of which he reminded me more than once. He told me to return to school to get a degree that would allow me to be more valuable. I returned to school for another degree, a Ph.D. this time. I didn't tell him what I majored in. I love Greek and Roman Art History. In my mind, it was very utile but not in his. It almost did him in. He was angry beyond words. He wanted me to major in business to enable me to join him as a haberdasher."

Doc laughed out loud at the memory of his conversation with his father. "The old man was not impressed. Then I got drafted. When the Vietnam

War started in the early 1960s, I received my draft notice a few days before Janey and I got married. Back then sometimes you could get a draft exemption if you were married or in school. I had obtained three college degrees and was married, but they informed me that I didn't qualify. I was to report for basic training in one month, and I would become Private McCrone. My new bride and I decided to take a honeymoon trip to California. Our parents financed our trip as our wedding present. We drove across the U.S. to view America and its incredible beauty along the way. We concluded our trip at Disneyland. It was new and very exciting. We'd never seen anything like it. We would have loved to have remained in Anaheim, but the war was calling. We headed back to New England, which would enable me to fulfill my military duty.

"I called my parents hoping that they would send me a bit more money. I told them that we were returning to New England and needed a bit more cash to make the trip. Mother informed me that a letter arrived from the draft board a few days earlier. I was worried that they moved my *report by* date up, and I missed it. If that happened, I might have been Inmate McCrone, instead of Private McCrone. The government took things like that seriously back then. Mother opened the letter and read it to me while we were conversing on the phone. It seems that they made a mistake and didn't need me after all. I was shocked, as I had never heard of that before. Most of my college classmates were already in Vietnam. But since then, I deduced that one of our parents provided some incentive not to be needed. Or maybe the marriage exemption kicked in.

"They wired us some money, which was lovely of them. We drove on to Reno and decided to celebrate. We had never gambled before and thought it sounded like a lark. We lost all our money in one night. We couldn't tell our parents that we gambled their hard-earned money away, so we drove a little farther and landed in Barrier. They needed a teacher and we needed money, so we decided to stay for a while. With my Ph.D., I didn't need a teaching certificate either. An added bonus. Barrier is an interesting town. It is very historical and filled with character. We like it here."

"Then you are Dr. McCrone. That's where Doc comes from. I should have guessed," Brick stated.

"Yes, I am Dr. McCrone but prefer my sobriquet 'Doc.' It seems more fitting in this village. If you call me Dr. McCrone, most will think I'm a medical type and want me to cure their colds and ague. 'Doc' works just fine.

"My parents were quite indignant that I didn't desire to manage MCC. They decided to drive out and convince me to return. When they got to the Hudson River, they determined that they hated the West. They turned around and never came back. Janey's parents died in a car accident shortly after we arrived here. They didn't make it either."

"Oh, I had no idea. I appreciate you telling me the story, and I am grateful for all the help you have given me." Brick reached over and shook Doc's soft freckled hand.

"It's been a pleasure to have someone to talk with these past few days. The teachers don't come in much if no students are around. Usually, it is Harry and me. Nobody else. But, since today is Friday, how about coming by for that toddy that we talked about earlier in the week? Let's say about 7 o'clock?"

Brick laughed, "That sounds good, as long as it isn't Oly. The Eldorado has one brand of beer, and although I like Oly, it isn't my first choice."

"No problem. We don't even have any beer," Doc retorted. "I guarantee that Janey will fix you anything else you like. She has developed exquisite bartender skills."

"Well, I need to get busy. I want to review the lessons for Monday morning. It has been a while since my student teaching days, and I want to make a good first impression."

Doc laughed aloud. "Do you think this group of youngsters will notice? They don't know the Greeks from the Romans and sure enough don't know the Civil War from Vietnam. I guarantee it. You can wing it. They won't notice a thing."

"Maybe you can do that, Doc, but I am a rookie. I want to be on top of my game next week."

Chapter 85

Las Vegas
18 Years Prior

Alice and Mary Grace turned the offices upside down trying to find the deed. This was a real problem. Mary Grace considered whether she should tell Alice about her call from The Bank of Las Vegas. She held off until they completed their entire search.

"Alice, I need to tell you something else. I don't want to because it can't be true, but..."

Alice interrupted. "What is it, Mary Grace? Did you misplace something else? Is something wrong with other parts of the audit?" She didn't blink her eyes. "What? Tell me."

Mary Grace relayed her conversation with Tim Smythe of The Bank of Las Vegas, ending it with "I don't know how this could be true. He has to be lying."

Alice plunked herself down in a chair with a thud, "Oh, my God, the deed was stolen, don't you think? Nobody but you and Fitz have access to the vault, right? No one else?"

"I wasn't aware it was missing until today," Mary Grace reminded Alice. "It's always been in the vault, and I lock it after I open it. Father Fitz has the combination, but I don't think he ever opened it. I know that he keeps the combination in his wallet. He's very careful. You know that."

"Let's go meet this Smythe guy and see what he says," Alice commanded. Smythe's office was but a few blocks away. Traffic was light, and they arrived within minutes.

Mr. Smythe was with someone, but Alice the Hun insisted to immediate attention, and he obliged. He was very cordial to the two women explaining, "The Cantina Regala CFO brought the deed in and announced to me that the corporation wants to move immediately to begin building a new casino on that site. The casino plans were drawn up and approved over a year ago, but they have been unable to locate a desirable enough location to construct it. It's been on hold. The Bank of Las Vegas is interested in this project because casinos are reliable sources of business. Ample, steady income is a given, and we have dealt with the Cantina Regala previously. We consider them among our best customers."

"The deed is most likely stolen," Alice countered, tapping her fingers on his desk and twisting her mouth into a frown. "Surely you can't use a stolen deed as collateral. The property does not belong to the Casino Regala. It belongs to the Diocese."

Tim Smythe peered at Alice over the top of his glasses before turning his gaze to Mary Grace. "I don't think it was stolen. It was signed over. It now belongs to the Cantina Regala. Unless it was forged."

"Who signed it?" Alice demanded. Mary Grace knew what was coming next and closed her eyes.

Tim Smythe opened his drawer and pulled out a facsimile of the deed. It was marked "copy." He handed it to Alice saying, "It was signed by someone named Patrick Fitzwater. Do you know him?"

Alice jumped up and headed for the door, glaring at Mary Grace and commanded, "Come on, Mary Grace. We've got to find him. Now."

Chapter 86

Barrier
Friday

Brick and Bridget crossed the hall to his classroom to spend some quality time on his lesson plans when realized he had left the teachers' editions in his Jeep. They retreated to retrieve the books but instead decided to take another tour of Barrier. Once again, he was searching for a place to live. He would try one more time before settling on the "murder house." They found a mobile home park with a sign reading, *Rentals Available*. Brick spoke with the manager with Bridget at his heels. A small mobile home was vacant, but the owners didn't allow dogs. That seemed odd since dogs are allowed everywhere else in Barrier. The school. The hotel. Restaurants. The sheriff's office. Probably at the hospital, too, if one existed in Barrier. Living in a mobile home wasn't high on his list anyway. Bridget was a keeper, and he wouldn't leave her behind. The cottage belonging to the school district was becoming more realistic.

Finally, Brick decided to call Superintendent Felton and ask him about renting the house once the sheriff completed her investigation. That wouldn't be for another couple weeks. He'd just stay in the Panorama until then.

Mr. Felton was ecstatic. For him it solved two problems. First, the house would be maintained warding off vandalism, and second, the furniture, which was of no real value, could remain in the house. Felton's silent bonus consideration was that it might entice Mr. O'Brien to remain in Barrier for a longer time. Brick hoped that Felton would offer it for free but no such luck.

They then went shopping. They visited Johnstone's Store and bought a Mr. Coffee, two coffee cups, and a container of a locally produced coffee for Brick. Rounding out the order were two bags of generic dog food, dog chews, and two bowls for Bridget. Maybe she would stop drinking out of the toilet and drooling water all over the floor and bed if she had her own water bowl. He doubted it, but it was worth a try.

On his way back to the Panorama with his purchases and books, he noticed that Maggie's rig was at the office and dropped by see her. It was noon, and he hoped they could have lunch together. It seemed that mealtimes were the only available times to spend with her. And they both needed to eat, right? He hoped that they would see more of each other after their first real date.

Maggie's office door stood ajar, and she waved him in. Her desk was piled high with boxes. She was reviewing a notebook with pictures, 141 of them. They were as disconcerting this time as they had been earlier. Two more boxes sat on her desk. She hadn't sorted or cataloged them. The unopened computer boxes, printers, and camera boxes were stacked on the floor.

"Want to help?" she whined miserably. "I'm sorting or rather trying to sort and label all these pictures and other items we took out of the garage. It's taking longer than I thought it would. Cagey started cataloging them, but we still have a pile to do. It's a two-person job, and he is back at the castle. This time, high school kids were playing Robin Hood with real bows and arrows. Shooting at each other. No one was hurt luckily. He'll call their parents, confiscate the weapons, and send them home. Then the parents will call me up and tell me to mind my own business and demand that we return the bows and arrows. Then we'll do a repeat in a few weeks."

Brick replied, "Now that's something I never saw in Los Angeles. Sure, I'd be glad to help. I was thinking of buying you lunch, but I can help you catalog for a while before we have our Eldorado Special." Brick shrugged his shoulders. "Or we can have a hot dog at the café. Whatever you want. Fine dining in Barrier."

Maggie laughed and then said, "By the way, I called the FBI for help with identification of these children. They will send a team out on Wednesday. That's the earliest they could get here. We're on our own until then."

Brick considered this. "Rural Nevada," he thought. "In California, they would have been all over it in a day."

Chapter 87

Las Vegas
Monday, 18 Years Prior

Mary Grace quickly followed Alice, who was marching out the door in a huff. "We've got to find him. Something's going on, and I don't like it. Where did you look for him today?"

"Everywhere. I drove by both his house and the church but didn't see his car. He wasn't anywhere I thought he would be."

Alice cut her off, "Try again. You phone him while I drive. We'll go to his house to see if he is home. I think I know where he keeps a key or at least where he used to. We can go inside if he doesn't answer. I'm getting worried that he might be hurt or sick and needs help. Also, try calling the Cantina Regala. I've seen him in the casino a few times. He plays craps mostly. He knows I work in the casino, and I think he avoids me. He plays in the mornings though, and I normally work in the afternoons and evenings after he's departed. I'm sure he doesn't know that I've seen him gambling. Ask for the manager's office. Tell his assistant that I'm asking this favor."

The manager reported that he hadn't been there all day. They rode in silence the rest of the way to his house.

Twelve minutes later, they were pounding on his door. He still hadn't answered either his cell phone or his landline. Alice pounded on the front door while Mary Grace scurried around the house to the back door. Mary Grace searched under the mat for a key but didn't find one. They both thumped on the doors harder and shouted his name.

Alice uncovered the key stone beneath a pile of dying garden flowers. It didn't exactly blend into his half-hearted attempt at a flower garden, but the key was wedged into the dirt and shined when she removed the stone. Alice opened the front door and yelled out, "Father Fitzwater. Are you home? It's Alice and Mary Grace. We're here to talk to you. Are you home?"

Mary Grace peered through the window of his garage and saw a bunch of boxes and his car. She circled back to the front of the house and followed Alice through the front door. They passed through the living room and went into the kitchen. "Should we check his bedroom?" she whispered to Alice. "A priest's bedroom? Do you think we should go in?"

"Oh, for heaven's sake, I'll go. You stay here," Alice yelped. She moved to the back of the house and opened the bedroom door. "Father! Wake up! Are you ok? Father Fitz! Wake up!"

"Is he sick?" Mary Grace queried peeking into the room. "Should I call a doctor or the EMTs? What do you think he has? He's not dead, is he?" She made the sign of a cross over her chest.

Alice cast her eyes over the length of his prone body and breathed in a deep lungful of air. He was lying on top the covers. He wore his blacks including a loosened white collar. She reached down and felt his pulse. "No, he's not sick. He's drunk. He's passed out. I don't know how much he drank, but I think he found the 'creature' at the bottom of the whiskey bottle. And here is the empty whiskey bottle." She reached down and used two fingers to pick up an empty bottle of Jameson from the floor.

"The creature? What creature?"

Alice regarded him disdainfully. "That's what the Irish say: 'There's a creature at the bottom of every bottle of Irish whiskey, and you have to let him out.'" She used a slight Irish brogue to explain to Mary Grace. "He found the creature all right. My father was an Irish whiskey drinker. He always threw the cork away when he opened a bottle to let the creature out. I wonder what precipitated Fitz's encounter with the creature."

Alice reached over and shook his shoulder. Hard. "Wake up, Fitz. Wake up." She continued shoving him until he began to move and groan. It took a several minutes.

His eyes flickered open, and he turned away from Alice slurring, "Who'ver ya are, go 'way. Don' wanna see ya. Go 'way." He half-heartedly pushed toward her hand and missed it. He tried to roll over but couldn't manage.

Alice persisted, "We are not going away. You need to rally. We have some questions, and we need the answers now." Alice wasn't about to wait until he was stone-cold sober. She'd dealt with drunks throughout her life and offered him no mercy. "We'll give you 10 minutes. We'll make coffee, and I'll be back in here then. Get up now." She pushed his shoulder again, which caused him to groan.

The two women exited the room and went to the kitchen. Mary Grace quickly located a can of coffee and began brewing it. "I can't believe this. I've never seen him drunk. I know that he has a drink now and then but never this much. And it's still morning. And why now? Right in the middle of this audit. It's crazy. Why is he doing this?"

"Good question. Let's ask him. Coffee ready yet?" Alice asked. "I'll go get him and bring him in here. If I can get him up, that is." She went into the bedroom, and he was gone. The bathroom door was closed. She heard him possibly, or rather undoubtedly, vomiting. She went back to the kitchen.

"Perhaps we should give him a glass of water." Mary Grace said. "And some ice. And can you find some aspirin or other pain reliever? I think he is in a lot of pain right now." Alice rolled her eyes.

Alice retraced her steps to the bedroom as he was exiting the bathroom. He eyed the bed and aimed himself toward it. Alice was not going to allow him to lie back down. She forcibly steered him into the kitchen and set him down at the table. Mary Grace gave him a glass of ice water and a cup of coffee. She took a hand towel from a drawer and dampened it for his blotchy face.

Father Fitzwater regarded them through vacant, reddened eyes and began to speak, but his words came out wrong. "What girls you doing? How'd the door let you in?" He was flushed and groggy with unfocused eyes. A few beads of perspiration dripped down his forehead.

Alice held the water glass while he sipped it. "I am sure you are dehydrated. Drink this down. And take these aspirin. They might help." He took the aspirin and tasted the water and then pushed her hand away.

Mary Grace slid the coffee cup over to him. "Try this. Coffee will help sober you up."

He drooled some saliva and wiped his mouth. "Not myself. No feel good." His words were slurred and almost imperceptible.

They continued this little assemblage for the better part of an hour until he began drinking the coffee for real. His eyes began to focus. Mary Grace added saltines to his buffet hoping to settle his stomach.

At last, he seemed ready to answer some questions. Alice started, "The auditors have been asking for the deed to the church. It should be at the Diocese, but we can't find it anyplace. It used to be in our vault. I forgot that we kept it there until the audit. All I want to know is where the deed is. Did you return it to the Diocese? Do you have it? Where is it?"

Father Fitzwater bowed his head, fingering his half-empty cup of coffee. He considered her question. His mind was still groggy. The truth was he didn't know exactly where it was. Lucinda took it. That's all he knew for sure, and he didn't know where she was. He was cognizant enough to know that he shouldn't tell Alice anything. He hesitated before speaking. "I don't know. I just don't know."

Chapter 88

Reno
18 Years Prior

Lucinda and her family kept a low profile during the two weeks she was in Reno. They played, went on walks, and saw some of the sights. The first weekend, they drove to Tahoe and enjoyed canoeing and a picnic on the beach. It was a wonderful time. Jack took a few days off so they could spend more time together. Lucinda and Jack met and married right after she moved to Vegas, but they had spent more time apart than together. Yet their relationship was strong.

"Why don't you stay here?" Jack cooed. "You can get a job in Reno and be home more often with all of us. I know you have a great job and your salary is tops, but the boys are growing up without you. You can't get these years back. Maybe after the boys graduate from high school and Mom dies, we could go back to Vegas. I can't go now. Not with her as sick as she is." Jack took her hand in his and kissed it.

He resumed his appeal, "The boys are both playing basketball and are pretty good at it. Jay plays especially well. I think they'll move him to the varsity team as a sophomore. Kenneth doesn't play basketball as well as Jay, but he'll make the JV team for sure. He'll play football, too. He's gotten big this year, and they need some size in the backfield. The coaches already have their eyes on him. And he seems better here in Reno than he was in Vegas. He seems to have put the incident behind him."

"I've been thinking about it. Speaking of Kenny's incident, I fixed it. My reason for staying in Vegas is over. Done. I feel free to move to Reno." She gazed past him into the lake. "We won't have to worry again."

"What do you mean you fixed it? What did you do? Did you kill him? Are you in trouble?"

Lucinda's cheerful face took on a sneer. "No, I didn't kill him, and I'm not in trouble, but somebody is. Lin and Fitzwater hurt Cagey. Lin was the one who abused Kenny, but Fitzwater took pictures. His deeds were just as evil in my book. Lin is dead so there was nothing I could do to him, but I fixed that bastard Fitzwater, and he is in big, big trouble. I don't think we'll ever have to worry about him again."

The boys ran up from the beach and dove into the sandwiches that Jack brought from home. "All together again. Isn't this lovely?" Lucinda wondered if she could get a job at the Harrah's in Reno.

Chapter 89

Barrier
Friday

Brick and Maggie continued to sort and record the pictures for a while longer. They photocopied all the pictures and put them in the sheriff's vault. "I'm still puzzled about the five pictures that are missing," Brick offered. "Did Cagey say anything about them? As you know, I'm detail oriented. I recounted the pictures that Cagey photographed on the walls. 146. Those other five are somewhere. We need to find them. We could compare his pictures to those on your desk to see which ones are missing, but that will be tedious. Missing photos means missing evidence. Not a good thing."

"I asked him, but he shrugged his shoulders. He was leaving to deal with the bow and arrow situation. He was distracted and left in a hurry. The caller said that he and his wife were hiking and saw some kids go into the castle with bows and a bunch of real arrows. The next thing he knew, an arrow flew toward him and his wife. It missed them by about four feet, and he decided to call our office. He didn't leave his name. He didn't want to get involved. Cagey headed to the castle as quickly as he could before somebody gets hurt. I'm positive the kids were drinking. I wish the county or city would tear the castle down. It causes me nothing but headaches. I think this is the third call we've gotten this week. It will help when the kids are back in school. Then they can be your headache. Not mine."

Maggie's tiny office was full of boxes of pictures and other items they removed from the garage.

They worked for a while sorting and cataloging. She was right on target. It was a two-person job. She numbered them while he filed them in plastic see-through document covers. They finally finished. In addition to the 141 pictures, they logged another 83 pictures. They had 224 images of children.

While Maggie returned the four phone messages she received, Brick shifted himself to the outer office to wait for her. He expected that it might take a while and decided to use the time to review one of his textbooks for Monday's classes. He stepped outside to retrieve the U.S. History textbook, then surveyed Cagey's desk.

Cagey's large, green metal desk was heaped with office paraphernalia, which made it difficult to set his textbook down. It was obviously a retired military issue desk. Its two broken legs were propped up on cinderblocks creating an unbalanced wobble. The top was scarred from age and coffee and other unknown blemishes of the past. It needed a thorough cleaning. Brick began to clear a spot, removing the usual items that covered a desk including pens, pencils, a coffee cup, and a stack of yellow pads. Two lopsided piles of file folders and a variety of journals and other reading material also sat on the desk's surface. A couple packs of lifesavers, peanut butter crackers, and a bag of unopened beef jerky completed the mess. He gathered all the paperwork into one big stack and moved it to a vacant chair. It was an old oaken office chair with armrests and wheels. The chair tipped as he set the pile down. Everything tumbled to the floor and flew in several directions. "Damn," Brick grumbled.

He stooped to pick them up and arrange them into some sort of order, but the pile tumbled off the teetering chair again. The file folders spilled open and out fell handwritten notes and some forms. And pictures. Brick perused them one by one. "Maggie!" he yelled. "You'd better come here. I think we found the missing pictures."

She came out of her office and asked, "You found them? Where were they?"

"They sat right here on his desk. These. At least I think these are the same ones," Brick said as he displayed five photos of a boy, maybe two boys in varying stages of undress. The boy or boys in the picture defied the photographer shooting eye daggers into the camera. He handed them to Maggie.

At that moment, the door banged open, and Cagey barged in. "Hey, what the fuck are you doing at my desk?"

Chapter 90

Reno
18 Years Prior

Lucinda spent her second week of vacation applying for management positions in Reno casinos. She was picky about where she worked and who she worked for. She reviewed every casino online and finally interviewed with three. She didn't want the Cantina Regala to know that she was seeking a different position and was careful about who she used for references.

On the spot, she was offered multiple positions, ranging from hostess to pit boss. None really suited her. She wanted management and kept searching. She called her boss in Las Vegas to ask for an extension of her vacation time, citing an ongoing emergency with Jack's mother. It was granted. Her boss told her of the continued requests by the patrons, especially from a man named Patrick Fitzwater, who seemed insistent on knowing where she was.

Lucinda, Jack, and their boys set off on another overnight road trip the next weekend. Lucinda had not visited Barrier since she moved to Vegas and was interested in knowing what it looked like today. The mining company repositioned the town before she arrived, but it still made a good story. They stopped at the shoe tree where the boys thought it would be cool to leave their shoes behind. Jack vetoed it. She told about the names written in pebbles in the sand at the sides of the road as they drove past. They stopped to examine the pebbled signatures, and the boys scrounged enough stones to write their names. She told them of Barrier's history and how Highway 50 was dubbed

"The Loneliest Highway in America." They debated how it could claim that title. Vijay said, "I was taught that Gettysburg was the bloodiest battle in the Civil War. I asked my teacher how they measured the blood, but she didn't answer. The loneliest highway might be the same."

They stopped at the castle and walked around it. The boys wanted to explore, but the fence discouraged them. Lucinda described it, "What I recall of the castle is that it was haunted, or at least that's what I was told. People rumored that the original owner, who was shot and killed by an angry miner, walked the floors at night. Now and then you could see a glow coming from the top floor. I saw the light once. I thought it was teenagers fooling around. I don't believe in ghosts, but it made me think. It was scary speculation."

Jack twisted his mouth and disputed her story. "That's the first I've heard of that. It is a tiny town. Run down and dilapidated. Do you still know anyone here?"

She considered the town and its vaguely familiar buildings. No new businesses were obvious, and several of the old ones were boarded up, but Johnstone's, the Eldorado Pizza Shoppe, a couple storefronts, and the Panorama were still in business.

"It's been a long time since I've been here. I'm not sure I will know anyone, but let's go to the Panorama. Maybe Harvey is still here. He was my sponsor. He'll be at the Panorama if he's still around. They have a good restaurant, and we can have lunch or brunch, whatever they are serving. You will be surprised."

The four of them trooped into the restaurant. It was bustling on this Saturday noon. Today's menu was a an all-you-can-eat smorgasbord. Jack joked, "They'll go broke trying to feed these two all you can eat."

Chapter 91

Barrier
Friday

Cagey furiously glowered at Brick and then at Maggie. "Why are you snooping into my stuff?"

Brick answered quickly, raising both hands in surrender. He glanced at the sheriff, "Whoa, there. I'm only borrowing your desk for a while, Cagey. I'm working on my lesson plans for next week. I didn't think you would be back this quickly. I'll move."

Sheriff Monroe took on a resolute sheriff persona. She held out the photos, splayed as Brick handed them to her. "What are these doing here in the file folders on your desk instead of being with the others? These are evidence, Cagey. You and I need to have a conversation." Her face turned a deep red. It was obvious that she was angry. Brick had never seen her angry, and he saw a new side to her. She motioned to Cagey that he should enter her office. She closed the door firmly behind them.

She began questioning him. They were both in argumentative modes.

Sheriff: "Why did you separate these five photos from the others?"

Cagey: "What's he doing at my desk?"

Sheriff: "They seem to be all of one or two boys. Do you know these boys?"

Cagey: "I dunno. What the fuck's he doing at my desk? Can't I have privacy around here?"

Sheriff: "He was trying to find some space to do his schoolwork prep. Do you know these boys?"

Cagey: "I dunno. Can't be sure. Are you firing me? And hiring him? Am I being replaced?"

Sheriff: "I need a little more information. You're a good deputy, Cagey. I need answers. You realize that when you separated these pictures from the others, you tampered with evidence, don't you?"

Cagey: Silence.

Sheriff: "Tampering with evidence can get you fired. You know that."

Cagey: Silence.

Sheriff: "Does this have anything to do with your brother, Jay Guzman?"

Cagey: Silence.

Sheriff: "C'mon, Cagey. Jay told me that you were brothers. That secret is out, but that's not the only secret that surrounds you and your brother. You hid these pictures and denied having them. You lied, Cagey. I don't know why you are keeping secrets from me. If you are covering something up, tell me. C'mon Cagey, tell me the truth."

Cagey: Silence.

Sheriff: "We are getting nowhere. You have to talk to me."

Cagey: "It's not important. It's nothin'."

Chapter 92

Las Vegas
Tuesday, 18 Years Prior

Mary Grace arrived at her job earlier than usual. She purchased a carafe of coffee and some donuts from Krispy Kreme. She was carrying them in when the audit team arrived in five Lexus sedans. The sun was shining. It would be a typical Vegas day, perhaps warmer than usual, but within the range of comfort.

The door was unlocked. *Oh, good,* she thought, *Fitz is already here. I hope he is back to himself.* But it was Alice who had unlocked the door. She parked in the rear of the building and entered through the back door.

The five men ushered Mary Grace into her office, confiscating the carafe and donuts. She scanned the room and questioned Alice with her eyes. Alice shook her head slightly. It wasn't even 8 a.m., and everyone was already here. Everyone except one person, that is. It could be a hellish day.

"I guess we're waiting for Pat. Have you heard from him?" The bishop directed his questions at both Mary Grace and Alice. For a half a minute, neither of them said anything. It was an awkward silence.

Alice answered first and spoke slowly, "Yes, we saw him yesterday afternoon. We talked to him. I am positive he will be here. He seemed a little out of sorts, but..."

The bishop interrupted Alice. "Was he drunk? Damned Irish priests. They think that Irish whiskey will solve all their problems."

Both women remained silent for a few more seconds. Mary Grace was still angry at the priest and didn't want to respond. She hoped Alice would do all the explaining and she did, "Yes, he was drunk, Bishop, but we sobered him up, and I'm sure he will be here. Mary Grace, could you give him a call, please?"

Mary Grace tossed Alice a couple eye moves that were close to eye rolls, but not quite. She reached for the phone. She wasn't in any mood to be kind to him. She wasn't sure that he would be sober enough even now to complete the audit.

Before she could dial, Father Fitz stormed through the door. "You thinkin' of starting without me?" he bellowed. "Let's get on with it. I need some coffee."

Chapter 93

Barrier
Friday

Sheriff Monroe sat silent for two or three minutes, waiting for Cagey to respond. She didn't budge. He didn't budge. She dealt the photos out like cards and placed them face up in a row, side by side. He glanced at them but didn't comment. She restarted the conversation.

Sheriff: "Let's talk about these pictures. Do you know who's in them?"

Cagey swatted them aside with his hand, knocking them to the floor. He gloomily admitted, "All right, God dammit. They're of me. These God-damned pictures are of me. When I was eight and nine years old. All five are of me, but at different times."

Sheriff: "These are of you? Oh, my God. Oh, God, Cagey. I am sorry. I am very, very sorry. I didn't know."

She rose and snatched them up from the floor, placing them in a stack upside down on the table, hiding the images from either of them.

Cagey: "Yeah, well, you didn't have anything to do with it. There were others who did though."

Sheriff: "Who? Who was it? Who took the pictures?"

Cagey: Silence.

Sheriff: "Father Fitzwater? Were you one of his victims?"

Cagey shook his head but didn't meet her eyes. His eyes started to tear, and he blinked them back.

Cagey: "No, not him."

Sheriff: "Then who? Why did Father Fitzwater have these pictures?"

Cagey: "He helped. The other priest molested me, but Fitzwater took the pictures. His name was Lin. Fuckin' Father Lin. He's dead now, but he liked to have his way with little boys. Fitzwater knew it but didn't do anything to stop it. I didn't know he kept the fuckin' pictures. I thought Lin had them. I didn't know what he did with them. Souvenirs? Trophies? I thought he destroyed them. At least I hoped he had. Then we went into the garage. It made me sick to see them. Not only me, but all those other kids, too."

Sheriff: "Where did this happen? You weren't raised in Barrier, were you? You grew up in Reno, right?"

Cagey wiped his eyes; the tears were too many to blink back. He still did not look at her. "No, we lived in Vegas until I was 10. Then we moved to Reno with our dad. Our mom was a casino manager and overwhelmed between work and family. Dad was finishing college and selling real estate. Mom and Dad encouraged us to spend time at the church. They thought it would be a good influence on us." He wiped his eyes again and gave her a weak smile. "Anyway, we were in the youth group and helped with chores around the church, you know dusting, putting things away. Chores. Lin, the fucker, always rewarded Jay and me by taking us to movies or the circus or stuff like that. He knew our parents were gone a lot.

"He liked to take us for ice cream or out to eat. When we got back to the church afterwards, he'd make a big fuss. He'd make me do awful things. Embarrassing things. Painful things. He never bothered Jay, who was two years older, but I was his target for two years. Two fuckin' years. He'd send Jay on an errand or give him a beer or a joint and a video game. Video games were new in those days, at least to us. Fuckin' Fitzwater would come in after and take pictures. He must have been doing this with others, I don't know. The bastard Lin taunted me. He always told me how proud he was of me, like I was his trophy. It was horrible then and still is. Just recalling it makes my stomach churn.

"He warned me that if I told anyone, he would inform our mother that Jay was drinking beer and smoking pot. And would tell God to send me to hell because I disobeyed a priest. I was eight and believed him. After one horrible afternoon at the movies, I told Jay, and then he told Mom and Dad. I think Jay knew all along, but he didn't ask me about it or say anything. They did this for two years. Two friggin' years. I didn't know how to make him stop. Jay never told our parents about the beer and pot though.

"When our parents found out what the priests were doing, they decided that we needed to leave Vegas. They couldn't or wouldn't confront the priests. Mom was a good Catholic and didn't want to go to hell. Dad knew if he confronted them, he would kill them. They decided that Dad would move to Reno, which was better for all concerned. Mom was employed in Las Vegas as a casino manager and didn't want to leave it. You know, money and status. She lived in Indonesia during the genocide and was proud to be a successful American.

"They decided to live separately. It wasn't a divorce or anything. They loved each other. They lived apart allowing her to continue her career. We lived with our grandma, and Jay and I attended school. Grandma was sick with a bunch of stuff, and Dad wanted to help her. Mom moved to Reno when we were first going into high school. She told me years later that she stayed in Vegas to get back at Fitzwater. It took her several years, but at last, she did. She disclosed that she saw Fitzwater in the casino all the time. She hated him but couldn't say anything for fear of losing her job. Finally, she did something to get even with him. She never told us exactly what she did, but Fitzwater got moved to Barrier a short time after she moved to Reno. Our mom's dead now, she and our dad died in a car accident a few years ago. They were hit by a drunk driver. She never saw Fitzwater again. When I came to Barrier to work here and live near my brother, I was too embarrassed and ashamed to confront him. The shame has kept me quiet all these years. I didn't want to risk losing my job. Who knew what people would say? It made me sick that he was the principal at the high school. I just prayed that he stopped doing all of that horrible stuff when he left Las Vegas."

Maggie got up from behind her desk and hugged Cagey and patted him on the back. "Oh, Cagey, I'm glad you told me. I was furious with you. I thought you betrayed me somehow, but I should have known better. I am so sorry. Sorry for you and sorry that I didn't trust you. This whole thing is awful, awful."

Chapter 94

Las Vegas
Tuesday, 18 Years Prior

All six priests went into the conference room and shut the door. Mary Grace and Alice were leery about what would transpire. Alice retrieved a cup of coffee for each of them not saying anything. The two women sat still without conversation.

Mary Grace saw another car pulling into the parking lot. She didn't recognize it and wondered who it was. She grimaced at the thought of anyone needing anything today. She felt unfocused and would rather not be here at all.

She sighed as she saw Tim Smythe and another man she had never seen before getting out of the car.

"This is not what we need," she whispered to Alice as they walked up to the door. "Not today. Please."

The two men entered, and Tim introduced the other man. "This is Fred Simpleton, the Acquisitions Officer for The Bank of Las Vegas. He deals with converting paper acquisitions to cash. He will be the one dealing with acquiring the church and property and transferring the ownership from the Diocese to the Cantina Regala. We called the Diocese, and they acknowledged that the bishop would be here. We would like to talk to the bishop, please."

Alice and Mary Grace simultaneously took a big breath and let it out as if choreographed. "He's here, but he's busy right now. I think you should make an appointment to see him next week or even the week after. That would be even better. You can call his secretary, and she'll arrange an appointment."

"We'll wait."

Chapter 95

Barrier
Friday Night

Brick took Doc up on his invitation for cocktails, or as Janey called them, cock-a-two-tails because she always made doubles. Janey and Doc lived in a log cabin. At least it was a log cabin on the outside. It cornered up to the mountain and oversaw the vast valley below. In the distance, the snow-capped peaks of the Humboldt-Toiyabe National Forest towered high and proud. Snow powdered the rims.

The six-room house represented five different countries in its design and decor. The living room was Asian. One bedroom was Scandinavian. The second was French. Tuscan décor highlighted the dining room. The kitchen was pure American, upscale in every way. A converted bedroom served as Janey's music room with a piano and several stringed instruments waiting for her attention. The last room was nicknamed Doc's Den with three walls of built-in bookcases. An enormous mahogany desk sat by a large window with a framed three-foot world globe adjacent. One wall held marble busts of Greek and Roman philosophers plus busts of Einstein and Janey. Janey had carefully choreographed the rooms, and she and Doc enjoyed a variety of foreign cultures within their own home. The details were authentic at least as far as Brick knew.

Sipping her own martini, Janey served cocktails in the spacious kitchen. She crafted a tall gin and tonic for Doc while Brick politely requested whiskey, whatever she had would be fine. Maker's Mark coming right up. Seconds were waiting. They sat on bamboo chairs with a glass table among them. The last roses of Janey's flower garden added color and ambiance to the little gathering.

She offered Swiss and Brie cheeses, a plate of saltines, and five different types of pickles completed the spread. Dill pickles, sweet pickles, gherkins, pickled jalapenos, and pickled mushrooms. "'Scuse the saltine crackers, Honey. That's all that Johnstone's offered today. Honey, do you have a girlfriend? I've been dying to know. Doc says he doesn't know. You two talk about school, and that's all."

Brick paused. He wished he could say yes, but he answered, "No, I don't. I was in a relationship a couple years ago. Women say they love cops, but they really don't. They like the uniforms and status but don't like the hours or the danger. They hate the uncertainty of whether the cop will come home after the end of a shift. So, no, no girlfriend. They might like teachers better, but I doubt I'll have better luck in Barrier. Not many people live here, but who knows?" He was thinking of Maggie. They hadn't even gone on a date although she seemed amenable to it. He wouldn't mention her to Janey. She might try to bump it up a bit.

"You might be surprised, Brick. When attractive men appear, women seem to find them. Bide your time, Honey. Don't forget about that lovely sheriff. She is a very nice young woman and so lovely."

"Oh, Janey, stop with the matchmaking. Brick's got things on his mind other than women. He's launching a new career. That will take precedence over anything else, I am sure. The classroom beckons with all the eager, young minds pining for knowledge." He laughed and shook his head, "To quote Cicero, *Semper idem*."

"Oh, Doc, don't start with the Greek quotes. You know I can't understand them. Talk like you were born in Barrier, Honey."

"Latin, Luvvy, remember? Cicero was Roman, a Roman lawyer, born before Christ was a twinkle in his mother's eye. *Semper idem* means, *Always the same thing*, and that's how it is with the young Barrier minds. It is always the same. They reject knowledge, but eventually seek it out. They don't comprehend that they want it yet."

Doc changed the subject leaving Latin and Greek behind, and happily so for both Janey and Brick. "What news have we regarding the demise of our leader, Principal Fitzwater? Do you have anything interesting to report?"

"I am out of the loop because I am not a law enforcement officer anymore. I have talked with the sheriff a few times, and she seems to think they are making progress. I don't think she's discovered a motive yet and is puzzled as to why someone murdered him. Was he honestly as fantastic as people say? I only met him a couple times. He and I got along, but I didn't know him. I mean truly know him."

Janey answered for Doc, "Honey, he was a lovely man. He used to come by now and then to say hello. He would have a cock-a-two-tail and chatter about things. We loved to have him over. He made me laugh, and he could keep up with Doc's random thoughts about life and love. It made a fun time to watch the two of them bouncing big words and thoughts off each other. He loved photography, you know. He took that beautiful photo." She gestured to a large framed photo of the mountain that arose near their home. "He preferred photographing people over landscapes, but never showed me any people pictures. We always enjoyed him. One time though, I was a little disturbed about something he said. We invited him to dinner, the three of us. Lamb stew. He loved lamb stew. We were chatting about school and kids and such. Doc and I couldn't have children. Father Fitz was celibate with no children.

"That evening he seemed to focus on children rather than the usual subjects of Barrier High School and our athletic teams. I went to the kitchen to retrieve something. Doc was in the bathroom. When I returned, Fitz was talking aloud to himself. His comments puzzled me. It was loud enough to be heard, but I don't think he meant it to be heard. He declared, 'I've had too many children. Too many. I shouldn't have had that many. It was wrong.' I asked him what he meant, and he snapped back at me.

'Nothing. I need to go now.' And he left without eating the lamb stew or finishing his drink or anything. It was odd. I always wanted to ask him what he meant, but it's too late now."

Chapter 96

Las Vegas
Tuesday, 18 Years Prior

The bishop excused the other priests from the room while he spoke with Father Fitzwater alone. His German temperament did not take a fancy to being put off by this young upstart of an Irish priest.

"Where were you yesterday? We needed to meet with you. In fact, we waited all day. We had to cancel some appointments and now the rest of the week is shot as well. You can't do that to this team." He was angry.

Father Fitzwater had planned out what to say. "I had obligations. Sick folks and meetings. Hazel Lake has cancer. Eugene Fillmore has the gout. Lucinda Guzman has disappeared, and her family is worried." These were sort of true and sort of made up. The bishop didn't know any of his parishioners and wouldn't know the difference. The Lucinda part was true. He wasn't family but was worried.

"Did Mary Grace give you what you needed? She isn't the most organized person I know. She seems to have her head in the clouds. I call her Mary Grace O'Klutz sometimes. Things are late, or she can't find them or forgets to do them. I have to remind her all time." He was lying. It was part of his strategy.

"Yes, she gave us everything we needed. I think she seems organized enough. Records were all up to date. The accounts were accurate. The personnel records are complete. She told us that sometimes her financial records are incomplete because she doesn't get the receipts and statements from you. You know, Pat, you should not be counting and depositing the money from the offerings. That's why you have a financial council. Alice would be excellent. She's a straight-arrow, and she and Mary Grace work together well. That recommendation will be in our report. The other thing we need is the deed. Father Lin took it from the Diocese before I was the bishop, and he kept it. We need it back. Today. Do you have it?"

Father Fitzwater stood suddenly and announced, "I'll be right back."

Chapter 97

Barrier
Saturday Morning

Brick drank the first cup of coffee from his new pot before descending the stairs to greet the day. Black and fresh, his coffee tasted good. Maybe not as flavorsome as Starbucks but good. "Great day for a run, right Bridget?" She laid herself down on the walkway, closed her eyes, and lowered her chin to her paws. The sun was shining. The geese and ducks flying above were headed somewhere. He didn't know where, and they probably didn't either. He stretched for a few minutes and began jogging toward the sheriff's office. "It's Saturday. Maybe we can go on a date tonight," he said to Bridget, not really thinking she would go.

Bridget reluctantly followed him at a not-so-fast pace. Her ears flapped in the breeze, and he waited until she caught up. Together they entered the building to invite Maggie out.

Maggie was in her office talking to someone on the phone. Jay and Cagey sat in the outer office, but they didn't acknowledge Bridget or Brick as they entered. Neither of them was smiling, in fact quite the opposite. Awkward was an understatement. Brick had hypothesized what was going on. When Brick departed her office the previous day, Cagey and Maggie were holding a conversation. He sensed the possibility that Cagey or Jay was in one of the five pictures but didn't know anything for sure. He wasn't certain that Maggie would tell him. He was a volunteer, after all. She still had not officially deputized him.

The three men sat staring at nothing. Their eyes roamed around the room gazing at each other and the wall with no direct eye contact. Cagey mindlessly moved papers on his desk from one pile to another. Bridget studied the three men. Her eyes shifted in a triangle to watch all three. No one said a word. Maggie finally came out of her office. Her face was taut as if she hadn't slept. She invited the two brothers to enter her office, which they did. Bridget rose and followed them, then raised her eyes to Maggie, reconsidered, and returned to a mat she discovered on an earlier visit.

"Brick, you're dressed for a run. Why don't you do that? I need to talk to Jay and Cagey for half an hour or so. When you come back, we can talk." Brick knew she had her hands full. He nodded and went outside. Bridget stayed on her floor mat.

Maggie started the conversation, "Thank you for coming in, Jay. When Cagey suggested that the three of us visit, I thought it was a good idea. Talking to you together might help me to understand the extent of the situation. Are you both okay with that?"

The two men nodded, and Jay answered, "Sure, we're brothers. No secrets. Ever."

Cagey agreed, "Yup, he knows everything."

Jay continued, "He told you about Vegas, I guess. That was a rough time for all of us. K. G., Mom, Dad, and me. Especially K. G. Nothing happened to me. It seems like a long time ago yet wasn't long ago at all. For K. G. it was probably yesterday or an eternity. Or both."

"Jay, can you tell me about what happened in Vegas? Cagey already told me, but I'd like to hear from you," Maggie stated carefully.

Jay repeated what she had already heard with a few differences, but not many. Cagey listened, now and then nodding his head or sighing, but he didn't interrupt. He looked fatigued, and his blotchy red face was obvious, even beneath his beard. His puffy eyes displayed anger and hurt.

"The two of you have known for a long time that Father Fitz was involved in pedophilia? At least 18 years, right?" Maggie queried.

Jay shook his head, "More like 25 or 26. Fitzwater's been here for what, almost 20 years, and he was hurting kids before that. I don't know who he's hurt here."

Cagey closed his eyes and interrupted, "July 4, 1985. I'm sure it happened to others before and after me, but that was the first time for me. Independence Day. That's a joke. That's the day I felt like I strapped on a large backpack with big friggin' rocks in it. Every time they approached me, I got two more stones. First the deed by Lin. Then the photograph by Fitzwater. Fitzwater didn't physically abuse me, but he took pictures of me after the other priest did it. It was a double whammy. The abuse followed by the humiliation of having my picture taken. Naked. Eight years old. And they were all laughin' and jokin' and telling me what a good boy I was. *You're such a good boy*, they'd say. God, I fuckin' hated them. I was eight years old and packing about 100 friggin' pounds of rocks, and they kept on coming."

"That's beyond awful. I'm sorry and don't even know what to say that might ease your pain." Maggie took a deep breath before continuing, "We can't rid ourselves of the past, and both priests are dead. Maybe that's a blessing or maybe not. But perhaps we can stop this from happening to others. That means that some of this will be exposed. Probably not all of it. I hope not. I don't know. It's sure to come out when we find the killer and go to trial. The bishops and priests and other church people need to understand the gravity of what he's done. Right now, they don't get it. And they need to."

"It's taken me over 25 fuckin' years of trying to get rid of that backpack full of weight, but some are still lodged in it, always pulling me down. They'll never go away. Every time I pass the sign on Highway 50 that reads, *The Loneliest Highway*, I laugh. I've been on the loneliest highway since I was eight years old. My mom and dad understood, and I think Jay did, but other than them, there was no help. No one to help me. Sometimes the weight of them fades, but then something happens, like this, and they come back heavier than ever. I am sick and tired of carrying all those fuckin' rocks."

Maggie's eyes filled with tears, and she tried to blink them away, "I understand, Cagey, and again I am so very sorry." She paused to wipe away her tears. "Did you tell Jay about the garage room and its contents?"

"Yes, I told him," Cagey answered. "I know it was a breach of my confidentiality and loyalty to you, Sheriff, and I apologize. But after I found those pictures, I needed to tell him. To tell someone. He knew about the pictures, but we both figured that Lin or Fitzwater destroyed them. Whoever would have thought that fuckin' Fitzwater would have brought these pictures with him?"

Jay patted his brother on the shoulder, "I couldn't believe it either. Until he showed me one of them. Un-fucking-believable. Fitzwater was such a dirt bag."

"That's for damn sure," Maggie agreed. "I want to ask your permission to let me share this with Brick. He knows about the pictures in the garage and some of the other stuff that we've discovered but not about you. He realized that you separated the five pictures of yourself from the others, but he doesn't know they are of you. Right now, he's probably thinking that you were intentionally interfering with this investigation. I know that's not the case, but that's probably what he's thinking. I know he can help. He has a lot of experience, more than either of us, in investigating murders. And wisdom. He is as tight-mouthed a cop as I have ever known. How about it?"

Chapter 98

Las Vegas
Tuesday, 18 Years Prior

Father Fitzwater streamed through Mary Grace's area and bee-lined it toward his office, ignoring the two men, the other priests, Mary Grace, and Alice. He didn't look at them, nor say a word, just passed through. Mary Grace thought about following him but reconsidered and didn't. Alice peered at Mary Grace but was silent. They heard the door slam shut but no one breathed a word. The priests seemed restless but were silent.

Tim Smythe spoke to Mary Grace, "Is the bishop available now? We won't take long. Fifteen minutes is enough time."

Mary Grace looked to Alice for support, but Alice didn't say anything. "No. Yes. No. I don't know, he's pretty busy." She was horrified and felt her job was on the line.

Bishop Schmidt poked his head out and summoned the pair into the conference room, "What is it, Mary Grace? If it won't take long, I can see them. Come on in, Gentlemen."

Mary Grace interrupted, "No, Bishop, you really shouldn't. You are much too busy. They can come back." She shook her head fiercely. Alice nodded in affirmation.

The bishop frowned at her and invited the men into the conference room.

The two men entered the office, shook his hand, and reintroduced themselves with the usual pleasantries. They handed him business cards.

"I'm not sure why you want to see me," the bishop started. "We don't have any accounts with The Bank of Las Vegas. I can ask, but we mainly use First National for our day-to-day banking. Of course, we use a variety of banks for other things, but I don't recall that your bank was ever mentioned. If you want us to start using your bank, you can set up an appointment with our CFO, Rodney Lewis."

"No, nothing like that. We are a medium-sized bank here in town, and we mostly handle things like defaults. Yesterday the Cantina Regala came in with a very different kind of request. It seems they have come into possession of a deed. To be clear, it is the deed for this church and the land it sits on. It was used as collateral for a gambling debt. It's all legal."

"What? That can't be true. Not a bit. The building and land belong to the Diocese. It couldn't have been gambled away." He dropped himself into a chair as he spoke, unable to continue standing.

"The Cantina Regala wants to build a new casino here on this property. It's a great location with lots of places for egress routes and parking, and it's already zoned for a business. The Cantina Regala thinks they can build soon with a target opening date of 18 to 20 months. They would need to start demolition of this building and begin construction by the end of the year. Is that time enough for you to make your arrangements to move the parish?"

The bishop looked at them in disbelief. "Would you please excuse me? I think I need to talk with our attorney."

Chapter 99

Barrier
Saturday Morning

The conversation continued, and the three debated the pros and cons of Brick being a party to knowledge of the abuse situation.

Cagey didn't like it. "I don't know about that. He's not law enforcement anymore. You can call him a deputy, Sheriff, but he's not a Washington County deputy like I am. He hasn't received a background check, training, all the stuff that we go through to get certified."

"He's not dumb," Maggie defended. "He's going to figure this out whether we tell him or not. We're better off telling him. He'll want to have the facts straight. I'll formally deputize him. He's a professional law enforcement officer, and the deputy badge will ensure his discretion. I do know that this investigation has moved forward more rapidly than if you and I handled it alone. The county isn't going to hire any more deputies for us, and the state won't send us any investigators. We're unfortunately on our own and could use the extra brain power and experience to find the killer."

"I like him," Jay agreed, observing Cagey. "I'm sure I don't get a vote, but I think he would help more than he would hurt."

Cagey frowned. He moved his eyes from Jay to Maggie, "I think he's hot on you, Sheriff. That's my observation. Are you sure that's not clouding your judgment?"

"What? No. No. I enjoy him, but that won't alter my professionalism in solving this murder," she didn't like this inference.

Cagey and Jay shrugged. She was the sheriff. It was her decision.

"It's settled then. I'll deputize him today and remind him about discretion. I don't think I need to, but I will. I also want to remind you two about discretion. It's the key to solving this case," Maggie declared. "One more thing. I'm curious. Are you half-brothers or stepbrothers or what? Why the different last names?"

Jay answered first, "Yeah, we're full-fledged, dyed-in-the-wool brothers. I'll tell you why we have different last names. It's a little confusing, but here goes. Guzman was our mom's last name, and Garrison was our dad's last name. We used Guzman when we lived in Vegas, but when we moved to Reno, the school required that we use Garrison. Our dad's name was Jack Garrison. My real first name is Vijay, which is a common name in the Pacific Islands. Mom was from Indonesia. She came to the U.S. during the Indonesian genocide. Vijay got shortened to Jay when we were kids. It was more American. But Mom and Dad always called me Vijay. I legally changed my name to Jay Guzman a few years ago to honor Mom. Everybody except our parents called me Jay anyway. And when I started buying businesses, a non-Anglo surname helped things. They sometimes considered me a minority, which helped obtain loans and licenses."

Jay stopped talking, and Cagey took over, "I kept my dad's last name, and my real name is Kenneth. When I got to Reno as a 10-year-old kid, I tried out different names, you know, like kids do. I wanted a new identity, to start over. Nobody knew about the abuse, but I thought a new name would help. I told people my name was K. G. The kids at school started calling me Cagey, and it stuck. Lucky for me that Father Fitzwater didn't recognize me or my name. He knew me by Kenneth Guzman, not Cagey Garrison."

"Thanks. I get it now. Getting a new identity makes sense. Jay, since your last name stayed Guzman, did Father Fitzwater recognize your name?" Maggie implored.

"Not at first," Jay replied. "He knew me by Vijay Guzman in Vegas. Not a lot of people know my real first name. At school the kids dubbed me with Jay. It was a good name during my basketball playing days. A name people remembered. One night several years ago, Fitzwater came through the tunnel to the Ranch. He visited several times before and made a point that he didn't want to be seen or identified by anybody from town. He never recognized me, but I recognized him. Community folks came through the tunnel occasionally. I was accustomed to clients barging into my office. Usually, they walked in and went directly through it to the upstairs area. He did, too. Usually.

"That time, however, he sat down and started asking me all kinds of questions. I was civil to him although it was hard. I was positive that he didn't recognize me. I offered him a glass of whiskey, and we talked for a few more minutes.

"Before he left, he noticed my high school diploma on the wall with *Vijay Garrison* on it with a photo of my mom when she first arrived from Indonesia hanging beside it. She never worked at the CDR, but she did work at the Panorama. The previous owner fell in love with her and kept her picture on the wall. I never took it down. Anyway, Fitzwater grabbed it and started to throw it to the floor, but I stopped him. He asked me if Vijay was my name and if I was related to Lucinda Guzman.

He must have remembered my name from Vegas. Vijay is not common. I couldn't lie. Regardless of how much disdain I felt for him, I just couldn't lie to a priest. Our mother had done something to him, and he was still angry about it. At that time, I didn't know what. His eyes blazed anger, and he wanted to know where she was. He tried to act all jovial and chummy and talked about wanting to see her again for old time's sake. He demanded to know about Kenneth, K. G., I told him the truth. He was a deputy in Las Vegas. That was true at the time. I didn't tell him where Mom was or what Kenny's last name was.

"Once he figured out who I was, he started coming to the Ranch regularly, maybe once or twice a week. He was a priest and the high school principal. It would not have been good if people knew. He argued about paying and refused to tip the girls. He thought if he was a priest, it was free, I guess. It wasn't good.

"One night a few weeks later, he came in again. He was drunk and told me that he found my mother and was going to kill her. He waved a pistol around and ranted for a while. He threatened to go upstairs and kill other people, too. He was wild. Almost maniacal. I couldn't call the cops.

"The last sheriff didn't want anything to do with the CDR, and I knew it was bad for business if cops showed up. Clients' confidentiality would be jeopardized.

"I knew money was his primary motivator, at least according to Mom. Eventually I got him to calm down. He wanted to make a deal. Part ownership in the CDR. Fifty percent, he wanted. I couldn't believe it. I didn't like dealing with this crook. He was a true slime ball and completely unstable. I didn't want anyone killed either, especially Mom. I offered him five percent of the Ranch if he would leave and never return. I didn't want to see him ever again. He wanted more. In the end, he got 33 percent. One-third of the Ranch. It was blackmail, pure and simple, but I knew he would kill my mom. We haggled, but he informed me that he found Mom. He could kill her anytime, now that he knew her last name was Garrison and she lived in Reno. He rattled off her address and phone number. I knew he was telling the truth."

Maggie's eyes opened wide, "Are you saying that Fitzwater owned one-third of the Chicken Dinner Ranch? A brothel, a whorehouse while he was a priest and a high school principal?"

"Yup, mind blowing, isn't it?" Jay sneered as he answered.

"Who else knows?" Maggie choked out.

"Nobody. K. G., you, and the lawyer who drew up the papers," Jay explained. "But that's not all. He got one-third of the take, which was paid daily. Plus, he wanted me to pay money to support one high school sport, which is basketball. That was no biggie because I love basketball and would have donated it anyway."

"You're telling me that Fitz gets money from the Ranch daily? As in every single day?" Maggie breathed aloud.

"Yup. That's right. He gets about $12,000 a month, between two and four grand a week. Sometimes more. I doubt that he pays taxes on it as we pay cash, and it was an under-the-table deal," Jay revealed.

Maggie asked the obvious, "And it is left on his kitchen table? Every day? Right?"

Jay agreed, "Every day. Occasionally it was every other day if we were busy. He didn't mind though as that meant more money for him."

"How did you get it to him, I mean, how do you put it in his house?" Maggie was still puzzled. "We found some of it, picked it up, and it is locked away, but it is a mystery because the doors to the house are locked."

Jay explained further, "Usually Mrs. Brownley took it. She's my assistant and drops it by on her way home. She's divorced and has a daughter named Reese who is in high school. He hired her to clean his house. It worked for him. She has a key. She would run it in, tidy up, vacuum, do a few dishes and leave. Fifteen or 20 minutes usually. He always gave her a twenty-dollar bill when she left the money. If he wasn't home, she tidied up and left the money but took a $20 from the pile anyway. I think she is saving that money for Reese's college."

"Does Mrs. Brownley know about his ownership of the CDR?"

"No, I don't think so, unless she figured it out on her own," Jay answered. "I guess that's possible, but I'm not sure."

Chapter 100

Las Vegas
Tuesday, 18 Years Prior

The bishop was livid and began shouting at Mary Grace. "Where did Fitzwater go? Find him now. I don't care if you have to call the state police!"

Mary Grace was horrified. No one ever yelled at her except the one time when Father Fitzwater cursed at her. Never a bishop. She had tried her best to keep Father Fitzwater there, but there was no way she could stop him from leaving. He was in a state. She hoped Alice would intercede, and she did. Alice spoke, "Calm down, Bishop, let's talk and try to figure out what's going on." She ushered him back into the conference room and closed the door.

Mary Grace was already on the phone, re-calling all the places she called before.

Alice knew what he had done. She had seen gamblers wagering their houses and businesses and property many times before. Usually, they owned the item they used as collateral, but not always. Gaming addiction was destructive to people, families, businesses, and relationships. One time she saw a gambler attempt to use his 7-year-old daughter for collateral. The daughter's name was Mercedes. He told the manager that he owned a Mercedes and wanted to use it for collateral. The manager thought it was an automobile because the gambler told him that it was in the parking lot. The manager agreed and required a letter of transfer as per protocol. She stepped outside to examine the car and found a small pony-tailed girl named Mercedes asleep in an old Ford pickup. She called child services, and he went to jail for the night. Mercedes went to child welfare.

Alice explained what she thought Fitz did, although it was difficult for her. She was feeling Catholic guilt and betrayal. He was a priest after all. Her priest. The bishop was shocked. He couldn't believe such a thing could happen, especially under his watch. How could a priest do this? He ranted and swore and turned red, then purple in the face. Fifteen minutes, then twenty. Alice nodded and tried to calm him. She had seen it all before.

Twenty minutes later Father Fitzwater strode through the door. "I told you I'd be right back. Get out, Alice," he ordered. "Out. Now." Alice exited.

Fitzwater faced the bishop and began his own rant. After all, this was the bishop's fault. He arrived a month early for the audit. Things would have been fine if he had stuck to the schedule.

"You realize that this is your fault," Fitzwater shouted. "If you stayed with the schedule that you sent out a couple months ago, everything would be fine. You arrived a month early, not telling anyone. When things weren't ready, you thought the worst and went crazy. It's your fault, Bishop. Your fault." Fitzwater sat down and folded his arms, confident that this was true.

Bishop Schmidt answered, "Hold it, Son. Your gambling is out of control. I talked with two men from The Bank of Las Vegas today. I can't believe what they reported to me."

Father Fitzwater considered the bishop inquiringly, "The Bank of Las Vegas? What are you talking about? We don't bank with them. What did they want?"

Bishop Schmidt stood and moved toward Fitzwater's chair. He said smugly, "I'll tell you what they wanted. It was unbelievable. I didn't think anyone would do this, especially a priest. You are entrusted with the body and soul of this church, Our Lady of Perpetual Tears. You gambled away the church and its property. You used the deed of the church as collateral for your gambling habit. The Cantina Regala owns it now." He paused to let his words sink in.

"They plan to build a casino right here on this property. They are going to tear down the church and construct a casino. Our Lady of Cantina Regala Casino. Un-fucking-believable."

Father Fitzwater glared at him suspiciously, "Not true. I loaned the deed to them. I have a receipt that says they will give it back. Wednesday. Things will be square Wednesday, maybe sooner."

"What you're saying then is that your gambling is not out of control? You did not gamble away the deed to the church? Is that what you're saying, Son?" The bishop could tell a lie when he heard one.

Father Fitzwater answered confidently, "That's correct. I loaned it to them. I must find Lucinda Guzman. She's the one who did this to me."

"Who is Lucinda Guzman?" the bishop asked.

Fitzwater countered, "She's not anyone important. She's just a woman who works at the Cantina Regala. This was all her idea," he explained. "I was gambling, that's true. She offered me a line of credit as my luck went south. I was due for a string of good luck though. She agreed to allow me to use my personal finance account, but the bank was closed. I borrowed the deed until Wednesday. On Wednesday, I can get my own money out of LVN and swap the deed for cash. It was a loan, don't you see? Just a loan. I'll be back on track by Wednesday." It was a lame explanation, but it was the best he had.

The bishop continued calmly, "I see. You needed a loan? How much did you need? How much did they lend you, Son?"

Father Fitzwater tried to minimize the situation, "Just $68,000. I can replace it easily.

My money is in the Reno branch of LVN."

Now Bishop Schmidt was shouting, "You asshole! You swapped the church building and property for $68,000? This property alone is worth at least a million and probably even more. The church building itself is worth another half million. That's a million and a half dollars, Son. Do you hear me?"

Chapter 101

Barrier
18 Years Prior

The Panorama brunch was everything Lucinda remembered. Wonderful food with a foreign flair. The boys ate, and after the third trip to the buffet, they were satisfied. They sampled food they had never tasted before and loved it. The servers were young ladies from outside the United States. Today's servers were from Russia, Singapore, and Rwanda. Lucinda was the first Pacific Islander to take advantage of the offer.

Harvey charmed the four of them, and to Jack's delight, the meal was on-the-house.

Harvey had recently renovated the old hotel, updating the bedrooms, bathrooms, and bar. He gutted and rebuilt the bar to resemble a movie set from a John Wayne movie. A giant mirror overlooked the saloon. It was framed with mahogany panels and hand-carved mahogany accouterments that were inserted into the frame. It gleamed and reflected the various liquor bottles on its glass shelves. Anyone could see it was a work of art. The bar itself glistened with countless coats of polish while the wall opposite was wallpapered with dollar bills autographed by patrons through the years.

The boys were spellbound with the history of the hotel, including Harvey's story about it being moved by wagons in pieces from Salt Lake City to Barrier during the 1800s. Harvey's stories were colorful and made for easy listening.

He embellished his tales and made up details that occurred in another time, another place, another age. No one was sure what was true and what was fiction.

He recited stories of the castle that intertwined with tales of the Panorama and the local brothel, the Chicken Dinner Ranch. Lucinda knew some of the stories, but Jack and the boys didn't. They were fascinated by the history according to Harvey. Vijay especially was mesmerized and asked lots of questions.

On the way out of town, the boys begged to stop again at the castle. They didn't let the fence stop them this time. They scrambled over it and through the moat and drawbridge opening. The large wooden door was unlocked. They bolted in and dashed up the stairs to examine it up close. When they returned, Vijay suggested that they could buy it and live in it. "This is way cool. It's history! We could be living history!" Lucinda and Jack didn't answer as they drove back to Reno. By the time they arrived in Reno, Vijay had declared that someday he was going to own the Panorama and the castle. Lucinda was glad that he didn't include the Chicken Dinner Ranch in his list of possible purchases. No one thought his pronouncement would come true.

Chapter 102

Barrier
Saturday Morning

Brick ran his three miles, switched clothes, and put together notes for his classes. He returned to the sheriff's office as Jay and Cagey were leaving. Jay nodded and mumbled something that sounded like "good luck," while Cagey skulked by, saying nothing.

"I've got a couple things to tell you," Brick said, as soon as he saw Maggie.

"Me, first," Maggie insisted. "Me, first. I'm starving, but before we go eat, I want to deputize you. It's been quite a morning. Raise your right hand."

Two seconds later, Brick could be called Deputy Brick with a badge. His ID would be ready later. "Still no pay," she reminded him. "Volunteer. Let's go eat."

The café was bustling. The booths were filled with a crowd of high school students, including a trio of girls who sat at a table toward the rear of the restaurant. These same girls had been at the parsonage on the day following the murder. They gestured at Maggie, and she went over while Brick ordered.

"We're just wondering," Marianne said, "did you find out who killed Father Fitzwater? We are worried that you won't find him."

"No, not yet, we're working on it though," Maggie responded. "You shouldn't worry. We'll get him."

Reese rubbed her brow, "What will happen to him? He won't get the death penalty, will he?"

"He might," Maggie answered. "It is a capital crime."

Reese fixed her eyes on Maggie. "That's harsh. What if he didn't mean to, or what if there was a reason? I mean a very good reason. Wouldn't that make a difference?"

"That's up to the courts," Maggie explained. "They decide what happens, not me. Now don't worry, girls. Most of the senior class is here. You should enjoy your lunch with your friends and not worry. School starts up again in a couple days."

Brick had ordered hamburgers, fries, and milkshakes. "Is it my turn yet?" he asked. He was unsure of what Cagey and Jay shared about their past and the CDR. "Can I take you to dinner tonight? Not the Panorama, the Pizza Shoppe, or this place. We could go to Altoona and have a real dinner. Doc told me about a new restaurant called, *Mag's Creek Pies*, and it sounds like it has some good seafood and steaks and also a good variety of other eats, including wine and chocolate pie. Altoona isn't very far away, and since the restaurant must be named after you, we should try it out."

"I've heard of it. It's named after Maggie Creek, however. A fishing-hunting-riding-backpacking haven. Is this going to be our date?"

"It can be, or we could have a different one or another one. Is that a yes?"

"Yes. This has been a mind-blowing day but, yes. I'm ready for a night off. I need to make sure my mom is okay first and then put on something more appropriate for a maybe date. How about if we leave here at 7 o'clock? You can pick me up at my parents' house."

"Does this mean I'll be meeting your parents?"

"Sure, why not? Mom's cool and Dad's…well, he doesn't care much about anything anymore. But he was cool when he was himself. You'll like them."

Chapter 103

Las Vegas
18 Years Prior

Las Vegas summers were long. The bishop felt the last week was interminable. The near 100-degree days didn't help. In addition, because of the situation at Our Lady, the Diocese was in disarray. Rumors were flying, and his office phone never stopped ringing. His assistants soft-peddled the concerns as rumors, merely rumors. The following afternoon, the bishop met with his lawyer Andrew Duncan.

"What do we do? What do we do?" the bishop repeated. "The church belongs to the Diocese, but the Cantina Regala has the deed in its possession and claims ownership. They are going to play hardball. They won't return it or even allow us to buy it back. It was signed by Fitzwater. And what do I do with Fitzwater? What a mess he has made."

Attorney Duncan had thought about this problem. He outlined it slowly. "First, Fitzwater had no authority to gamble away or sell the church. He had the deed in his possession, but the Diocese didn't care enough to retrieve the deed. Your lack of interest and action to regain it might sway a jury that you surrendered it. Second, you can try to buy it back, but I doubt that it's for sale. Not for $68,000. You can bank on that. Third, you could claim that the signature was bogus, but I don't think that would work." The bishop frowned. None of these seemed good.

Attorney Duncan commented, "Do you know what a prime location that property is for a casino? My God, I'm surprised you have been able to hold onto it for as long as you have. It is ideal. Close to the Strip but not on it. Centered among several nice subdivisions, the property is big enough for a good-sized casino plus parking. Every casino corporation dreams of luring locals away from Fremont Street. Land is tight, and it's impossible to find properties large enough to build on. The casinos lose a huge number of patrons since the locals gamble downtown, which means loss of profits.

"I think the best option is to negotiate with the casino, not fight them. Your new super-church is only a couple miles away. It's big and beautiful and spacious. You can claim that the church isn't needed here to serve your parishioners. Incoming parishioners already migrate to the new church. Closing this one shouldn't be a hardship. Parishioners can be moved easily enough to the new church. We can negotiate for more cash from the casino. They won't want to be viewed as taking advantage of you. That would be bad for their business. I know they'll bargain. If we can get them up to a million or even more, you could use that money to build a school: The Bishop Schmidt School. A real feather in your cap." The bishop's frown turned upside down at the thought of The Bishop Schmidt School. This seemed like a great idea.

"Another issue that you need to consider is the publicity. Local church goers put their hard-earned money in the collection plate only to have a priest steal it and gamble it away. I can see it now: PRIEST GAMBLES AWAY CHURCH, BISHOP CLAIMS IGNORANCE. How's that going to play to your members? I don't think it's something you want headlining the newspaper. It would make the front page of the *New York Times*, for Christ sake."

"I never thought of that, but it might be the biggest issue. We have enough trouble with donations. They might dry up completely. I like your idea though. It might work." Bishop Schmidt changed the subject. "What about Fitzwater? What am I going to do with him? I can't fire him from the priesthood. It's a calling. And he does well with the congregation. They love him, but we sure can't leave him in Las Vegas. He would most likely start up again. Maybe I can negotiate his future as well."

Chapter 104

Barrier
Saturday Afternoon

The sheriff and her newest deputy returned to the office where she debriefed him on her morning's conversation with Jay and Cagey. Brick sensed that some of the pictures might have been of the brothers, but when she shared the story about the priest/principal as part-owner of a brothel, he was nothing short of shocked.

"One-third? He owned one-third of the Chicken Dinner Ranch? That's unbelievable. A priest owning a brothel. That's one for the books. Honestly, I thought I'd seen it all in California, but Barrier has more oddities than any town should."

"We've figured out the money issue, including where it came from, but we haven't talked with Mrs. Brownley. Maybe she has some info. Maybe she saw something. Maybe she knows something. I'll bring her in for an interview this afternoon. Do you wanna join me?"

"Sure, but it's your interview. I'm only another set of ears."

Two hours later, Mrs. Brownley shuffled in. She stood 5 by 5. Five feet tall and five feet around, but her face was a ray of sunshine. Her ear-to-ear smile lit up the whole room, and it was easy to see why Jay hired her.

Maggie introduced Brick to Mrs. Brownley who said, "I've heard a lot about you, Mr. O'Brien. From Reese. You've met my Reese. She is very excited to have you for a teacher and everybody in town is talking about you and basketball. We can't wait," she said. "But this whole thing about Father Fitzwater is awful. What a beguiling man he was! He was charming with a magnetic personality. You know he was godfather to my Reese. She'll be a senior this year and then off to college next year." She reminded Brick, "She'll be in your government class, Mr. O'Brien. She's a good student. I mean, I already told you she's going to college."

Maggie interrupted, "I need to record this. Are you okay with that?"

Mrs. Brownley laughed, "Honestly, I don't know what I can tell you that you would want to listen to again, but yes, it's okay."

Maggie began the interview, "Can you tell us a little about yourself, your family, and your job?"

Mrs. Brownley answered, "Let's see. I'm divorced. It's me and Reese. I lived in Las Vegas for a long time but moved here 12 years ago when Reese was about to start kindergarten. My husband finished school, and we decided to be pioneers and live off the land and so we moved to Barrier. We knew a couple people who lived here, which made it an easy move. I finished my education several years before. I have an MBA from UNLV. We found that living off the land in Nevada wasn't easy. My husband also tried his hand at gold mining on his own, not with a company. It didn't pan out," she smiled at her pun.

"He enjoyed the Chicken Dinner Ranch, but in other ways than I do. When I discovered what he was doing, I booted him out. Reese and I get along fine without him. Then Jay offered me a bookkeeping job, which was right up my alley, and I've loved it. I think he felt sorry for me because of my husband. I was lucky because not very many jobs are available in Barrier anymore. Unfortunately, the Ranch doesn't need me full time. I supplement our income by cleaning houses and such. Mindless work, but it pays well, and I don't mind it. I always schedule my work so that I could spend time with Reese. I arrange my schedule around hers. I cleaned Fitz's house, too. He was somewhat of a slob, but I got him trained."

Her grin broadened, and she laughed a robust laugh. "It's hard enough to train a man. A priest is worse."

"Can you tell us about your work at the Ranch?" Maggie asked. "What all do you do?"

Another guffaw. "I'm not one of the girls, if that's what you're asking." She winked at Brick. "They're nice girls, but they think a little differently. Most have had trouble in their lives. Jay is good to them. That part of the business is for him, not me. My job is accounting. I keep the records. The state government requires a lot of information, and I fill out forms and write reports. I do office work, that's all. It's mostly a cash business, but we do take credit cards. Someone else cleans, though. I don't have to do that. I work about 20 hours a week."

"I understand that you carried money from the CDR to Father Fitzwater's house a few times a week. Is that correct?"

"Yes, I do. That is, I did before he got murdered. I'm not sure why Jay wanted me to do that. He never told me to stop until a couple days after he died. I thought it was a donation to the church or to the school for basketball. You know Jay. He's crazy about basketball. I never thought that Jay was religious, but maybe I don't see that side of him. In addition to the Ranch, he owns the Panorama. Maybe he combines the two businesses in his charity. I know the Global Girls are required to attend church. But I don't know why he was giving money to Fitz. He never told me."

"How much money did you take to Fitz?"

"It averaged out to about three or four thousand a week, which is quite a lot, especially by Barrier standards. I asked Fitz once, but he didn't answer. He ignored the question. He might've thought I was too nosy."

"How did you get along with Fitz? Did you and he ever talk?"

"Oh, yes, we talked all the time, not as much as we did when we both lived in Vegas. I knew him in Vegas. Did I tell you that?"

Maggie replied, "No, you didn't tell me, and we need to talk about that. Before we do though, I forgot to have you state your name for the record. What is your whole name, Mrs. Brownley?"

"Mary Grace. Mary Grace Brownley."

Chapter 105

Las Vegas
Friday, 18 Years Prior

Father Fitzwater missed his daily masses the rest of the week. As directed, he appeared at the Diocese office early on Friday morning. He arrived even earlier than requested and sat in the waiting area with the administrative assistant. She greeted him coolly and didn't offer him coffee or a donut, although a plate of them sat on the table near her desk.

The bishop made him sit and wait for two hours before admitting him to his inner office. When he finally entered, the bishop was alone. "Okay, Son, this is what's going to happen. It pains me to do this, but I have no other choice."

Father Fitzwater resented being called, "son." He felt it was condescending and humiliating. The bishop used it exactly for that reason.

"I have talked every which way to our attorneys, and we are trying to retain Our Lady as a church; however, it looks grim. Our attorney says we have lost it, and it now belongs to the Cantina Regala. They're not going to give it back. And most likely, they're not going to sell it to us either. Son, you are now a man without a church. Lucky for you, though, I found you a church. Nevada needs ministers, and I know you will serve well. I call this a win-win, Son. I don't need you bringing us negative press. And, clearly, new scenery is just what you need. Washington County is up north. I think you will like it."

Father Fitzwater pictured a map of Nevada in his head and reviewed his limited knowledge of which counties were which. Washington County. Washington County. That's Reno. That'll be good.

"Not that you deserve it, but you'll find lots of recreation available. Hunting, fishing, climbing, hiking. A National Forest isn't far. No priest has served that parish for several years, but the population is predominantly Catholic. With your talents, you will be able to build the membership. In addition, there is a high school, not a Catholic School, but a public school. At one time it was Catholic, but the population diminished, and the public schools absorbed it into their system. The principal died last year, and they have not been able to find a replacement. You still have your certification credentials, so I called the Department of Education and talked with the school superintendent. He is excited to have you. The school and community are both small so, trust me, you'll have plenty of time to do both jobs." Fitz pondered the bishop's words silently, *The last time I heard, "Trust me," that damned Lucinda did me in.*

"It is filled with history and is one of the more interesting communities in Nevada. It even has a castle. I know you enjoy photography, and it is scenic. It lies in the Humboldt-Toiyabe National Forest with mountains, lakes, and streams. Anyway, because time is of the essence, you should go home and pack. I'll have your furniture shipped to you this week. The school district provides housing for the principal. Oh, and before I forget, the name of the town is Barrier."

Chapter 106

Barrier

Saturday Afternoon

Maggie and Brick ended the interview with Mrs. Brownley and were satisfied that she told them the truth. "She's a happy person," Maggie observed. "It sounds like some hard luck has followed her, but she seems at peace with herself. Most people who live in Barrier have had some misfortune. Otherwise, why would you move here?"

"To teach school," Brick answered without thinking. "Or to be a sheriff. For me it seemed like the right decision at the moment. And I think it was a good decision. Even better if we have dinner tonight."

Before she could respond, the sheriff answered her ringing phone and said, "I'll come right now."

She disconnected the call and looked at Brick, "The castle calls. Again. Wanna come?"

Without a word, the two walked out the door. They got in the sheriff's cruiser and headed out.

"What's going on now?" Brick queried. "This makes three times this week, if I've counted right. But who's counting?"

She explained, "BBW. I was surprised it didn't appear earlier in the week."

"BBW? What's that?" He looked at her with a puzzled look.

"Beer. Boyfriends. Whoopie. The usual, kids being kids."

When they arrived, it appeared that half the school was already inside. Half a dozen cars and a couple motor bikes sat empty in the parking area. A keg of beer sat on the steps. It was leaking out of the tap, and the steps were wet with foam. The kids were upstairs and didn't hear the sheriff's car drive up.

"Here's what we're going to do. First, we empty the keg. That'll piss the hell out of them. Then, I'll go upstairs and confiscate their phones and keys and pull their IDs. Some of them will try to leave. You stay here. You can greet them as they run down the stairs trying to get to away. They don't know you yet. Surprise. Surprise. Make them sit down, and you can pull their stuff. Keys, IDs, and phones. Then, I'll call their parents. Some parents will be angry, others won't care, but I'll call 'em anyway. A few parents will thank me. Then we'll wait for them to come and take them home. They're good kids; they just like BBW."

And so, they did. The 14 kids belonging to nine families were retrieved and taken home. "I suspect you've done this before, Sheriff."

Chapter 107

Barrier
Saturday

The drive to Altoona for their dinner date was pleasant. The sun faded, and the air was cool, but not cold. They drove with the Jeep's top down with Bridget nestled in her bed in the backseat. The fresh air felt good. He would have to put the top up before they returned to Barrier. Brick drove under the speed limit, which meant more one-on-one time with Maggie.

A small flock of big-horned sheep was crossing the road with two rams guarding them from cars or other menaces. The flock trailed up the mountain behind a third ram. "See how they cling to the side of the hill," Brick exclaimed. "I've seen big horns before but haven't seen a whole flock climbing." They watched it for several minutes before the two ovine sentries allowed them to pass. The two rams raced up the hill behind the rest of the flock, forcing the trailing lambs to move faster. In a matter of minutes, the entire flock disappeared behind some Mesquite trees. Brick was thankful Bridget slept through the whole ordeal.

They drove a little farther, and Maggie suddenly cried, "Turn right at the next road. That one." She pointed at a dirt road with fence posts on each side. He turned onto the well-traveled dirt road. It was dry, and dust bounced up behind them.

"Here? What's here?"

"You'll see. I want to go for a swim."

"Swimming? Where? Are you sure?"

"Keep driving. It's about a mile."

"Is this where you rescue me from a pit?" He asked but obeyed her command. Two turns later a grouping of boulders emerged. A few pine trees surrounded the boulders and aging wild flowers rippled in the breeze.

The air smelled like fresh pine.

"Park anywhere," she ordered. "Anywhere."

"Parking now," he answered. "Yes, Ma'am."

Maggie jumped out of the Jeep and ran toward the boulders. Bridget jumped down from her back-seat bed and began chasing her. She ran a few steps, then stopped and picked her way through the uneven ground. Brick turned off the motor. "Hey, wait, you two. Where you goin'?"

Maggie disappeared into the boulders, and he heard a splash. A cloud of steam floated up from behind the rocks. He moved more quickly and rounded the large stones. Maggie had already stripped and was treading water in an enormous natural hot water pool. She had abandoned her clothes on the stones. "What are you waiting for? This feels terrific! It's been years since I've been here, but it feels the same. Warm and tingly. I'm waiting," she teased.

Brick joined her in the water a few moments later. She had smiled as she watched him strip down. Bridget sat on the bank observing them and dipped her paw in the water, but didn't go in. She found some warm mud and burrowed herself into the soft ground.

The kisses started slowly at first, then faster and harder. They wrapped themselves around each other, touching, exploring, searching, caressing. The darkening sky and moonlight created an ambiance, prodding them to do more. And they did. They devoured each other, making for a divine dinner, followed by an even better dessert.

Chapter 108

Las Vegas
Friday, 18 Years Prior

Father Fitzwater stopped at the church. He kept a bottle of Irish stashed in his office. He wanted, no, he needed, a drink. He didn't intend to see Mary Grace or anyone else at the church. He hoped she had already gone home. He entered through the back door, picked up the half-empty bottle, and started back outside when he heard, "Can I do anything for you?" It was Mary Grace's oh-so-cheerful voice. It didn't sound as cheerful as usual, but she was there. He had not escaped unseen after all.

"No, I came in to get something. I'll catch you later," he called to her.

She answered, "We've got a few things to go over. What time are you coming back?"

He shook his head at her and responded, "Actually, I'm not. I've been relieved. They are sending me to a god-awful town in northern Nevada, someplace called Barrier, wherever the hell that is."

"Are you kidding me? That can't be true. They wouldn't relieve you. The parish loves you. They wouldn't dare." Mary Grace thought he was kidding.

He continued, "They did. I'm not kidding. I'm out of here. I've been removed. Removed from Vegas ministry. I'm going to someplace in the middle of nowhere."

"What will we do without you?" she voiced. "Oh, my God, you are the foundation of this parish. What's going on? Should I call Alice?"

He shouted, "Do whatever the hell you want. I'm done." He slammed the door without responding and headed to his car.

When Fitzwater arrived at his house, a car and a small moving van sat out front. He didn't know to whom they belonged. He had never seen them before. The house was unlocked and three people he didn't know were moving around inside. Several suitcases sat by the door, and a variety of boxes were stacked near the front wall, taped up and labeled. He inspected the boxes and picked one up before he went into the bedroom where two men were removing more items and boxes from his closet. "What's going on? Who are you?" he roared. "Get out. What are you doing with my personal property?" Fitzwater stared in horror at another battered cardboard box with the name *Fr. Lin* written in magic marker across the top. The name was faded, but it was still legible. The tape had come loose and the corners of a couple black and white photos peeked out. He kicked the box hoping the photos would slide back down. Lin had taken a risk asking him to take photos that day, but Fitz succumbed easily to the temptation.

A man whose name tag read, *Otto* responded, "You must be Father Fitzwater. We're from Vegas Van. We were hired by Bishop Somebody to come and pack your property and then ship it to Barrier, wherever that is. Didn't they tell you? Anyway, we had a cancellation and came today." Otto held out his hand to Fitzwater.

Fitzwater didn't take the hand and scanned the boxed items. He was horrified. He shoved several boxes out of the worker's reach and pushed them behind him. "Don't touch my stuff," he bellowed.

"But we're almost done packing. We'll load the van today, and it should be in Barrier by next Friday night at the latest." The worker reached over to take the box that Father Fitzwater still gripped in his hands. Fitz's face was red and getting splotchy with anger.

Otto offered, "Let me take that for you. We'll put it on the truck with everything else."

"No, you can't have this one or any of these. They're full of mementos. Keepsakes. They're personal. I'll take them myself. They are some old photographs that my friend Father Lin gave me."

Chapter 109

Barrier
Saturday Night

It was well after midnight when Maggie and Brick returned to Barrier, feeling satisfied and excited, but still hungry, having forgotten dinner altogether. Mag's Creek Pies would have to wait for another date, if they could get past the swimming hole. They dressed and wrapped themselves in scruffy towels that were lying on the floor of the Jeep. Brick decided not to put the top up and all three were shivering, even though the heater blasted high all the way home. Bridget was covered with mud and needed a bath.

"I've got to get warm and regroup. We can't go to my parent's house. We can't go to the Panorama. We can't go to the sheriff's office, and Barrier has no other hotel. I feel like a teenager sneaking out of my bedroom."

Brick was thinking the same thing but came up with an idea. "This might sound morbid or sleezy, but how about Fitz's house? I've agreed to rent it. I'm on hold until the investigation is completed, but couldn't we borrow it for a little while? Just to get warm. I have keys. Maybe we can find something to eat, or we could go to the Eldorado after we warm up."

She teased him with a flirty surprise. "Are you hungry? We had such a yummy dessert," she laughed. "Well, I know it isn't recommended in the sheriff's handbook, but I can't think of a better option than Fitz's house." Maggie agreed.

The cottage was dark, but the moonlight twinkled on the whiskey-bottled walls giving it a festive feeling.

They turned on every light in the house. They figured that Bob Givens would think it was being burgled if only a couple lights were lit. Brick's Jeep plus all the lights represented official business to the neighbors.

No one told Mrs. Brownley to stop cleaning the priest's house, and it was shipshape. It sparkled. She had shifted some things around, and it seemed bigger and fresher. Dirty towels were washed and folded. No money lay on the table. The milk drool was gone, and the floor sparkled. It would need another scrubbing after Bridget had trailed in remnants of the swimming hole.

Maggie got into the shower to warm up. She was unable to stop shivering. Brick sat on the lid of the toilet and admired her through the transparent shower curtain.

She peeked out at him, "I need shampoo. Do you see any in that cupboard?" Brick found green shampoo and conditioner and handed them to her.

As he sat down on the toilet again, he knocked over a large square basket that held magazines, spilling them to the floor and unveiling a half-full package of birth control pills, a small array of Trojan gels, creams, and a stash of condoms. "Sheriff, we missed this stash under the magazines. Was he living with someone?"

She poked her head out of the shower and said, "You've got my attention now. I don't know, but we didn't know a lot of things about him. Give me a sec." She rinsed her hair, toweled it off, and wrapped the towel around her. She stared at what was on the floor.

"I think we must have overlooked the basket." Without thinking, she lifted the lid of the dirty clothes hamper and said, "Whoa, I think we missed more than the basket. Lookee here." On top of the dirty clothes was a pink kerchief, identical to the one around Bridget's neck. She pulled out the remainder of the items one by one. Some were obviously the priest's, but there were also women's undergarments all XXL in size. They were followed by a pair of black shorts, a pair of jeans and two T-shirts. All women's XXL. At the very bottom of the hamper lay a .38 pistol that was wrapped in a pink kerchief.

Behind the door hung a pale green XXL T-shirt nightgown reading, "Nitey-Nite."

They looked at each other and exclaimed almost simultaneously, "Mary Grace Brownley? Who else could wear these?"

Chapter 110

Las Vegas to Barrier
Friday Night, 18 Years Prior

The Cadillac made a smooth and easy ride from Las Vegas to Barrier. The drive was four hours flat without any sign of police to caution him. A couple jackrabbits and a coyote crossed the road, slowing him down, but other than that, it was a quick trip. He had four hours of thinking time. He spent them trying to figure out what happened to him over these past few years. What led to this situation? Lucinda. She must have done it. She connived a way to abscond with the church building and give it to the Cantina Regala. This was all her fault, and he would get even with her. If he ever found her. In his mind, he nicknamed her Lucifer. She was evil. She seduced him. And then she disappeared. Exactly like Satan.

It was past sundown when he arrived in Barrier. He was anxious to see where the bastard bishop had sent him. He wanted to view the town and drove from one end to the other and then back again. It took but a few minutes. It was mostly dark. He saw the school and church, but they were black. No cars in either lot. A few lights shined in the town's buildings, but most businesses were already closed. Some neon signs and porch lights glowed. A pizza shop, a restaurant, and gas station were the sole businesses that showed any sign of life. He didn't see a casino.

He saw a medieval-looking castle and noticed some lights flickering in it. Flashlights he thought as they jumped around. A couple four-wheelers sat outside. I can check it out in the morning, he thought. He saw a couple stores, but they were closed. It didn't take long to see everything to be seen. Damn. This assignment was the worst. The bishop outdid himself in finding a way to punish him. Vegas was a dream job, and this was a nightmare. Damned German bishops.

He parked and entered the only hotel that he saw. The Panorama. It was massive. It was the largest building in town by far with lights and music to boot. Maybe they did have gambling. A long wooden bar hosted a few drinkers. He registered with the hotel and went to his second-floor room. He wanted to find out how to get into the house that the bishop told him about.

Dinner in the ornate dining room puzzled him. It was not the usual Vegas fare. Eating with Lucinda meant the best cuts of steak with a variety of side-dish accompaniments and spectacular desserts. When he ate alone at a restaurant, he alternated Mexican, Chinese, or plain home-cooked American food. Tonight, two dishes were on the menu: Coq au Vin with Chocolate Banana Crepes as a dessert. Or Irish Stew, which was made from scratch, the server told him. He loved Irish Stew. Irish Stew it was. And a glass of Irish whiskey, a double.

After dinner he drove to the address that the bishop gave him. The street was dark with no street lights. He saw a couple other houses on the cul-de-sac. Lights shone inside, but not outside. He opened the trunk of his car and felt around for a flashlight. He flicked it on thankful that it held a steady beam.

He was concerned what his salary would be. The priest salary would be lower than Vegas. He knew that. He might get a salary for being the principal, and if the house was a part of the school district's benefit package, it might work. He thought he might as well use the house.

The door was unlocked. He entered and flipped on the lights. It was small but quaint with a liquor-bottled wall. Odd. Eccentric. He had never seen one before. Still, he might be able to get used to it. A few pieces of furniture, a bed, couch, and a kitchen table were left by the previous owner. It would be enough to allow him to exist for a few days until Vegas Van arrived. Maybe this wouldn't be such an awful place after all. He hadn't seen a casino although the Panorama must have some gaming somewhere. It was big enough, but he hadn't seen any slots or other signs of gambling. He meandered through the backyard in the dark relying on his flashlight and the moonlight. He discovered a small garage hidden in a small grouping of trees. The garage was small, but big enough to store the boxes of mementoes he had brought with him. The Cadillac would fit, but the door was locked.

Behind the garage a man stood smoking and dusting himself off.

"Who are you?" the priest demanded. "What are you doing here?"

"I'm Sterling Allen. I'm having a smoke before I go home. It always wears me out when I pass through the tunnel. The air's rather stale, and I need to revive myself. The tunnel's air doesn't bother you? Oops. Father? I didn't notice the collar. You probably don't partake."

"Partake? Partake in what? What's in the tunnel?"

"Why, it's the tunnel to the Chicken Dinner Ranch, our brothel."

Father Fitzwater stared for a moment then smiled. "Is that so?"

Chapter 111

Barrier
Sunday

Maggie and Brick arrived at the sheriff's office at approximately the same time on Sunday morning. The sky was mottled with clouds, but it didn't feel or smell like rain. Maggie was back in uniform and looking official. Brick wore fresh jeans and a clean T-shirt. They kissed lightly and then stepped apart. They agreed to put aside the prior evening's dip-in-the-pond and tend to business. They whole-heartedly agreed to do it again though. Soon.

Maggie had bagged the pistol as well as the clothing from the hamper and the cabinet's contents.

Brick said, "We need to speak with Mrs. Brownley again. It appears that maybe, just maybe, she and the padre were closer than she let on. I'll go by her house and bring her back here. Figure out what you are going to ask her, and maybe we can get some answers. It's no crime for her to sleep with somebody, even the priest, but perhaps she knows more than she let on."

He exited the office with Bridget who still dripped sand and mud with every step, saying, "Bridget, you need a bath."

When he arrived, he could see Mrs. Brownley curled up on the couch with a blanket draped over her. She was drinking coffee and doing the Sunday crossword puzzles. She still wore her nightgown, a pale-yellow T-shirt that also read "Nitey-Nite." Her robe strained over her ample bosom.

"Good morning, Mrs. Brownley. I hope it isn't too early. Sheriff Monroe wants to speak with you again. Could you get dressed and come with me? I'll drive you to her office and bring you home when you are finished."

"Call me Mary Grace. Anything I can do to help. I'll be only a few minutes." She left the living room as Reese entered through the back door. "Oh, Mr. O'Brien, I wondered who was here. Where's Mom? What's up?"

"Nothing really. The sheriff wants to talk with your mom for a few minutes. I'll bring her back in a while. Are you ready for school to start tomorrow?"

Reese didn't respond immediately taking her time to answer, "I'll say. I can't wait to see my friends again."

Brick answered with a question, "Are you busy, Reese? Bridget is outside and needs a bath in the worst way. If you aren't busy, could you clean her up for me? Spraying her off with the hose would help. She rolled in some sand last night, and it's still sticking to her. I'll pay you. Twenty bucks? The Panorama told me that she couldn't come back without a little grooming. I'll pick her up when I bring your mom back." He pulled out a $20 and offered it to her.

"Sure. For $20, I'll even perfume her and brush her teeth. She'll be sparkling, and even Harry Bird will want to pet her."

Chapter 112

Barrier

Saturday Morning, 18 Years Prior

Father Fitzwater awakened early and decided to go on a walk before people were out and about. He called the superintendent. Saturday morning. No answer. He'd try again on Monday. He put on Dockers and a flannel shirt and hoped no one would see him. No one would recognize his face, but if he wore the white collar, it would be a dead giveaway. The collar would draw people who undoubtedly would ask questions. He reasoned that the house was within walking distance, and he wanted to see it again in daylight this time.

The cottage was as quiet as the night before. Two bedrooms, living room, kitchen, laundry room, small yard. He thought the whiskey bottle wall was interesting and knew that each of those bottles had a story. Those stories were from long ago and would remain untold. He settled in his mind that this would be his new home.

He thought about the brothel. The Chicken Dinner Ranch. What a name. Brothels were not legal in Las Vegas, and his knowledge of them was rudimentary. It was something to learn. Something to look forward to. Would he visit it? Should he visit it? Maybe. Maybe not. Well, maybe. He didn't have to decide today.

He hadn't noticed a brothel last night. He had imagined it would be lit with flashing neon lights: *Brothel! Come On In*. Was it far out of town or on a different road? It couldn't be too far if the tunnel connected to it. How did the tunnel connect to the brothel? His cul-de-sac was on a slight hill and offered a view of the town and Nevada ranches, but he saw nothing resembling a brothel. Could the brothel be below the ground? That didn't seem reasonable, but it was worthy of a check.

The hatchway to the tunnel was positioned flat on the ground, a solid piece of wood, painted camouflage to blend in with the terrain. It was about two feet square with a rope grip. He tugged on the handle, and it released easily. It was pitch black, but he could see a ladder that abutted the trap door. He would need to bring his flashlight.

Chapter 113

Barrier
Sunday Morning

Maggie was waiting for the pair when they arrived at her office. Cagey was seated at his desk and eyed Brick warningly as they entered. Cagey greeted Mary Grace, but not Brick.

Brick offered Mrs. Brownley a cup of coffee and poured one for himself. She asked for cream and sugar, and he scrounged around until he found some.

"Let's talk," Maggie invited, "Please come in. Deputy O'Brien, could you come in also?"

"Sure thing, Sheriff," Brick said. He glanced at Cagey, whose eyes were glued to Brick's face.

Mrs. Brownley waddled into the office with her coffee cup grasped firmly in both hands. She plopped down and then quickly traded chairs when she realized that Brick would have to crawl over her to sit down.

"Deputy? I thought you were a teacher?"

"He's a reserve deputy. He helps our office when we need him. I have some more questions," Maggie began. "About your relationship with Father Fitz."

She paused for a second to discern Mrs. Brownley's expression before continuing. "How close were you? You knew him first in Vegas and later here. Is that correct?"

Mrs. Brownley paused before replying, eyeing them both, twisting her lips, and rubbing her hands together. "Yeah, I was his assistant when we were in Las Vegas. I knew him then. I wouldn't say we were close because he was very demanding."

"Demanding in what way?" Maggie urged.

"The whole situation was demanding. The Diocese sold the church, and I lost my job. That was just before I got married to Wayne. Fitzy, that's what I called him then, called me after he got here. He wanted to see us and told me what a nice town it was. Wayne and I decided to move out of Vegas. Reese was just out of diapers, and we wanted to raise her in a small town. Wayne was handy and got work easily. He finished a degree in Construction Management at UNLV. We went to Mass on Sundays, and Fitzy came to dinner now and then. I started cleaning his house after we moved here. Every Monday. He always called it Mary Grace Mondays." She smiled at the remembrance. "Anyway, he was always messy, somewhat of a slob, never put anything away, not even washing the dishes. He would wash one dish and one fork when he needed it. He would put them back in the sink when he was done and wash them again when he needed to eat. It was gross."

Maggie probed a bit more, "I see. Did you ever go anywhere together? Do anything?"

"He helped me through my divorce. He couldn't understand how a man could go to a brothel. He was totally disgusted by the whole idea of legalized prostitution. He even wrote letters to the editor of several Nevada newspapers saying that prostitution was bad, evil. He talked about going to the legislature to get brothels banned. He was very angry with my husband. Ex-husband."

"Did you two ever sleep together? Have some sort of physical relationship?"

Mrs. Brownley snapped, "No, never. Are you kidding? He was a priest, celibate. Why would you ask that?"

Maggie pulled out the *Nitey-Nite* nightgown and the other clothes they found in the hamper and draped them over a vacant chair. She continued, "Do you know who these belong to?"

Mrs. Brownley was silent. Brick had the next question, "This nightgown is the same as the one you were wearing this morning when I picked you up. But today, yours was yellow, wasn't it?"

Mrs. Brownley's cheeks flushed red, "Well. No. I mean...I think I might have given him some of my old clothes for a charity or something. It was a long time ago. I'm not sure. Lots of women in Barrier probably have that same nightgown. Johnstone's doesn't have much variety."

"We found these items in the bathroom hamper as well as birth control pills and condoms and some feminine products. And we found this," Maggie laid out the bagged pistol on her desk.

"Do you know anything about the pistol or these clothes?"

Mrs. Brownley's eyes widened and filled with tears. "I never went into his bathroom to clean. He never let me clean it. He called it private. And I don't use birth control pills."

Brick was direct, "Is this your pistol?"

Mrs. Brownley flashed back quickly, "Do you think I killed Father Fitz? That fine man? No. NO!"

Brick repeated the question, "Is this your pistol, Mrs. Brownley?"

"No, I don't have one. It looks like the one my husband, ex-husband that is, owned, but I am pretty sure he took it with him when I kicked him out. He used it to kill jackrabbits like everyone else in Barrier does. Are you accusing me of something?"

The questioning continued for a few more minutes, but the sheriff could see she wasn't going to get anywhere. Mrs. Brownley was near tears, and the sheriff had exhausted her questions. Brick drove Mrs. Brownley home. She had given them some food for thought, but they didn't have anything concrete.

Chapter 114

Barrier
Saturday, 18 Years Prior

Father Fitz walked back to the Panorama to have breakfast and figure out what to do. He didn't like staying in a hotel. It seemed to be a waste of money when he could stay in the house instead.

He was hungry and requested corned beef hash, eggs, and coffee, but that was not available. The breakfast menu today was fresh fruit, yogurt, and croissants with preserves and tea. He ate what they served but inquired about other dining options in Barrier.

After breakfast he went to Johnstone's to see what food and bedding were available before returning to the house that he was to call home. He purchased a few items and then drove back to the house. He dropped off the newly purchased items and his luggage. He considered locking the door, then remembered that he didn't have a key. He was technically a non-paying guest. It was best to leave it unlocked. Besides hardly anyone lived in this scrawny town.

He opened the trap door to the tunnel again and flashed the light around trying to see where the tunnel went. He lowered himself into the tunnel and stepped down the ladder to the floor. No signs or arrows indicated which way to go or how far. Flashlight in hand, he began walking.

Half an hour later after some ducking down and stooping low, he found himself crawling on his hands and knees. A yardstick-sized ceiling discouraged him from continuing, but he did. He crawled a few more yards before he was at a door, which he opened and entered.

A large burly man greeted him. "Aren't you the new priest? And I heard you're going to be the principal at the school. I'm Harvey Cooper. Welcome to heaven. We haven't seen a priest here before. To my knowledge anyway. But then people don't always reveal their identities. I've heard about you. You're coming from Vegas, right? Barrier's a small town, and news travels fast. Are you in the market? Or simply checking out the recreational opportunities in Barrier? Hunting and fishing are the main interests, but the Chicken Dinner Ranch runs a close third."

"I'm browsing," the priest answered wryly. He glanced over the photos on the wall and focused on one in particular. "I've never been in a brothel. It's on my bucket list, a carnal experience. I would appreciate my presence being kept secret. The parishioners might object. God might, too. I don't know for sure."

"Oh, your secret is safe with me. The exit to the tunnel lies on the school district property. Another partial tunnel passes from the school's house to the main pathway. You can pass through it, but it's a tight squeeze. It's unfinished."

"There's a second tunnel? From the house? If both entrances to the tunnel are on school district property, I should receive a discount. It's called rent. As I'm sure you're aware, priests always get discounts. It'll be good for business."

Harvey didn't know how it would be good for business, but laughed aloud and answered, "I'll think about it. Nobody has ever asked that question before."

"I was noticing the photos on the wall. What beauties. Who is that one? She's gorgeous," Fitzwater drooled. Fitzwater knew damned well who she was.

Harvey reached up and patted the picture with his index finger. "That one? She's gone now. She's married and lives in Vegas. She was never a working girl. I like to look at her. Her name is Lucinda."

Chapter 115

Barrier

Sunday Morning

Brick returned with Bridget who was sparkling clean, but still damp. She smelled like a flowery perfume. Her collar was clean, and she wore a new pink scarf. Harry Bird would be happy.

Maggie, Cagey, and Brick sat down in the sheriff's office. Cagey was angry. He didn't like being shut out, and he had remained quiet for a long time. "You wanna tell me what's going on? Or have I been demoted to your second-string deputy? It seems like all you want me to do is tend to the hassles at the friggin' castle."

"No, Cagey, you're still my chief deputy, but those pictures might implicate you in some wrong doing." Cagey dropped his eyes to the floor. "I mean it might seem that you have revenge issues or something. No one would blame you. I deputized Brick because we need help in this case, and the Feds and State Cops are still not addressing our needs. Wednesday, they told me, maybe Thursday. Brick's assistance will no doubt be diminished starting tomorrow when school starts again."

Maggie filled him in on what they found in the bathroom. Cagey reluctantly agreed that they might have missed searching the bathroom. Maggie continued, "Let's talk about what we have and various ramifications and possibilities. If we put our heads together, maybe we will steer ourselves in the right direction. All the evidence points toward Mary Grace Brownley.

I can't see anyone else. How about you two?" They both nodded, and Maggie resumed talking, "The .38 pistol belongs to somebody. We don't know who. She says it might be her ex-husband's, but I don't think he is in Barrier any longer. We need to have a ballistics test run to see if it was the murder weapon. Somebody must take it to Forsythe. I'm sure the clothes in the hamper are hers, but she denied it. Birth control pills? Maybe, but probably not. She lied about the clothes, but she was adamant about the pills."

Cagey said, "I need to go to Forsythe to grab some antibiotics for one of Jay's employees. Somebody gave her the clap. I'll drive the pistol over and will have them run the ballistics. I'll run my errand and then wait for the results so I can bring the pistol back with me."

"We didn't really find anything out about the clothes in the hamper, but I think she was lying. I'll go back to the Brownley house and ask Mary Grace about them again. Brick, could you come with me? I want you to talk with Reese while I'm questioning Mrs. Brownley. Maybe she'll be able to fill in the gaps about her mom and Fitzwater."

Chapter 116

Barrier
Sunday Morning

They drove two vehicles to the Brownley residence, the sheriff's car and the Jeep. The small home was adobe. One wall had been constructed with bottles, much like Fitz's. The front of the house had been created out of bright blue and green bottles with a few yellows, woven into the shape of a peacock's tail. It was framed with brown whiskey bottles. The bottles reflected the afternoon and evening sun and crafted a luminous glimmer. The front door was positioned to the right of the art work. Its bright colors matched the radiance of the peacock tail.

Maggie knocked on the door, and Reese answered within a few seconds. "Oh, Sheriff Monroe, now what do you want? You upset Mom badly."

"I need to speak with your mom again, Reese. We have a few more questions for her. Where is she? Is she here?" Maggie asked.

Reese uttered, "She's lying down. She has a massive headache after you practically accused her of murdering our principal. She took some Tylenol and is resting. She loved him. She didn't have anything to do with killing him. How could you accuse her?"

Mrs. Brownley emerged from the bedroom fuming. Tears dampened her cheeks. "What do you want now? Leave us alone. Please."

Sheriff Monroe spoke, "Reese, I want to visit with your mom alone. Could you and Mr. O'Brien go outside? I know he has some questions about school and the students. Perhaps you can answer some of them and help him have a good first day of school." Reese frowned at being excluded from the conversation, but the two exited the house through the back door. Mary Grace sat down and gestured for the sheriff to do the same.

"Mary Grace, we want to clear up a few details about the clothing we found in the bathroom hamper. And the pistol. We can go back to my office if you want, or you can answer them here. Your choice."

"I don't want to go back to your office. I'll answer them here. I prefer not to answer them at all. Are you sure Reese is outside? I don't want her involved in any of this."

Maggie replied, "Yes, she's outside with Mr. O'Brien. Were those your clothes in the hamper? You know I can have them tested for DNA, but if you'll answer me truthfully, perhaps we won't have to go that route. It might make it easier for you."

Maggie could see that she was livid. At the same time, she seemed to have developed a calm over her. Mary Grace sat still for a full three minutes without speaking. She wrinkled her brow and twisted her mouth and tapped her fingers and surveyed the room. Her eyes avoided Maggie. She remained silent. Maggie didn't speak either.

Maggie finally prodded her. "I know you want to say something, Mary Grace. What do you have to tell me? What is it?"

She whispered, "Yes, if you must know, those are my clothes. Fitzy and I had an arrangement. We had a fling, more of an affair in Las Vegas years ago. And then after I booted Wayne out, it was easy to start up again. We met a few times to talk. One thing led to another and…Reese doesn't know, and I don't want her to know."

Maggie cut in, "Know what?"

Mary Grace's eyes fell to the floor unsure of whether or how to answer. After another long pause, she told a story, "She is his daughter. I got pregnant while I was his assistant in Las Vegas. I was his secretary, and he claimed that it was a part of my *administrative duty*. Mary Grace Mondays he called them. As a young man Fitzy was very handsome and charismatic. The most charming man I ever knew. I loved him. I thought he loved me. I even named Reese after him. Her real name is Patricia, and Reese is her nickname. Wayne always called her Reese though. You know, Patrick, Patricia. He was also her godfather. What a con man he was. Wayne never knew. He never figured it out. He still doesn't know.

"The church where he and I worked closed, which meant that I didn't have a job any longer. Father Fitz was falsely accused or set up by a woman he knew. Something gambling related. He never told me exactly what it was. The bishop moved him to Barrier, and I lost my job. He didn't want to come here at first but then began to enjoy it. I'm not sure what changed. I convinced Wayne to move here. I wanted Reese to know Fitz as a priest, and I wanted him to know her as a daughter. After Wayne left and I got my divorce, we started seeing each other again on the sly. It was easy because I cleaned his house and took the CDR money to him. I was at his house several times a week. We always enjoyed a good relationship, but I told him that I wanted to break it off because I was afraid Reese would find out.

"Then he betrayed me. This year Reese is a senior. She's popular, smart, and pretty, and he told me that if I continued to have sex with him, he would guarantee that she'd be selected Homecoming Queen. The students believed their votes determined who won, but he selected the queen. That's what he always did. He liked to control what happened in the school. He counted the ballots. He could skew them anyway he wanted. I believed him, but he chose another girl, Cassie something, a new girl in town. I couldn't believe it. He betrayed me. Betrayed Reese, his own daughter, his goddaughter. I was glad to see him dead, but I didn't kill him." Mary Grace's eyes were streaming with tears.

Maggie was stunned at the story and articulated her doubts. "Reese was his daughter? But you didn't kill him? Do you know who did?"

Mary Grace vigorously shook her head, "No, I have no idea. He was well loved, and I am totally at odds about who might have done it."

"I did," came a feeble and quivering voice from the kitchen. "I killed him. I hated him, and I still do. He got me pregnant and then told me I had to get an abortion. It wasn't right."

Reese entered the room, eyes red, face blotchy, seeming somewhat shrunken with Brick towering behind her. "I heard you, Mom. I'm sorry. Very sorry. He told me last summer that I if I slept with him, I would win the crown. I wanted it so badly. I didn't know that he was my father. He knew it though, and he still wanted to sleep with me. That's repulsive. I told him no, but he kept asking. I finally agreed and slept with him once. Then he wanted it again and again and again. He kept begging, *Just one more time, and you'll win. I'll make sure of it.*

"Then a few days before school started, I found out I was pregnant. I didn't tell you, but I told him. He laughed and said, *What a good girl you are, but you'll never get the crown now, Darlin'.* He told me he was done with me, and he would pay for an abortion. I don't believe in abortion. You taught me that, Mom.

"I didn't know what to do. I couldn't tell you, and Daddy's gone. Daddy would have killed me or Father Fitz anyway. I went back to plead with him. He called me a slut. 'You're exactly like your mom,' he said. Then he told me that he was my father and named after him. I didn't understand and left. On my way home, I figured it out. I knew where Daddy kept his gun hidden when he was still living with us and so I checked that spot hoping he forgot it when he left. The gun was still there, so I took it, went back to Fitz's and shot him. He deserved to die, and I'm not sorry."

Mary Grace rose to embrace her daughter, completely encompassing her as if to shield her. "Oh, no, Reese."

Maggie arrested Reese and took her to the holding cell in the jail. She would transport her to Forsythe the next day.

Chapter 117

Barrier
Sunday Afternoon

Mary Grace called an attorney on Sunday afternoon. He arrived from Reno early to represent Reese. She was sure to go to trial and would need help. She was still 17. That would be in her favor. She might be treated as a juvenile, although the judge could decide to designate her as an adult. No attorneys practiced in Barrier, and those in Forsythe dealt solely with real estate laws and wills.

Maggie and Brick sat in her office with the door closed, debriefing each other. Maggie stretched out behind her desk with her hands clasped behind her neck. She was thinking aloud. "How on Earth shall we handle this? The town thinks he's a saint. They're going to learn about his relationship with Mary Grace and Reese in detail at the trial. That will shock them, for sure. It sure as hell shocked me."

Brick interrupted, "Yes, Ma'am. Some will accuse her of lying, but at the trial all the secrets will be revealed. Some might protest because they believe that Reese fabricated the story, but others will figure it out. Another issue, which you have some control over, but not total control, is the issue of the pictures of the children. How much does the community need to know about the issues with the kids? All the pictures he took, and the lives that he and Lin ruined, including Cagey's? This is a huge and extremely complicated problem. You can be sure the Catholic Church will want it covered up, and they'll do their best to accomplish that goal. The news media will be all over it, but the Catholic Church has a lot of power."

"I figured out that my crash course on 'how to be a sheriff in a small county' wasn't worth diddly squat. Murder, rape, incest, pedophilia, and pornography all wrapped up together in one enormous case. It's a horror show. And to think, it all started with the issue of who would be the high school Homecoming Queen for this year. What a waste."

"A few days ago, I was talking to Doc. You know how erudite he is. That's his word for himself. He leaves me behind sometimes. He referred to PEALAGS. I didn't know what he was talking about. It's a pneumonic for the seven deadly sins: Pride, Envy, Anger, Lust, Avarice, Greed, and Sloth." He ticked them off on his fingers. "It's a pretty slick way to remember them. When you think about Fitzwater and Lin, what they possessed and what they desired. They each owned all these sins. They craved everything, power, sex, money and then used children and their positions to grab them. And they covered it up during all these years through lying and cheating and stealing. It's abhorrent."

Chapter 118

Barrier
Sunday Afternoon

It wasn't long before Cagey returned with the pistol and the ballistics results in hand. He was anxious to report what the test results determined, and they were anxious to tell him about their morning. His drive to Forsythe tempered his mood. The antagonism disappeared, and he remained cool.

"Ballistics are positive. Undoubtedly, it is the gun that killed Fitzwater," Cagey reported. "Now we have to connect it to the shooter."

Maggie was next, "We got a confession, Cagey. We know who killed Fitzwater."

"Did Mary Grace confess? I didn't think she would. She's a tough gal. Did she say why?"

"Not Mary Grace, Cagey. Think again."

"Who? I don't know. Some drifter? What was the motive? Who else would have a motive?"

"Try Reese. She confessed. We thought Mary Grace killed him because, apparently, she and Fitzwater were romantically involved about 18 years ago. That tryst resulted in Reese. Then Fitzwater started a *thing* with Reese, who claims it wasn't her idea. This *thing* resulted in another pregnancy: Reese's, who is currently pregnant. When she confronted him, he told her to get an abortion. She said no and shot him and killed him. And it was all because Reese wanted to be Homecoming Queen. Go figure."

Brick had dealt with sensitive issues before, but it was still shocking to learn about such an aberrant deed by a priest. Maggie was also stunned. She had always trusted and respected Father Fitzwater. Not that it mattered then or now. In Maggie's pre-sheriff days, such acts were unheard of, and she hoped never to hear of them again. But obviously as sheriff, she was sure she would.

Chapter 119

Barrier
Monday

Brick arrived at school early Monday morning and left Bridget in the Jeep. He put up the top, but left off the windows, allowing a free flow of crisp air. His sweatshirt remained in the Jeep, and Bridget snuggled down. He left a small bowl of water on the floor and reminded her to stay.

The students began entering his classroom shortly after the first bell rang. In turn, each of them eyeballed him with some interest. They nodded to him as they entered, and a couple greeted him with "good morning." Most had attended the funeral and were familiar to him. First period was a government class. The seniors filed into the room, 18 boys and seven girls, with one absence. They took their seats, and he introduced himself.

Brick had given some thought about how to approach these students, especially the seniors. Father Fitzwater served as their principal for their entire high school career. It was clear at the funeral that many students thought highly of him.

Brick introduced himself and told the students about his past as a police officer and how he found Barrier. He told them some stories, mostly true, with quite a few omissions about his visits with the priest. Most of the students laughed and talked freely about their relationship with him. It didn't take a genius to know that they adored him. Brick watched the silent ones though and wondered about them. Were they? Could they have been?

The students were curious about Bridget and what he was going to do with her. He glanced out the window, and she was still in the Jeep stretching her neck to view the second story window. Apparently, she knew where he was and would keep her eye on him.

At the end of the hour, not much government was taught or learned, but Brick felt good about the class. He wanted to gain their respect and trust. Open conversations were a good way to do that. One or more of the pictures included in the binders on Maggie's desk could be of someone sitting in this very classroom today. Brick wanted them to trust him enough to talk to him.

The remainder of the day passed pretty much the same. The social studies curriculum didn't advance much, but the rapport with the students was positive.

After school, his room filled quickly with boys who were curious about the basketball program. He saw most of the boys throughout the day, but they were now differently focused. They asked questions and gave opinions. They were eager to start practice, and he gave them some suggestions for getting into shape. He had a feeling he was really going to enjoy this.

Epilogue

Barrier

Three years later Maggie was easily re-elected to her second term as sheriff. She received 48 more votes than before, stealing them from Mickey Mouse and Donald Duck. Clint Eastwood was still in contention. Since the murder and Reese's conviction, no major crimes traveled across her desk.

Brick was at BHS starting his fourth year. He took the necessary course work for principal certification and accepted the job. He still coached the boys' basketball team, and his first two years at Barrier his team had come in second in the state tournaments. The following year, they won the state championship, lifting the town's spirits. He convinced the superintendent to place white boards in all the rooms invigorating the faculty and sealing his popularity. He made sure Harry Bird had new cleaning supplies and the building continued to sparkle.

The castle ceased to be the main cause of frustration. Jay purchased it and turned it into a medieval-themed bed and breakfast. He embellished its interior with the works: castle guards, swords, and suits of armor. He walled the moat with rock, cemented its floor, and filled it with water, turning it into a sort of water park. Guests donned bathing suits and waded through the slow-flowing stream. He added small waterfalls where kids could swim and splash. On weekends, authentic medieval dinners were served by costumed waiters. He added shooting and archery ranges and a horse-riding academy.

Occasionally he offered jousting tournaments if proficient riders wanted to try. Most weekends large crowds filled the 10 guest rooms. The visitors loved the opportunity to experience this unique adventure that was handy to their California and Las Vegas homes. Mary Grace took over the management, and the Castle Inn thrived.

The citizens of Barrier were devastated by the testimony at Reese's trial. They were angry at Fitzwater, at the Diocese, and at themselves for being taken in by Fitzwater's charm and magnetism. At first, they disbelieved Reese and Mary Grace's testimonies. When additional victims from Las Vegas testified and the truth was laid out, they were horrified. How could this have happened in their small town?

The Barrier Catholic Church never recovered. The parish dissolved as those who wanted to continue to worship could not bring themselves to attend Mass in Barrier. Some went to Forsythe, and others quit attending Mass altogether. The Diocese of Reno closed the doors to the Barrier Catholic Church, and it fell into disrepair after only a few years.

After testifying at Reese's trial, Cagey went into counseling to resolve his many issues. He continued in his position as chief deputy and was elated that the hassles at the castle disappeared.

Doc retired from teaching, but not from life. He became a master storyteller at the castle gatherings. He related stories about the Greeks and the Romans and the various gods and goddesses. Occasionally he took to costume and recited soliloquies from various Shakespearean tales. Janey played her lute and sang ballads and ditties from the past. The Doc-Janey pair billed themselves as The McCrone Crooners and became a popular attraction at the castle.

Toward the end of the fourth year, Maggie and Cagey drove to Las Vegas to return Reese to Barrier where she was to serve out her two years of probation. She served four years of a 10-year sentence at the women's prison in Las Vegas after being convicted of voluntary manslaughter. She was given time off for good behavior and completed her high school diploma. She earned as many junior college credits as allowed, majoring in computer repair. While in prison she gave birth to a baby boy. Mary Grace cared for him during the years of her absence. Having the toddler in her house allowed plenty of grandma time, and she cherished her days with him.

Brick and Maggie married and purchased the cottage from the school district and renovated it. They razed the garage and built another in its place. They sodded the yard and blocked both tunnel accesses to the CDR.

Bridget. Well, Bridget still pouted and glared at everyone disdainfully, even more determinedly after Brick and Maggie's twins were born.

Read on for a sneak peek at the next book in the
Maggie Monroe series: **Murder Almost**

Chapter 1

Charlie
Present Day

My name is Charlie Walker. I am forty-three years old and ready to restart my life. I have a couple things to do first though, and I'm in a hurry to finish them. I have not been home in over twenty-five years because I was in prison in Fenwick paying my debt to society, so they claimed, for a crime I mostly didn't commit. Sure, you might say I participated, but I didn't do it. My best buddy did, but he skipped town. So now I resolve to make the son of a bitch pay.

***

I grew up in Barrier, Nevada, a jerkwater town, although the population loomed larger in those days than today. Barrier grew gold as its main crop with no end in sight, until it ended. The multiple mining corporations stripped the gold clean while I served out my prison sentence, and now with the loss of mining, its population has dwindled. Returning to my hometown, I didn't expect much, maybe a few lowlifes who couldn't or wouldn't leave their roots.

I'm a good-looking guy with black, wavy hair, brown eyes, and bushy eyebrows starting to gray. I'm six feet tall, the same as when I entered prison, but I've beefed up a lot. I have a prison physique and can handle myself in most situations. When I wasn't working in the prison library, I bulked up my body and my self-confidence by pumping iron, and when all of my tattoos are exposed, I am especially imposing. Mostly, though, I keep my tats hidden, with one exception: Patsy, with a heart on my bicep. She had been my high school friend and occasional girlfriend when both of us were horny, but I hadn't seen her in a long time.

Right now, my face is mostly covered by a graying beard, but I might shave it off before it gets too gray, going naked as they say in the big house. You need a beard in prison before they'll respect you. No beard, no respect, and the guards aren't any different than the inmates.

The prison gave me a set of civilian clothes when I left, they called them civvies, but I'm sure people will recognize them as prison clothes. A pair of wranglers, a t-shirt, and a plaid flannel shirt, none of them new, but by wearing them, I suppose I looked like a regular Nevada guy. They gave me a new pair of tennis shoes with laces and a green mesh ballcap that read Sammy's Feed Store.

Fenwick, a high security prison located in the middle of the Nevada desert, had no redeeming features. I passed through the town of Fenwick when they first drove me to prison. It had nothing, and, if even possible, was worse than Barrier. When I first arrived, the guards dumped me in the maximum-security unit in a single cell. I spent a sleepless night listening to other inmates shouting and clanking and farting. The hard bed had a flimsy mattress with no springs, and they gave me one blanket and a pillow with no case. Too many lights flickered outside my cell, further interrupting my attempts to sleep. I had finally fallen asleep when the guard awoke me by clanging his keys on the cell door and shouting, "Wake up, Newbie, time for chow." He said this same thing every single day during my time in the joint. After about a year, he replaced Newbie with Walker and a few years later Walker with Charlie.

Three days after Judge Little banged down his gavel and sentenced me to twenty-five years with no parole, I rode the bus to Fenwick. I considered his sentence a lifetime because it was longer than the eighteen years I had already lived. I was angry. I was a kid, just a kid, and I needed help.

I spent most of the first morning pacing my nine by seven-foot pale green, concrete cell wondering what would happen next, until a guard escorted me to the counseling office where the welcome-to-prison counselor, Ms. Clara

Moneyjoy, explained what was what. An old, grayheaded lady with a wrinkled face and leopard hands, Ms. Moneyjoy didn't move too fast because she limped in her clunky black shoes. Even still, I noticed she smelled of old books as she passed me. Her charcoal gray pantsuit was speckled with tea or coffee, and her faded, navy blue blouse looked older than she did. I didn't have anything in common with her, that was for sure, and resented having to see her, but what else did I have to do? I had never spent time with a counselor before and didn't think I would like her, but what she said somehow stuck and has remained with me through all these years.

On our first visit, she removed a nickel from her drawer, carefully set it on its edge, and drew her hand away. "This coin is you, Charlie, on your first full day in prison. You can stand tall, or you can fall flat and, believe me, prisons offer many ways to fall." She flipped the nickel onto its side. "Gangs, disobedience, fighting. But prison also offers positive opportunities. While you are here, you get to choose. Nobody's going to select for you. Counseling, education, learning of all types are all available. The gymnasium is a positive outlet for frustrations that might arise, and a chaplain comes to Fenwick several days a week. I call this nickel The Coin of Your Life, as Carl Sandburg said."

I had never heard of Carl Sandburg and wouldn't understand the depth of her lecture for a year or more, but I did get the you get to choose part, which my stepfather, Eugene, who had been a Marine drill instructor, attempted to hammer into my head from the first time he met me. It hadn't worked.

The other inmates heard I had killed a cop, a rumor I didn't work to clear up. I hadn't killed anyone, but if I laid my story out, I would be targeted as a fraud. Inmates hate police in general and honor those committing crimes against cops, which I knew would be useful to me. Telling guards or inmates the truth would have been bad for business, with me being the business.

Doing time is a drag. Bad food. Bad bed. Good gym. Every day the same. I started my time in Fenwick working toward earning my GED. This was part of the sentence mandate, so I complied and worked as fast as I could to get it done. It wasn't hard. While getting that degree, I filled the endlesshours of boredom working in the library where I discovered a few books that looked interesting. Reading became my lifesaver. I read everything, particularly biographies. As Ms. Moneyjoy said, You can stand tall, or you can fall. Characters in some biographies stood tall; others fell. I learned from the books and decided I would work to emulate the standing-tall folks.

I didn't know how easy this would be. Were there any other inmates hoping to turn things around? I wasn't seeing it. Most of the prison inmates looked ready for a fight. I had heard terrible things and didn't want to get beaten up or hurt anybody else, so I behaved myself and didn't cause trouble, and the guards left me alone. One guy, who considered himself tough, attacked me once, but I managed to clean his clock, although honestly, I'm not sure how. For an unknown reason, he held a grudge against me and came after me in the shower during my first week at Fenwick. We were the same size, but the fight ended when I threw a knee into his nuts. He had trouble walking for a long time after. From then on, everybody left me alone because they thought if I had killed a cop and had a long sentence, I must be a bad ass. I didn't even get rotated to other prisons like most inmates did and lived in the same cell at Fenwick for my whole sentence.

The staff allowed me to visit Ms. Moneyjoy as often as I wanted, and I learned from her. A grandmotherly type, she treated me kindly and even made me laugh. Several years later she gave me a metal coin, a challenge coin with *Time is the Coin of Life* embossed on it. It resembled the red and yellow Marine Corps challenge coin Eugene kept in his pocket. She said it violated prison rules for her to give it to me and made me promise to keep it hidden from the staff. I cherished the coin, my singular real possession for the time I resided at Fenwick. I later learned she told the correctional officers on my floor what she had done and threatened them if they bothered me about it.

The staff also had me visit a re-entry counselor a few times, but we never discussed release from prison, rather what I did to be sent to prison. I didn't hurt Sarah Hudson and wasn't going to admit I did. So much for innocent until proven guilty. Railroaded. That's what I was.

How I arrived at Fenwick is a compilation of bizarre events and bone-headed mishaps, and I paid mightily with twenty-five long ones. Many people in the big house say they didn't commit their crime, but most of them did. Not me though. I really didn't.

Chapter 2

Charlie
Twenty-Five Years Ago

I had recently turned eighteen and acquired a dangerous combination of stupidity and immaturity. My best buddy, TwoJohnny, and I wanted to go to Las Vegas to gamble. We had brand new IDs, hot off the press, and we both knew how to play craps and convinced ourselves that we were pretty damn good. Problem was, we needed a car to drive to Las Vegas. We didn't have a car, so obviously our only choice was to steal one, which TwoJohnny volunteered to do since he had previously hijacked a few cars. He picked a sleek, beautiful, canary yellow Porsche 911 with under 2,000 miles on the odometer. It sat in the old lady's driveway that night with the keys dangling from the ignition. Why would anybody leave the keys in a brand-spanking new Porsche? She deserved to have it stolen. Maybe she wanted to have it stolen.

The theft itself was a cinch, but just as TwoJohnny was driving out of Barrier by way of Highway 376, he noticed the yellow light announcing he was about out of gas. "It looks like we have about two gallons of gas left. And that's if we're lucky." "We've gotta go back. Nothing's out here," I told him. "On Highway 376, a person could drive 100 miles and never run into a gas station."

He flipped a U-ie and aimed the car back the direction he had come. He glanced over at me and smirked, "Uh, money? Do you have any extra money? How do we pay for the gas?" He could be so clueless.

I barked back at him, "Where do you think? The old lady who owns this car, Dumbass. She has all that money from her dead husband's insurance policy." Devising the best plan that my eighteen-year-old-brain could come up with, I continued, "We go back and ask her politely to lend us a few dollars. We'll pay her back when we take her car back because we'll win big in Vegas. No doubt about it."

"What if she says no?" TwoJohnny snapped. "She might say no." I shook my head and retorted, "She won't. She's old and not smart. She left the friggin' keys in the car, didn't she? Plus, I kind of know her. She works as the juvenile probation officer. I had to meet with her when the cops arrested me when I was twelve. I'll wait in the car, and you go ask her. Politely. Her name is Sarah Hudson. Mrs. Hudson. Go ask her. I can't go in because she knows me from that bogus arrest, and last week I helped her move crap out of her laundry room and kitchen into the garage. She paid me twenty bucks, so I can't go in. You'll have to do it."

TwoJohnny pulled the car into the driveway and squeezed out of the Porsche, taking the keys with him. He went around the house to the side door. An unlocked screen door met him, and he vanished into the house. A long minute crept by. Then another. Suddenly he burst out the door and shouted, "Go! Go! Go! Start the car. We've gotta go now."

"You have the keys, Dumbass," I shouted. "You took 'em." He leapt into the car and fumbled with the keys. Finally, he keyed it up and ripped down the street.

"What happened?" I shouted over the roar of the car. "Did you get the money? How much did she give you?"

Chapter 3

Maggie and Brick
Present Day

A quiet town, home to few thousand residents, Barrier drew more than its share of transients looking for an idyllic small town where they could live out their dreams. Speeding tickets, weed busts, and barking dogs had been the town's only high crimes and misdemeanors when Sheriff Maggie Monroe was first elected to office a few years ago. But that easy spell of crime solving ended quickly when she found herself in the middle of a murder case involving the town's beloved priest. When the case turned even uglier, with pornography and pedophilia at its center, Maggie had been baptized by more than fire; it had been a volcanic eruption, shattering her youthfulness and naivety. The entire town had been spellbound by a charismatic priest, but everything changed after his murder. The publicity and community gossip not only transformed Maggie, but it also changed the town's aura, as the whole of its small population seemed to bubble with a newfound cynicism that hadn't lived there before. One good thing to come of the murder case was a whirlwind romance with former LAPD detective Brick O'Brien. A wedding and twins followed quickly.

Brick had come to Barrier in search of a calmer life. After serving in L.A. as an officer for ten years, the number of near misses started to rattle him, and he decided to move on. He arrived in Barrier to head up the high school's basketball team and to teach a few high school classes, a much safer career choice. All that changed when his soon-to-be boss was murdered in cold blood on the very day Brick arrived. So much for a quiet, safer life.

Brick stood around six-foot-three with black hair and blue eyes. From the moment he arrived in Barrier, he was at Maggie's service. With only one deputy to help her, Cagey Garrison, Brick was deeply involved in a murder before he began to unpack.

Today found Maggie at her desk, rifling through a pile of letters and emails that had accumulated during the past week. Nothing seemed important, and she mindlessly sorted them in two folders, to do and done. It seemed enough.

Deputy Cagey Garrison entered her office and closed the door. He held a sheet of paper in his hand and sat down. A no-nonsense deputy, Maggie knew something was up the minute he closed the door.

Cagey waved a paper around and said, "Do you remember Charlie Walker? He was the one who robbed and hurt a local juvenile probation officer named Sarah Hudson. This happened a quarter of a century ago. Back then, he swore up and down he didn't do it. Neither of us was old enough to remember it, but I have heard people talking about it over the years. Anyway, court documents say he assaulted her with an iron. He knocked her out and left her for dead. Because Mrs. Hudson worked as a law enforcement officer and Walker showed no remorse, the judge sentenced him to twenty-five years fixed, a long sentence for a kid of eighteen, especially since it was his first serious offense. The prosecutor called Walker a real bad ass."

"I vaguely remember him from my days at UNLV. We studied a lot of court cases and Walker's was one of them. What kind of iron was it again? A tire iron?" Maggie asked.

"No, it was a clothes iron, as in pressing clothes, the housework type. Walker swung it by the cord and thwacked her in the head, knocking her out, and giving her a concussion. Her eye and face were burned, but she could see well enough to identify him."

"Which prison did he go to?" Maggie asked.

"Fenwick and the bad news for us is that he got out two days ago," Cagey answered.

Maggie said, "The assault happened around the time my parents moved our family to Barrier, but since I was only five years old, the only memories I have about it were from college. God, I'm over thirty. If he had a twenty-five-year sentence, he must have topped his time. Twenty-five years is a long time."

Cagey summarized the rest of the email, "Well, our problem is that he is out of prison. And, on his way out, he told a guard that he planned to go to Barrier, and he's gonna kill the SOB who cost him twenty-five years of his life."

About the Author

Helene Mitchell is an Idaho native and retired educator. She served as a Marine Corps officer during Vietnam. She taught school for many years, eventually graduating into positions of leadership including principal, superintendent, and Director of Education for the Idaho Department of Correction. She lost her husband of 51 years during Covid and began writing for pleasure rather than for work.

She and her new husband Robert Mitchell met online accidentally and now live on the Montana side of Yellowstone Park with Cody their wonder dog. They travel often, and she says, "Gotta do it now, not getting younger, not getting healthier."

The *Maggie Monroe* series currently has five books, moving Maggie's adventures from rural Nevada to rural Montana.

She also writes blogs and books under Gail Decker Cushman. The *Wrinkly Bits* series is available on Amazon and her website: **gailcushman.com**

Gail Cushman's other books

Wrinkly Bits Series, a senior hijinks:
- *Cruise Time*
- *Out of Time*
- *Wasting Time*
- *Flash of Time*
- *Bits of Time*

Made in the USA
Middletown, DE
07 November 2023

42049992R00195